Al Hess

SHAKE OUT THE GHOSTS

ANGRY ROBOT
An imprint of Watkins Media Ltd

Unit 11, Shepperton House
89-93 Shepperton Road
London N1 3DF
UK

angryrobotbooks.com
Kiss prints on a mirror

An Angry Robot paperback original, 2026

Copyright © Al Hess 2026

Edited by Desola Coker and Shona Kinsella
Cover by Sarah O'Flaherty
Illustrations by Al Hess
Set in Meridien

All rights reserved. Al Hess asserts the moral right to be identified as the author of this work. A catalogue record for this book is available from the British Library.

This novel is entirely a work of fiction. Names, characters, places, and incidents are the products of the author's imagination or are used fictitiously. Any resemblance to actual events, locales, organizations or persons, living or dead, is entirely coincidental.

Sales of this book without a front cover may be unauthorized. If this book is coverless, it may have been reported to the publisher as "unsold and destroyed" and neither the author nor the publisher may have received payment for it.

Angry Robot and the Angry Robot icon are registered trademarks of Watkins Media Ltd.

ISBN 978 1 91599 896 5
Ebook ISBN 978 1 91599 897 2

Printed and bound in the United Kingdom by CPI Group (UK) Ltd, Croydon CR0 4YY

The manufacturer's authorised representative in the EU for product safety is eucomply OÜ - Pärnu mnt 139b-14, 11317 Tallinn, Estonia, hello@eucompliancepartner.com; www.eucompliancepartner.com

9 8 7 6 5 4 3 2 1

You are not a snow shovel

CONTENT WARNINGS

mentions of past physical assault; non-consensual kissing/touching; PTSD and on-page panic attack; depression and anxiety; brief violence; kidnapping; mentions of death ideation; vomiting; language; smoking and alcohol; consensual closed-door m/nb sex and sexual elements; morbid humor; "ghosts"

1

MIRROR IN THE BATHROOM

Cosmo - Three Years Ago

Cosmo's hand shook as he brought a cigarette to his lips. He wasn't sure if he wanted to keep crying or just throw up all the champagne sloshing around in his stomach, but this balcony was suitable for neither. The lights from the city bobbed and blurred like dying stars.

"I just want" – he sniffled and took a drag – "I just want someone who will love me enough not to cheat on me. Is that really so much to ask?"

Déjà leaned her elbows on the metal railing. There was glitter in her Bettie bangs, and he vaguely wondered where it came from. "You know what I'm going to say."

"But I love him."

"And I love *you*, but if you keep going back to Zedd, he's gonna keep cheating, and you'll keep ending up here – standing on someone's balcony during a party, drunk, with mascara running down your face."

He swiped at his cheek. "That's harsh, darling."

"No, it isn't. *Dump him.*"

"I did."

"And this time, don't take him back. No matter how much he begs and cries and tells you you're the most wonderful, beautiful creature he's ever known."

Cosmo let out a sob. Only three days ago, he and Zedd had gone to the theme park in Fairview, fed each other spoonfuls of gelato, and gotten lost in the funhouse. A mannequin dressed in the most dreadful outfit had popped up in his path, and he'd shrieked. Zedd punched the thing on instinct and knocked its head clean off. He snatched Cosmo by the arms, pushed him against the wall, and said, *I'll protect you to the ends of the earth, gorgeous. No mannequin is a match for my love.* And they laughed and made out and flipped a coin to decide who would take the giant stuffed alligator home. Cosmo lost, but Zedd had let him take it anyway.

He wiped his eye, and his finger came away black. He should have worn the waterproof mascara, but he hadn't planned on Zedd breaking his heart – *again* – at the party tonight. "I want to die."

"Don't be dramatic."

"In case you haven't noticed" – he gestured to himself, then lost his balance and dropped the cigarette – "dramatic is what I am. I feel things deeply. Can't you see my electromagnetic field right now?"

She hunched her shoulders. "I can."

She'd told him his aura was what drew her to him in the first place. So vibrant that he outshined everyone in the Art History lecture hall, radiating magenta and orange. Right now, he probably looked like cloudy paint water.

"At the moment, I don't want to feel anything at all. I want to crawl into a hole and pull the dirt down on top of me." He picked up his cigarette, which had burned nearly to the butt, and took a drag. A chilly breeze flung his curls into his face. "You should go back inside. Find your new crush."

Déjà was always put-together, but tonight she'd worn a black lace dress that accentuated her voluptuous figure-eight shape, and the low neckline barely contained all that light brown cleavage. She had on fine mesh fishnets and the sequined pumps with flamingo-shaped heels that he couldn't borrow because his feet were too big. She looked weird and hot and was wasting the effort on him instead of... "What's their name again? Wheat? Barley?" It was something that reminded Cosmo of bread.

"Rye." Déjà kept her gaze on him, and it was hard to look away when her severely painted eyebrows and sharp cat-eye liner pinned him in place. "And I will, but you're not going to get out of my lecture that easily. This hurts now, but just like any wound, it will heal. As long as you stop poking at it! Going back to Zedd is self-harm, and I will not stand by and let you destroy yourself. Take out your feelings on your art; have a one-night stand with some fun thing who also thinks you're a beautiful creature – and, let's face it, everyone does – then let's throw a party."

Cosmo blinked at the sliding doors leading back inside. The lights doubled and bled together. A pop song throbbed through the glass, and people drifted past like wraiths trapped in a bottle. "We're at a party."

"Not like this. Bunch of snobs insisting they understand the meaning behind that turn-of-the-century floating snow shovel–"

"Duchamp's *Prelude to a Broken Arm*." He steadied himself against the cold balcony railing. Cars rushed by far below, and his stomach lurched. Pushing back, he sat in a folding chair and hung his head between his knees. "It's not hard to understand, given both the object and the title. You walk outside to shovel the drive, then slip on the ice and break your arm."

"That's not art," Déjà said. "I could put a hammer in a plexiglass box and title it *Prelude to a Smashed Thumb*."

"It's Dadaism."

"It's stupid. All I'm saying is we can throw a better party, in your honor, where we hype you up and send you on your way toward a brighter future *without Cinereous Zedd*. Prelude to Cosmo finding the love of his life who will fuck the brains out of his pretty head, treat him like the queen he is, and never cheat on him."

He didn't see anyone like that in his future. But an event was a great idea. No art show after-party. Not a birthday. Not a trite celebration where people attended to congratulate him for making it one more turn around the sun but in reality only came for the booze.

There was only one way to shake loose of his life clinging to Zedd and his counterfeit affections. It had to be a farewell, a send-off. And it had to be *dramatic*. The grandest display possible to demonstrate that there were plenty of people who loved Cosmo, even if a soulmate wasn't in the cards.

Every end was a new beginning.

Cosmo needed to die.

Micah - Present Day

Distorted synthesizer thumped through the dark studio. The bass wasn't strong enough to rattle the frames on the walls, but it prodded a tender spot in Micah's brain. Sweat dried to his forehead as he stared at the ceiling, one foot growing icy beyond the edge of the sheets. Faint lyrics drifted, Mark Almond singing about being desperate for love and attention.

Someone was playing Soft Cell. Again.

Groaning, Micah shoved off the comforter and donned his glasses. He snatched the broom from its habitual spot near the headboard and rammed it against the ceiling. Ximena had taken his complaint seriously, but the memo she'd taped to all their doors, reminding people to keep the noise down after nine, hadn't been given the same consideration.

He switched on the light, then rubbed his face and staggered into the kitchen. The clock on the microwave said *2:24*. After downing a glass of water, he dropped into his chair at the drafting table and blinked at stray pencil shavings.

After three weeks of the same songs recycled through the midnight hours, the lyrics and beats were familiar enough that he should have been able to sleep through them. But it didn't happen every night, and the volume fluctuated, so it wasn't predictable enough to anticipate.

Micah picked up a kneaded eraser and squeezed the gray putty between his fingers. His eyelids sagged. Snippets of song floated, and he questioned again whether it was really the upstairs neighbor. The sound almost seemed like it was coming from the middle of the front room. He'd pounded on other walls though, and the tenants had called him an asshole and complained that he'd woken them up.

The song changed, slinky synth and bright sax filling the room. He was never going to fall back to sleep with this going on. A stretched canvas sat on a nearby easel, the half-finished landscape staring at him judgmentally. Making a dent in it would at least be productive; he hadn't touched it in so long that the thick oil strokes were probably dry by now. He should have said no to it to begin with, but all his portfolio submissions so far had ended in rejections, and he needed any commissions he could get. When someone asked for a painting of a field, it hadn't seemed like a challenge. Blue sky, green grass, her grandmother's barn in the background. But clouds were weird, and trying to paint tiny, thin-stemmed plants was torture. The curves of a body, the way shadows fell on defined thighs or the tendons in a hand, was much easier to get right.

Who was he fooling? He wasn't going to work on the painting when there was something far more tempting he could be doing if sleep wasn't an option. After poking through his pencils and selecting an HB, he tore a sheet of paper from the drawing pad and set the materials to one side.

As always, he started this guilty pleasure by opening his phone and scrolling through contacts. Sometimes he dialed random numbers. Those were the most fun, because the conversations could go anywhere, the calls lasting for as long as he and the other person wanted. But most people thought he was either a pervert or a scammer. And starting the conversation with *I'm definitely not a pervert or a scammer* tended to be the opposite of reassuring.

Customer service lines hardly ever worked. Those people only wanted to help him with his credit card, or his health insurance, or computer issues. But sometimes bored restaurant hosts would humor him while they took his order.

The sex hotline was expensive, but it was much easier to find someone willing to tell him whatever he wanted, especially this late at night.

He clicked the number and wedged in his earpiece.

A sultry robo-voice purred: "Thanks for calling, lover. Our operators are aching to talk to you. What gender are you interested in?"

"Surprise me."

"Hang tight while I find your perfect match." There was a click, followed by legalese about call privacy and how much he was being charged per minute.

A silky baritone entered his ear, drowning out the beats of Soft Cell. "Hey there. I'm—"

"I don't want to know your name. Not even whatever pseudonym you use. You can tell me pronouns, though."

"Alright, you got it. Pronouns are he/him."

"Mine too. How are you?" Tension unspooled from Micah's shoulders, and he relaxed into his chair. He sketched loose gestures onto the paper, building a boxy masculine frame.

"I'm good. I'm good. You lonely tonight?"

"Yeah. Can't sleep."

The operator's chuckle rumbled through the earpiece. "I'm sorry to tell you this, but I plan on keeping you up. Want to know what I'm wearing?"

Micah tapped the end of his pencil against the desk. "No. I want to picture you nude."

"Eager, are we? Well, I'm at your service. What are you in the mood for?"

The only problem with calling a sex hotline was the operators expected him to, well, want sex. He'd tried making small talk with them as he sketched, the way he used to with his life-drawing models. In the past, the models would come to the studio and sit on a stool, lounge on the couch, or stand gracefully beside a chair, telling him about their favorite restaurants and pets and hobbies while he drew.

But trying to ask an operator the name of their goldfish while they were faking an orgasm didn't work very well.

"Describe yourself, please. Give me details that I can picture."

"I'm Black. Twenty-three. Dark eyes, dark hair. Athletic build. Thick thighs and a bubble–"

Micah sighed. "Is that the only script they give you?"

"You don't like twenty-something guys with thick thighs and bubble butts?"

"I didn't say that, but this happens every time I call. I want to know what *you* look like."

"This is fantasy, babe."

"I'd rather imagine a real person. All bodies are beautiful."

There was a pause, and the operator's voice lost some of its gloss. "Not mine. Better to stick to the script."

"I don't want to make you uncomfortable or dysphoric, but I'm also not going to pay three eighty-nine a minute to listen to you read a script. I'll hang up."

"If I describe myself, you'll do that anyway."

"I promise I won't."

"I'm not anyone's fantasy."

Sketches on the wall fluttered in the draft of the ceiling fan – some were busts, others full body exercises, with models both clothed and nude. There were downy lashes and sparse ones. Hooked noses and broad ones. Barely-there breasts and huge, sagging ones spidered with veins. So many curves, muscles, rolls, wrinkles. "That's not true."

The operator clucked his tongue. "I weigh three hundred pounds, and I'm going bald. Twenty-three passed me up a long time ago."

"I'm listening."

"I've got a big gut and flabby pecs."

Micah sketched broad shoulders, a wide chest, and prominent stomach. "Strong arms? Square jaw?"

"You're into this? Shit, man. Alright. Um. More round, I guess. I've got a beard."

"It's good. I like details." Micah blocked in the operator's face and brawny arms. His left eye ached, struggling to focus on the fine lines, and he looked away, blinking hard.

"There's a long scar on my thigh from a car wreck five years ago," the operator said.

"I bet you have nice hands. Wide palms. Thick fingers."

"I guess. Never really thought about it."

"Hands are my favorite. Keep talking, please. I like your voice." He sketched the suggestion of veins winding across the backs of the operator's hands, little shaded canyons between the tendons, and half-moon strokes for knuckles.

A deafening crash came from down the hall. Micah jumped. His heart rocketed into his throat, and he strained for more sound, but the beats of "Tainted Love" and the operator saying something about his pinkie finger made it impossible to hear anything else.

He ended the call abruptly and slid off the stool, so much adrenaline lightning through him that his legs were unsteady. No one was in here with him. It was only something falling over. Even so, groping beneath the drafting table and finding the knife he'd duct-taped there was immediate comfort. He peeled it off, the handle gummy with tape residue, then padded past the kitchen. Something rolled across the floor in the dark hall, and he made a noise in his throat.

No one was here. The windows were always locked, the slide chain and two deadbolts secure on the door, and the motion sensors he'd installed months ago hadn't gone off. And if all of that somehow failed, the intruder would at least trip over a potted plant or two in the dark. Micah was alone. He shook out his tingling fingers and reminded himself to breathe, then tightened his grip on the knife – just in case. Switching on the hall light revealed a bottle of pills amid bits of something glittery. He peered into the bathroom.

"Oh god."

Shards of glass from the cabinet mirror littered the tile and sat at the bottom of the toilet bowl. The cabinet stood open, and combs, eye drops, floss, and a host of other things from the shelves scattered the floor. What a mess. Micah hadn't felt the bass from the neighbor's music, but maybe the slight vibrations had been enough to shake the mirror loose. Ximena wasn't going to be happy about replacing it. The two am synthpop was a terrible enough invasion of his privacy; the idea of letting maintenance people inside to install something sent fresh electric panic racing through his body.

He blew a slow breath through his nose. Ximena preferred someone present when maintenance was working but surely she'd make an exception for him. He could make a day of it and visit the new aquarium or catch a movie in that luxury theater that provided mystery boxes to be opened at certain points during the viewing. If Ximena wouldn't budge on the issue, he'd just do without. She could have the mirror installed when he eventually moved out.

Crisp xylophone notes and bursts of drums drifted through the front room. Micah rounded the bookcase that doubled as a room divider and collapsed back into bed. Some small toiletry hit the floor in the hallway and bounced away. More bass rattling the bathroom cabinet. Well, let the whole place fall apart if it wanted to – he wasn't getting back up.

He must have eventually fallen asleep, because morning light streamed through the window when he opened his eyes. After texting Ximena and cleaning up as much of the bathroom mess as he could, he pulled out the vacuum.

Bits of mirror sparkled against the baseboards, and he ran the vacuum hose along the edge. Half the toiletries that had been littering the floor were now in the trash; some were expired pills and others were makeup compacts and flowery lotions that his ex must have left, even though he couldn't recall her ever wearing sparkly chartreuse eyeshadow.

He shut off the vacuum and stopped before a prescription bottle that had rolled into a corner. *Tobramycin and dexamethasone ophthalmic suspension. Instill 2 drops to the affected eye(s) three times a day.*

The shit had been necessary to stave off an infection in his injured eye, but it made his eye weep and created halos around lights, so it had been impossible to draw or paint. When he'd complained to his brother, Everett, he told Micah he shouldn't be trying to draw after what happened anyway. Said he needed to relax, maybe watch TV instead. But art *was* how he relaxed, and he didn't even own a TV.

He lobbed the bottle of eye drops down the hall. It sailed into the garbage can with a satisfying *thunk*.

A knock came at the door. He stiffened, then tried to calm his racing heart. It was okay. It was Ximena certainly. She wasn't going to push her way in, and she would have told anyone with her that they couldn't step foot into Micah's place while he was inside.

He shook out his hands and stared at the knob, prepared to snatch it like a poisonous snake. The doorbell chimed and he gasped.

"Stop working yourself up. Just open the damn door." After unlocking the deadbolts, he tugged open the door as much as the slide chain would allow. A Latina woman with steely gray hair – Ximena – stood on the balcony in black heels and a polka dot blouse that looked a little too thin for the weather. Two maintenance people stood beside her, and a large panel swaddled in bubble wrap and plastic leaned against the railing.

"Hey." Micah pointed through the gap in the door to the wrapped panel. "Replacement mirror already? Don't tell me you want to install some cheap generic thing in my bathroom." With a shaky grin, he added, "It'll throw off the aesthetic. My delicate creative genius can't function under those conditions."

Ximena recoiled, and the tote bag she held slapped against her leg. "Generic? Don't insult me, mijo. I had an extra laying around from the last time this happened."

"The last time?" The building was old, and maybe whatever adhesive was used to affix the mirrors to the cabinet doors was losing its hold after so long. That was bad news for everyone else.

Micah glanced at his sweatpants and sandals. "Um, give me a few minutes to dress and I'll head out." The aquarium was only five minutes away. But the parking was probably atrocious, and what if there were screaming, hyperactive kids there on a field trip?

It was too early for a movie, and besides, there likely wasn't anything good playing. Plus, buying anything at the concession stand would require selling both his kidneys.

"How long do you think this will take? An hour?" He'd just nap in his car in the parking lot. Lord, he was still so tired.

"No, no. Fifteen minutes. Promise." She beckoned. "Come stand out here with me. It's a nice morning."

Her smile was warm, bunching her round cheeks, and all of the patience in it made Micah want to slam the door and lock it. How ridiculous he must look, afraid to let innocent maintenance people into his bathroom.

After shutting the door and pulling away the slide chain, he stepped outside and nodded to the men as they carried the mirror into the studio. The light stabbed at his left eye, and he shielded it, squinting.

A cool breeze rustled his hair, and a dove made a soft *coo* from a nearby tree. His place was on the second floor by the stairs that wrapped around the outside of the complex, and it gave him a lovely view of the city. In the distance, the tops of buildings scratched the bellies of fat clouds, sunlight turning windows and peaked roofs into the brilliant facets of gems. He inhaled, and a little of the tightness in his chest eased. It really was nice out this morning.

"The silicone won't be cured in fifteen minutes," Ximena said, "but they're going to put tape around the edges of the mirror to hold it to the cabinet door. Leave it for, like, three days, just to be certain, okay? I hope you didn't clean up the mess last night. Sweeping at night is bad luck."

"So is breaking a mirror. And I've fulfilled my quota of bad luck for the last year already."

She patted his arm. "Yes, you have." Her gaze hung on him, and he imagined how she must see him, with his blown pupil and the scars snaking over his cheekbone and through his eyebrow. They had waned from their deep mauve, but they were still far pinker after nine months than the doctor had promised. Micah's face would never be the same again no matter what, but the scars' stubborn refusal to fade to white felt like an additional sign to others that he was not okay. Evident by Ximena looking at him like this fragile, damaged thing that needed to be coddled. Or maybe she was remembering how he looked after returning from the hospital, swollen and stitched and covered in gauze.

Holding out the tote bag, she said, "I brought you chicharrónes con pico de gallo."

Micah sighed.

"You don't like it? Or you don't know?" she asked. "I can't remember if I brought you some before."

"You have, and it's delicious. But you don't need to bring me food anymore." After he came home from surgery, she'd ordered delivery every night and had the driver leave it at his door, until he called to tell her that though the gesture was lovely, he couldn't stomach any more greasy burgers and congealed mac and cheese. She'd replied apologetically, *I don't really know what white people eat.*

After that, it had stopped being delivery and instead handmade tamales, pozole, and thick sheets of chicharrón with salsa. He hadn't had the energy to protest then, since he spent most of the time lying in bed, hoping that if he didn't move, he'd be absorbed into the mattress. But needing to give her the dishes back had motivated him to get up and wash them, sometimes tidying the kitchen a little while he was at it.

But he wasn't trying to assimilate into the furniture anymore, and he didn't need incentive to clean, do laundry, or shower.

Ximena pushed the tote bag at him. "It's no trouble."

"Stop feeling sorry for me. It's been almost nine months."

Lines bracketed her mouth. "What did you eat for dinner last night? Did you cook? Did you go out to a restaurant?" She shook her head and waved her hand as though erasing her last question. "You didn't go anywhere."

"You're worse than my grandma used to be."

"And I'm sure she'd be thanking me for saving you another day of eating microwave ramen from the back of your cabinet. You love my food. I love that you love it. I don't have to feel sorry for you to bring you some."

She was lying, but he took the bag and peeked inside. "Thanks. I'll bring your dish back later."

"I know you will." She smiled. "Is it quiet at night now?"

"No," he muttered. "Someone is still playing music in the middle of the night. It sounds like it's being piped directly into my studio. I can't sleep."

Ximena pinched the bridge of her nose. "Okay. Well, I've already talked to Randi, and she's never home at night, either working or staying at her girlfriend's place, so it's not her."

"Which one is she?"

"Directly above you."

No wonder pounding on the ceiling didn't do any good. But if it wasn't her, then who? "Maybe I need to buy a white noise machine or a louder fan."

"No. I'll figure it out."

"Just ask them to show you their playlists. Whoever has Soft Cell set to repeat is your culprit. You can ask them when you're installing more mirrors that have fallen down from crumbling silicone."

She shook her head. "This apartment is the only one I've had trouble with."

"You said you had to replace one of the mirrors before."

"Yes, here! Same thing happened to the last tenant. He said it fell by itself in the night."

"That's... odd." He chuckled. "He wasn't tormented by eighties music at two am, was he?"

"Not that I remember. But he was weird. And his sculptures were" – she wrinkled her nose – "grotesque. Garish."

"He was an artist too?" This neighborhood was called the Artists' District for a reason, but he'd met plenty of people here who weren't. Or they wrote horrible poetry, which was worse.

"Yes, of course. And he was a polite boy. Friendly. But his art was not tasteful like yours. It wouldn't surprise me if he broke the mirror in the bathroom on purpose as part of some experimental, artsy thing."

Making garish and grotesque art to channel complicated feelings wasn't any worse than what Micah was doing – except that he was able to hide his peculiar habits from everyone but his phone company.

Ximena peered at her reflection in his window and tucked loose strands of hair back into her updo. He didn't think she was *that* much older than him, maybe ten years, but her gray hair and motherly concern threw him off. Turning back to him, she said, "That wasn't right. Forget I said any of that. I shouldn't be talking about the dead."

"The last tenant died?"

"Yes." She clutched her elbows and shifted uncomfortably, her gauzy blouse rippling in the wind. "I came out of the office one day to see people moving furniture out of his place. They gave me an invitation to the funeral, but I didn't go."

"Damn. What happened to him?"

"I don't know. There was an obituary, but they never tell you in those things. Shame, though. He couldn't have been more than twenty-six, twenty-seven."

The door creaked open, and the maintenance men walked out. "All done," one of them said. "Hey, your art is really good. Do you draw those from live models?"

"Dead ones. It's a little tricky getting a corpse up the stairs, but I can pose them on the couch, and they'll sit still for me for hours. They never complain that they have a cramp or that it's too drafty…" Micah trailed off at the man's blank expression, then said, "That was a joke." Maybe not a very good one in light of the previous topic. "And no, I didn't draw those ones from live models, but I used to. They'd commission me to do their portrait."

"Some of those women you've got up there are super hot." He whistled. "That's a sweet gig. They pay you to look at them naked basically. Wish I knew how to draw."

Micah pursed his lips and hoped it resembled a smile. "The people who came to my studio usually stayed clothed. I appreciate you stopping by this morning." He nodded to Ximena. "Thanks for the chicharrónes."

He carried the bag inside and set it on the kitchen counter. As he reached in for the food, the front door swung open, and the maintenance man stepped over the threshold and onto the carpet.

"I forgot the silicone."

Micah screeched, and his heart caught in his throat. No no no. No one could be inside with him.

Get out!

Get out!

His vision tunneled, limbs going rigid. The oven handle scraped into his side as he pressed against the counter, but he barely felt it. Though his mind screamed at him to flee, or to grab a weapon and fight, he was paralyzed. He needed to tell the man to leave, but each word crowded in his throat until he was certain he would choke on them.

A hand – Ximena's – snatched the man's shirt sleeve and yanked him outside. The door slammed shut and she shouted, "I'm so sorry, mijo!"

Breaking from his cemented position, Micah rushed to the door and threw the deadbolts and the slide chain. He trembled, nerves short-circuiting and terror pumping through his veins. His cheek pressed against the door, eyes watering, and he slowly sank to his knees and thudded his forehead against the grainy tile. Tremors quaked his chest, dust bunnies and a pencil shaving stirring from his frantic breath.

Footsteps clanged down the stairs outside, the maintenance man's mutters of "I'm sorry" standing no chance against Ximena's sharp admonishments.

Shame plunged into Micah's gut amid the other mess of signals his body was sending him. That guy didn't mean any harm. He didn't deserve Micah's reaction. *Micah* didn't deserve Micah's reaction.

He balled his fists, intent on taking this energy out on something, but he'd already stomped on half-painted canvases and flipped over his drafting table after returning from the hospital, and it hadn't made him feel better.

Pushing to his feet, he ran his hands through his hair, slapped his cheeks, and walked to the bathroom. The new mirror looked exactly like the old one, save for the strips of tape on each corner. The silicone sat on the toilet tank. He could return it with Ximena's dish later, and maybe he could get the maintenance guy a six-pack next time he went shopping.

A shadow drifted in his peripheral vision, and he tensed. Great, now his body was in overdrive, imagining intruders who weren't there.

Everyone left. He was alone. He'd locked the door.

Even so, he peered down the empty hall. Nothing. But when he turned back toward the mirror, he gasped. Written across it in cheery pink was the phrase:

EVERYTHING WILL BE OKAY

2

SOMETHING IN MY HOUSE

Micah - Present Day

Tubes of oil paint rattled in the drawer as Micah rummaged through. He set out cadmium red, phthalo blue, yellow ochre, and titanium white.

The floorboards creaked, and he paused. His bed sat beyond a plant-laden bookcase; the covers were a bit sloppily tucked in, but the bed looked the same as always. The thick leaves of his biggest monstera crowded the corner, tangled in shadows. Like always.

Turning back to the paints, he pulled out lamp black and burnt umber. This was more of an effort to continue the landscape painting than he'd made in the past month, and he applauded himself for–

Ice tumbled into the receptacle in the refrigerator, and he startled. He shut his eyes and blew out a breath.

This was silly. His studio wasn't haunted. The late-night eighties music was from a neighbor, even though he couldn't pinpoint which one. The broken mirror was due to deteriorating silicone, even though his studio was apparently the only place with this problem. And the marker on the mirror was… not so easy to explain away.

It hadn't been there when he walked into the bathroom. Shaken as he was with the maintenance guy trying to come back inside, he distinctly remembered staring at the mirror, a clean and identical replica to his previous one, and seeing nothing amiss.

The last tenant died. Not necessarily in the studio, but maybe it was a familiar place he was pulled back to. Could that shadow have been him? A ghost who liked to write saccharin platitudes in pink block letters?

Leaning back, Micah wiped his hands down his face. He got up, walked back to the bathroom, and stared at the message. *Everything will be okay.* Maybe that was written specifically for him. He already had the pity of the landlady and his family; he didn't need it from a ghost. *He* wasn't the dead one.

He swiped at the message. It faded, but only slightly, and a fine powder of marker dust coated his fingers. Scrubbing at the glass with a wad of tissue did nothing, and neither did applying rubbing alcohol.

Ximena would be pissed if he couldn't get that off. Actually, she'd probably take it in stride, thinking it was some therapy technique Micah had been ordered to practice.

It was hard to be frightened by an entity writing such an upbeat phrase, but it was still an invasion of his privacy, and he couldn't take any more nights of Soft Cell. Maybe he needed some fresh air. The coffee shop on the corner had the best muffins, but for some reason the thought of walking over there made his palms sweat. He'd already had several cups of coffee anyway, and going there for a single muffin seemed unnecessary.

There was a gallery showing a couple streets down, and today was the last day. But that was another activity that involved leaving his apartment. He wiped his hands on his thighs, jaw clenched. The gallery didn't open until five, and rush hour was a bad time to go anywhere. Waiting until the crowd thinned out, maybe at seven, would be better. Except at that point, he'd be in his sweats with dinner and a book. That was fine. He didn't really want to go anyway.

But it would be nice to have someone to talk to about what was going on. He picked up his phone and scrolled through his contacts. Courtney was a no. She called once a month to check up on him, which was more than Micah ever expected of an ex, but she was too grounded to believe in ghosts, even with evidence. Dad and Mom? They worried about him enough as it was. They'd want to send him to some mental health retreat, which might help his anxiety, but it wouldn't solve his current issue.

Oh, Grandma… If only. She wouldn't have second-guessed a ghost's presence. She'd claimed to have sensed many in her lifetime, including Grandad after he passed.

Reaching the bottom of the list, he pondered Ximena's name, but what would she do? Charge the ghost rent?

Closing out of his contacts, he opened Face2Face and hit his brother's picture. After a moment, Everett answered, the screen filled with an unflattering angle showcasing his nostrils and the underside of his chin. He glanced down.

"What's wrong?"

"Nothing's wrong." Micah dithered in the hall, eyeing the bathroom. "Why would something be wrong? I can't call my favorite brother in the middle of a weekday when I know he's at work and busy?"

The clack of a keyboard filled the speakers. Everett said, "Seriously. Did something happen? You look anxious. Hey, did you get that list of therapists I sent you?"

This was a bad idea. "I did, yeah."

"You haven't called any of them, huh? Want me to do it? I'll book you an appointment, no problem."

Micah moved the phone away from his face so Everett couldn't see his expression. "I don't need help with it."

"Okay." His tone called Micah a liar, but he didn't push it. When they were kids, Everett was the carefree one, dragging Micah along on dangerous, sometimes illegal adventures. But he'd become so much like Dad as he got older that Micah hardly recognized him sometimes. The keyboard clacked. "So, what's going on?"

If Micah mentioned the message on the mirror, it would only make Everett more concerned, which meant he needed some other reason for calling.

The half-finished painting on the easel caught Micah's eye. It had been sitting beside the drafting table in its current state for so long that he no longer had any concept of its quality.

"I just need your opinion on something."

Everett's upside-down face pulled into a smile. "You met a guy."

"No."

"A woman."

"No."

"A non-binary person so unbelievably hot and fantastic that you need my help picking out engagement rings."

Micah sagged. "God, I wish. No, I need you to look at this painting I'm doing and give your honest opinion."

Everett stopped typing. "You're kidding, right? Everything you create is gorgeous. And a little creepy. But gorgeous. And you've never been insecure about your art before."

"This one is different. Honest opinion."

"Different how? It's not a portrait?"

"Portrait, yes. I'm trying to summon Beelzebub with it, but I don't think I got the nose right."

Everett made an indecipherable noise. His brother never knew how to take his jokes, and that was part of what made them so funny.

"If it's not good," Micah said, "but you lie and say it is, you'll only be wasting my time, not saving my feelings."

"And your demon summoning will fail. Gotcha. If it's ugly, I'll tell you."

A thud came from behind him, and he gasped and nearly dropped the phone. The sound of a closet door slamming closed came from the other side of the wall. For god's sake. Just the neighbor.

Pressing a hand to his pounding heart, Micah turned the screen to face the landscape.

"It's ugly," Everett said.

"I knew it."

"Not technically. It's very skillful, just like everything you paint. But it's boring. A field and a barn. I think I would have preferred Beelzebub."

"That's what the client wants. I'm doing it from a photograph."

"In that case, I'm not sure what you want me to say."

That it was soul-crushing for him to be doing this. That he needed to get over his problems and let people into his studio again so he could draw them. That he needed a new therapist. All the things Dad would tell him.

He must have paused for too long, because Everett pulled his phone so close to his nose that Micah could practically see up into his brain. "Are you low on money?"

"What? No, no. I'm... fine."

"You sure? You have money for food? For prescriptions?"

"Yeah."

"Are you still getting commission profit from that gallery you're in?"

"I'm not in a gallery anymore. I missed a couple of networking receptions, and they dropped me." He'd also missed the yearly art fair and had turned down the chance for a group exhibit, the lure of staying in bed much more tempting.

"What the hell? Don't they know what you've been through? Let me wire you some money. I have to get some emails sent, but after–"

"You don't need to do that. I'm getting this commission done and have others lined up." He didn't, and skinning his own hands with a potato peeler sounded more appealing than painting another landscape, but he wasn't going to take Everett's money. His emergency credit card would just have to do more heavy lifting.

Micah dropped his arm to his side and turned in a circle. "I'm managing, but I feel like I'm stuck in limbo. I haven't made any progress on getting my life back on track–"

"It's been, what, nine months? You're not lying in bed twenty-four/seven, unwashed and barely present. You're making art again. Your studio looks clean. That's progress."

He wanted to argue that he wasn't progressing fast enough. That he should be able to let people come inside. He should be able to go on dates or hang out with friends, or even attend a life drawing event somewhere other than his studio, in a group setting in the safety of other people. But saying that would only reinforce that he *did* need a new therapist, and he wasn't ready to attempt that again.

He realized Everett was saying his name. "Sorry, what?"

"I have to get back to work. Want me to call you later tonight?"

"No. Thanks for your perspective. I'll let you go."

Everett bent over his phone and looked into the camera. "Hey. Hang in there."

Everything will be okay.

The screen blinked off, and Micah was staring at his own reflection. He scowled and tossed the phone on the bed. He'd rather stare at the ten thousand blades of grass he'd be painting than look at himself.

Dropping onto the stool, he pulled up the client's field photo on his computer, then mixed greens with blobs of crimson and ochre, and layered the strokes over swipes of deep evergreen. After a break to stretch his back and eat some of Ximena's food, he went back at it, determined to make enough progress that he could snap a picture to prove to the client that it was getting done.

Something thudded down the hall, and Micah's hand jumped, creating a dramatically long blade of grass. He stared at the canvas. That wasn't his imagination, and this time, it wasn't the neighbor's closet door.

He groped for the knife under the table, squeezed the comforting grip of the handle, but left it there and crept into the hall.

"Hello?"

Faint music from someone's TV drifted; a car door slammed from the street below; ragged breath whistled through his nose.

A sudden cacophony of metal jangling against metal thundered from the bathroom. A hard thud reverberated off the tub.

Micah screamed, imagining Jacob Marley using his shower. He hurried back to the drafting table and ripped the knife free. This was ridiculous. Ridiculous. But whether it was an intruder or the Ghost of Christmas Past, they were going to get a knife in their gut.

Squeezing the handle until his fingers cramped, he inched toward the bathroom and hoped his voice sounded aggressive. "Who's there?"

After pulling in a steadying breath, he lunged through the doorway, only to be met with a bathroom as spotless as it had been earlier. He peeked behind the door, then turned to the tub. The frosted shower door was closed. Had he left it that way? He certainly hadn't kicked the bathmat into the corner.

Light flared off the trembling blade in his grip, and he was certain he wouldn't be able to hear anything else beyond the roar of blood in his ears. He reached for the handlebar on the shower door, straining for shadows moving beyond. The glass shuddered as he flung it open.

The knife pointed at empty space. Micah stared at a blue glob of body wash on the tile, then glanced down. A cherry red metal hoop sat in the bottom of the tub. He picked it up and turned it over. Hard water deposits laced the enamel surface. A shower curtain ring.

Micah slid the glass shower door closed and open, then turned in a circle, perplexed.

Pocketing the ring, he strode for his phone. Ximena was going to think he'd lost his mind.

He typed, <*Did my apartment used to have a shower curtain instead of a door?*>

All of the apartments in the complex were designed in a similar manner, but it had been so long since he'd entered a neighbor's place, let alone used their bathroom, that there was no way to remember if all the tubs were the same.

His phone vibrated. <*Yes. Some still do, because we normally wait until the tenant has moved out before doing that kind of work. Is something wrong with your shower?*>

<*Hypothetically, how much drain cleaner would it take to get rid of ectoplasm?*>

<*I don't understand what that means.*>

<*Sorry. My shower is fine. You wouldn't happen to remember if the tenant before me had a curtain, would you? It's silly, I know, but I found a shower curtain ring and was just thinking about what you said about him. The funeral and everything.*>

It took a moment for Ximena to respond. <*Mijo, are you sure you're okay? You aren't sitting in the bathroom thinking morbid thoughts, are you? Should I call someone??*>

He snorted. <*I swear I'm not doing that. I was only curious.*>

<*We started installing the shower doors four years ago, and probably did the one in your apartment after Cosmo passed away, so yes, there would have been a curtain.*>

<*Okay. Thanks for indulging me. Have a good afternoon.*>

Micah took out the curtain ring and turned it over in his hand.

Cosmo.

3

WHEN DOVES CRY

Cosmo - Three Years Ago

Cosmo sliced through a particularly tough bundle of twine holding a set of paintings together. Bubble wrap popped and deflated, and he carefully pulled it away. He set down the X-Acto and shook shreds of plastic from his gloved hands.

After giving the idea some thought, he'd wondered if it was selfish to throw his own funeral party and invite people to attend. People didn't throw their own baby showers or retirement parties. But they did throw their own birthday parties and wedding receptions. Cosmo wasn't asking people to buy something off a gift registry at Shady Meadows Funeral Home. He wanted them to enjoy themselves and in return get a little support.

It was tempting to start drafting a eulogy first, but the obituary would come before the funeral. And he needed invitations, of course. Decor. Flowers. A burial outfit. There was so much to do!

Was food served at funerals? It had been so long since he'd attended one that he couldn't remember. But it wouldn't be a party without food and booze.

Foie gras. No. Not after learning the poor ducks were force-fed through a feeding tube to fatten their livers.

Pâté then. And brie with those crackers that–

A hand closed over his shoulder, and he gasped.

Royce stepped back. The director's tie was crooked, the back room's fluorescent lighting washing out his fair skin and glancing off his balding head. The gaunt cut of his jaw and his intense blue gaze made him look intimidating, but when he smiled, a little of the harshness dissolved. "Didn't mean to startle you. I said your name three times."

"Ah, sorry. Lost in thought." Cosmo turned back to the unwrapped painting and blew a shred of bubble wrap from the thick impasto strokes. Hopefully Royce didn't think he was slacking off. Identical Dog was one of the most prestigious galleries in Lemon Disco, and it was only Cosmo's second week. He and Royce had both been at the party the night before, and Cosmo's public breakup with Zedd likely hadn't made the best impression.

"The packaging on Allen's block prints was horrendous. A piece of masking tape was stuck to *two* of them; I believe I sweated out half my body weight trying to peel it off without damaging the prints. I wasn't completely successful." Cosmo picked up the damned strip of tape, flecked here and there with blue paint and a bit of paper.

Royce waved a hand. "Take photos of the prints and the tape, but don't worry about it. We aren't responsible for Allen's poor packaging." He turned his gaze to the impasto, but Cosmo sensed all of the director's attention was on him.

Cosmo peeled away another sheet of bubble wrap. "Is there a problem? Have I made a mistake?"

"Mistake? Not at all. I wanted to see how you were feeling after all that champagne last night." He cocked his head, now in perfect symmetry with his crooked tie. "Do you want to break for lunch at the pub across the street? Maybe a Bloody Mary will help the hangover. My treat."

"Aw, that's sweet of you." Cosmo tugged on one dangle earring; the hard points of the geometric charms dug into his fingers. Midday on-the-clock cocktails didn't seem like the best idea, even if it was sanctioned by the boss. "But I don't have a hangover. And I really don't drink that often. Not *that* much anyway. But…"

"Your boyfriend."

"*Ex*-boyfriend." Although he couldn't blame anyone for not knowing which one it was at any given time.

"I heard part of the argument."

Cosmo cringed. He couldn't remember the exact words he and Zedd had hurled at each other, but it had still felt like a script Cosmo was doomed to repeatedly act out in some sort of tragic play, his punishment for being shitty in a past life. Well, no more.

He went back to unwrapping the impastos. "I'm putting him behind me." Which was another reason he didn't want to sit in a noisy pub with the director. He needed to get back to funeral planning. "Thanks for thinking of me, but I had a huge breakfast. I want to get all of these paintings opened and mounted before the end of the day."

"You know, you don't need to work so hard to impress me." Royce winked. "If you change your mind, do let me know."

Cosmo nodded, then set the unwrapped paintings on a cart. Royce's loafers clacked against the tile as he headed back into the gallery.

What to do about that giant stuffed alligator from the theme park? He could give it to Zedd... Or maybe he should stab it repeatedly until the stuffing hemorrhaged out. *Then* give it back.

And there were Zedd's shirts, his toothbrush, a pair of shoes. Trash, all of it.

After unwrapping the rest of the paintings, he pushed them on the cart toward the west wing of the gallery. A wheel squeaked as he passed Isaäk's blown glass raven skulls, mixed media neoplasticism pieces that took up entire walls, and surrealistic acrylics in eye-watering color combinations.

He stopped at a blank spot of wall and measured the first painting, then divided the number in half and added one hundred and fifty centimeters. He marked it down, then measured the painting's drop.

The gallery seemed to be empty – at least in this wing – which was welcome at the moment because he had so much on his mind. Despite only working here for a little over a week, patrons had stopped to chat him up on multiple occasions. Aside from yawn-inducing lines about the art being nothing in comparison to his own beauty, what he heard most often was *What's your favorite kind of art?*

It was such a broad question. Did they mean his favorite medium? Favorite style? Or did they actually mean art form as in fine art, cinema, architecture, literature, or music?

It really didn't matter, because he had the same answer for all of them: weird. Déjà had been right – there was nothing beautiful or impressive in the construction of *Prelude To a Broken Arm*. It was a snow shovel hanging from the ceiling. But the concept was the point of Dadaism. It was amusing and absurd, and people remembered it.

Cosmo wanted the unusual, the memorable.

He was unusual and memorable. But like Duchamp's shovel, people were often only fascinated by him on a superficial level. He drew attention, but only enough for people to want him as an interesting party guest or to fuck him a couple of times until they grew bored and moved on to someone else.

He wasn't anyone's true love.

He was a goddamn snow shovel.

But no one was going to say that at his funeral, he'd make certain of it. They were going to talk about how wonderful he was. God, hopefully people cried. That would be fantastic.

Swiping curls from his eyes, he mounted a painting and checked it with the spirit level. The bubble bobbed in the green liquid, then settled in the middle. Royce needed one for his tie.

Footsteps neared, and Cosmo turned. A wiry white guy in sunglasses and motorcycle boots rounded the corner. Cosmo's chest clenched, mouth growing dry as he stared at Zedd. He squeezed the level, trying to decide if it would work better as a blunt weapon or a piercing one.

Striding for Zedd, he jabbed a finger at the exit sign. "Get the hell out."

A single red rose dangled from Zedd's hand. Sinus-clearing cologne wafted around him. He pushed up his sunglasses. "I am so sorry."

"Get out. I'm working."

"Please. It wasn't my fault. I need another chance."

"I'm not having this conversation again. We're through."

"I'm completely committed to you. Look." Zedd pulled off his leather jacket and rolled up the sleeve of his shirt, revealing a band of plastic cling film. Beneath it, in weeping tattoo ink, was *COSMO*.

Unbelievable. "You put as much thought into your tattoos as you do your fidelity." He turned back to the cart and tried to pick up a nail with shaking fingers. "Please do me a favor and spontaneously combust."

Holding out the rose, Zedd's voice cracked as he said, "I love you. I love you more than anything. More than–"

Cosmo snatched the rose, bit off its head, and chewed viciously. Petals flew from his mouth. *"Get. Out."*

Zedd gaped. His jaw clamped shut, nostrils flared. "You'll come around. You always do." He turned away and slammed into Royce.

The director gripped him by the elbows and practically hurled him down the hall. "Come back – ever – and I'll call the police."

Tears stung Cosmo's eyes, his mouth full of rose petals. He pulled a wet breath through his nose. Should have worn the waterproof mascara.

Royce returned, straightening the lapels of his suit jacket. He stared at Cosmo, lips a tight line, then plucked out his pocket square and offered it. "I think you could use that Bloody Mary now."

Cosmo swallowed petals and dabbed at his eyes. He probably could. But all he really wanted to do was finish his work and go home. And if he accepted the drink offer, he ran the risk of crying on Royce or boring him to death with his woes.

His phone vibrated, and he opened it. A text from Déjà scrolled across:

<u ok>

Royce waited ahead, hands clasped behind his back. Green light from the exit sign settled into the creases of his face.

"I need a moment to compose myself," Cosmo said. He headed for the restroom and replied to Déjà: <*No, I'm not ok*>

<*i knew it. you were getting morbid at the party last night, talking about the beauty of burial caskets n stuff*>

<*Zedd showed up at my work and tried to get back with me*>
<*what!! call me now*>

As he dialed her number, he stopped in front of a mirror in the restroom and dabbed his smeared mascara with the edge of a paper towel.

She answered immediately. "What happened?"

"The same typical bullshit. It's not worth getting into; he's already left. I'm going to flip a coin and either work straight through my break so I can get out of here early or go have a slightly unprofessional cocktail with the director while on the clock."

"Um, *what*? Isn't he like sixty? Ew, ew. You are vulnerable and hurting, and I will not watch you go down in flames like this. Sleeping with your boss who is almost forty years older than you is nasty and not a solution to your problems!"

He scoffed. And she thought *he* was the dramatic one. "I have no intention of doing that. I don't know where you got that idea from."

"He flirted with you at the party last night. He wouldn't stop talking about your sculptures, and he kept calling you stunning and unique."

Cosmo had no recollection of that, but it didn't matter. "Those aren't flirts, darling. They're facts."

"Pompous ass."

"I get comments like that all the time. Even from you." He lowered his voice and glanced over his shoulder at the stalls, but they were empty. "And what does it matter if they are flirts? They only mean something if I want them to, and I don't. Especially not now. If I can't have the version of Zedd that I keep convincing myself is real, then it's no one."

The disgusted noise coming through the speaker was so loud that Cosmo pulled the phone away from his ear. "Excuse me, but Zedd should not be the litmus test for a loving, happy relationship. Not even your version of him that doesn't exist. He's average. *Average.* Nothing about you is average, and you deserve someone on your level."

Cinereous Zedd had seemed anything but average in the beginning. As the lead singer of Snake Milk, they'd met after an energetic performance in which Zedd had vaporized his eyebrows by getting too close to the pyrotechnics. Conversation had been hard because Cosmo had to shout into his ringing ears, but it hadn't mattered much when experimental punk rock and the intensity of their physical chemistry filled up the deficit.

But music and sex weren't enough, even if you fell in love. Cosmo needed conversations at one am while he and his love stared out at the glittering city. He needed someone to try his baking and tell him if there was too much icing. Someone to read to him and stroke his hair as they lay in bed on a Sunday morning.

Déjà's words were lost to the sound of his heartache. It sounded a lot like Zedd's music, and Cosmo didn't want to hear it. This was not the time to dream of things that couldn't be. He had a funeral to plan. And maybe when he got home, he'd put on *Non-Stop Erotic Cabaret* and play "Tainted Love" as loud as possible over and over until the stylus on the turntable wore out. Especially if his neighbor was on the phone – which he always seemed to be. He wasn't sure whether it was the guy in number twenty or number twenty-two, but godawful "on hold" music was always penetrating the walls. The poor man must have a lot of issues that required calling customer service.

Cosmo tossed his paper towel in the garbage and leaned against the sink. "I don't want to talk about Zedd anymore. We're going to throw a party, remember?"

"That's the spirit."

"Oh, it will be. It's going to be downright spectral."

4

SPIRITS IN THE MATERIAL WORLD

Micah - Present Day

The shower curtain ring sat on the drafting table, and Micah kept expecting it to disappear, to be absorbed back across the veil into the afterlife. But every time he picked it up, which was frequently, it was still as solid and unimpressive as a curtain ring should be.

Photos of it and the marker message on the bathroom mirror didn't look like much evidence. Maybe he needed to install cameras. But who was he going to show? Everett? Between keyboard clacks and high-definition views of his brother's sinuses, Everett would tell him the shadow he'd caught on film was simply that, a shadow. Some play of light from a passing car and Micah really was paranoid and did he call any of those therapists yet?

Scrolling through his contacts, Micah pressed the number for the hotline and wedged in his earpiece.

"Thanks for calling, lover. Our operators are aching to talk to you. What gender are you interested in?"

"Surprise me."

"Hang tight while I find your perfect match."

Sultry music piped through the earpiece. Micah twirled the curtain ring between his fingers.

A deep baritone rippled in his ear. "Hey there. I'm–"

"Don't tell me your name. Anonymous is better. But pronouns are okay... How are you tonight?"

There was a pause. "Can't get enough of me, huh?"

"Mr Satin Voice, we meet again."

"Looks that way. I'm glad, actually. The stuff you said last night about how everyone's body is beautiful, and how I probably have nice hands and what not... That made me feel really good about myself, man. You don't even know."

Micah smiled. "Good. I meant it."

The operator purred into the earpiece. "Now, you tell me what I can do for you tonight."

"If I want to talk about something other than your body, will you hang up on me?"

"Nah. If you wanna beat it while we talk about football or something, I'm not going to judge."

"I don't ever touch myself during these calls. But the topic on my mind is rather unusual."

"It's your dime, baby. Try me."

"I think my apartment is haunted."

He expected the operator to laugh or adopt an "I'm humoring you" voice, but his tone was sincere. "What makes you say that?"

"The same eighties songs have been playing out of nowhere in the middle of the night for three weeks, and yelling at the neighbors has done nothing. There are loud noises, things falling down, and a weird message appeared on my bathroom mirror."

The operator would be amused now. He'd tell Micah they were unrelated events, that ghosts weren't real, that someone had to have written that message when Micah wasn't looking – the same things Micah had been telling himself.

"The last house I lived in was haunted," the operator said. "We heard footsteps up and down the hallways at night, and we thought it was one of the kids. It sounded like a kid running. But when we checked their rooms, they were fast asleep. And once the bedroom door opened and then slammed shut again."

Micah glanced over his shoulder at the dark room. "So what did you do?"

"We moved the hell out of there. That house had bad vibes."

"I can't move. My lease isn't up, and I like this place besides. It's a steal for what it is. Anywhere else would be twice as expensive for half the amenities."

"You got bad vibes being in there?"

Micah pursed his lips. Maintenance had shampooed the carpets while he was in the hospital –after the police got the evidence they needed, not that it amounted to anything – but it hadn't removed the bloodstains. Ximena had given him a rug to cover them up.

"The worst thing that could happen to me already did, and it wasn't caused by a ghost," Micah said. "My life is already bad vibes."

"Don't say that. It can always get worse."

"That's not comforting."

"Not supposed to be. But I've got this friend who does house cleansings. She's real in tune with otherworldly stuff. She could probably help."

"Will she burn some sage in my living room then charge me fifty bucks?"

"Nah, she mostly does this stuff for free. Aside from cleansings, she has EMF meters, EVP recorders, and all kinds of tools for detecting and communicating with ghosts. I moved out of my last place before I knew her, but her clients swear by her. Lemme give you her website."

Micah wrote down the address as the operator gave it. The ghost hadn't done anything threatening, but he couldn't sleep, and his mind registered every unusual noise or shadow as an intruder. Cosmo had to go.

Sitting on the rug with a strange woman, a crystal ball between them, was out of the question, but if she had any investigative tricks or suggestions of things he could do to fix this, that would be useful.

"Her name is Déjà Solano. Tell her Darryl referred you."

"Darryl." Micah never wanted to know their names. Anonymity kept a safe distance between them. They could chat and he'd draw and then they'd go their separate ways. But now he felt compelled to introduce himself. "Thanks. I'll send her a message. I'm Micah, by the way."

"It's been a pleasure, Micah. You wanna keep chatting, or you have your fill for tonight?"

He wasn't sure what was worse – drawing in silence at his desk, or lying wide awake in bed to a ghost playing eighties synth.

"I'd like to, but I think I need to address this ghost problem."

"Gotcha." Darryl's voice lilted. "Talk to you tomorrow maybe, huh?"

Micah smiled. "You never know."

He ended the call, then opened his laptop and navigated to Déjà's website. He'd expected something with casual fonts and horrid color combinations, coupled with a cheesy headshot, simply because "freelance ghost evictions" didn't sound like something that came with an air of professionalism. But a soothing scheme of navy and smoky gray splashed across the screen. A pop-up greeting directed him to the navigation bar. It listed options with various prices:

> *Paranormal Investigation – buy me a coffee*
> *House Cleansing – cost of materials ($5-10)*
> *Séance – $50*
> *Automatic Writing – $200*

What in the world was automatic writing and why was it so much more expensive than an investigation?

He took off his glasses and rubbed his eyes, suddenly incredibly weary. Even the thought of reading a paragraph on a website was exhausting.

An investigation seemed unnecessary since he already had evidence of ghostly activity. And a séance was out because didn't you have to hold hands at a dining table for that? They couldn't both be in the studio at the same time. Maybe he could just email the woman and see what she recommended. He found her contact form and listed all his evidence, along with pictures. Hesitating, he mentioned that Darryl had talked highly of her, then hit submit on the form.

After climbing into bed, he propped his hands behind his head and stared at the ceiling. Déjà would show up with her sage and magic charms, letting psychic energy guide her to the source of Cosmo the Ghost. She'd wave a quartz pendulum and tell him it was okay to let go, to stop suffering.

If that's all it took, it almost seemed unfairly easy. Micah's bottom lip pushed up, a sudden and unexpected ache in his chest. Crystals and kind words didn't work on the ghosts inside of *him*.

He pressed a pillow over his face, hoping it would absorb the tears in the corners of his eyes so he could pretend they were never there.

His phone vibrated with an email notification.

*Darryl!! I haven't talked to him in months. He's got a
birthday coming up. I'd better get him something.
Sounds like you need a cleansing. Happy to help you out.
Shoot me your address and I can be there tomorrow morning.
—Déjà*

Micah sniffled. He wasn't sure how much faith to put into a... well, whatever Déjà called herself. The idea of a ghost haunting his studio was strange enough, and how a person would know what to do to get the spirit to leave was beyond him. But it was a problem with the promise of a solution, and that was at least something to focus on.

He supposed Déjà knowing how to banish ghosts wasn't any different than knowing the particulars of his own profession. Muscle memory and years of practice meant he didn't need head count theory to get the proportions of his figures right. Knowing where shadows would fall on a face – beneath the brow bone, at the join of the chin and lower lip, in the intertragal notch – was instinctive.

Exhaustion pulled him back down into the sheets. After sending a reply to Déjà, he shut his eyes and tried not to think about the idea of the ghost standing over him while he slept.

In the morning, when he was on his second cup of coffee, a knock came at the door. He forced his heart back into his chest and answered. Déjà was a curvy Latina woman in leopard-print pants and oversized sunglasses who looked like she stepped off the set of *Crybaby*. She stood on the welcome mat in black platform pumps, a backpack slung over one shoulder.

Micah joined her on the step. He shielded his left eye from the light and held out his other hand. "Pleasure to meet you."

She shook it. "Likewise. The artist world here is so small, isn't it? My ex lives in this complex." Her smile sagged. "An old friend lived here too."

"Oh really?" He thought of commenting that the artist world was *too* small in that case, but the look on her face made him change his mind. "Are you an artist too?"

"Yeah. I paint ghosts."

"Of course you do."

Peeking through the gap in the open door, she said, "The music going on right now?"

"No. Thank god." It had taken him a while to fall asleep, but once he did, it had been so deep and restful that he didn't wake up until nearly ten. "I can't believe this ghost doesn't own anything other than Soft Cell. Do you think I should buy him some Dead or Alive?"

"Nah. This should be quick and painless, and with any luck, they won't bother you anymore. Ready to get started? I need to grind some herbs if you've got a table or counter space I can use. Works best if they're fresh."

A bolt of anxiety shot through his chest, but he ignored it – he was okay. He pushed open the door and spread his arm. "Be my guest. I won't be going in with you, though."

A smile tugged at her lips, and she gave him a onceover. "You scared?"

"Not of ghosts."

She looked him up and down again, then pushed up her sunglasses. "What is this? Some kind of prank Darryl coerced you into? Or somebody is waiting behind the door to rob me as soon as I walk in?"

"No! Not at all."

Her gaze narrowed, emphasized by her sharply painted-on eyebrows. "Then you'd better explain because I don't like being messed with."

A knot formed in his chest, the words tangling in his mouth, but he had to say something or Déjà was going to leave. "I… was assaulted. And ever since then, I have to be alone in the studio. If someone is in there with me, I panic. Maybe not a family member – I don't know, they live too far away – but acquaintances or strangers?" He shook his head. Everett had flown in to bring Micah back from the hospital, and he'd come again a month later and stayed for a week, but Micah had been so out of it that he barely remembered.

Déjà's expression changed to the same damn one Ximena always wore – pity. "Sorry to hear that." She pushed open the door and kicked off her pumps. The heels were clear and liquid-filled, and little faux goldfish swirled around inside. She sat on the rug and opened her backpack. "Well, this won't take long. Don't want you standing on the step all day."

"It's nice out right now," he muttered. It was, but he would have said it even if there was a blizzard.

Déjà pulled out a small brass dish with a wire mesh top. She dropped in a black object that looked like a charcoal briquette and lit it with a lighter. It crackled, and a thread of smoke spiraled to the ceiling. Setting it aside, she took out a mortar and poured in herbs. She ground them with the pestle, and the scent of lavender floated through the doorway. "So, how do you know Darryl?"

"Oh. Uh." Shit. What was he supposed to say to that? He couldn't say he was a work friend or that their kids went to the same school. And he had no idea what kind of social life Darryl had. "Fender bender. I was backing out of a parking lot and ran right into him. We exchanged information and..." Micah shrugged.

She raised her eyebrows. "And you invited him to your old white man country club or what?"

"Nah. Phobophobes Anonymous."

"A fear of fear? Is that a thing?" Her expression shifted, eyes crinkling in a knowing smile. "If Darryl's Lexus got dented, you'd sooner be a stain on the pavement than friends with him. You got a crush on him, huh? Call him on his hotline? He's got that smooth voice that makes everyone wanna spread their thighs."

Heat flared in Micah's cheeks. "It's not like that. I'm not–"

"You don't need to justify it to me. Darryl's got back problems and needs a sit-down job that pays well enough for him to provide for his family." Déjà added more herbs and ground them with the pestle. "Far as I'm concerned, you're providing for his kids."

"Would you use that same argument if I was an alcoholic and showed up every night to the bar he tended?"

"No. Because calling his hotline isn't harming you, unless it's a sex addiction and you're using your last dollar to do it. Is that the case?"

"No. Not at all."

"Then I don't see any reason for you to be embarrassed. Everyone gets lonely. It's okay to need comfort."

Micah's throat constricted, and he hugged his arms to his chest. Maybe she *did* know how to reach the ghosts inside him. One of them, anyway. "You sure you want to serve paranormal eviction notices? Maybe you should be my therapist instead."

She barked a laugh. "I doubt I have the bedside manner for something like that. And your face has turned into a cherry tomato, so I'm sure you want me to change the subject. But seriously. You shouldn't feel ashamed."

"Thanks. I appreciate that."

Hopping up, Déjà poured the contents of the mortar onto the briquette in the brass jar. The heady scent of lavender, sage, and something with a woodsy citrus bite filled the room. Micah leaned his head against the doorjamb and drew in a lungful of the fragrant air. A flush still throbbed in his cheeks, but some of the tension left his shoulders.

"Even when activity seems localized to a specific room or hallway, ghosts like dark, enclosed places that don't have much activity – attics, closets, storage cabinets," Déjà said. "So I like to get every corner. Is it cool if I walk through your place?"

"Yeah. Sure. The music always seems concentrated in the front room, and the message is still on the bathroom mirror."

She paused. Smoke coiled from the brass jar in her hand. "By the way... Not sure you want to hear this, but this won't be an 'eviction,' per se. Pretty much every building hosts dozens of ghosts. They're here all the time, everywhere. It's just that they usually don't make a fuss. I can't kick them out. I just calm down the rowdy ones."

"Oh." That wasn't exactly reassuring. "What a bunch of freeloaders. They could at least chip in for the electric bill or let me know when I'm running low on milk. Do these calm ones watch me shower? Laugh at me when I spill salsa down my shirt?"

"Hard to say. Not much we can do about it if they do, but I've always gotten the sense that they're barely aware of our world anymore and couldn't care less about our human affairs."

This sparked a whole new tangent of thought about what most ghosts *were* aware of, and what purpose their post-death form served, but that seemed more like a question for a priest than the woman in his studio.

If the other ghosts weren't bothering him, they could hide wherever they wanted. He hadn't noticed their presence in the three years he'd lived here. He just needed the music and noises to stop. And no more shattered mirrors.

"There are mites that live on our eyelashes and in our oil glands," Micah said, "and the idea is kind of gross, I guess, but they're harmless. A handful of ghosts hiding inside the bathroom nook where I keep my toilet paper isn't any more stressful."

Déjà curled her lip, her nose wrinkled. "That's great for you, but now I'm going to be thinking about bugs all over my face."

She stopped by his art desk, wafting smoke toward his supply drawers and the narrow closet. After disappearing from view, she said, "You were right about the nook in the bathroom. Dark alcove with unfinished wood and a hard-to-open door. They're definitely in there."

Micah crossed his arms and leaned against the doorframe. "I guess if they come out of there while I'm taking a shit, that's a *them* problem."

He hadn't said it very loud, but Déjà snorted with laughter. "You're real chill about this, y'know? A lot of people aren't. You sure you want to stand outside? I'm not going to do anything to you."

"I'm sure." He retreated from the door and rested his elbows on the railing. Low clouds backlit by the sun hung over downtown, refracted in the windows of a nearby bank building. After a few minutes, footsteps and the heady scent of incense filled the doorway. Micah turned around.

Déjà tapped her nails against the brass jar, a furrow between her brows. "Okay, so whenever I enter a place with calm ghosts – which is pretty much everywhere – it's like... a soft draft of air, or cool water on a hot day. It gets stronger the closer I get to the source. In your case, that's the bathroom nook and your back closet. But a rowdy ghost is like someone sitting on my chest. I don't physically have a hard time breathing, I'm not in pain, but it feels constricting, suffocating."

She was going to tell him this ghost was strong, that his presence was crushing her, and that a simple cleansing wouldn't do the job. She was going to need to fumigate the place with weapons-grade sage, then she'd charge him a hundred dollars. This was probably her go-to shtick. The process was free on the surface, but there would *always* be a roisterous ghost who "resisted" her normal methods. This should have occurred to him much sooner.

"Let me guess–"

"There's nothing here." Her voice was flat, matter of fact, without any of the warmth it had contained before.

"What?"

"There's no rowdy ghost. I checked every corner, every cabinet and closet. You don't have one."

He scratched his head. Did she think he was wasting her time? "Well... Could he have gone into one of the other apartments? Maybe he saw your incense and snuck out for a while."

"That would be a first."

"Maybe it's easier to detect him at night?"

"It makes no difference for me... I'm going to be straight with you. I don't think you've ever had a rowdy ghost." She tapped his chest. "You have a lot of murky red and black going on here – anger, anxiety, and grief – in what is otherwise a very sweet and creative electromagnetic field. The manifestations are likely coming from within you. Your trauma has turned into negative psychic energy."

"*I'm* the ghost?" He huffed and balled his fists. "My anxiety is so bad that I'm shattering mirrors with my mind and writing cryptic messages to myself? And somehow, I've generated songs from an eighties band that I haven't listened to in years? That's preposterous."

She put up her hands. "No need to get defensive. Now that you know the source, you can take steps to stop it. I have some items that can help, but the best thing you can do is talk to a therapist–"

"Thank you for your time," he snapped. "What do I owe you for the materials?"

Déjà blinked. "Nothing." She picked up her backpack and slipped on her heels, then walked through the door.

Micah pulled a slow breath through his nose and worked the tightness from his throat. Therapy had been useless. He wasn't going to give up art so he could become a dog walker or some other damn thing he didn't want to be.

And something about this wasn't adding up. Maybe Déjà just wanted to get this over with as quickly as possible because his apartment reminded her of her ex. No matter the reason, he never had guests, and he didn't want this one leaving on a sour note.

"Hey, wait a second." He slipped inside and retrieved a twenty-dollar bill and the sketch in the top drawer of the drafting table.

Déjà stood on the stairs, her fist tight around the strap of her backpack.

Holding out the money, he said, "Please. For your materials and gas."

"I walked."

"Get an expensive coffee with the rest of it then. There's a great shop down the block."

She reluctantly plucked the twenty from his grip. "I hate to leave you without a solution, but you don't want to hear my advice."

The music could still be a neighbor, the mirror a random occurrence. But the message and the curtain ring... "Do you think your cleansing would have gotten rid of the ghost, even though you couldn't detect him?"

"If they were in there, the cleansing should have taken care of them, yeah."

"Okay." He waited a beat, expecting her to say something like, *If it doesn't work, don't hesitate to contact me again, and I'll attack this from another angle.* But of course she wasn't going to say that, because she thought the ghost was *him*.

She nodded to the sketch in his hand. "What's that?"

"It's Darryl. That's what I do when I call the hotline. Did I get him right?"

A small smile appeared on her face. "I've never seen him naked, but yeah, it looks like him. This is beautiful. You have a lot of skill."

"Will you give it to him for me if you happen to see him? Stick it in with his birthday present or something."

"You do have a crush on him, huh?"

"No, but I've never had the chance to give the drawings to anyone I've called."

She opened her backpack and carefully slid the drawing inside. "I'll be sure to give it to him. He'll love it."

"Thank you."

Déjà pulled out an herb sachet tied with a string of gemstone beads and brass charms. "I want you to have this, but you have to promise to use it. Don't you dare toss it in the trash."

"Is there a dried finger inside?"

She snorted. "No. But I put a lot of intention into making them. The charms are buried in cleansed dirt during the new moon and dug up after thirty days. Amber beads for comfort, howlite to relieve stress, and" – she plucked out a dark stone with subtle striations and pressed it into his palm – "rainbow obsidian. It'll help cleanse the negative energy and fill your darkness with radiance."

A soft sheen rippled off the stone as he tilted it. "Did you walk over here with a backpack full of rocks?"

"Yes." She handed him the sachet. "Promise to use it."

A bag of potpourri and a chunk of volcanic glass seemed like silly trifles to pit against his wall of bad vibes, but the sincerity in Déjà's voice made him squeeze them tight. "What do I do with these things?"

"Do you have a localized point of your pain in the studio? A certain spot or object?"

He swallowed, thinking of the box buried deep in his closet. "Yeah."

"Place the sachet and the obsidian there."

"Alright."

She nodded, then clanked down the stairs in her platform fish tank shoes. He couldn't imagine her walking very far in those things. The one time he'd done drag, he'd nearly broken his ankles.

The potent scent of incense still hung in the air as he walked back inside. He let it fill his lungs and bathe his insides as he headed to the closet and dug out the box. His stomach clenched as he pulled out a ceramic replica of Maurizio Cattelan's *Comedian*. Just looking at it summoned up memories he'd tried to bury much deeper than a closet was capable of. The sculpture of *Comedian* he'd had before was probably still in some police evidence locker downtown.

For some godforsaken reason, Everett thought buying Micah a replacement was a perfectly appropriate birthday gift. Micah had wanted to hurl the fucking banana across the room. Instead, he'd thanked Everett, insisted it would put his studio back the way it was supposed to be, then shoved it in a box.

After finding a screwdriver, he screwed the sculpture to the closet's back wall – a spot where he wouldn't have to look at the horrible thing – then draped the sachet over the top and slid the door closed.

5

FLESH FOR FANTASY

Micah - Present Day

YOU LOOK FABULOUS

Micah blinked at the message on the mirror. The previous phrase had vanished nearly a week ago, and this one looked so fresh that the marker wasn't yet dry. He swiped his hand through the words and his fingers came away stained mint green, though that didn't erase the phrase.

He wouldn't ever call himself "fabulous," but there was a certain refreshment to his face that hadn't been there in some time. It helped that there hadn't been any Soft Cell at night recently, but apparently hoping that meant the ghost was gone was too much to ask. Though Déjà's cleansing had kept the ghost away for days, Micah's studio no longer smelled like sage and lavender. As silly as it was, he kept the chunk of rainbow obsidian under his pillow. That he felt fresh and upbeat this week was a placebo effect surely, but maybe that was okay.

No matter what Déjà had been right about, the idea that these mirror messages were coming from himself, and that he'd manifested a random shower curtain ring in the bathtub, was ludicrous. He had a rowdy ghost, and it was too bad Grandma wasn't here to tell him what to do about it.

He could get herbs of his own and hang potpourri everywhere or burn a shit-ton of it so often that Ximena would be convinced he was a complete stoner. But that didn't seem like a long-term solution.

He traced the letters on the mirror, trying to imagine the hand that wrote them. Slender fingers or thick and sturdy? Wide palms or delicate and narrow? Prominent knobs of knuckles, ropy veins, freckles, or scars? Did Cosmo bite his nails or wear polish or chunky rings?

Trying to imagine the ghost's appearance almost felt like drawing the strangers he randomly called.

Fishing a dry erase marker from a drawer, he wrote beneath the ghost's message:

And what do <u>you</u> look like?

After staring for a moment and praying the ghost wouldn't appear in the hallway as a half-decayed corpse, Micah left the bathroom, then stopped at the closet, pushing away his button-up shirts to reveal the replica of *Comedian* screwed to the wall. The potpourri sachet hadn't melted the duct-taped banana or eaten into it like acid. No evidence that Déjà's magic charm was destroying the evil that the sculpture embodied. But looking at it didn't come with quite the pain that it had before.

He closed the closet, then peeked into the bathroom and did a double take at the mirror:

VERY FUNNY ♡♡

Micah's confusion of what the answer meant momentarily overshadowed the fact that the ghost had *replied*. He was communicating with a dead, twenty-something tenant named Cosmo. Who needed the latest iPhone when you had a supernatural medicine cabinet?

He walked out of the bathroom, ran a hand through his hair, then walked back inside. Did *very funny* mean Cosmo thought he looked funny? Or the concept of him looking like anything at all was funny because he no longer had a body? Maybe once you died, you lost all concept of who you'd been, the life you'd led, and what you looked like. That was depressing.

The people Micah called, like Darryl, were sometimes reluctant to describe themselves in an honest manner, or they used padded language that skirted around their insecurities. But Micah always meant it when he said all bodies were attractive. The human form simply was. That concept had always been easy to apply to others, but far harder to attribute to himself when he spent his teens struggling with the incongruence of his inner and outer self. His body hadn't been bad or unattractive, it just wasn't the right one for *him*. With hormones and surgery, he'd reached a place of acceptance, though.

His face with its scars that refused to fade to white… not so much, but he'd had them less than a year. Maybe in time they too would be something he'd come to accept.

He pulled the cap off his marker and wrote beneath Cosmo's message:

You're beautiful

Maybe Cosmo would think that was funny too, but if he'd forgotten what he looked like in life, someone needed to tell him.

He stared into the mirror, waiting for letters to form. This needed to be recorded. It would be better evidence than any so far. Maybe convincing enough to show Everett. He hurried out of the bathroom and snatched his phone. By the time he made it back, there was already a reply:

XOXOXO

Cosmo was certainly friendly. Flirty? Then again, Micah *had* called him beautiful. Maybe he'd had no one to talk to in the three years since his death.

What a miserable thought. Micah's phone was his main source of socialization, and just the idea of someone taking it away made him want to curl up on the floor in the fetal position.

Which begged the question, why were the messages only showing up now? Because the mirror shattered? The nightly music had only been going on for a month, and there were no strange noises before that either.

There were dozens of questions that begat a dozen more. And none of them had a definitive answer. He could ask the ghost, but there was only so much space on the mirror, and he needed to choose his phrases wisely.

Please stop playing Soft Cell. It keeps me up.

Aiming his phone at the mirror, he waited. After a few minutes, the screen went to sleep, and Micah realized he was staring at his blown pupil and how his biggest scar distorted the edge of his eyelid, tugging it down and breaking the symmetry of his face. He turned away, woke up the phone, and pointed it back at the mirror without looking at his reflection.

He had a tripod somewhere, but searching for it would require leaving the bathroom. Shaking out his aching arm, he said, "Come on, Cosmo." It wasn't like a ghost was busy, right? Unless he didn't plan on replying.

A knock came at the door, and Micah jumped. The phone fell from his grip and clattered into the sink. Who the hell could that be? He hurried to the door and peered through the peephole. Ximena's distorted, fish-bowl face stared back. Hopefully this would be quick.

She smiled as he opened the door. A grocery sack dangled from her hand. Food again?

"Buenas tardes, Micah. How are you doing today?"

Shielding his eye from the sun, he glanced over his shoulder at the dim hall. "I'm fine. How are you?"

"Good, thank you. But I got a scolding from the mailwoman because your box was full again. She couldn't fit anything else inside, and didn't want to have to send it back. I told her I would take it all up to you, which I don't think is probably legal, because it isn't my mail or my–"

"Wait." He pointed to the grocery sack. "All of that mail is mine? Did the universe vote to make me the next Santa Claus?" It couldn't have been that long since he'd been down to check it.

She handed him the sack. He pawed through the sheaf of letters – hospital bills, car insurance, a flier for an event in the park on August sixth. That was over a month ago.

"Sorry. I'll leave myself a reminder to check it more often."

Ximena's brows pushed up. There was that pitying expression again. She opened her mouth, but he said, "I've just been busy. And distracted. Tired, too. I won't let it get to that point again. Thanks for bringing it by."

"Now I have to have maintenance check someone's base heater. It scorched the leg of their nightstand, which is what happens when you put furniture too close, but for some reason they're claiming it's the heater's fault." She sighed. "There's always something. I'm making enchiladas, so come by later and get some, hm?"

"Alright." He waved goodbye, then shut the door and hurried back to the bathroom. The mirror didn't say anything new, and he sighed in relief. The sack of mail still hung from his arm, and he flipped through it. He paid all his bills online, so most of this was unnecessary. There was a birthday card from Mom and Dad; his birthday was in July. He hadn't checked his mail for two months? It was easy to excuse it away as the card getting lost, but he left the house so rarely that the days bled together, indistinguishable from one another. If he was being honest with himself, it was entirely likely that he hadn't checked his mail since July.

The deafening distortion of "Desperate" suddenly blasted from the front room. Crisp green block letters formed on the mirror.

This was it! Fumbling his phone with shaking hands, he hit record and aimed. Looking at the mirror through the phone's screen removed it one step from reality, but it was still tempting to flee the bathroom and slam the door behind him.

The fork of a K appeared, slightly slanted Es, the swoop of a P. Mark Almond's breathy lyrics floated above heavy bass.

I LIKE KEEPING YOU UP

Micah's jaw fell open. Oh, this ghost was cheeky. Maybe the dead didn't need to sleep, but–

As if they were leaning out of a frantically roiling mist, someone's upper half appeared at the sink directly in front of Micah. He glanced at the phone screen just long enough to confirm the ghost was in the shot, then turned his attention back to what was happening before him. Buoyant umber curls framed Cosmo's head, and the wide neck of his striped sweater had slid off one shoulder. His fair skin didn't have the bloodless pallor of ghosts in movies, but was a healthy bisque. He pressed a hand against the mirror, then leaned in and kissed the surface, punctuating his last message with a pink lipstick print.

Heart pounding harder than the max-volume eighties beats, Micah reached out and grazed the ghost's bare, warm skin. Cosmo turned around. His hazel, eyeliner-rimmed eyes widened. He shrieked and dropped a tube of lipstick. It bounced off the tile and rolled into the hall.

When Micah looked back up, Cosmo was gone. Soft Cell abruptly stopped, Micah's quickened breath filling the silence.

"He obviously screamed because you put your hand on him," the customer service operator drawled. "Poor thing's probably forgotten what human touch feels like."

Micah erased a smudge from his sketch of the operator, then continued on her hair. "You said you have bangs, right?"

"Yup."

She'd said she had "big hair," and he couldn't help but picture her as Dolly Parton. "I didn't think it would be possible to even touch a ghost."

"Well, you never tried before, did you?"

He wasn't sure how to answer that. Cosmo's tube of lipstick sat on the drafting table in the same spot it had occupied for the past three days. That the curtain ring he'd found in the tub was a physical object made sense… he supposed. It was a part of the apartment. But why lipstick belonging to a ghost was just as real and solid and didn't disappear along with Cosmo was perplexing. Shouldn't it be just as ghostly? Which led him to a strange thought he still wasn't sure what to do with: after the bathroom mirror shattered, he'd thrown out a handful of makeup and cosmetics that didn't belong to him. He'd presumed they were his ex-girlfriend's, even though they didn't seem like Courtney's style. But what if they were Cosmo's? He could certainly picture Cosmo wearing something as daring as chartreuse eyeshadow. Maybe those cosmetics and the lipstick now sitting on the drafting table had always been here, overlooked when Micah moved in and something Cosmo still liked to use even in death.

He felt bad for throwing the others out.

Sketches of the ghost hung on the wall in various poses, showcasing his angular jaw, his halo of dark curls, his sweater hanging off his shoulder.

The messages and kiss print had disappeared from the mirror; only Micah's half of the conversation remained. The recording on his phone was definitive proof, but if he shared it with people he knew or posted it on the internet for it to be sensationalized, then it would no longer be an experience he got to keep all to himself. Right now it was something intimate just between him and Cosmo. And, well, this random operator, who he could speak freely to and then never hear from again.

She said something into his earpiece.

"Sorry, what?"

"I said, 'he's cute, huh?' Wish I was haunted by a flirty young thing who left kisses on my mirror."

"Do you think he was flirting?" Micah wasn't sure why he was even asking. Cosmo was dead, and Micah had scared him off anyway.

"Well, duh, honey. He's been starved for affection for years since his tragic death, and he latched onto you because you're kind and handsome and he gets to watch you walk around your apartment in your boxers."

This was a mistake. The operator was turning this conversation into her own personal fan fiction. "You've got it all wrong. I wear briefs."

"Bet you have a six pack."

He glanced at his soft gut. She'd described herself for her sketch, but she probably didn't want the same amount of truth from him. "I don't think he's going to come back. Thought I'd be happy about that, but..."

But he couldn't get Cosmo out of his head.

Cosmo was a person – or had been – who'd intruded into Micah's studio. The ghost's appearance hadn't brought the same fight-or-flight response that normally came with someone walking into Micah's place, though. Which was confounding, because Cosmo could manipulate objects and had at least a partially solid body. He could hurt Micah just as easily as a mortal intruder. Easier, even. But for some reason, Micah wasn't afraid.

"Get a... What are those things called?" the operator said. "The board game with letters and a little pointer that the ghost controls?"

"Ouija board. The pointer is called a planchette. But I don't see how that would be any different than communicating via mirror. He doesn't want to talk to me."

"Write him an apology. Or get him some flowers. Do guys buy other guys flowers? Or play the music he likes."

Micah groaned. He was *not* summoning Cosmo back with Soft Cell. "I'm thirty-eight. Too old to be buying a twenty-seven-year-old flowers."

"Technically, he's thirty now, right? You said he's been dead for three years."

"Okay, but..." Did ghost logic work the same as vampire logic? A never-aging appearance, but mentally and emotionally they were far older?

It didn't matter. What he needed to do was forget about the whole experience and get on with his life. Things were improving – he was nearly done with the stupid grass on the client's landscape painting; there was no more music at two am.; no sudden noises that threatened to be intruders; and placebo or not, that piece of rainbow obsidian beneath his pillow every night and the sachet hanging off *Comedian* in the closet brought him a modicum of comfort. None of that was a replacement for the way his life had been before the assault, but it was still something.

"Thanks for chatting with me. And for letting me draw you. I should go now so I'm not holding up your line," he said.

"Oh honey, it's a slow night. I've got plenty of time to hear about your hot ghost."

He pursed his lips. "I appreciate that. Getting late for me, though. Maybe I'll try out one of your suggestions tomorrow."

"Well... Alright." The operator sounded like someone said her favorite soap opera had been canceled. "Good luck. If something develops, you can for sure call me on this line. Ask for number forty-six."

"Right." Not that she would need that with her running head canon. "Goodbye."

After pulling out his earpiece, he hung the operator's sketch on the wall with the others.

Forget about him. That's all there was to do. Micah's studio was his alone again. Everett was proud of him for the small steps he was taking toward living normally again, and he could continue that by finishing this commission. He needed to send out more job applications and submit his portfolio to other galleries, but every rejection was a harder kick to the gut, and it was difficult to summon up the motivation to keep trying.

He shut off the lights and climbed into bed, then opened his phone, finger hovering over a folder of social media apps. After detouring down to his photo gallery instead, he opened the video of Cosmo. Skipping to second twenty-three, he advanced frame by frame. "Fog" wasn't the best term for the substance that Cosmo leaned out of, but it was hard to describe it any other way. His upper half assimilated from nothing, soft sprays of agitated particles fringing his terminated torso.

Second twenty-seven: his reflection's eyes half-closed, pink lips pursed as he leaned toward the mirror.

Second thirty-four: Micah's hand on Cosmo's exposed shoulder.

Second thirty-six: Cosmo turned at three quarters, wearing a wry smile.

Micah had already touched him at that point, so why was he still smiling? It wasn't until second thirty-eight, when he locked eyes with Micah, that his expression shifted.

He hadn't expected Micah to be able to see him. That was it, wasn't it?

After rewinding to second twenty-seven and lingering on Cosmo's pucker face, he hit play. "Desperate" thumped through the phone's speakers. Desperate for love and attention.

I like keeping you up.

Cosmo was still accomplishing that whether music was playing or not. Micah opened the internet and typed *"Lemon Disco death Cosmo"*; he was met with articles about a cartoon show and the popularity of Cosmopolitans being on the decline.

Maybe Cosmo wasn't his real name. It would help if Micah knew how he died. But those articles sometimes didn't mention the person by name at all.

He typed *"Lemon Disco artist death."* The first hit was about a seventy-eight-year-old quilt-maker. Nope. The next result was an investigation into the death of an avant garde ceramics artist–

The phone sagged in Micah's hand. He knew her. *Had. Had* known her. He'd attended an art show with her, where they'd discussed their exhibits and how hard it was to get featured. She'd mentioned with disgust that the director of a now-defunct gallery had not so subtly suggested that if she could perform a certain talent other than clay throwing, he'd consider her submitted portfolio. Micah had never been asked to suck someone's dick to get into a gallery, thank god.

He skimmed the news article about the woman's death.

–found asphyxiated in her bathtub, the tie from a decorative shower curtain knotted around her throat.

"Christ." The police were questioning suspects at the time the article was written, but another internet search suggested they'd never arrested anyone, and the case had gone cold. How awful.

Sitting up, he flung off the covers, then picked up the shower curtain ring on the drafting table. Before it appeared, there'd been a loud jangling, like the rings clanging together as the curtain was ripped down, then a hard thud. Had the same person who killed the ceramics artist killed Cosmo? Strangled him in the bathroom?

No, no. That couldn't be the case. Ximena would have known about that. Even so, Micah couldn't help checking the deadbolt and window locks.

He sat on the bed, his traitorous imagination conjuring up an image of Cosmo in the bath, candles melting down the sides of the tub and wet spirals of hair clinging to his cheeks as he leaned back and shut his eyes. Then a dark shadow in the doorway. Cosmo wouldn't notice; he was listening to Soft Cell and thinking about his current work-in-progress or ice cream or a lover. Fishing wire dangled from the intruder's hand.

Micah bunched the sheets, his heart hammering. Just an ordinary day, then your entire life destroyed in an instant. Micah hadn't died, but he knew too well how that felt.

The intruder would stride into the bathroom and snatch Cosmo by the hair. Cosmo would shriek, he'd splash, fight back. He'd grab the shower curtain for leverage, but it would rip off the rod, and he'd fall, cracking his head on the edge of the tub. Blood would run into the bath water. The intruder would loop the fishing wire around Cosmo's neck and pull tight–

Tears fell onto Micah's leg, and he realized he'd balled the sheets so tightly in his fists that his hands were cramping. Shallow breath whistled through his nose. He pulled the rainbow obsidian out from under his pillow and squeezed it.

Maybe Cosmo had started visiting Micah because he realized their trauma was similar. And his fright upon Micah seeing him had been some kind of post-traumatic reaction. He didn't want to come back because he was afraid. But what if Micah was the only one who could help Cosmo move on to some better afterlife? Talking with a therapist about the shit Micah had been through had been awful, but the idea of doing it with the ghost – with someone who'd experienced something kindred – didn't seem so bad, especially if it was helpful.

Crossing into the bathroom, Micah erased his messages from the mirror, uncapped his marker, and wrote:

Here if you want to talk

6

TAINTED LOVE

Cosmo - Three Years Ago

Tapping the straw of his matcha milkshake, Cosmo stared at Déjà from across the diner booth. "I think my studio is haunted."

"Hmm?" Déjà flipped open one of the funeral home brochures spread out on the table. She pursed her lips, her lipstick as dark and glossy as her Guiness-and-cocoa milkshake.

As incredible as it would be for Cosmo to bid goodbye to his old life from inside a silk-lined, mahogany casket, it was simply too expensive, and he'd already dropped a hundred dollars on the obituary.

Déjà pointed to a brochure. "I just had a thought. What about cremation instead? We can get an urn, and then instead of ashes inside, people can write down the things they most love about you and put them inside. Then whenever you're feeling down, you can pull them out and read them."

He grinned and clapped his hands. "I love that. But you didn't hear what I said."

"You can get an urn for like thirty bucks."

Swiping away the brochures, he said, "I think my studio is haunted."

Déjà chewed on her straw. "Of course it is. You live there. Cosmo the Flamboyant Ghost."

"You don't believe me." He thought she of all people, with the ability to see auras, wouldn't make fun of him for such an idea. "Right, so an urn. Do they come in red?"

"Hang on. You're serious? What happened?"

A waitress in a car hop dress skated past with a tray of sodas. College students crowded the central counter, and someone at the jukebox started up a rockabilly version of "Walkin' After Midnight."

Cosmo slid into the other side of the booth beside Déjà and pulled his milkshake over. "Things have been a little odd for a while now. I thought the voice I keep hearing, always on the phone with customer service or a hotline, was a neighbor. I've been playing music to drown him out. But last night, I slipped on my bathmat and grabbed the shower curtain for leverage. The whole thing ripped down, along with the shower caddy." He scrubbed at the sudden goosebumps on his arms. "When it happened, someone let out the most dreadful shriek from the front room."

"You sure it wasn't you shrieking?"

He licked whipped cream from his straw and turned up his nose. "Fine. I suppose I'll withhold details about the shadow and the footsteps in the hall because you don't want to hear about my spooky new friend." The bathroom door had creaked open on its own, then a long silhouette drifted across the wall. Cosmo had almost called Déjà then, but opted for crawling under the sheets and shielding himself with the stuffed alligator from the theme park.

Déjà collected the pamphlets, shuffled them, then slapped them back on the table. "They're everywhere."

"What are?"

"Ghosts." Her teeth pressed into her bottom lip. "They're in my apartment, they're in yours. They're in this soda shop."

Cosmo stared. "Now *this* is more what I was expecting from you."

She regarded him uncertainly, looked out the window, then pushed the brochures into a neat stack. "You don't think it's weird?"

"It's very weird. Tell me more. Why would they haunt a soda shop? I mean, they do have incredible milkshakes, but... Do you think someone died in my studio?"

Her hands seemed to have taken on a nervous energy, fussing with the greasy salt and pepper shakers and laminated menus sitting askew in their rack. She rescued one of the maraschino cherries from her milkshake's wilting cream and bit it off the stem. "They – they go wherever they want. It doesn't mean they died there. Sometimes they're rowdy and people can hear and see them."

"But you see them all the time?"

"No. Just feel them. But I don't... I don't really want to talk about this. I've never told anyone."

Déjà looked smaller than Cosmo had ever seen her, her shoulders hunched and fingers nervously picking at the corner of a brochure. They were brochures for a party in his honor. She was here for *him*, while struggling with something in secret. Cosmo always garnered attention, but it wasn't fair for his gravity to be sucking up all the focus of their friendship.

He patted her leg and said, "You are fascinating and lovely. And I'm a shit friend. I'm sorry that I'm not a safe enough space for you to share that kind of thing with me."

"You're always safe." She gave him a squeeze. "And you're not shit. I just never knew how to bring it up before, I guess."

"You introduced yourself by telling me what colors my aura is made up of. If that's not a weird ice breaker, I don't know what is, and I knew then that we'd get along great. I'm always here if you want to talk about this, and I promise I won't judge." He waved a hand. "And even if the studio is haunted, it's constituent to my upcoming party. I haven't even died yet, and I'm already hanging out with ghosts." He tugged on a curl. "I'm thinking of wearing a black veil. Is that gauche?"

Déjà's pinched features softened. "Not nearly as gauche as painting your face white or wearing a bedsheet with eye holes cut out."

"Ugh. How vulgar. Can you imagine?"

She stared out at the car-studded parking lot, a hand on her chin, as chatter and rockabilly music filled the space between them. When she turned back, she said, "Do you like Rye?"

"I prefer white to be honest."

"You racist."

"Hot and thick. Slathered in butter. I want to really be able to sink my teeth in." He waggled his eyebrows.

"Sounds kinky. Why don't you invite me to these parties?"

"Because you don't want my white bread."

She snorted. "You're right, I don't. I love you, but I don't want your baked goods."

He smirked as he fished a thick curl of candied lemon peel from his milkshake. "Rye seems interesting. And as long as they're good to you, I like them." He wasn't sure how much those words were worth when they were coming from him. He'd gone back to Zedd again and again. But it didn't make them less true. Déjà too deserved someone to treat her like a queen.

"You haven't told them about your ghost-sensing ability?" he asked.

"No! They love my art, but I don't know how into me they are. And I don't want to ruin it by revealing some morbid quirk about myself that I can't shut off."

"Darling, you paint still lifes of things that have no business being at a picnic. If Rye loves them – which they'd better because your work is fabulous – then I'm sure learning about this talent of yours isn't going to faze them."

The jukebox fell silent, and Déjà's nails clicked against her milkshake glass, but most of her nervous energy seemed to have evaporated. She smiled and squeezed his hand. "You know, I don't know why I built up this 'talent' so much in my head as a terrible thing I shouldn't talk about, but I always thought if I told someone, they wouldn't want to be around me anymore. I'm not sure about telling Rye, but I'm glad I told you. Thanks. Really."

"We're always getting in our own ways, aren't we?"

"I can't see the ghosts but often I" – she leaned back and looked at the ceiling – "I get an image that accompanies one. It's never something I've seen in real life, but–"

"Your paintings." The things sitting on the picnic cloths amid glossy fruits and wine glasses in Déjà's still lifes had an unsettling organic quality, like something an untrained AI would render if asked to depict human organs. He shivered involuntarily. "Ghost picnics. I am thoroughly creeped out now, and I mean that in the best way! It's marvelous. You've got to tell Rye."

"No!"

"Have you even told them what colors their aura is?" The look on her face said that no, she hadn't. He swiped a lock of hair from his eyes. "Next time you see them, lead with that. They'll think nothing could be sexier than someone who can see not only who they are on the outside, but their *essence*. And then when art comes up, you seduce them further with your inspiration for your paintings."

She laughed. "No way. Not everyone has a hard-on for strange things."

"But the people who matter do. And Rye had better. If they don't, they're no good for you anyway."

They finished their milkshakes amid talk about Rye and the upcoming funeral party. When Cosmo mentioned that his sixty-year-old boss who maybe flirted with him on occasion was on the guest list, Déjà made no comment, which was a relief. He'd much rather talk about *her* budding relationship than the shambles of his own love life.

He hugged her goodbye and drove home, absorbed with what candles would melt the prettiest on the steps of the abandoned church out on Cherry Lane.

Ximena, his landlady, stood beside the rose bushes at the edge of the parking lot. Wearing a sun hat and gardening gloves with a pinstripe dress and pearls was certainly a statement. As he parked and stepped out of the car, she shook a pair of pruning shears at him. "Mijo, that boyfriend of yours is sitting on your doormat bawling his eyes out. I told him you weren't there, and that only made him cry harder. Please take him inside or get him to go away."

Shit. Cosmo stared at the fleshy pink roses blooming on the bush beside Ximena, certain he could still taste petals in his mouth. He pinched the bridge of his nose and muttered under his breath. "He's my *ex*-boyfriend. And I do not want to deal with this."

She snipped off a scraggly branch and tossed it onto a pile in the dirt. "Should I call maintenance to escort him away? Or the cops?"

"Cops? No, no. He just... He does this."

Ximena put her hands on her hips. A grid of light filtered through her sun hat and onto her irritated expression. "My ex was the same. I got a restraining order. Best decision I ever made."

Hopefully it wouldn't come to that. He said, "I'll keep it in mind. Love your look today, by the way. Very nineteen-fifties Better Homes & Gardens."

Her gaze slid down his body, and she wrinkled her nose. Today he was wearing green hotpants, a crushed velvet sport jacket, and chunky glass earrings shaped like lemons. "Er, thank you."

She didn't want his compliments. Fine. He headed past her and climbed the stairs. Hoarse sobs drifted from the second level. Zedd sat on the welcome mat in ripped jeans and motorcycle boots, his cheek pressed against Cosmo's door. Tears and snot ran down his face, and he clutched a striped sweater in a white-knuckled grip. So that's where that went.

Cosmo stopped at the mat, jaw clenched. "Go away."

Zedd looked up. His breath ratcheted, coming in wet gasps, and his whole body quaked. Though his throat worked, no sound came out. Dropping the sweater, he snatched the lapels of Cosmo's jacket and bawled into his stomach. "I thought you were dead!"

"Not until next week."

Wiping his nose on his sleeve, he said, "But the obituary. I couldn't believe it, but – but I went to your gallery and your boss said it was real."

Props to Royce for getting in the spirit, but the obit wasn't supposed to be printed until Friday, *after* Cosmo had passed out party invitations. "The obituary was in the paper?"

"On their website. Juan saw it and texted me. I don't understand. Is it some kind of performance art?"

"Something like that." Cosmo picked up his missing sweater, then fished for his keys.

Zedd kept his grip on Cosmo's jacket. "I didn't know what I was going to do. You're the love of my life."

"Uh-huh." Where the hell did he put his keys?

"I was sitting here thinking about you dead, laying on a tray in a morgue locker, with a sheet pulled up over you and your lips blue." Zedd rubbed his eye. "And all I could think was that there better be room for two people in that locker, because I was going to crawl in there with you."

Cosmo paused, hung up on the image. "You were going to break into a morgue and climb into a body locker with me?"

"Yeah." His breath hitched. "Just shut the door behind me and lay next to you under the sheet."

"That's... incredibly romantic." And the pain and sincerity in Zedd's face was genuine. Much more authentic than flowers and an impulse tattoo. Sitting up here sobbing against the door couldn't have been a performance if he'd truly thought Cosmo was dead.

I'll protect you to the ends of the earth, gorgeous.

Maybe Cosmo had made a mistake. His heart yearned for the love they once had. For all of the good that had been in their relationship. For there *had* been good. Zedd had had such an intense focus on him, and not just on his beauty like everyone else seemed to. He'd been interested in cracking Cosmo open and seeing all of the dark and dirty things that made him up, and he wanted to share his own with Cosmo. It hadn't been Cosmo's romantic visions of taste-testing pastries and reading books in bed, but it had been raw and true.

Zedd struggled to his feet, gripping the metal balcony railing for support. He searched Cosmo's face with bloodshot eyes, then caressed his jaw. Cosmo instinctively leaned into the touch and sighed.

"I'm so relieved that you're okay." Zedd dropped his hand and turned away, then stuffed his hands into the pockets of his leather jacket. "I'll leave you alone now."

After fishing out his keys, Cosmo unlocked the door. An ache throbbed in his chest, and the phantom sensation of Zedd's caress lingered. He pressed his nose to the soft wool of his sweater and inhaled a hundred days of eating takeout at Zedd's window seat while they talked about the tragedies of brilliant musicians. A hundred nights of falling asleep secure in the arms of another, with love bites purpling on his neck.

Cosmo was a forgettable novelty. He was Duchamp's snow shovel, and there was no soulmate for him, no love of his life. Not if it wasn't Zedd.

He drew in a slow breath and swung open the door. "Do you want to come in?"

Cosmo pulled on his missing sweater, then found his hotpants. Zedd let out an obnoxiously loud yawn and shut his eyes, burrowing into the pillows. One of Zedd's socks hung from the head of a mixed media sculpture. Cosmo frowned and flung the sock at him. "You going to sleep in my bed all day?"

"Better than sleeping with you in a morgue. It would have been nice if you'd given everyone a heads up that the obituary and all this death-planning stuff was just for a party."

"I didn't know the obit would be on the website." It made things rather awkward. It was a local paper, and no one outside of the city was supposed to see it, but having it on a website meant that anyone could. He needed to email the paper and have them take it down. God forbid someone send the link to Mom.

Stopping in the bathroom, he stared at his reflection. His hair was a bit frazzled, cheeks pink, and lips swollen and chafed from being kissed too hard. After taming his curls, he plucked a marker from the cup on the back of the toilet tank and wrote on the mirror:

YOU LOOK FABULOUS

He had to be careful with how hard he pressed the marker. This new mirror was probably fine, but he was still paranoid about the whole thing crashing down after what happened last week. To think Ximena accused him of breaking the mirror on purpose. Who needed that much bad luck?

That milkshake wasn't nearly enough to sustain him after an emotional conversation and vigorous makeup sex. He rummaged through the fridge, then called, "How does pizza sound?"

Zedd made a consenting noise. Cosmo found his phone and placed an order, then finished dressing. He tugged at his bare lobe. What happened to his other earring? Searching the floor, he headed into the bathroom, then raised his eyebrows. Beneath his compliment to himself was:

And what do you look like?

"Ha ha." He hadn't even seen Zedd get up to use the bathroom. Sneaky bastard. It was so nice to have things back to normal between them. It was tempting to tell Déjà, but she'd only yell at him about how Zedd was average and would merely cheat on Cosmo again. The thought cramped his stomach. Zedd hadn't even promised that he *wouldn't*.

But no, it had to be different this time. Zedd wouldn't sob on his doorstep and commit to wasting away beside Cosmo's corpse if he didn't love him. And if he loved him that much, he wouldn't hurt him.

The other earring sat on the floor beside the toilet. Cosmo threaded it through his lobe, then turned to the mirror and wrote:

VERY FUNNY ♡♡

He paced through the kitchen and texted Mom that he was not, in fact, dead, and she shouldn't believe anything that said otherwise. After hitting send, he decided that more of an explanation was probably warranted lest she still worry. He sent her another text, stared at the screen for a moment with no reply, then pocketed the phone. Zedd had written another message on the mirror in the meantime, telling Cosmo that he was beautiful.

With a flutter in his chest, he headed down the block to pick up the pizza.

What was he supposed to do about the party now? The point was for his old life to die so he could move on – without Cinereous Zedd – and be reborn into a better future. But there was no telling what was waiting for him out there. Zedd was what he knew.

His phone rang, "*MOM*" filling the screen. He answered, and she said, "I'd better be invited to your funeral."

"If it were real, of course you would be. I'm just having a party. My artsy friends will be there."

"I'm artsy."

He rolled his eyes. She was, but her beautiful watercolors of flowers that won blue ribbons at the fair weren't the same as his trompe-l'œil skulls, or Déjà's picnic ghosts, or Rye's chairs made out of barbed wire. "Remember when I threw a Halloween party and there were chocolate-covered crickets in the snack bowl and a display of jarred pig fetuses I'd stolen from Science class?"

She made a strangled noise. "Y-yes. Is this the same thing?"

"Absolutely not. That party was terrible. It didn't even have a theme. But my point is we don't have the same tastes, and you would still find *this* party and my friends utterly grotesque, Mother. We're all weird and gay."

The bell on the door to the pizza place jingled as he pushed through. Piercing 8-bit sound effects from an arcade game made it hard to hear Mom's reply. He turned up the volume on his phone as she said, "Did you break up with Zedd again?"

He swallowed and nearly bumped into the person behind him in line. "Why would you say that?"

"Because you always do the most dramatic things when you're hurting. I might not understand the appeal of decorating with dissected animals–"

"There won't be anything of the sort this time–"

"–but I want to be there for you no matter what."

He sighed, tucking the phone against his ear as he picked up his order and left the restaurant. He loved Mom, but there was a clear divide between the activities he engaged in with her, and the ones he didn't. Baking with her on the weekend or going to a flower show? Absolutely. Taking her to a Snake Milk concert or a showing of an independent horror film in an abandoned warehouse? Definitely not.

Mom was still talking. "And as for the other part, I have a whole stack of erotic sapphic paintings I did in college."

Cosmo paused, staring at a fire hydrant on the corner. "You're... You're bi, Mom?"

"Honey, why do you think I kicked your father out after what he did to you? Aside from the fact that I love you unconditionally and would have done it regardless."

Dad had been begrudgingly tolerant of Cosmo's feminine traits as a kid, but he'd tried to throw Cosmo out at sixteen after catching him kissing a boy on the doorstep. Mom had thrown Dad out instead.

His heart swelled, and he crammed the memory back into the vault it came out of before he teared up on the sidewalk. No wonder she'd kept those paintings hidden.

"Why didn't you ever tell me?" he asked.

"Eh, it's one of those things that just... I don't know. I almost told you after kicking your father out, but I didn't want to take away from what you were going through. You had queer friends your own age who you could probably relate to better. I figured if I ever got a girlfriend, though, I'd let you know."

He chuckled. "You can come to the party. If you want. Of course you can."

"I want to decorate."

"Absolutely." He said goodbye, then tucked the phone back in his pocket. Mom's revelation floated with him as he walked home. Snores drifted from the bed as Cosmo came back inside. Hopefully Zedd didn't have anywhere to be this afternoon.

Detouring into the bathroom, he was met with yet another message that Cosmo needed to stop playing Soft Cell. Odd. Soft Cell wasn't even going right now. And that wasn't much of a flirt.

Well, the lug needed to get out of bed and eat anyway. Cosmo slid his pink LP of *Cruelty Without Beauty* out of the sleeve, flipped it to side B, and set it on the platter. He pushed the power button on the receiver, cranked the volume knob, and set the stylus on "Desperate."

Zedd startled at the sudden blast of synthesizer, then sat up in bed and rubbed his face. "Jesus. What time is it?"

"Pizza time, darling. Put some clothes on."

Zedd pulled on his pants, shook a cigarette from his pack on the coffee table, and walked out onto the balcony. Cosmo headed into the bathroom and picked up his marker.

I LIKE KEEPING YOU UP

He ran a blush-pink lipstick across his lips, then kissed the mirror. Things were going to be okay. It was different this time.

A gentle hand grazed his shoulder. He smiled and turned, prepared to kiss the rest of the lipstick off on Zedd.

A bespectacled white man with dark, tousled hair and an eye socket of scars stood directly behind him.

Cosmo screamed. He scrambled for the door, certain the man would slam it shut and trap him in here to do god knew what. But the man *evaporated*. Some unperceived mist swallowed up his wide-eyed face, and he disappeared.

Clawing at the doorframe, Cosmo lunged for the hall. His foot slipped on something cylindrical, and he slammed into the ground. A marker rolled away, stopping at Zedd's foot.

"Shit. You okay?" Zedd gripped Cosmo by the arm and pulled him up. "What the hell is going on?"

His shoulder and wrist throbbed from the impact with the floor, but he barely processed it. "There was a m– A man. In the bathroom."

Zedd poked his head into the bathroom then ran into the front room and ripped open the curtains. "Where'd he go?"

"Disappeared. A ghost."

"The hell he is." Zedd flung the sheets away from the bed and peered underneath. "I know he didn't go out the front door, because I was smoking out there. Where'd you go, asshole?"

Cosmo picked up the marker he'd slipped on. Black, like the writing on the mirror. "Did you write the replies to my messages in the bathroom?"

"What?" Zedd yanked open the fridge door as if someone could actually hide inside.

"Did you write 'You're beautiful' and 'Stop playing Soft Cell. It keeps me up' on the mirror?"

"No?" Zedd slid open the closet and shoved clothes away. He looked back. "That guy left you a message that you're beautiful? I'm going to smash this creep."

Cosmo pressed a hand to his still-throbbing heart. This ghost was watching him, listening to his music, leaving him messages. Cosmo had been planning his own funeral, caught up in the romanticism of death, and the first thing he did upon seeing an actual ghost was scream.

Zedd opened the front door and stared out. "Wherever he went, he's not here now. Must have slipped inside when you were getting the pizza."

"He's a spirit."

"No such thing."

"I need to call Déjà." Cosmo picked up his phone and opened his contacts, but his fingers trembled and he clicked on the wrong name.

"That witch who's always telling you to leave me? She's putting weird thoughts in your head. You don't need her."

"Excuse me?" Cosmo put a hand on his hip. "You don't get to choose who my friends are."

Zedd closed the door and stopped before Cosmo. "You sleeping with her?"

Cosmo scoffed. "You've got to be kidding me."

"That's not a 'no.' And why else would you hang out with her so much? Why else would she try to drive a wedge between us? She's making you all morbid, writing up obituaries and planning a death party. No wonder you think you're seeing ghosts. She's probably making a voodoo doll of me that she'll stab in the balls anytime I get near you."

The band constricting Cosmo's chest ratcheted tighter. He thought of her hunched shoulders in the soda shop, confessing that ghosts were everywhere. Encouraging him to find someone who would treat him like a queen. Zedd was treating him like anything but.

When Dad had caught Cosmo kissing his date on the doorstep, he'd yanked Cosmo inside and slammed his fist into the drywall right beside his head. He'd called Cosmo the f-slur and swore Cosmo wouldn't spend another night in the house. Mom had loved Dad, but she didn't hesitate for even a second to start throwing his clothes out on the lawn. In the end, Dad had gotten on his hands and knees, crawling after her and sobbing like the pathetic worm he was.

Mom had been married to him for close to twenty years, and in a split second she'd mustered up the conviction to throw him out. She never took him back.

Cosmo's throat welled with rage as he stared at Zedd. "Get out."

"What?"

"You will not bad mouth my dearest friend, and I won't stand one more moment of you treating me like shit. The audacity of you! Accusing *me* of being the one to cheat when your cock is in every willing participant you find! Maybe I would have fallen for Déjà because she is warm and wonderful and mesmerizing, but she isn't into men." Cosmo wasn't so sure he was a man, but that was beside the point. "You can forget crawling into a body locker with me; I will rise from the dead to drive you away. *Now get out!*"

He flung open the door, snatched Zedd's shirt, shoes, and cigarettes, and hurled them over the balcony.

"Goddamn it!" Zedd clanked down the stairs after his items.

After hauling the giant stuffed alligator out the door, Cosmo punted it over the balcony railing. It bounced off a rose bush, then rolled into the parking lot.

Tears needled his eyes, but he sucked them back. He was not crying over this fool again. Zedd wasn't average, but he wasn't any good either, and Cosmo was an idiot in a haunted studio, clinging to love that didn't exist.

He grabbed his phone, his keys, and the pizza, and hurried down to his car. Zedd was pulling on his shoes, but he abandoned one and strode towards him. Cosmo jumped into the car, put it in drive, and hit the gas. It lurched onto the sidewalk and Zedd leapt away, cursing. The car thumped over the stuffed alligator. Cosmo backed over it, then peeled out of the parking lot.

7

DEAD MAN'S PARTY

Cosmo - Three Years Ago

Soulful synthesizer filled the church. Candles twinkled from windowsills, orange light bobbing against cloudy, cracked panes. Spiderwebs fluttered in the draft like confetti streamers. Holes gaped in the roof, and pigeons lurked in the rafters. It had taken some scrubbing to get rid of the worst of the bird droppings, but Cosmo didn't mind the slightly decrepit ambiance.

Between Mom insisting on decorating, and friends handing out invitations and even moving things out of his apartment, he felt utterly useless. His attempts to help had been swatted away because Déjà said dead people weren't in charge of hosting their own funerals. Luckily, he'd prepped all of the food in advance before anyone could take the task from him.

He hadn't planned on moving, and he'd had to break his lease to do so. It was easy to explain it as just another part of his mission to bid farewell to his old life, and *not* because he was terrified of living in a studio with a ghost who liked to sneak up behind him in the bathroom.

Stevie hammered the keyboard beneath water-warped prints of the Virgin Mary. The funeral music dissolved into an enthusiastic rendition of "Tainted Love." Bless her.

"There are spirits here, yes?" Cosmo didn't mind – he expected it, really – as long as none of them followed him home like lost puppies.

"Yeah." Déjà tied red strands of confetti to the bare curtain rods over the windows. Chains with moon phase charms jangled on her netted headdress. "But here, more than usual."

"Rowdy ones?"

"No. They seem quite at peace."

That was a nice thought. If he died and had the ability to haunt people, he absolutely would, but peaceful ghosts seemed like appropriate guests for his send off to his new life.

Cosmo set his urn on a pedestal at the head of the room, then turned it until the little placard with his name on it was facing forward. Flower-laden photos of him on easels flanked the urn. "I'm half-expecting the ghost from my studio to appear in a pew during our party. Do you think *he's* at peace?"

Déjà set a jar of pens and a tray of paper strips next to the urn. "No. He made noise and opened doors and touched you. He's rowdy. The rowdy ones aren't at peace, otherwise they wouldn't be doing that."

She said she didn't know how she knew these things, but that they were true. Cosmo didn't question it. He was grateful she was opening up to him at all about it. Some things you couldn't keep bottled inside, and you needed the right friend to tell them to. Déjà had been that person for him many times, and it was long overdue for him to return the favor.

Something tugged on Cosmo's veil, and he gasped, imagining the bespectacled phantom from his studio pulling it off his head.

"Hold on, girlfriend. You're going to rip it." Déjà held him steady and plucked the veil free. "Snagged on a splinter. Everything here is splinters."

"A waist-length veil was maybe not the best choice, but the short ones didn't drape right over my hair." And how was he supposed to appear spectral if his veil looked like a napkin he'd placed on his head?

A full moon charm waggled between Déjà's painted-on eyebrows as she adjusted his halo of a headband. She stepped back and smiled. "I hope we all look so good when we move on."

He hadn't told her about sleeping with Zedd. When he'd arrived at her apartment, she'd chalked up his emotional state and his refusal to return to the studio to being touched by the ghost. The truth itched on the tip of his tongue, but there was no point to speaking it. He'd thrown Zedd out, changed his number, and wasn't going to give him an ounce of his thought ever again. It was Cosmo's funeral, but Zedd was the dead one.

Mom approached with a sack hemorrhaging Halloween garland. Metallic orange jack-o'-lanterns winked amid black tinsel, and thick clots of faux cobwebs were stuck to some of it. It looked like something she'd pulled out of the storage unit. He could clearly picture her digging through tangles of Christmas lights and glittery craft stick ornaments he'd made as a kid, looking for decor that paired with her only child's funeral party. Getting interrupted by that nosy neighbor – what was her name? – and Mom listening politely with her jacket pulled tight around her.

Did she keep her erotic sapphic paintings in the storage unit? Cosmo could only imagine the look on the neighbor's face if she happened to see them while Mom was looking for decorations.

After brushing a stray curl from her face, Mom fished inside the bag of the garland, and even though Cosmo didn't want the church to look like a suburban haunted house, if she wanted to put it up, he wasn't going to stop her.

She pulled out a cardboard box and handed it to him. "There's another in here."

He prized open the lid, revealing a ceramic skull with an open top, a candle holder nestled in the bottom.

Mom retrieved a second one and poked her fingers through the eye sockets. "When the candle inside melts, the wax runs through the holes and makes it look like it's crying. Which is more sad than grotesque, but I figured with your artwork…" She shrugged.

"Oh, how fun. They're very cute. I'm sure we have candles in here that will fit."

He started to turn for the bags of decor clustered beside a collapsed pew, but the church door creaked open, and Royce walked inside. He put his hands behind his back the way he did when surveying Cosmo's installation work in the gallery, then nodded approvingly.

He stopped before Cosmo. His silky charcoal tie was patterned in black embroidered paisleys. And it was crooked. "There's the man of the hour. You look like a gothic bride."

"Thank you."

"And where's the groom?"

Déjà grunted and threw Royce a glare. She protectively linked her arm in Cosmo's. "That position isn't available."

"Ah. Then are you a friend? Or a *friend*?"

"None of your business."

Cosmo glanced at Mom, intent to put this conversation to rest before anything mortifying came out of someone's mouth, but Royce said, "It *is* my business when Cosmo's romantic affairs seem to infiltrate the gallery on a regular basis."

Good heavens. That wasn't true; Zedd had only shown up the one time, but once was bad enough. "Déjà has been my best friend since Art History 101. You met her at the Night Gallery afterparty, remember?"

"My attention must have been elsewhere," Royce said.

"Yeah, on Cosmo." Déjà squeezed his arm. "Because he'd been drunk on champagne, and you probably thought there was an opportunity to—"

Cosmo put up his hands. "We're going to start soon. Royce, be a love and dump the ice into the coolers, please. The tiny wines need to be chilled. Déjà, some of the candles have gone out. Can you relight them?"

Royce headed to the hors d'oeuvres table and ripped open a bag of ice. Déjà pursed her lips, adjusted Cosmo's veil, then pulled a lighter from her pocket.

Now he needed something for Mom to do that was out of earshot of anything else potentially embarrassing. People from different social circles mixing was a point of awkwardness he hadn't considered when planning this thing. And being alive for your own funeral meant you were witness to it.

Mom took the skull votive from his hands and headed toward a bare windowsill beside the drink cooler. She touched Royce's shoulder and said something. When he turned to her, she smiled that tight smile she got when she wasn't sure if someone was friend or foe. Cosmo wiped his hands down his face. It was too bad he didn't have that casket, because there was a good chance he would prematurely expire if this kept up.

Well, it was his party; he could die if he wanted to.

More people filtered in – art colleagues, old coworkers, people from parties, cousins, friends-of-friends, and even that girl from the coffee shop down the block. He couldn't remember inviting some of them, but that was okay. There weren't a lot of sturdy pews, but still plenty of places to sit.

A curvy Black person with a short, fluorescent orange afro approached, their hair color a sharp contrast to the muted church walls. They looked like a model for a commercial where the product wasn't even shown, but whatever they were selling, you needed it before it sold out.

"Hello, Rye," Cosmo said.

"Hey. Pretty sure I've been to all of the same parties you have in the last year," they said. "This is by far the most incredible, and it hasn't even started yet. Did you have to clean up a lot of trash to get this place ready?"

"There were some beer bottles and a couple junkie needles, but it was practically untouched. No one comes in here because it's haunted, you know." He paused. "Do you believe in ghosts?"

"Yes." They whispered the word as if saying it any louder might summon one, but their eyes glittered. "I'm drawn to all of that paranormal stuff."

He'd thought so. "Isn't it thrilling to be able to experience something past your notions of the world? To touch beyond that barrier, even in a small way." He brushed back his veil, then gripped Rye's jacket and leaned in, hoping his face looked pained. "Rye…"

Rye frowned. "Are you okay?"

"Rye…" Cosmo gasped and let his knees buckle enough to tip Rye off balance and make them lean closer. "You– You have to do something for me. It's my last wish as – as I leave this mortal coil."

They scoffed, the concern in their eyes replaced with amusement. "I guess I can't refuse that."

Cosmo clawed at Rye's jacket. "It's Déjà. You must…"

At the mention of Déjà, Rye straightened and glanced around the room. "Yeah?"

"You must give her the love she deserves."

Their eyes bulged. "Is it that obvious that I like her?"

"Yes. And she wants you too."

"She does?"

"Please, Rye!" Cosmo threw the back of his hand against his forehead like an expiring Shakespeare character and fell into Rye's arms. "My only wish is that the two of you fall madly in love and–"

"Okay, okay! Shhh! I get the message." Rye pushed Cosmo upright, a finger pressed to their lips. "Déjà is going to hear you."

Déjà appeared beside them so suddenly that Rye squeaked. Her gaze darted between Rye and Cosmo, suspicion etched into her face. She turned to Cosmo. "We're going to start. Get your spooky ass up front."

If Cosmo lingered any longer he was either going to get himself in trouble or cramp the romance, so he pulled the veil over his face, then sat in the front-most pew beside Royce and laced his hands together. Mom sat next to Cosmo, and he couldn't tell if her claustrophobic proximity was because she was contemplating that this was his funeral – no matter how alive he was – or because she didn't like Royce. If it were the latter, Royce didn't seem to notice, his attention on his phone.

After this, Cosmo would be someone new. He was embracing death, finality, and the unknown, so he could step *into* the unknown. It was rebirth, a fresh start, a rise from the ashes. It was frightening, but not so bad with friends and family by his side.

The ghost in his studio hadn't gotten to choose when his end time came, and judging by the scars on his face, it hadn't been a peaceful way to go. Cosmo almost wished that man *was* here, so he could move forward too. Being stuck in Cosmo's old place couldn't be the ideal afterlife experience.

And if he showed up, Cosmo wasn't going to scream this time, damn it.

Déjà stepped up front and opened her arms, revealing chiffon batwing sleeves and an ouroboros drawn on each of her palms. "Welcome, cohorts! Death of any kind – of love, of familiar comforts, of the life we saw clearly laid out for us in our dreams – is violent and painful. Change hurts. But we have to move on because there is no other way. The universe won't let us be static.

"We are gathered here tonight for our beloved Cosmo Koslov, because it's his time to move on. The person he was, the person we knew, has come to an end. Cosmo has touched us all in some way, and we are better for knowing him. He needs your love and support to start his journey into a new beginning. If you're moved to do so, please come up and tell us how Cosmo has affected you, whether it's his sincerity, his compassion, his art, or simply an amusing story. Or if you'd rather keep it private, there are strips of paper and an urn so you can write him a message."

Déjà pressed a hand to her heart. "What I love most about Cosmo is his authenticity. Both in his interactions with other people and how he presents himself, he is never fake. He is earnest and passionate in everything he does."

Cosmo smiled. Déjà started to sit down next to Mom, but Cosmo tugged her into a hard hug. "That means so much to me."

Others came to the front, sharing stories of how they'd met Cosmo, how he'd influenced their art or their lives. Ava said Cosmo's use of mixed media had inspired her to try her own hand at it, and one of her new pieces had sold to a collector for enough to pay her rent for several months. Bodhi confessed that Cosmo's unabashed self-expression had prompted vir to come out as non-binary and wear things that ve would have been afraid to otherwise. Mason said Cosmo had said something so profound to him at a party that he'd decided not to go home and take his life like he'd been planning. Cosmo had no idea what he'd said or even that Mason had been hurting so much.

By the time people were finished speaking, tears streamed down Cosmo's face unchecked. He'd daydreamed about this party being affirming and giving him a much-needed boost of support, but this? This was far beyond the impact he would have expected to have simply by living his daily life, and it meant that there had been plenty of good in his old life.

So many people wrote on the paper strips to fill the urn that Mom had to cut more. Those messages would be perfect reminders that not every one of his past decisions had been a poor one, and he didn't need to get rid of all aspects of himself in order to start anew.

Stevie hammered at the synthesizer, kicking it into a full gear party, and people took the cue to get up, drink, and sample the hors d'oeuvres. Cosmo composed himself enough to join them, but Déjà took him by the arm and pulled him from the church. Starlight bled through the gauze of his veil, and he pulled it back from his face. Crickets sawed in the weeds, and a soft orange glow tumbled from the broken windows and into the night. Stevie's rendition of "You Spin Me Round" floated with Cosmo as he and Déjà walked around the side of the church.

She stopped behind the building, and he blinked, waiting for his eyes to adjust. City lights glimmered in the distance, and cows lowed from a nearby field.

A wooden cross jutted from the soil at the head of an open grave. It wasn't six feet deep, but Cosmo wasn't planning on crawling into it and pulling the dirt down on top of himself. Not anymore.

"Did you dig this yourself?" he said.

Déjà snorted. "And break my acrylics? Stevie dug it. She likes that kind of thing. I'm not sure what you want to put in it, but I figured you needed one to complete the illusion."

It was too bad he didn't still have that stuffed alligator from the theme park.

"You got anything of Zedd's on you?" she asked. "Not sure why you would, but that would be appropriate to toss inside."

Cosmo had thrown it all off the balcony and already trashed the gifts Zedd had given him, except the garnet ring on his index finger. He tugged on it.

"Why do you still wear that?" Déjà nodded her head at the grave. "Drop it in."

"I like it."

"But doesn't it remind you of shit times with Zedd?"

"Not really."

"Well... Do you want to spit in the hole or something instead?"

"Spitting on my own grave doesn't seem appropriate."

"But I thought the point of this was to–"

Footsteps crunched through the brush. Cosmo turned, and his heart caught in his throat. Zedd approached, hands in the pockets of his suit jacket. Zedd had never worn a suit in his life. Coupled with his slicked hair and completely unnecessary sunglasses, he looked like a high school's biggest douchebag headed to prom.

"What the hell are you doing here?" Déjà spat.

"I'm here to pay my respects, what else?" Zedd said.

Cosmo walked toward him and balled his fists. There was so much adrenaline pumping through him that he could barely feel his fingers. "You were not invited, and you can't be here."

"I can't come to my own boyfriend's funeral? I have rights."

"'Rights' my ass." Déjà shoved him. "Cosmo isn't yours."

"Oh no? Then why, after he said he didn't want anything to do with me, did he invite me into his place last week? Why did he tell me he loved me? Why did we spend the afternoon in his bed?"

Déjà's mouth fell open. She turned to Cosmo. "He's lying. Right?"

Cosmo shrank and spun the garnet ring around his finger. Goddamn it, Zedd. "That was a mistake. And we are not–"

"Cosmo!" Déjà's voice broke. Her nostrils flared, and even in the dark he could see the utter disappointment in her face. "I've watched this asshole break your heart over and over. And every time, I let you fall apart on me. I helped you back up and reminded you of your worth. And still, and *still*, you go back to him."

He backed against the church and put up his hands. "You don't understand what happened."

"Oh, I understand plenty! I helped plan this whole thing for you! I wrote you an obituary and bought you an urn and how are all those people inside going to feel when they find out this whole event is a sham because you aren't moving on? Your old life isn't dead at all. It's *un*dead, in the form of this stinking, rotting tumor of a man standing here. And I'm a complete fool for thinking things would ever change." She wiped her hands down her face, and the ouroboros inked onto her palms smeared onto her cheeks.

"It's different this time. It'll never happen again." Cosmo's throat constricted, tension coiling in his limbs. He bared his teeth at Zedd. "Get the hell out of here. *Now*."

Zedd scoffed. "Do we have to do this every time we have a little spat? When I went to talk to you, I had every intention of leaving you alone afterward. But *you* invited me inside. *You* climbed on top of me and said you needed me because I was the only one who was ever meant for you."

He'd done that, but no one was listening to him when he said it had been a mistake. And Déjà didn't know the horrible things Zedd had said afterward that cemented that realization into Cosmo's mind. He turned to Déjà. "I took him back too many times. I know that. But I thought about how my mom had thrown my–"

Déjà let out a snarl and jabbed a finger at Cosmo. "I can't do this anymore. I can't watch you ruin yourself time and again over this unfaithful malignancy. It's self-harm, and I won't be a part of it."

His mouth fell open. "But you're my dearest–"

"No. Not anymore. I can't." Whirling on Zedd, she said, "The next time you play with explosives during a gig, I hope you blow your dick off."

"You goddamn witch." Zedd shoved Déjà, and she fell on her backside in the dirt. "Somebody should burn you at the stake."

Cosmo slammed his fist into Zedd's jaw so hard the impact vibrated all the way up his arm. Zedd stumbled back, his sunglasses askew. He pressed a hand to his face and tried to speak. Blood bubbled from his lips. Cosmo swung hard and socked him in the eye. Zedd swept out his leg and kicked Cosmo in the ankle. Cosmo folded, and his head cracked against the ground. White stars burst in his vision; the pain in his skull throbbed so hard he was too stunned to react. Zedd snatched a handful of Cosmo's veil and yanked. It tightened around Cosmo's throat, and he let out a strangled gasp.

Zedd's knees dug into the dirt on either side of Cosmo, the taffeta wrapped around his fist. His split lip shone glossy in the candlelight. "Why are you doing this? I *love* you. We're going to be together forever."

He jerked the veil – and Cosmo with it – toward him, then planted a kiss on Cosmo's mouth. Blood ran down Cosmo's throat, and he gagged. Groping through the dirt, he grasped the wooden cross. Splinters jabbed into his fingers as he ripped it from the ground and smashed it into Zedd's head.

Zedd groaned and lost his grip. Cosmo shoved him away and backed into someone's legs. Royce scooped an arm around Cosmo and hauled him up, then strode for Zedd, who was doubled over on the ground. Royce kicked Zedd in the back. Crying out, arms flailing, Zedd fell into Cosmo's grave.

"Get up, and I'll kill you." Royce scraped a pile of dirt into the hole with one shiny loafer. "Get near Cosmo again, and I'll kill you. If I ever see your face again, I'll kill you. Do you sense the theme here?"

The skin at Cosmo's throat was raw, the back of his skull throbbing and broken nails aching. Royce put his arm around him and led him toward the church. He leaned into the protective hold. Thank God.

He scanned the dark field, hoping Déjà was still nearby. Was she okay? She couldn't have meant it, that she was cutting him out of her life. They'd been friends for years. It couldn't just end like that. But if she needed time away from him for her own emotional health, he needed to leave her alone.

He wasn't going to go back to Zedd, but that didn't repair the gaping cracks inside him. Déjà had tried to hold them together, but they were too great. And maybe she was right, that the best thing to do was for everyone to leave Cosmo in his disrepair until he broke apart entirely.

Royce led him to the church doors, then lightly took Cosmo's chin and stared into his face. It was hard to keep eye contact with Royce's intense blue gaze, but it pinned Cosmo in place. "This is your party. You buck up and hold your head high. Understand?"

He nodded and struggled to swallow the lump in his throat.

The doors opened with a groan. Cosmo squared his shoulders and sucked back his tears. Guests gasped as Royce escorted him up the aisle, then they erupted in applause.

Rye lifted Cosmo's filthy, shredded veil, their eyes dancing with delight. "Assemblage sculptor, my ass. *You* are a performance artist. Fantastic!" They raised their drink and turned to the crowd. "Cosmo has crawled from his grave, resurrected!"

Someone pushed a glass of wine into Cosmo's hand. People patted him on the back and squeezed him in hugs. They showered him in congratulations and wished him well in his newborn life.

But Cosmo wasn't reborn. All he saw was death.

8

YOU MAKE ME FEEL (MIGHTY REAL)

Micah - Present Day

Micah lay in bed, burrowed in the sheets. A car sighed past on the street below. The fridge kicked on, its hum filling the dark studio. Someone coughed in a neighboring unit. Shutting his eyes, he strained for more sounds, but each car that passed, each noise from his neighbors, only made the emptiness in the studio more acute.

His thoughts drifted to fantasies he'd played until they were threadbare: sometimes he was standing at the bathroom sink when mint green block letters appeared on the mirror, spelling out a new flirty message. Sometimes he was hunched over the drafting table and would catch a moving shadow in his peripheral vision. Occasionally he was leaning against the kitchen counter with a cup of coffee when footsteps padded down the hall. No matter the setting of the reverie, the enchanting specter haunting his apartment would always–

Something gripped his arm. He yelped and sat up, staring into the dark. He scrambled for his glasses and inadvertently knocked them on the floor. Cursing, he found them and put them on, then waited for his eyes to adjust, the sensation on his arm lingering.

"Hello?"

The only sound cutting the silence was his thudding heart, then a voice drifted, soft and lilting: "It's you."

Micah slapped a hand over his mouth. As his eyes adjusted, he could make out a silhouette cut through with moonlight. It seemed to solidify the longer he stared at it. Cosmo stood with slightly hunched posture, gripping his elbows. Interestingly, instead of the sweater he'd worn previously, he was in acid-washed dad jeans and a busy button-up shirt.

He was back, and he was talking. Okay, Micah had thought about this... a lot. He had to choose his words carefully. *Be smooth.*

"Um... Hi." Christ. That wasn't smooth. He scooted back against the pillow and tugged up the sheets. In his daydreams, Cosmo would always touch the portraits of himself hanging above the drafting table, and Micah would have the opportunity for an easy icebreaker about art. He hadn't expected the reality to be closer to that Dolly Parton operator's cheesy fantasy of Micah in nothing but his briefs.

He couldn't sit here and have a conversation in his underwear. After sliding out of bed, he hastily pulled on a shirt and a pair of sweats, then ran a hand through his hair. "I'm – I'm sorry for frightening you. Before. In the bathroom." He suddenly wondered if Déjà's incense and bag of herbs were hurting Cosmo. "Have I caused you harm?"

"No, I've done it to myself."

"Ah." The syllable sounded trite and callous in response to something so heavy. Micah smoothed out the comforter, then sat down and patted the space next to him. "I've never tried to hurt myself – not consciously anyway – but I know very well how it feels to not want to exist anymore. You don't want to die, you just don't want to be here."

"Oh, too true." The foot of the bed creaked as Cosmo sat down – he seemed capable of becoming solid at will, which was an interesting concept to ponder later. Right now, he focused on the idea that he might be the only one who could help Cosmo move on to something better than the state he was currently stuck in.

"Do you want to talk about what happened?" Micah asked.

The moon limned Cosmo's curls and the slope of his nose. He was silent for so long that Micah was certain asking the question had been a mistake. Cosmo sighed and said, "I killed my old life, but I'm still here. What's changed? All I did was destroy the good thing I *did* have. Now I have to face the future alone, not knowing what's waiting for me... What's your name?"

"Micah."

"I'm Cosmo."

Micah swallowed. This was happening. Cosmo was company. *Inside* the studio. And it felt okay. Maybe it was the darkness between them, the ease of speaking to someone who wasn't actually there, or the fact that they might have similar experiences, but he didn't want him to go.

Clenching his teeth – whether from giddiness or fear, he didn't know – Micah pulled in a slow breath and said, "I'd offer you a drink, but there's only one kind of spirit around here."

Cosmo let out a surprised laugh, rich and velvety, and Micah's insides melted. Cosmo turned, his amusement shifting to interest. "I told you mine," he said gently. "You tell me yours. What happened to you in this studio?"

It was only fair. And he wasn't a therapist who was going to tell Micah to give up art. "I, uh, I let someone in that I shouldn't have. I fought back, but–" A sudden sting filled his sinuses, and he cleared his throat. "It wasn't good enough."

Moonlight kissed Cosmo's sharp cheekbones and webbed his lashes. "Well, then. Here's to no more bad decisions. Whether they be accidental, or" – he tapped a long, slender finger against his heart – "self-inflicted. We can toast with our own spirits."

"Cheers... So what now?"

The ghost's sigh was the sound of wind whispering through bare-branched trees. "We move on, I guess. No choice."

A tiny surge went through Micah's heart. Maybe he *was* helping. Although he was a hypocrite, because *he* wasn't moving on. Everett and Ximena would say so. Otherwise he would be in therapy and checking his mail. "Do you have a grave somewhere?"

Cosmo leaned back on the bed. "What a strange thing to ask. How did you know?"

It seemed obvious, but before Micah could reply, Cosmo said, "At the end of Cherry Lane. But there's nothing inside but my disillusions. Let's promise each other something. We won't be hung up on the past. We'll move forward, unafraid of the future."

"I can't keep that promise."

Cosmo tugged on his bottom lip, staring at the space between his feet. "Then we promise to try. Please. We're haunting ourselves, darling, and it's not a good look."

"Haunting ourselves."

Was that what Micah was doing? Haunting himself in this studio with the door locked and curtains drawn? When had he actually gone somewhere? He thought about doing it all the time – heading to the aquarium, the theater, going out on dates. But he always made excuses not to. When was the last time he'd traded houseplant propagations with someone or actually bought a muffin from the coffee shop on the corner? The farthest he'd been in weeks was taking trash to the dumpster.

His therapist said his trauma had turned into agoraphobia, and Micah had scoffed. He wasn't afraid of going outside, he was afraid of letting people *in*. And yet... He never left unless he had to.

"Are baby steps okay?" he asked.

Cosmo smiled, his pearly teeth floating in the dark. "I think that would be just fine."

"Okay. Then I promise."

"Good. As do I." Moonlight pierced Cosmo's face, diffusing him into a frantic mist. Micah reached for his hand, hoping to keep him there a little longer, but he snatched at empty air.

"Thank you for the stimulating chat, handsome. I'll let you go back to sleeping like the dead." Cosmo's laugh faded into the dark.

It took Micah a long time to fall asleep.

In the morning, he walked outside, locked the door, and headed down the steps to the sidewalk below. A muffin. He was going to buy a muffin. No, two. And a coffee. There was nothing monumental about it, but the tightness in his chest eased as he pulled in crisp fall air and the perfume of Ximena's rose bushes. She stood on the sidewalk, prodding at a sprinkler head in the grass.

"Buenos días." Micah stuck his hands in the pockets of his jeans. "Something wrong?"

Her mouth fell open. "Buenos días, mijo! The timer on these sprinklers isn't working. Not coming on when they should. Where are you off to?"

"The Seventh Circle of Java. It's a pain to avoid the pitchforks and open flame pits, but they have the darkest roast you can get."

"Sounds wonderful."

"Do you want something? Coffee? A muffin? Only costs your soul."

"Is that all? It so happens I have a couple extra from tenants who were late on rent. Not doing me any good. I'd love a latte and a blueberry muffin."

"You got it."

She squeezed his arm. "Micah!"

He chuckled. "What?"

"It's just... so nice to see you out and about this morning. You look well." There wasn't any pity in her face today; instead, her smile threatened to burst at the seams.

"I feel pretty good."

"Has the music at night stopped?"

"I haven't heard it in a while." He thought of the slender fingers on Cosmo's hands. Of Cosmo calling him *darling* and *handsome*. Maybe he wouldn't complain so much the next time Soft Cell started up.

"Oh, I'm so glad," she said. "I sent out another memo. This one must have gotten through."

"It must have. Thank you."

"Let me go get my purse, and I'll give you some money for my order."

"Absolutely not. It hardly makes up for all the food you've brought me over the months."

The sprinkler hissed, and an errant stream of water lashed Micah's jeans. He jumped back and so did Ximena.

She wiped at the skirt of her dress. "Twenty minutes late."

Behind them, water bubbled from ground tubing beneath the rose plants. Micah glanced at the frilly petals. "I, uh, want to pay my respects to someone later. Can I take a few flowers?"

"Take as many as you'd like."

Which ones? Blush? Mulberry? There were more bushes farther down, with other colors. "Can I ask you a weird question? The tenant who passed away, Cosmo... What color do you think was his favorite?"

Ximena's gaze drifted from Micah to the roses. "You've been thinking about him a lot, huh? Maybe I shouldn't have said anything. I don't want you getting depressed and morbid."

"I swear I'm not." He shrugged. "Well, not any more depressed than I have been. Today, less so, actually."

She folded her arms and tapped her chin. "He wore the most outrageous outfits. Greens and purples together. Cowboy boots with… things that don't go with cowboy boots. The tiniest shorts you've ever seen" – she gestured to her crotch – "that left nothing to the imagination."

"Wow." Cosmo liked to make a statement. "I can work with that. Thanks."

"I can't say I understood his style or his art, but he was always polite, and I think it's sweet that you want to visit his grave."

Micah nodded and continued down the sidewalk. A soft breeze toyed with his hair, and a kaleidoscope of scents – flowers, exhaust, someone's spicy cooking – filled his lungs. Cars honked in the distance, a chihuahua yapped, and a smoke alarm let out a shrill beep. Lemon Disco was alive. So was Micah. He needed to start acting like it.

When he reached the coffee shop and opened the door, he was inundated with the rich bite of coffee and sparkle of sugar. The last of the tension in his muscles unraveled, and he found himself rocking back on his heels as he waited in line. People sat at tables, typing on their laptops and chatting with friends. There was an incomparable comfort to being at home, safe, amid his art, but right now the studio seemed dismal in comparison to the energy in The Seventh Circle of Java.

Stooping to the pastry case, he surveyed the selection. Though there were no open flame pits, their hot pepper jelly muffins had made him feel like he was tongue-kissing Satan, and he wouldn't be making that mistake again.

"Micah? God, I haven't seen you here in forever. I thought you moved away."

It hadn't been *that* long since he'd been here, had it?

He looked up. The cashier's surprised smile decayed. She stared at his face, blinking rapidly as though if she did it hard enough it would make him less disfigured. Yep, apparently it had been that long.

"Still here." He focused on the pastry case. "Can I have two medium lattes, please. Also two blueberry muffins, an angel muffin, and a poppyseed. Gotta get fat for hibernation."

The cashier let out a strange laugh. "Yes, of course." She filled his order, trying to fit all of the muffins into a tiny paper bag. "I think you might need another bag."

"For my face?"

A flush flared in her cheeks, and she stammered and dropped the poppyseed muffin on the counter.

"Sorry. Still working on my routine of self-deprecating jokes." He opened a bag and put the poppyseed muffin inside.

After paying, the cashier thanked him and urged him to come back more often. This had gone awkwardly, but he would try. Baby steps.

Stopping at Ximena's office, he traded her a latte and muffins for a pair of pruning shears, then clipped the most vibrant roses possible from the complex's bushes. Cosmo might not see them since it was doubtful any ghost wanted to spend their afterlife beside their own grave, but that wasn't the point.

Purple at the center, flanked by orange and yellow, fringed at the edges with lavender herbs that had been growing freely beside a fire hydrant. After tying the bouquet together, he set it gently in the car and drove for Cherry Lane.

GPS gave him the fastest route there, but failed to come up with the location of a cemetery. Buildings thinned out, replaced by swaths of alfalfa and corn. Orchards and cow pastures rolled by. Maybe what Cosmo considered his grave wasn't a proper burial spot, but the place of his death. He'd said there was nothing inside the grave at all.

A decaying church sat at the end of the road. Faded graffiti marked the double doors, and windows that once would have reflected the blue sky gaped as black, broken-paned holes. A strand of something sparkly was caught on the jagged glass, flapping lazily in the breeze.

Micah parked and got out, shielding his left eye from the sun. Weeds and beer cans crunched under his shoes. He stopped at the church and plucked a scrap of Halloween garland from the window. Little sun-bleached jack-o'-lanterns grinned on black tinsel. He peered inside. Shafts of light pierced the gloom from holes in the roof, illuminating more partiers' trash, collapsed pews, and candles melted to window sills.

He walked around back, startling a crow. Seedheads quivered, and branches on nearby trees rocked slowly. A wooden cross jutted from amid the weeds and broken bottles. There was only one, leaning against the church as though it didn't have the will to continue standing on its own.

Party streamers tied to the crossbeam caught the light as Micah picked up the cross. The bottom was splintered and jagged, caked in dirt. It had clearly marked a grave at some point.

A heart, drawn in marker, adorned the back of the cross. Micah squinted at the faded lettering within:

DÉJÀ

+

COSMO

He gasped. Did she know it was Cosmo the entire time she was in the studio? Maybe that's why she'd said there wasn't a rowdy ghost and tried to pin it on Micah. She didn't want to deal with a friend who'd passed away. He snapped a picture of the writing on the cross, then attached it to an email and sent it to Déjà with the phrase, *You know my ghost.*

After setting the cross carefully back where it came from, he headed to the car for the bouquet. He wasn't sure what he wanted from Déjà. Her admission wouldn't prove that the ghost wasn't himself – he already knew that – and he no longer needed help getting Cosmo to leave. He didn't *want* Cosmo to leave. And more details about his life, his art, his music, his outfits, were only going to get Micah more worked up about the fantasy in his head. Still, maybe it would help Déjà to know that Cosmo was making efforts to move on to a place he'd be more at peace.

As he reached for the door handle, his phone vibrated. He opened Déjà's reply, met with: *Cosmo Kozlov isn't your ghost. He isn't dead. Where did you get that cross? It was from a party we threw years ago.*

Micah stared at the message.

He isn't dead.

It was a mix-up, then. But how could that be? There were too many coincidences for it to be the wrong Cosmo. He typed back, *White artist with curly hair and hazel eyes who wears eccentric outfits and calls people "darling"?*

He climbed into the car, the phone growing clammy in his grip.

Déjà wrote, *That's him. But he's very much alive. Go check his Flashbulb profile.*

Blood pounded in Micah's temples, his finger hovering over the attached link. This made no sense. Cosmo had materialized in the studio at least twice, once with half his torso missing. Moonlight had shown through his incorporeal form, and he'd vanished before Micah's eyes.

As he tapped the link, a profile appeared, displaying a grid of photos. Cosmo, with his arm around a woman's waist, a mixed media sculpture on a pedestal beside them. Cosmo, pouting seductively for the camera, his pursed lips glossy and heavy earrings pulling at his lobes. Cosmo, a cigarette between his teeth as he arched his neck, the strap of his dress falling down.

Micah expanded the image, ensnared in the curve of his throat, his bare shoulder, his smoldering I-know-how-hot-I-am gaze.

He scrolled through dozens of comments, most of them flirty, some outright propositions.

Someone wrote, *Damn, sexy! I'm sorry I missed that party.*

Beneath it was a reply from Cosmo, dated only the day before: *It was positively dull. I had to make my own fun. Would have been much better if you were there!* 🌿🌿🌿

A torrent of confused feelings howled through Micah. He raced home, hands clenched on the wheel. When he got back, he emailed Déjà and attached both his phone number and the video of Cosmo appearing in his bathroom.

His phone rang, and before he could say hello, Déjà said, "What the hell is this?"

"You tell me."

"I don't have a clue."

"But this is Cosmo. Isn't it? Your same, very alive Cosmo? Appearing out of thin air in my bathroom. He used to live in my studio."

"He isn't mine, and he may as well be dead to me. I see him around, but we don't hang." She sighed. "I don't understand this."

Neither did he, and if Déjà didn't have an answer, the only other one who might was the "ghost" himself. Micah paced the front room, then picked up the tube of pink lipstick from the drafting table. "He was in my room last night. I saw moonlight go right through him." It sounded delusional, and he was grateful he had proof of one appearance.

"What time?"

"Around midnight."

"He was at a gallery event until one last night. There's a video on his Flashbulb."

"You aren't friends, but you stalk his Flashbulb?"

"What I'm saying is he can't be in two places at once."

Micah turned the tube of lipstick over in his hand. No explanation he could come up with – a dead twin, astral projection, alien bodysnatching – was remotely comforting. "There's a serious glitch in the Matrix then."

He didn't mean it literally, but she said, "I don't believe in Simulation Theory. And I don't have the answer just because I'm a medium. At first I – I didn't realize your studio was the same one Cosmo used to live in because I'd forgotten the apartment number and it had been remodeled. But your switch plate in the closet is made of polymer clay. Turquoise blue with eyeballs. He made a bunch of light switch plates in college, and that was one of them."

Micah walked into the closet and flipped on the light. Of course Cosmo had made this thing. "The first time I reached into the closet to turn on the light, I felt the lashes on those eyes and thought I'd accidentally touched a huge spider." There was no way Ximena had seen that when remodeling, or she would have replaced it. But Micah had liked it; this strange, gaudy surprise tucked away in the closet.

"When I realized it was Cosmo's place, I just wanted out of there," she said. "But I was telling the truth when I said that you don't have a rowdy ghost."

"I don't suppose you can ask Cosmo for an explanation."

Déjà's voice flattened. "Mm, no. He's a big boy in charge of his own life. And as a matter of fact, so are you. You two sort it out. He works just down the block from you at Identical Dog."

So close this entire time. Micah wiped his hand down his face. What should he do? Showing up at the gallery unannounced would be awkward. If he sent a message to Cosmo's Flashbulb account, it might get filtered into a spam folder and lost, and he didn't want to wait around for Cosmo to find it. He wanted to talk to him *now*.

"Okay, well–" He paused, then glanced at the phone screen. She'd hung up on him.

It would be easy to go back to his life and forget the whole thing ever happened. One of those bizarre, unexplainable events, like a child remembering a past life as a World War II pilot; seeing a UFO; or being struck by lightning on more than one occasion.

But he'd done good today. His promise to Cosmo had gotten him out of the house to *two* places. And he wanted to see him again.

Realization poured over him like ice water. Cosmo was alive, and it would be much easier to interact and have conversations with a live person than a dead one. It was possible to have an actual relationship with a live person. Except... The idea of Cosmo being a ghost had made their interactions intimate and special; he'd been a secret daydream for Micah alone. In reality, he was out living his life, partying and being flirty for thousands of Internet admirers. And he was so much younger. Micah didn't fit into that narrative. Micah was on a completely different plane of existence from that. How could he expect to compete for the affections of a gorgeous young artist when he had a fucked up face and couldn't even invite someone into the studio?

He opened Cosmo's Flashbulb profile and scrolled down. Cosmo in front of a gallery installation that made it look like it was raining in the room. Cosmo licking a drippy pink ice cream cone. Cosmo in – Oh, god, there were those hotpants Ximena mentioned. And by the likes on the post, they were a hit. All the comments were variations of: *Damn, sir!* 💋💋💋 *It is illegal to be that hot.* 🔥🔥

Cosmo replied with hearts and kiss emojis, even to the blatantly gross comments that made Micah wrinkle his nose.

He sank into his desk chair and called his brother. Everett's Adam's apple and the underside of his chin appeared on screen. Keyboard clacks filled the speakers. "Yo."

"I met someone."

Everett looked down at the camera and grinned. "You did?"

"I need to go talk to him about something important, but I'm crushing hard, and he's way out of my league."

"Is he hot?"

"Not just hot. Weird-hot."

"What's weird-hot?"

"Unusual. Not conventionally attractive. All people are beautiful in their own way, but Cosmo..." Micah blew out a breath. "And he's younger than me. Like twenty-eight, twenty-nine. He already gets tons of attention, and just because we sat together on my bed–"

"Wait, what?" Everett leapt out of his seat and twirled around so hard he bumped into his desk and sent the phone sliding. It came to a stop beside the wall of his cubicle, beneath a calendar that hadn't been changed since March.

Everett picked up the phone and held it properly. The office lighting gave his skin a sallow cast and highlighted the salt and pepper stubble on his chin, but his grin lit up his face. "Like four people just saw me dance, and I don't care how cringy it was. I'm so happy!"

Micah shook his head. "The problem is I don't think it means anything–"

"The hell it doesn't! You let your hot date inside your apartment."

Oh no. He was picturing Micah welcoming someone over his threshold, and that wasn't what had happened. "It wasn't a date, and I don't know if that counts. He kind of came in without asking, and I just let him."

"Well, did you have a panic attack?"

"No. I liked having him here."

Everett let out a squeal and the phone shook in his hand. Someone in the background said, "Jesus, Wildsmith, save it for the club."

Maybe Micah shouldn't have called. Everett was giving him more credit than he was due. "It's only worked with him so far, though. Even thinking about letting in my sweet landlady who adores me cramps my stomach."

"Hey, don't downplay this. This is amazing progress."

"I went outside today. Went to the coffee shop down the street."

Everett laughed, his eyes suddenly glossy. "I'm so happy for you."

"Thanks, but now I don't know what to do. This crush of mine is flirty, but it seems like he's flirty with everyone, and I can't compete for his attention with" – he waved a hand in front of his face – "this Phantom of the Opera thing going on."

"Stop it. Did he tell you that you're horrifying?"

"He called me handsome."

Everett leveled his gaze at the camera. "Then you are worried about problems that don't exist. Go sweep him off his feet."

Micah blew out a breath. That vibrant bouquet of roses sat on the edge of the desk, still waiting to be offered to a beautiful ghost.

"Okay." He set his jaw and looked at Everett. "I'm going to go now, before I lose my nerve."

9

ALIVE AND KICKING

Cosmo - Present Day

Passed over for registrar *again*. Cosmo stomped on cardboard boxes with more force than needed, then tossed them onto the pile for the recycling bin out back. Dahlia seemed lovely, and her experience at Wegmann's Gallery certainly made her a sound hiring decision. But he'd been the art handler for three fucking years, and no matter how good of a job he did, no matter how much he helped out with tasks that weren't in his job description, like mopping the floors and scrubbing the walls, he was always turned down. This was a student's job. He needed to move up, but he was doing something wrong, and it was maddening that he didn't know what it was.

Royce hired and transferred the employees, but he said it was between him and the gallerist to finalize decisions. The gallerist, Hina, was a contemplative woman who always praised Cosmo's installations and handling of the artwork, and had even given him a space in the gallery for his own sculptures. So if it wasn't her that didn't approve, then it was Royce, which didn't make any sense.

Royce's loafers clacked against the tile. He stopped in the doorway, arms folded. "You really need to get a restraining order against Zedd. He's getting creative."

Cosmo groaned. He'd tried that, and the cops said there was nothing they could do other than give Zedd a scolding.

After the last incident, he hadn't expected Zedd to get anywhere near the gallery again. Royce was in commendable shape for someone his age, and had literally picked Zedd up by his shirt and waistband and thrown him out on the sidewalk.

Cosmo tossed another broken down box on the pile. Though he wasn't sure he wanted to know, he said, "What happened?"

"He sent someone to give you roses."

"Like, a delivery person?"

"No. A man with a bouquet showed up, wanting to talk to you. Normally your admirers orbit the same parties and gallery events you do, but I've never seen this man before."

Admirers didn't bring Cosmo flowers. They laughed at everything he said whether it was funny or not, spewed pick-up lines like they were rehearsing for the theater, then slipped a hand under his shirt.

There'd been Marla, of course, but she didn't last. No potential new love ever lasted when Zedd was heavy-breathing in the background of Cosmo's life.

"What was this man's name?" Cosmo said.

"Didn't ask."

"What did he look like?"

Royce shrugged. "White guy. Glasses, brown hair, a scar on his face."

Cosmo saw so many people on a given day that it could have been anyone. Maybe Royce was right, and it was another of Zedd's delusional efforts to win back Cosmo's affections.

"Well, thanks for scaring him away. I don't want to deal with that today."

Royce picked up a bundle of boxes and dumped them in a cart. "I'll take these out for you. Zedd could be hiding in the dumpster for all we know."

"Thanks. You're sweet. I'm sorry this is such an issue." Maybe that's why Cosmo was always passed over for promotions. And really, who could blame Royce for not wanting to give him more responsibility when his damn ex-boyfriend constantly showed up and made a scene?

Zedd was destroying every aspect of his efforts to move on. His death party should have been more final. He could have quit his job, changed his name, and moved to a different city.

"It is an issue, but I don't mind." Royce pressed down the stack of boxes, then wheeled them toward the back door. "Let me take care of this, and we'll go get a drink."

"So thoughtful." Royce acting as an impenetrable barrier made the gallery one of the only hassle-free spaces Cosmo could be. He'd turned down Royce's drink offers in the past, but now Marla was gone, and he couldn't bear to sit in a bar alone.

Royce disappeared out the door, and Cosmo helped close up. This wasn't technically part of his job, but complaining was certainly not going to get him promoted to something other than art handler.

He walked outside, tugging his jacket around him. Champagne pink bled from the setting sun, and buildings cut sharp silhouettes against the sky. Someone approached from Cosmo's peripheral vision. The brilliant roses he clutched to his chest made the sunset a diluted facsimile. He wore a pale blue sweatshirt and his–

Cosmo screamed. He lunged for the gallery doors, but the ghost jumped in front of the entrance, an arm barring his way.

"It's me!" Micah said.

"I know!" Cosmo clutched his heart and backed up. He misjudged the edge of the sidewalk and sharp pain lanced his ankle. The bouquet of roses hit the ground and a firm hand steadied him before he went down.

Micah's grip was solid, his body and proximity anything but spectral. Breath rushed in and out of him, his features strained. He licked his lips and looked like he wanted to say something, but no sound came out.

Of all the people Cosmo had expected to be waiting with flowers, it wasn't the ghost who haunted his old studio. At times, he'd asked himself if any of it had even been real. Maybe he'd been too preoccupied with death and dreamed it all up. But there was no disassociating from *this*.

"Why are you here?" Cosmo whispered.

Micah let go of his arm. "You're not dead."

"Am I supposed to be?" His stomach clenched. "Did I miss my window, and you're here to push me in front of a bus?"

"What? No."

"Or you know it's coming any moment, so you're here to usher me into the afterlife so I won't be alone." That was kind of sweet, actually, but Cosmo didn't plan on going anywhere except to the bar, then home to his sculpting.

"No, I..." Micah picked up the roses and tucked an errant strand of lavender back into the raffia holding the bouquet together. "I just want to know what's going on."

"With flowers?"

A flush bloomed in his cheeks, and he adjusted his glasses. "They were for your grave, but then I found out you aren't dead, so I figured I'd bring them with me instead of leaving them there where you'd never see them. Why did you scream?"

Yes, how embarrassing. "You startled me. I saw your face and–"

"Right." Micah's expression fell, and he looked so much like a kicked dog that Cosmo wanted to apologize, though he wasn't sure for what.

"I have a bit of a thing for the macabre, and to be honest, I'm ashamed now. Screaming at a ghost is the equivalent of a herpetologist screaming at a snake."

Micah frowned. "I'm not dead."

A ghost who wasn't aware he was one. That was a thing, wasn't it? They lived out their afterlife performing things they'd done when they were mortal, never realizing the cycle they were stuck in. This certainly seemed off-script, though. "I hate to break it to you, but you aren't a part of the land of the living anymore. I saw you disappear on two occasions."

"I saw *you* disappear on two occasions. And you wrote messages on my mirror. You – You played Soft Cell all hours of the night, and I could never sleep."

The poor dear was really confused. But Cosmo knew how he had died, and it looked like he was going to have to break it to him.

The gallery doors swung open. Royce scowled at Micah. "I told you to leave!"

"You can see him?" Cosmo asked. "Well, of course you can. You told me he was here."

"I'm not dead!" Micah protested. He pulled a wallet from his back pocket and flipped it open, then aimed his ID at Cosmo.

His photo was taken before he possessed his scars, which only proved Cosmo's point. "Ask Ximena, ask the maintenance men at the complex. I live in your old place."

"Of course you do. You were there when I was living there."

"No. I moved in after you moved *out*. Well, Ximena said you died and your friends moved your furniture out, but when we were talking last night–"

"Last night? I haven't spoken to you in years."

Micah blinked, and something in his brain must have completely broken, because he stared through Cosmo, the flowers sagging in his grip. Cosmo hoped he didn't end up this rattled once he passed on.

Royce pulled out his phone. "I'm calling the cops."

"No, no. It's okay." Cosmo leaned toward Royce. "I'll have to take a raincheck on the drink. I need to get him back where he belongs."

"Is he schizophrenic?"

"Just very confused. See you tomorrow."

Royce's face creased. He glared at Micah, then strode toward the parking lot.

Cosmo took the bouquet from Micah and pressed his nose to the petals. "These are lovely. Let's take a walk and figure this out."

Micah nodded. They headed down the sidewalk in the direction of Cosmo's old complex. He said, "I hate to tell you this, but you were assaulted in your studio. There are scars on your face–"

"I know that," Micah snapped. His bottom lip pulled up, tendons jumping in his jaw. He pulled out his phone and opened a browser. After typing something in, he held it up to Cosmo. The headline screamed: *MAN HOSPITALIZED AFTER ASSAULT IN LEMON DISCO'S ARTISTS' DISTRICT*. He scrolled down, revealing a blurred photo that said *graphic content*. When Cosmo clicked on it, it clarified, revealing Micah with a bruised and bloody face, gaping gashes spidering away from his swollen eye. Cosmo cringed.

"Look at the date," Micah said.

"January of this year? But I moved out years ago. How could I have seen you with your scars three years ago if the assault only happened this year?"

"Exactly."

Now Cosmo was probably the one who looked like his brain was broken. "You're not dead."

"Coffee helps."

"Well!" Cosmo slapped his thighs. "I could use a drink or two or seven. Care to take a lady out for a good time?"

"I'd love to." Micah rubbed the back of his neck. "How about dinner first?"

If this was a come-on, it was the most original Cosmo had ever received. "I'd love that. There's a delightful bistro down the street. Have you been?"

"No."

Trying to understand how an interaction that had happened last night for Micah was years ago for Cosmo made his head hurt, and he didn't want to think about it all until he had a couple drinks in him. Instead, he turned his attention to Micah. There was something oddly cozy about him. He was slightly disheveled, his carob-colored hair a bit mussed and dried paint on his sweatshirt. He looked comforting, like a home-cooked meal, a favorite chair, the softest sweater.

Cosmo squinted at his face. "I thought your eyes were two different colors, one darker than the other, but they're not. You have a dilated pupil."

Micah shrank, tucking his hands in his pockets. "My iris is paralyzed. From the assault."

"Like David Bowie." It gave him a unique allure, like behind the comfy man who painted Kinkade-esque landscapes was someone with strange secrets.

Micah scoffed. "I look nothing like Bowie."

"I'm giving you a compliment. Who wouldn't want to be compared to such a bicon? I find it sexy."

Blood rushed to Micah's cheeks. Flustered seemed to be his default. He pulled off his sweatshirt, revealing a plain black tee; strong, veiny forearms; and an ass that perfectly filled out his jeans.

"Now that I know you aren't a ghost, you're far less frightening." Cosmo's gaze lingered on Micah's forearms. "I'm sorry for screaming."

"Last night, or, well, the last time we talked, you didn't seem frightened. We promised each other we'd try to move on."

"We did, didn't we?" That was going just swimmingly. "I was in a rather dark mood at the time. I walked into the studio to get the last of my belongings, and when I saw a bed – with a person inside – in my otherwise empty apartment, I thought a new tenant was moving in already." At the time, Cosmo had felt so lonely that he hadn't cared who the person was. Maybe they'd wake up and be company for a while. "When I realized it was you, well. I was still scared, I guess, but not enough to leave."

"Why were you writing messages to me on the mirror? *'Everything will be okay.' 'You look fabulous.'*"

Cosmo laughed. "Those were for me. I used to write little uplifting things to myself all the time. And when you started replying, I thought it was my ex."

A line formed between Micah's brows. "Oh."

The bistro sign glowed ahead, but Micah slowed and looked like he'd had a change of heart. Cosmo pressed his thumb into the thorn of a rose. He'd thought Cosmo had been flirting with him with those messages. And now he was disappointed. Aw.

The fact that Micah had believed Cosmo was a ghost and was still into it was the exact brand of weird Cosmo could get behind. And he was good-looking company Zedd hadn't yet scared away.

Plus, he simply had to have an explanation for what had happened in the studio – if there *was* an explanation.

Cosmo quickened his pace. "I'm starving. Are you vegan? Allergic to fish? Gluten-free?"

"God, no. I ate two muffins for breakfast."

"Then you must have the lobster toast. It's incredible." He dug his cigarettes out of his pocket. "Mind if I smoke?"

"No. Go ahead."

He poked a cigarette in his mouth, but fumbled the lighter. It clattered across the sidewalk. Micah retrieved it, but instead of handing it back, he flicked it on, cupped a hand around the flame, and held it toward Cosmo's cigarette. Oh, Micah was a doll.

"Thank you." Cosmo took a drag. "You don't smoke?"

"No."

"Good on you. Nasty habit. I only allow myself two a day. What is your drug of choice?"

"I don't think I have one."

"Everyone has one. Whether it's coke or sex or working out."

"There's the torture dungeon, but it's more of a closet. You know how small the studio is."

Smoke rolled from Cosmo's mouth as he laughed. Avoiding the answer. Intriguing.

They passed a secondhand clothing shop, a record store, and an ebike rental kiosk. Soft jazz floated down the sidewalk as they approached the bistro. Micah opened the door and ushered Cosmo inside. It had been a while since he'd been here – hopefully they didn't have a dress code. Micah probably had some crisp button-downs and slacks hiding in his torture dungeon, but his harried I'm-busy-being-artsy look was cute.

Globe lights hung over tables of dark, glossy wood, and the scent of French onion soup drifted. Cosmo tucked the rose bouquet under his arm and checked his hair in the glass of the wine case. Merlot sounded fantastic.

Micah leaned toward him. "You look great."

It was a reassurance, an insistence of the truth, not a flirt with an unspoken part two: *You look great, and I'm dying to ravish you.*

Micah stared at his reflection – unless it was the wine selection he was frowning at – then brushed hair from his brow and pushed his glasses up the bridge of his nose.

They were ushered to a table, and once they both had wine before them and an appetizer of fromage fort on the way, Cosmo turned his thoughts to their peculiar situation.

They swapped details: Micah had heard Cosmo's music, and Cosmo had heard Micah on the phone, but it fluctuated, sometimes only faint and at other times incredibly clear. Both of them dissolved into some kind of otherworldly mist. The marker Micah had been writing with had remained in Cosmo's possession, and Micah had a shower curtain ring and a tube of Cosmo's lipstick.

"Oh!" Micah pulled out his phone and slid over in the booth until he was next to Cosmo. He hit play on a video and held it out. "Desperate" thumped from the speaker, and Cosmo's disembodied handwriting formed on the bathroom mirror. After the video played through, Cosmo started it again. God, he looked young and in denial, and he'd lost that sweater again.

The waitress set the fromage fort, crudités, and crackers on the table. Micah spread melted cheese on a seeded cracker and took a bite. "What do you think?"

"I can see how you thought those messages were addressed to you. And this is a different perspective than mine, but merely reinforces what we already know. I don't see anything here that might give us a clue to what's going on. What do *you* think?"

He popped the rest of the cracker in his mouth. "That the canned cheese I have at home has little bacon bits in it, and this doesn't."

Cosmo wrinkled his nose, and Micah said, "That was a joke. My canned cheese doesn't have bacon bits." He pointed to the fromage. "It's delicious. Great choice."

"You're going to keep me on my toes with your jokes. I never know when they're coming."

"Would you like a warning beforehand?"

"No. Thank you." Cosmo smiled and dunked a wedge of radish into the dip. "Are we dealing with some kind of time travel? From your perspective, you've been interacting with past-me. The me of three years ago. But I was interacting with future-you. A future ghost."

"Well, we all are, aren't we? Future worm food. Future ghosts. But I see what you mean." He frowned and squinted at the globe light over their table. "I haven't had much time to process any of this, but time travel hadn't crossed my mind. I had jokingly thought earlier that maybe we're in a simulation, but maybe it isn't a joke."

Cosmo was open to a lot of odd ideas, but that wasn't one he personally believed in. "I've gone through too much in my life to have those experiences cheapened by the fact that none of it was real."

"They'd still be real to *you*. But I'm just tossing out ideas. And I think I like that one because it's simple. 'Whoops, the universe had a glitch.' Makes my head hurt less than anything else."

Nothing about this seemed simple. Radish spice tingled in Cosmo's mouth, not quite tempered by the cheese, and he chased it with a swallow of wine. A dull ache settled in his chest as he thought of Déjà. It was times like these that he really wished he could call her. She might not have an answer, but her presence alone soothed the anxiety of the unknown. And this certainly wasn't the first time he'd had that wish. After breakups, during shopping trips, when he went to the movies. Lying alone in the dark at night, staring at the ceiling. He had other friends, and he certainly didn't regret taking Mom on some of his stranger outings, if only for her reactions, but no one quite filled the absence that Déjà had left. "I wish you would have known more about me when we'd first started interacting in the studio. You were essentially from the future; you could have warned me that my decisions were ghastly and the consequences I wouldn't be able to bounce back from."

Micah scooped cheese onto a snap pea. "I was waiting tables at the Supper Club over on Highland Street three years ago. I wish a future-someone could have told me to listen to my gut when it came to who I eventually let into the studio to draw. I had a weird vibe from him, but…" His mouth pulled to one side. "He had such an interesting look. I wanted to do his portrait, so I pushed away the feeling."

"I'm so sorry." Micah wanting to draw a stranger was far more innocent than Cosmo deciding to take Zedd back for the umpteenth time, but whether the universe was a simulation or not, it certainly didn't care if your decisions were harmless or self-destructive. You could still be hit with awful consequences.

"I didn't mean to turn this conversation into a downer," Micah said.

"You're perfectly fine. So, you do portraits? I pinned you for a landscape painter."

"God, I hate doing landscapes."

"Maybe you could do *my* portrait some time."

A drop of wine sloshed out of Micah's glass as he brought it to his lips. He took a sip that seemed uncomfortably long for a wine this dry. "I've already drawn you. A few times."

Cosmo tugged his earring. "I'd love to see."

"I could bring them by the gallery sometime."

Really? No, *Why don't you come home with me so I can show you*? No, *My drawings of you will outshine every installation in Identical Dog*?

Even Marla, who'd wanted a relationship and not a one night stand, had flirted Cosmo into submission on their first real date. He'd presumed this was an opportunistic date, but maybe Micah was just lonely and wanted attention and a friend wherever he could get one, even if it was in the form of a ghost.

The waitress arrived with their lobster toast, and Cosmo cut through the soft wedges of meat adorned in béchamel and salmon roe.

"Unless you think coming to the studio might help our situation somehow?" Micah cut into his toast and his knife squealed across the plate. "I don't want it to cause some kind of inter-dimensional rift that implodes the universe. That's not a joke. I don't know what we're dealing with."

Cosmo wasn't sure what he was dealing with either. Something within the studio had connected them both, but he didn't know Micah's exact intentions, which left him on unsteady ground. People normally didn't make him guess.

He brushed his knee against Micah's. "And if I did come over, what would you propose we do?"

"It's a little short notice to go haunt someone together." Micah's fork quivered as he brought it to his mouth. A chunk of lobster fell off and hit the table. He set down his fork, tucked his hands into his lap, and gave Cosmo a tense grin. "But I could show you my portraits – I'd love to know what kind of art *you* do – and maybe write out a list of theories about our situation."

No suggestive banter. Hmm. "I want to figure out what's going on, and the studio seems like the best place to start. But I'd like to know a bit more about you first. Are you queer?"

Micah blinked. "I thought that was obvious. Please don't tell me I give off hetero vibes. I'm trans, by the way. And that reminds me that I've forgotten to ask. Are your pronouns he/him? I saw pictures of you in dresses on your Flashbulb, and of course cis people can be gender non-conforming, but I don't want to assume one way or the other."

"I find that trying to put a name to who and what I am only invites people to make assumptions."

Micah nodded. "I get that. Everyone in my family is tall with a strong jaw, and I've been on testosterone since I was seventeen, so I don't fit what some people 'expect' trans masc to look like. Like it's only one thing."

Cosmo sipped his wine. This was a refreshing conversation in comparison to what he was asked at parties, and Micah deserved more than a party answer in return. "I'm not cis, and I've been thinking about trying different pronouns, but I'm not ready for a label yet. Perhaps that will change in the future. But I don't care what gendered language you use for me, darling."

Parties used to be fun. *Life* used to be fun. Working at the gallery and attending art events had been stimulating; nights were spent with Zedd or mingling with creatives; there were day dates with Déjà and parties and dancing. But then Cosmo went and killed his old life and everything had gone downhill from there. His career at the gallery was stalled, the creatives were tedious, Déjà hadn't spoken to him since the funeral, and Zedd constantly turned up like a cancer.

Meeting Micah felt like the burst of inspiration Cosmo got right before creating one of his favorite sculptures. Green paint lined the edges of Micah's fingernails. A single hoop earring hung from his lobe, and a small beauty mark punctuated the corner of his tea rose lips. Dark chest hair curled from the neckline of his shirt.

Cosmo lightly touched his wrist. "Let's head back to your place. I'm willing to risk implosion. And I'm quite eager to see your portrait style."

Micah's throat flexed, and he downed the rest of his wine. "You don't want to see the torture dungeon?"

"I didn't say that."

"It's a little cluttered. I'm not usually expecting... company."

"We can't all have spotless torture dungeons."

"My maid refuses to go in to polish the handcuffs."

Heaven's sake, the blistering innuendo that would spawn from this banter if it were someone else. Coming from Micah it sounded downright G-rated. There had to be a NSFW version of this man beneath the soft sweatshirts and gold-rimmed glasses. It was refreshing not to see it during a first date, though.

After finishing their meal, they headed toward the entrance. A group of diners walked toward them, and Micah pressed his hand against the small of Cosmo's back to guide him away from a collision. The touch was electric, racing up his spine.

He had no idea what to expect when they reached Micah's studio, and the thought was exhilarating.

10

THE ART OF FALLING APART

Micah - Present Day

This was not a baby step. *Not a baby step.* Micah's heart was a runaway train, barreling through the dark.

Cosmo clutched the rose bouquet as they walked, his other hand so close to Micah's that their knuckles had brushed, and his train-of-a-heart was going to end in a fiery explosion if it happened again.

He'd touched Micah during dinner too and gazed at him with interest, but all Micah could see when he closed his eyes were Cosmo's kiss emoji replies to every suggestive Flashbulb comment he received.

Everett's encouragement of *Go sweep him off his feet* sounded like a rallying cry for a battle Micah couldn't win, but Cosmo *was* coming back to the studio, and dear lord, hopefully the place was clean.

"Damn it. I left rose clippings all over the counter." He hadn't meant to say it out loud, but it was better than announcing that he couldn't remember the last time he'd cleaned the fridge.

"You arranged this yourself?" Cosmo asked.

"Yeah. They're the complex's roses."

"I'm not sure why, but I assumed you bought it." He pressed his nose to the petals. "I like it even more now."

Breathe, Micah.

The complex loomed, art deco molding catching the soft light of twilight. For the first time in nine months, Micah was going to be able to invite someone in. He could stand next to them at the drafting table and talk about his sketches and compare mediums. He could offer them a drink and a place to sit. The gin he'd bought earlier in the day might not be Cosmo's drink of choice, but Micah was certain he'd at least made the bed and done the dishes.

Even though it was only one specific person he could invite inside, it was a start. Cosmo was giving Micah nerves of a completely different sort, and he needed to calm down.

Ximena stood outside her office, a stack of manila file folders in her arms. She turned around, then stared at Cosmo. Color drained from her face. The folders slipped from her arms and crashed across the ground, but she stood frozen in place.

Micah cleared his throat. "Guess who I found."

Ximena screamed, crossed herself, and scrambled for her office door. She fumbled her keys and shook the locked knob, then ran around the side of the little building, disappearing beyond the bushes and into the dark.

Cosmo pinched his lips closed. "That happens on occasion."

"She said you had an obituary." Micah bent to collect Ximena's folders, tucking the papers back inside. He was going to have to text her an explanation. Hopefully she didn't send him a priest or an eviction notice before then.

"Yes, but it wasn't supposed to go out until after I handed out the funeral invitations – which made it clear it was a party."

"She didn't know it was a party. She thought it was a real funeral."

Cosmo helped pick up the mess, and his voice took on an irritated edge. "Then she didn't look hard enough at the invitation or was never actually handed one. My execution was certainly lacking in some aspects of the event. Now I get people randomly screaming at me when I'm trying to buy shampoo in the grocery store." He stacked everything neatly, set it in front of the office door, and placed a rock on top so nothing blew away. "Chasing her down to give her the folders seems like a bad idea."

"I agree." Micah started to direct him up the stairs to the second level, then caught himself. "I was about to tell you where my place is, but of course you already know."

"I don't remember, actually. It's been three years since I lived there. It's twenty-something. Twenty-four?"

"Twenty-one." Keeping in mind that so long had passed for Cosmo was going to be difficult, though his hair was longer than it had been in their ghostly interactions, one lock always hanging in his eye.

"How old are you?" Micah headed up the stairs and dug his keys from his pocket. "Twenty-nine?"

"Close. Twenty-seven."

Micah suddenly felt ancient, and he was certain Cosmo could see every line on his face and the slight regression of his hairline. It only reinforced that he couldn't assume Cosmo's flirts meant interest, and working himself up was only going to end in heartbreak.

"And you? Wait – I'm going to guess it. Thirty-one."

A laugh barked from Micah's throat. Cosmo frowned and said, "I'm quite far off? Twenty-eight, then."

Twenty-eight! "I'm *thirty*-eight."

Cosmo smacked Micah's arm. "You are not."

"I am."

"You don't look it."

Micah unlocked the door and swung it open. He shook out his tingling fingers. This was it. Cosmo was coming in. Everett's coworkers were going to hate him for all the dancing he'd be doing.

He stepped over the threshold and turned to welcome Cosmo inside. Cosmo placed his foot on the carpet. Micah's chest seized up. He slammed his hand against the doorjamb, blocking Cosmo's entry. Cosmo flinched and stepped back.

Oh no. No, no, no. Micah let out a ragged breath. "I'm sorry. Hang on. Just... Just a moment." He tried to calm his quaking limbs, but his mind was screeching unnecessary warnings. *Bad! Danger! Run! Bad! Stop! Bad! Bad! Bad!*

Cosmo let out an uncertain chuckle, as though this were another of Micah's jokes that took him by surprise. "I don't mind if it's a little cluttered."

Fighting through his racing thoughts, Micah reminded himself that Cosmo had been sitting on his bed just last night, and it hadn't induced panic. This was the same Cosmo, only in the flesh, and there was nothing bad or dangerous about letting him inside.

He squeezed his eyes shut, dug his nails into the doorframe, and commanded himself to step out of the way and let Cosmo pass. But the more he insisted, the harder his hand cramped around the frame, his legs the stubborn roots of an ancient oak.

"You're genuinely worried I'll break the universe by coming inside?" Cosmo asked. "If it helps, I'm not scared, and I don't believe something will happen."

This phobia was not going to keep ruining his life. Not tonight. Not with Cosmo. Micah just needed to do something differently. He stepped outside, then turned and faced the open door. "Why don't you try going in first?"

"Oh, I see." Cosmo grinned and tugged on one tortoiseshell hoop earring. "You're not worried about me. You just don't want to be collateral damage." He stepped into the studio, opened his arms, and turned in a circle. "I don't think my atoms are being rent apart. Seems safe to come in. Look at all these plants! Your space is lovely. Very cozy."

Lovely and cozy, and Micah could share that space with Cosmo. Cosmo was safe company, and he was already inside. Micah could walk in and shut the door behind him. It was easy. Nothing to it.

He clutched the doorframe and stepped onto the threshold. His heart pumped madly, body vibrating so hard it was going to shake his soul loose. Throat tightening and tears stinging his eyes, he clenched his teeth and pain zagged through his jaw. Just. Walk. Through.

Flinging himself away, he gripped the cold balcony railing and screamed. "*Fuck!*" It echoed across the parking lot, bouncing back at him. His voice broke. "God *fucking* damn it!" He yanked at his hair and kicked the railing until it rang like a tuning fork.

No matter how much he liked someone, no matter how safe they felt, he was never going to be able to share their company in his home because his brain was utterly broken. The assault had nearly robbed him of his eye, and it was still robbing him. There was no way to go back and be the man he was before, and there was no point to living as this one.

He smashed his fist into the railing, again and again. Blood smeared the metal, and the bars warped.

A hand grazed Micah's shoulder, and he crumpled. He pressed his forehead against the concrete and let out a fractured sob. "I'm sorry. I'm so sorry."

Cosmo's shoes scraped across the pavement. "Should – Should I leave?"

Micah pulled in a wet breath. "Yes. Just go. I can't do this."

Cosmo said something, but it was too low to make out. He hurried down the stairs, and his footsteps receded.

Micah picked himself up, walked inside, and slammed the door behind him.

Each throb of his heart sent pain shooting up to his elbow. Scrapes and lacerations ran across his knuckles, and they were already starting to swell. He wouldn't be able to draw or paint for days. But who cared? He might as well shut himself up in here and never come out again.

The portraits of Cosmo stared back at him from the wall. He took off his glasses, slumped over the drafting table, and sobbed into his arm. His chest hitched and he fought for breath, praying that the next gasp of air wouldn't come. Then, in a month, when he didn't pay rent, someone would find his bloated corpse and take him away from this cursed studio and put him in a grave – the grave he should have ended up in after his assault. He'd survived, been doped up and stitched up, and sent on his way. But he wasn't fixed. All the hospital's horses and all the hospital's men couldn't put Micah back together again.

A soft knock came at the door, and Cosmo's voice drifted. "Micah?"

His heart surged. He wiped his face and sucked back his tears. After raking a hand through his hair, he drew in a deep breath and opened the door.

Cosmo stood on the step, one hip jutted out and a cigarette dangling from his fingers. He took a drag, and smoke curled from his nostrils. "Well, the good news is that since you're unable to invite people inside, you'll never have to worry about vampires."

"I'd gladly trade the risk."

"You should have told me."

Micah blinked at the city lights through the blear in his eyes. "I thought it would be different with you."

"Is it only company in your place that gives you an attack? We were in the bistro together and you were fine. Can you go into other people's houses?"

"I think so. But I can't remember the last time I've done that."

Cosmo shivered, then tugged his jacket around himself and sat on the step.

"You're not leaving?" Micah asked.

"I tried. Ximena said if I wasn't actually dead, she'd make me wish I was if I didn't come back up here and spend time with you. I explained about the funeral party but managed to slip out of her grip before she grilled me on anything else."

Micah sighed. "I'm sorry."

"She really likes you."

"Yeah." He pulled the blanket off the foot of his bed, then sat on the step and handed it to Cosmo. "But she goes overboard. I don't mind her acting motherly, but I'm sick of the pity."

Cosmo opened the blanket, but instead of wrapping it around himself, he flung it across both of their shoulders. He scooted next to Micah until their thighs and shoulders touched. His warm scent of raspberry and clove filled Micah's nose, and Micah was certain any moment his heart would stop beating.

Curls brushed his cheek as Cosmo pulled the blanket tightly around them. "You won't get any pity from me. I hate that it happened to you, but it did. And it's okay to not be okay."

Micah shut his eyes and pulled in a slow breath. "Thank you for understanding."

"Darling, I killed myself over an ex-boyfriend. Not literally, but…"

"But sometimes keeping death close is a comfort. Maybe that's why the thought of you as a ghost intrigued me so much. I liked you in my studio."

"Of course you did, since you can't let a mortal person inside." Cosmo sucked his cigarette, then stubbed it out on the step. "Am I less intriguing now that you know I'm not dead?"

"No. Am I?"

Cosmo smiled and shook his head. "May I see your art?"

"Sure. Most of my recent figure studies are above my drafting table in the front room."

Pushing away the blanket, Cosmo stood and walked inside. Cars sighed past on the street below, and cheesy comedy music drifted from a neighboring unit. Everyone on the block had probably heard Micah's outburst, but hopefully Ximena wasn't eavesdropping from the rosebushes below or sitting in the parking lot with binoculars.

Cosmo walked out with a drawing clutched to his chest. "Your portraits are beautiful. And strange. There's something... coercive about them. They're eidolic and ethereal, and you've created that with bodies that society often *doesn't* consider the ideal. It's like you're swaying the viewer to your vision simply by depicting it. It's not at all passive art, and I am in awe."

Micah's mouth parted. He'd heard all the typical praise for his art, but no one had ever called it *eidolic* or *coercive*. "Thank you. Truly. You work in one of the best galleries here, and to think that about my portraits when you must see so much fantastic art on a daily basis..."

"It is fantastic, but I don't choose the exhibits, and they don't often move me in an emotional way. Your art does."

"Wow. I'm flattered."

Cosmo sat and revealed the drawing he held. It was one of himself, showcasing his long lashes and exposed shoulder. "Can I buy this from you?"

"Definitely not. It's yours to keep."

Streetlight pooled in Cosmo's eyes, turning them into chips of agate. His teeth pressed into his bottom lip, and he rubbed his knee against Micah's. "I don't live that far away. Do you want to come back to my place? I have more wine."

Shit. Blood throbbed in Micah's temples in time with the pain in his hand, and it was suddenly very warm beneath the blanket. In the past, he'd tried to orchestrate first dates that had no hope of ending in sex so that he could broach the topic of his sexuality later.

"I'm ace."

A fine line appeared between Cosmo's brows. "Ah, that makes sense. So... You *are* attracted to me, but not sexually."

"Yeah. I've had sex with partners in the past, but I have to fall for someone with my heart before I ever can with my body."

Cosmo's expression fell. The blanket slid off his shoulder, but he didn't seem to notice. "I see."

"You're disappointed." They often were, so it wasn't surprising, but that didn't take away the sharp sting of it.

"You're lovely and attractive – when you aren't destroying balcony railings – and I'm of a mind that trans/trans relationships and sex are better than any others. In my experience, anyway, there's been more mutual understanding. More consideration of the other person's identity and body, their comfort and pleasure, no matter whether their parts are the same as yours or not."

"So why am I getting the sense that sex is all you want? Are you aromantic? Or I'm just too old for you."

"No. It's neither of those. What I am is cursed." His mouth wavered. "My loves–"

Something clattered inside the studio. Micah startled, and Cosmo snatched his arm. Micah stared back at him then pushed up and stopped at the doorway. "It has to be you, right? Past-you?"

"I never went back to the studio again after seeing you in the bed," Cosmo replied.

As much as Micah wanted to point to a glitch in the simulation as the cause of all of this weirdness, the laziest explanation wasn't necessarily the right one. He instead considered what Cosmo had said about time travel. Three years ago, Cosmo had moved out and…

"Is it *me* moving in?" The front room was undisturbed, and he strained for moving shadows. "I never saw myself when moving here, so that means if I go inside, I'm not going to see myself now. Right? Unless by choosing to go inside, I alter the past, and I'll suddenly have an old memory of seeing a ghost who looks like me."

"You seem like you're dealing with a lot of ghosts as it is. I'll go see." Cosmo walked inside, then leaned into the hall. "Do you hear that creaking?"

It was faint, old wood groaning. "A chair? Or a cabinet opening?"

"It sounds like loose floorboards. You have tile in the kitchen and hall, but I had wood when I lived here. It always seemed so noisy when I got up to pee at night."

"Then it can't be me." When he'd moved in, the tile with its mosaic sun patterns had immediately impressed him. "Maybe you should get out of there."

Either Cosmo didn't hear, or he ignored Micah, his footsteps receding. "Oh, you have a shower door. It's so chic. They made a lot of renovations after I left."

A voice drifted, so soft it could have been the whisper of the wind. It could have been anyone – someone who walked inside to survey the apartment after Cosmo moved out; a homeless man who'd made his way inside; or maybe the timeline was reversing and it was the tenant before Cosmo. No matter who it was, alarm bells rang through Micah's mind. He curled his toes in his shoes. "Cosmo, come back out here."

Glass popped and shattered. Cosmo shrieked. Micah lunged inside, imagining an intruder smashing a lamp against Cosmo's face. He ripped the knife free from under the drafting table, then ran into the hall. Curved shards of glass glittered on the tile, and Cosmo covered his head with his arms. Micah rushed over the glass, grabbed his sleeve, and pulled him through the studio and out the door.

After slamming it behind him, he forced Cosmo's arms down. His eyes were wide, and bits of glass hung in his hair. A thin red cut ran along one of his high cheekbones. Micah plucked out shards and flung them away. "Are you hurt?"

"They were lightbulbs. They exploded in midair." Cosmo looked down at himself, then brushed a bit of glass from his shirt. "I've never seen anything like it."

Micah's hand cramped around the knife handle. What intruder would be carrying lightbulbs?

"It's past-Ximena." Cosmo tried to peer through the window, but the curtains were drawn. "I heard her say, 'Ay dios mío!' after the lightbulbs shattered. Probably trying to fix things up before you moved in, but I don't know what would have made the bulbs break before they hit the ground. Maybe there was a... A box or a ladder I couldn't see because it was still back in the past. This is fascinating, Micah."

Only Ximena. The knife seemed foolish and unnecessary now. Micah was getting worked up – again – over people who wouldn't harm him.

It had been hard to sleep with Soft Cell going on, but he didn't know how he was going to relax if there were ghostly maintenance workers ripping up the flooring and installing the shower door. And what would happen when past-him moved in? Did that mean *he* was destined to move out? His lease wasn't up, and he didn't have enough for a deposit on a new place.

He set the knife on the ground. "Things seem to appear at random. The shower curtain ring, your lipstick. I bet there are other things that I haven't noticed."

"You came inside while I was in there."

Micah stared. He had, hadn't he?

Cosmo cringed and pressed a hand over his mouth. "Perhaps I shouldn't have pointed that out."

There hadn't been time to think about it; Micah was only concerned with keeping Cosmo from enduring a similar fate to his own. "I wasn't going to let anyone hurt you."

"You are so sweet." Cosmo gave him a radiant smile.

Before he could stop himself, Micah blurted, "Will you go out with me again? Please?"

"I can't. He'll ruin it."

"Who?"

Cosmo sighed. "My ex. I've tried seeing new people in the past, then they dump me out of the blue. Either they send me a message breaking it off, or they disappear and I never hear from them again. Zedd will see a photo of me and my inamorate on social media, or he'll hear that I was kissing someone at a party, and he finds them and drives them away." Cosmo swept a lock of hair from his vision and let out a deep sigh. "I can't handle a broken heart again."

Diffused light from the window painted Cosmo in soft strokes, highlighting the smudge of eyeliner at the corner of his eyes, the angular cut of his jaw, and the graceful arch of his neck. He liked Micah. He didn't tell him his art was tasteful and refined – he said it was *strange*. And Micah's blown pupil didn't make him look disfigured, it made him look like Bowie.

This was the closest Micah had been to romance in a long time. The closest he'd been to letting someone in. And he'd be damned if some pathetic ex-boyfriend was going to ruin it.

"You run through my mind constantly." He brushed a bit of glass from Cosmo's shoulder, then slid his thumb along the seam of his jacket. "I want to see your art. I want to get to know you. As far as your ex is concerned, I don't need to be your inamorato – I'm just an art colleague, your asexual friend who wants to take you on a picnic in a graveyard."

"That's rather morbid."

"This weekend?"

Cosmo looked like Micah had asked him whether he wanted the arsenic or the cyanide in his tea. "You're going to ghost me eventually, just like everyone else."

"I mean…" He gestured to himself. "We're already doing the ghost thing. And I wasn't going to let a triviality like death get in the way of my crush on you."

"I noticed." Cosmo pulled out his phone. "Saturday. Give me your number so we can make plans. I'll bring wine and dessert."

Oh, this was happening. He gave Cosmo his number, then took the blanket back inside. Bits of glass glittered on the hallway floor, but not nearly as much as he expected.

He crept past the mess, peering into the kitchen and bathroom, but they were empty.

Cosmo hung at the doorway, typing on his phone. "Will you be alright in here? I don't want past-Ximena to mace you while you sleep."

"Well, what's a little excitement in my life?" His phone vibrated, and a message appeared from Cosmo:

👹👹 🍷 🍷 💐💐💐💐 🦊 🦊 😽😽😽😽

That was a lot of emojis. Micah opened his keyboard, finger hovering over a kiss-blowing smiley he'd seen Cosmo use so many times on Flashbulb. He clicked it and hit send.

"It's getting late," Micah said. "Want me to drive you back to the gallery so you can get your car?"

"I'll walk. But you can join me."

Micah locked the door and followed him down the stairs. "Your ex doesn't hang around the gallery, does he?"

Cosmo sighed. "Unfortunately, yes. Though I haven't seen him in a while. I'm grateful for Royce. He's the only one who can scare Zedd away."

"The director?" When Micah had first walked into the gallery, Royce had snarled at Micah to leave before he even had a chance to explain why he was there. He was almost certain Royce was the director who asked artists for head in exchange for portfolio consideration, but that conversation with the departed ceramics artist had been so long ago. "I guess I can't blame him for being hostile when I show up with flowers and you already get harassed by your ex. He doesn't ask you to do... like..."

"Do what?"

Micah stared at Cosmo's lips and swallowed hard. "He treats you professionally, doesn't he? He's a good boss?"

"He's always been good to me. I consider him a friend, honestly."

It was hard to decide whether that answer was relieving or not. "How friendly of a friend?"

"Why are you asking this? Are you jealous? Because I get more than my fill of that from my ex."

Micah put up his hands. "No, I'm sorry. I've just heard things about him, and I'm hoping that they aren't true."

"Are you certain you're an artist?" Cosmo squinted at him, but an amused smile played on his lips. "The first thing I learned upon breaking into the art scene is that there are rumors about everyone. And that more often than not, the truth is far more outrageous than whatever gossip is slung at parties."

"Does that apply to you?"

"No, in fact. I *am* outrageous, but what you see is what you get, darling. I don't hide it."

Micah gazed at Cosmo for a long moment. "I like what I see."

Grinning, Cosmo linked his arm with Micah's and leaned into him. They passed rose bushes, their footsteps echoing off the sidewalk. Micah lost himself in Cosmo's touch, and when Identical Dog appeared on the corner, it seemed too soon.

They stopped at the lone car in the parking lot, and Cosmo turned to him. "Well, my attractive asexual colleague, this has been a hell of a bizarre evening, and I mean that sincerely."

Now was the point where a date would squeeze Micah's ass or stuff their tongue down his throat. But if Cosmo tried to shake his hand, that would be even worse.

Micah leaned in for a hug. Cosmo pressed his lips against his cheek, and it sent a spark through his nerves. Micah clutched his jacket and breathed him in.

"Take care of that hand. No more punching innocent balcony railings." Cosmo stepped back.

"Looking forward to being weird with you again."

A light flush tinged Cosmo's cheeks, and his eyes sparkled. Footsteps clacked on the sidewalk behind them. Someone in a hoodie passed by. Cosmo's smile faded, his expression wary, then he climbed into his car.

Micah waved as Cosmo pulled away. If a stranger on the sidewalk elicited that much suspicion from Cosmo, Micah was going to need to know what this ex-boyfriend looked like – just in case.

11

GAME ABOVE MY HEAD

Micah - Present Day

Something clattered within the studio.

Micah stood outside the open door at the dented balcony railing, a chilly morning wind licking at his ears. Goosebumps erupted on his skin; he hadn't grabbed a sweatshirt, but it was too late to go back in. Having ghostly maintenance men pull up ghostly wood planking wasn't panic-inducing, but it was damn annoying.

The disturbances weren't going away – if anything, they'd gotten more prominent. Cosmo's time travel idea seemed to be the right one, or at least close enough, which meant Micah couldn't stay here any longer. Unearthing dusty memories of his conversations with Ximena when he'd been apartment hunting gave him a rough estimate of where the timeline was at. By his calculations, his past self would be moving into the studio in two weeks. He didn't plan to cause himself more trauma than he'd already been through.

His phone vibrated. He scrubbed at his arms, then expanded the email notification.

Thank you for submitting your portfolio to Identical Dog. While your work is intriguing, it isn't right for our gallery, so we'll be stepping aside at this time.

He'd expected that, but he'd had to try. There were still four other galleries he was waiting on responses from. Wait. Another unread email sat in his box.

Thank you for letting Half-Empty Gallery review your portfolio! We're going to pass! Good luck!!!

"Christ." With a name like that, you'd think they'd be falling over themselves for his art.

No matter how beautiful Cosmo found Micah's portraits, they weren't going to help him come up with enough for a deposit on a new place unless he could get into a gallery and start selling his work... or get an hourly job. The odds for either weren't looking good. Leaving the house had been an incredible struggle, and freelancing didn't work well when he couldn't bear to have a live model pose for him. For some reason, people who wanted him to draw a portrait from a photograph expected to pay him an insultingly small amount of money. He'd be stuck with more tedious landscapes that he couldn't concentrate on with construction noises in the background.

Wood cracked and splintered from inside, and a faint voice drifted. Micah peeked through the door, met with a crowbar sitting in the middle of the room.

He shivered and stamped his feet. This was ridiculous. He was going to have to call Everett and ask for money.

Unless...

Clutching his elbows, he hurried down the stairs and stopped at Ximena's office. He was about to knock when he remembered her concern for his mental well-being whenever he mentioned Cosmo or the strange things happening in the studio. She'd already been worried about him getting depressed and morbid as a lonely shut-in, but now he was going to seem downright delusional unless he could show her what was happening in person. And even though the phantom construction noises had been going on all morning, it would be just his luck for them to stop as soon as she entered the apartment.

Before he could leave, the door swung open, and Ximena exclaimed, "Oh! Micah! I was just coming to talk to you. I know your social life isn't my business, but I–"

Her words dissolved into white noise as he scrambled to tell her why he was there. He gave up and said, "Will you come up to my studio right now? I need to show you something."

"Is it an emergency?"

"Kind of."

She shrugged on a sweater and followed him to the steps. "Did a pipe burst? Oh! I didn't grab my phone. I'll have to call maintenance."

He lightly took her elbow and urged her on. "Remember my mirror shattering? And when I told you I found a shower curtain ring even though I don't have a shower curtain?"

"Yes."

"And Cosmo–"

"I didn't give him a lot of thought over the past years, but I *did* feel bad for him, and it seems like a nasty trick to make people think you're dead. He never even told me he was moving out. All that being said..." She paused as they stopped before Micah's apartment. "What's that noise?"

Wood clattered, and someone laughed. Well, here went nothing. Micah opened the door and said, "Maintenance is already here. They're ripping out the wood flooring."

Ximena frowned. "You don't have wood flooring."

"Not anymore." He peered inside. The crowbar still sat on the carpet. "After Cosmo moved out, do you remember breaking a bunch of lightbulbs all over the hall?"

She stared, and her frown grew deeper. "No. What is this about?"

The hairs rose on the back of Micah's neck, and it didn't have anything to do with the cold. "I don't know how else to say this, but the timeline from three years ago is intruding into this studio. The past is bleeding into the present."

Breath whistled through Ximena's nose. Her eyes were wide, and she looked like she might bolt down the stairs. "I don't understand what that means."

She took a step inside, her knuckles white as she clutched the doorframe. The high-pitched whine of a drill came from the hall and she gasped. Someone said, "Do you know how much it costs to rent a pony for a birthday party?"

Ximena backpedaled so quickly that she ran into Micah. She crossed herself and gripped his arm. "That's Rick. But he's dead! He died of a heart attack. I went to his viewing." Her face grew ashen. "His granddaughter loved ponies. He showed me the pictures from that party."

Well, at least she hadn't screamed and run away this time. "You're hearing past-Rick. Rick from three years ago, when he was pulling up flooring before I moved in."

Ximena clutched her throat. "The music playing in your place at night..."

"It was Cosmo."

"How is this happening?"

"I don't know. I know there isn't a clause for intruding timelines written into my lease, but I'd really love to move to a different unit before I end up coming face-to-face with myself."

"You have to!" She reached over and slammed the door, as if that would stop the timewarp inside from spilling out onto the balcony. "Otherwise the man who beat you will show up again. Won't he?"

Oh god. Micah clenched his teeth. How he wished he would. How he wished he could come up on his attacker straddling past-Micah on the carpet, rip the blood-coated replica sculpture of Cattelan's *Comedian* from his grip, and smash the man's face in with it. This time, Micah would shatter *his* eye socket. He'd scar *his* face. Paralyze *his* iris. And there'd be no going to the hospital for *him*. He would bleed out on the floor while the neighbors called the cops. Micah would cradle his past self in his arms while they waited for the ambulance, and Micah would tell him that it was okay to not be okay.

That's what he wanted to do anyway, but that's what he'd wanted to do while it was happening. And he'd failed. He couldn't risk freezing up and letting himself down again.

"Micah?"

He blinked and looked at Ximena. The expression of pity on her face wasn't quite as grating today, because he needed it if he was going to get out of here. "What?"

"I said, twenty-six is empty and ready to be moved into. It's a one bedroom, not a studio, but I won't charge you any extra. I have some cardboard boxes and milk crates you can pack your smaller things into, and I'll get some people up to move your furniture and plants, okay?"

"Thank you." He sighed, and knots in his shoulders unraveled. "You know what this means, though. Any new tenant who moves into twenty-one is going to be haunted by the ghost of

Micah-Past." Except... That couldn't be the case because he didn't remember a future tenant appearing in the studio.

So it didn't come as a surprise when Ximena said, "No! I can't let anyone else move in there. It's cursed."

"Yeah, I don't think sprinkling holy water on the rug is going to help. You going to call the news?"

"And have them all up in my business, harassing the tenants? No. Does anyone else know about this besides Cosmo? I don't want this to become some... some *meme*."

That probably wasn't the word she meant to use, but Micah said, "I don't want that either." The last thing he needed was more people knocking on his door. "I told an acquaintance about it, but she doesn't want anything to do with it."

"I can't say I'm surprised." She patted his cheek. "Go get your essentials packed up. And your art – I don't want anyone else touching it. I'll send some people for your bed, your desk, whatever you need today."

Micah started to thank her, but her mouth parted, gaze darting to his front door. "Oh no. Twenty-two was mad that the base heater had scorched the leg of their nightstand, and they wanted maintenance to check it. They said it kept kicking on even when it was *unplugged*. I didn't believe them, of course, but now... And someone else mentioned phantom smells. I've had far more strange complaints than normal lately." She rubbed her face and leaned against the balcony railing. "I think I need to lie down."

He supposed it made sense that the apartment next to his was affected, though how one would figure out the magnitude of such a hiccup in spacetime was beyond him. Did it extend beyond the complex to the street below? There could be a specific spot in the parking lot where a car from the past might suddenly appear in a driver's path, or a rose bush that seemed to always have roses no matter how often you cut them. "This is the Artists' District. Maybe you can market it as a feature instead of a bug. The eccentric ones will go for it."

Ximena shook her head, mouth pulled into a grim line. "I should retire early is what I should do."

"Who lived in twenty-six three years ago?" The last thing he needed was to move into a new apartment with more disturbances than his current one.

"A little old lady with a cat. She was a fiber artist. Very nice. Quiet. Lived there for years before moving into a retirement home."

"I'm not sure we'll have much in common, but maybe she can teach me to crochet."

"You aren't scared by all this?"

"'Scared' isn't the right word. I don't know what would happen if I met myself, and I don't want to find out. But having Cosmo haunt my studio only succeeded in giving me a crush. And he thinks the whole thing is fascinating."

Her laugh was exasperated but not unkind. "You're right. The eccentric artists will probably be fine."

"Coffin Crew, this is—"

"Don't tell me your name. I don't want to know." Micah twirled a pencil between his fingers, the phone pressed to his ear. "But pronouns are okay."

"Is this a robbery? Because there's only like sixty bucks in the till, and I don't have the key to the safe."

"Not a robbery." Micah leaned toward his laptop screen and expanded a picture of a cemetery. "I just have some questions I was hoping you could answer."

Static rustled through the speaker. "Are you the old guy with the fro-yo sitting on the bench by Epic Shoes? Look, man, I've seen you eyeing the neon fishnets in here more than once, and it's totally okay for you to buy them. The orange ones would probably look rad on you."

Micah smiled. "Orange sounds like a great choice, but I'm nowhere near the mall. I'm taking someone on a date, and he's kind of into the gothic thing. He planned and attended his own funeral party, with an obituary and a grave and everything."

The cashier made an appreciative noise. "Damn. That's cool as hell."

"We're going to picnic in a graveyard, but I'm not sure what to wear."

"Ooh. Okay. Well, you don't want something too fancy because you'll be sitting on the ground. A button-up shirt is always a good choice. And it doesn't have to be black. Red or purple, maybe. Leave the top button undone, roll up the sleeves to your elbows. Wear some nice black jeans."

Micah jotted down notes. "This is good. I thought I might have to dress like Vincent Price."

"Nah. Plus, you want to be your true self for your date, right? If you go overboard, it's going to look fake."

"So I should save the plastic fangs for the third date?"

The cashier chuckled. "I gotta go. Fro-yo guy is coming this way. Oh, hang on. You've got cologne, right?"

"Er, I have some of that body spray stuff in the can."

"Ew, no. We've got one here called Moonlight. It's super sexy but not obnoxious. Trust me, he'll love it."

Micah was going to have to add the mall to his list of errand locations. His phone beeped with an incoming call. He said goodbye to the cashier, then answered.

Déjà's sandy voice came through the line. "Did you find Cosmo in the flesh?"

Strange that she was asking when she didn't seem to want anything to do with him or the situation. "We have a date in a graveyard."

"That doesn't answer my question."

He snorted. She could do morbid humor too, apparently. "Yeah. I found him in the flesh."

"You figure out what's going on in your studio?"

"Sort of. You want the working theory?"

"Maybe later. Right now, I need you to promise me three things." He started to speak, but she continued. "One. You don't ever cheat on Cosmo."

"Okay. I can promise that. But why do you–"

"Two. You treat him like the queen he is."

Micah wanted nothing more. "I promise."

"Three. You fuck the brains out of his pretty head."

"Uh." He scrubbed at his eyebrow. "I'm ace. I can't promise that."

There was a beat of silence. "Huh, I thought I was saving the easiest one for last. We can't have a promise with only two parts. Then you promise to pay attention to his physical needs, whether that's food or cuddling or getting him a sex toy."

"What about my needs?"

Conviction filled her voice. "Cosmo has a tender, giving heart. He will shower you in adoration and baked goods. Unless you hate brownies, you'll be fine."

"Well, I was on the fence, but the brownies sealed it for me. I promise." He paused. "I know it's not my business, but maybe you should reach out to him. It's obvious you still care."

"Text me later. Tell me about the studio. I'm curious." There was a click, and the call ended.

Déjà's sudden and active interest in Cosmo's well-being surprised him, but it shouldn't have. When Micah had broken up with Courtney, she'd cut off all communication with him, never even acknowledging his requests for her to pick up her things from his apartment. He never saw her in the places she used to frequent, and she changed the password on the music app they'd jointly used, locking him out, even though *he* was the one who'd been paying for it.

A year and a half later, the assault had happened. A month after that, Courtney called. She'd called every month since then to see how he was doing, and had even invited him to go get a coffee, though he'd declined.

Maybe she did it out of guilt or pity, or maybe it was because the wounds that had sundered them weren't as fresh as they once were. He wasn't going to ask what had happened between Déjà and Cosmo, but he hoped that if one of them reached out to the other, that the outcome would be positive.

A knock came at the door, and his heart filled his throat. He crossed through the hall and into the living room. He'd lived in a studio for so long that keeping his bed and drafting table in separate rooms was too strange, and he wasn't sure what to put in the living room at all. Right now it held milk crates and unframed paintings, but maybe he'd come around to the idea of making it his studio area.

He shook out his hands, drew a slow breath through his nose, then opened the door. Ximena stood on the step with a box and a stack of his shirts and jackets draped over one arm.

"Geez, you don't need to do this." He picked up the jackets by their hangers, then set them on a crate just inside the door. "I was going to get more stuff out of there later."

"I don't mind helping. The sooner everything is out of there, the better. Not sure what to do with the space now, but that's a worry for another day." She stepped over the threshold and into the living room.

Micah's chest seized, limbs vibrating with the energy of a nuclear reactor. Alarm bells rang through his mind, and a strangled noise tore from his throat. He needed to *go*, to push past her out the door, but he couldn't move.

Ximena dropped the box and the side burst open, hemorrhaging kitchen utensils and spice shakers. She threw her hands over her mouth and backed out the door. "I'm so sorry! I'm so, so sorry. I wasn't thinking about this being like your old place, and I don't know why."

He worked the lump from his throat and flexed his fingers. A shaker had popped open, and pepper covered the floor. After a few deep breaths, he said, "It's okay."

"No, it isn't." She stared at the mess like it was taking every ounce of her willpower not to lean inside and clean it up.

Bending down, he gathered everything back into the box with quivering hands, then set it on the kitchen counter. Ximena stared at the pepper on the floor, her eyes watery. Micah stepped outside, then pulled her in a gentle hug. "It's okay."

"I'm sorry, mijo."

Ximena was sweet and wouldn't do anything to hurt him, but the fear came anyway. Had it been past-her dropping lightbulbs everywhere, he wouldn't have panicked.

It made no damn sense, and he couldn't keep living like this.

"I need help." He walked into the living room, planted his feet firmly on the carpet, and said, "Will you step back in? Just stand over the threshold and–"

"No!" She waved her hands and backed into the balcony railing.

"If you do it a few times, maybe I'll get used to it and won't panic."

"No! I'm not going to hurt you a second time." She sniffed and wiped her eyes, then hurried across the balcony and down the stairs.

Damn it. It might not have worked anyway, but he was never going to know without someone to assist him.

He shut the door, walked back to the bedroom, and dropped into the desk chair. Hopefully the mall had gift baskets, because Ximena deserved one. Something from the cooking store.

If Everett was here, he could practice with Micah, but it probably wouldn't work. It was Everett, so Micah wouldn't panic to begin with. And Everett would have to take time off of work and fly in, and Micah couldn't put that burden on him.

Maybe what he needed was the help of a beautiful ghost.

He opened his phone, hesitated, then typed, <*Hi. 🐙 How are you today?*>

After a moment, Cosmo replied. <*Helloooo 🍩🍩 I'm having the most dreadful time at work. I cannot figure out how to mount these sculptures with the instructions the artist provided. I'm going to call her and if she says "with telepathy" I won't be surprised.*>

<*That sounds like an ordeal.*>

<*No matter. I'm glad for a break. What's going on with you?*>

<*I need a favor.*> He started to type his request, then thought about Cosmo speeding down the stairs after Micah's awful outburst, only returning because Ximena threatened him. He hadn't known Cosmo long enough to ask him for something so big, especially if it might scare him away for good.

Instead he wrote: <*I'm going to rob a bank, but I need a getaway driver.*>

<*Omgodddddd. 😄😄🎉🎉🎉 Let me take the license plates off my car and I'll be right there.*>

Micah laughed. <*Do you have a chic ski mask you can wear?*>

<*Naturally. 🎿 🐩 You're just full of date ideas, aren't you?*>

<*Well, I try.*>

<*Is this the only reason you texted me?*>

<*Don't worry, we'll split the money 50/50.*>

<*😄😄😄🐙🐙🍩🍩 Micah, darling, you're positively droll. Truly, you make my day better. 😺*>

His heart fluttered, and he leaned back in the chair. Saturday couldn't come soon enough.

A crash came from the kitchen. He gripped the armrests, the breath snatched from his lungs. What now? Leaving the comfort of his knife below the desk where it was taped, he crept down the hall and told himself a little old lady would be much more frightened of *him* appearing out of nowhere while she was trying to watch *Murder She Wrote*. That thought didn't slow his pulse, however, and it took all his effort to peek into the kitchen. The box he'd set on the counter lay on the floor; ladles, egg beaters, wooden spoons, and spice tins were strewn across the tile.

"Hello?"

Something brushed against his leg, and he yelped.

A white cat with heterochromic eyes stared up at him, purring loudly. He drew in a steadying breath, then sat on the floor. The cat immediately hopped into his lap.

"Wow. You're friendly." He tentatively scratched behind her ears, and she kneaded her paws into his thigh. Her coat was silky, and she wore a collar that looked brand new. "What's your name, little phantom?"

The cat mewed loudly and butted her head against his chest. He chuckled and leaned back against the oven, stroking her fur. She'd surely vanish soon, but not before getting him completely hairy and possibly knocking over something else. That was alright. This was a haunting he could deal with.

12

OBSCENE PHONE CALLER

Cosmo - Present Day

Wearing velvet leggings instead of actual pants was a mistake, and Cosmo knew he should have grabbed a heavier jacket. Dead grass and fallen leaves covered the ground. Bright sun filtered through massive maples, casting dappled light onto headstones and monuments pitted by time and the elements. A brisk wind curled around him.

Micah, clearly, had thought his own outfit through. He wore a crisp button-down the color of dried blood, and the collar hung open, revealing a peek of dark chest hair. Black jeans hugged his ass and thighs, and an alluring scent of jasmine and amber floated around him. He'd slicked back his hair, but it was rebelling, his bangs teased by the wind and curling across his forehead.

He looked so fuckable, and the reminder that he was ace kept popping up in the back of Cosmo's mind. Certainly, he'd met ace people before, but he'd never had a relationship with someone who was. The thought kept knocking him off balance because he didn't want to do anything that would make Micah uncomfortable.

The thought of Zedd catching wind of his new inamorato and scaring him away took up even more of Cosmo's headspace. He'd never seen Zedd threatening one of his love interests firsthand, but he still half-expected him to pop out from behind a tombstone and hiss at Micah. And the poor love didn't need any more encounters with menacing men.

Cosmo stumbled over uneven earth, and Micah snatched his hand. His grip was clammy, fingers chilly. He smiled, his eyes bright and cheeks rosy from the brisk air. "Careful."

He could have chosen a newer, maintained cemetery with manicured lawns and paved paths, but Cosmo wasn't sure how much trouble they would have gotten into if they were found by a mourning party or the groundskeeper. And besides, the weedy tracks and overgrown graves felt more welcoming. Most of the deceased here had likely suffered their second death – no one still alive who remembered them or spoke their name – but they weren't completely forgotten. Nature was still working on bringing them home, folding the dead back into her bosom.

Micah rubbed his hand on the leg of his jeans, but didn't offer it back to Cosmo. It was cute that he got so worked up over each of their interactions. Cosmo *meant* something to him. It was obvious in all of his glances, in each flush of his cheeks, and in the slight tremble in his voice. And those portraits he'd done of Cosmo... There wasn't anything provocative about them, but the intensity and care with which they were drawn did something to his insides.

How long had it been since *Micah* meant something to someone? How long since Cosmo had been the one with clammy hands and shortness of breath? If he fell too hard, he was going to get sloppy, and Zedd would find out. But if he didn't, if he kept a barrier between himself and Micah to spare them both future heartache, that was going to hurt Micah anyway.

Cosmo wanted to fall for someone. He wanted love in return. But it never worked out, and if it was going to this time, he had to be careful. No mentioning Micah by name, no pictures of him on social media, and if they attended any parties or gallery showings together, it had to be as friends only.

"I wish the weather were a bit nicer." Micah shifted the basket hanging from his arm. White lilies peeked from the top. "But I do have a backup plan if it gets too cold. We can climb into a coffin together. I'm sure the current resident won't mind if we move them."

How romantic! Cosmo imagined cuddling Micah in a silk-lined casket, his nose pressed to his chest hair, and the warmth from his skin soaking into Cosmo's bones. Their quickened breath filling the confined space, Micah's lips against Cosmo's ear– Okay, this was becoming sexy. "I rather hope the temperature drops."

A shy smile formed on Micah's face. Goodness he was cute.

They stopped at a patch of grass with enough space to spread out without sitting on top of anyone's grave. Crows hopped along tree branches; leaves in butter yellow and vermilion shivered on the trees, backlit by the sun. Cosmo unfolded a blanket, and Micah took the bundle of lilies from the basket.

He slid one out and handed it to Cosmo. "The others are for everyone else here. Don't be jealous, okay?"

"That is so thoughtful." Cosmo clutched the lily to his chest. The dead here had been forgotten, but not by Micah. It was a struggle to resist snapping a photo of them both for Flashbulb and captioning it, *Feast your eyes on this sweet morsel of a man I'm with!* But even if he kept the wording benign, he was attracted to multiple genders, and people wrongly assumed that meant he couldn't have platonic relationships. The only caption that might work was, *On a picnic with my very heterosexual cis friend!* But he couldn't say such a horrible thing about Micah.

They sat on the blanket, and Cosmo pulled out a bottle of pinot noir and plastic, stemless glasses. Micah produced finger sandwiches and sliced watermelon. Cosmo twisted the corkscrew into the cork. This wine wasn't the only thing he'd been reserving for the date. Micah had mentioned other apartments in the complex seemed to have crossed timelines as well – including the new one he'd moved into – and over the past few days, Cosmo had been pondering the situation. He looked forward to giving Micah an answer, even though it didn't do anything to solve it.

"There are two schools of thought when it comes to how time functions." Cosmo popped out the cork, then poured Micah a glass of wine. He surveyed their items, then untied the decorative twine from around the bunch of lilies and placed it in a straight line on the blanket. "Imagine spacetime is a piece of string. Some people believe in presentism, in which the future doesn't exist until we reach it. The string would represent all of history that has already happened, with our present moment at the very edge of the string. As the days/months/years proceed, the string grows longer."

"Makes sense," Micah said. "From our perspective, that's what's happening."

"Right. But the other theory is eternalism. That we live in a static block universe, and all points of time that have ever happened or *will* happen are already on the string." He pressed his finger to the twine. "If we are in the middle of the string, that doesn't mean that everything ahead of us doesn't exist. It just means we can't see it from where we are. All of time exists simultaneously, and what it is for us – past or present or future – is completely relative."

Micah's wine glass hovered at his lips. It was hard to tell whether he was giving any credence to the idea, but he finally said, "So past-Cosmo would still exist the same as you do. Past-me would still be here too, and he'd be moving into the studio likely in less than a week. That fits. But why are the timelines melting together? If time is string, we should be too far ahead to see or interact with our past."

"I thought about that." And Cosmo was quite pleased that he had an answer, even if the theory of time as string was a rather crude comparison. "String can get tangled. I don't know how, but I propose that a knot has formed in the timeline directly within the apartment complex." He made a slipknot in the twine, then placed it back on the blanket. "The past has looped over the present, and these moments are crossing into each other. Maybe it fluctuates and at moments it's very strong, like when you and I were able to see each other and objects passed through, and at others it's fainter. Only sounds or scents. And I don't think this is the first time in history it's happened."

Micah's gaze was distant as he clutched his unsipped wine. "Certainly not. I've seen ghost hunting shows where this idea fits perfectly. A bar in a ghost town randomly fills with jaunty piano and the scent of cigars."

"Exactly!"

"In one, the investigators asked a ghost where they were, and the reply they caught on audio was, 'I'm right here. Where are you?'"

Cosmo pushed curls out of his eyes and scrubbed at the goosebumps on his arms. Micah must have thought he was cold, because he pulled off his jacket and draped it over Cosmo's shoulders. The sleeves of his button-down were rolled up, showcasing his solid forearms, so Cosmo didn't push the jacket back at him.

"I wonder if all the ghosts people have ever experienced were just a timeline tangle," Micah said. "That's kind of sad, because maybe there isn't an afterlife for us or any of the people in this cemetery. They're just dead. Then again, that means they're still existing at multiple points on the string, and will be forever."

"I don't believe that. I had a dear friend who could sense ghosts, and she knew for certain that they were the spirits of the dead."

"Déjà."

Cosmo stared. "You know her?" Lemon Disco's art scene was tight, but Cosmo wasn't sure how Micah would know her if he never went to parties or gallery showings.

"She did a cleansing in the studio when the disturbances started. Told me I didn't have a 'rowdy ghost.' Which makes sense now that I know you're alive."

Déjà had done a cleansing to get rid of Cosmo. Wasn't that just fitting? Cosmo said, "Did she tell you we weren't friends anymore?"

"Yeah. And I'm sorry." Micah scooted a little closer. He looked like he might say more, then shook his head and finally took a sip of his wine.

Cosmo topped off his own. His past self was still friends with her. They were still going to parties and drinking milkshakes and painting each other's toenails in the living room of her apartment. It didn't bring him much consolation, because her absence *now* still actively hurt. And it meant that some version of Cosmo was still crying over Zedd. Some version of him was still breaking up with Déjà. Some version of Micah was still being beaten within an inch of his life.

Crows chattered in the trees, the sigh of the wind cutting through the lull in their conversation.

Micah picked at his sandwich, then brushed off his hands. "Want to hear a secret?"

"You know what to say to a boy. Do tell."

"I dial random numbers and make the person on the other end describe themselves to me. That's how I've done most of the portraits on my wall."

Cosmo gasped. "Micah! How peculiar."

A flush crawled up his neck, and he chuckled. "I don't know why, but I thought you might like knowing that."

"I do!" Cosmo imagined answering an unknown number and Micah's breathy voice coming through the line. Requesting that Cosmo talk about his body in detail so he could turn him into a piece of his gorgeous, coercive art. He shifted and pressed his thighs together. Leggings were definitely not the best choice today. "I want you to draw me this way."

Micah's blush deepened, now the color of his shirt. "*'Draw me like one of your French telemarketers.'*"

"Will you? Call me this evening and say to me whatever it is you say to them."

Micah's throat clicked as he swallowed. "I'd love to."

His right pupil was a small black point in the light of the afternoon sun. The other was an event horizon, swallowing the amber of his iris. Cosmo was in danger of being pulled in, and he wasn't sure he wanted to be rescued.

He slid his hand over Micah's knee, and Micah pulled in an audible breath. His gaze hung on Cosmo, and he raked his teeth across his bottom lip. From someone else, these would be clear signs of desire. Micah was romantically attracted to Cosmo, but he had no idea if that meant Micah was interested in kissing. If he wasn't, Cosmo would look foolish, but he couldn't resist leaning forward and tilting his chin in invitation, letting his eyelids fall as he parted his mouth.

His phone let out a shrill jingle.

Micah sat back, and a crow launched from a tree. Damn it.

He thumbed down the ringer without looking at the caller. "Sorry."

"You don't need to see who it is?" Micah asked.

"I know it isn't you, and you're the only person I want a phone call from at the moment." But thinking about that too hard right now in these leggings was going to turn the date inappropriate really quickly.

Cosmo stood and picked up the lilies. "I'm getting a bit of a cramp. Do you want to walk with me and place these on the graves?"

"Yeah."

They strolled past chipped and discolored headstones with motifs of skulls, angels, and crosses. Cosmo set a lily before a drunkenly-leaning marker. Micah stopped at a stone that had broken off its mounting and cracked in half. Weeds sprouted through the division, and chunks of sandstone littered the surrounding area.

"That's a shame." Micah draped a lily across the broken marker.

Cosmo's phone jingled again. He sighed and pulled it from his pocket, intent to turn off the ringer. A text from Royce sat in the notification bar.

<There's a lot of prep that needs to be finished for the Night Gallery event. I need you now. Call me.>

Identical Dog and Night Gallery sometimes collaborated on events, but Cosmo didn't help with prep unless it required moving artwork or setting up installations, and that was always done days ahead of time. Dahlia was the registrar. Cosmo had been passed up for that position – again – so why was Royce falling back on him to help?

Micah walked ahead, setting flowers on graves. Cosmo sighed and dialed Royce.

Royce answered immediately and said, "This is going to be a shitshow if you don't get down here."

Cosmo scoffed. What had crawled up Royce's ass all of the sudden? "Excuse me, but it's my day off and I'm on a – an outing with a friend."

"Too bad. This is Night Gallery's biggest charity event of the year, and if it doesn't go well, it will reflect badly on all of us."

"I'm just the *art handler*, and I don't care for your tone. Where's Dahlia?"

"She may as well be an exhibit for all she's doing to help. And the registrar of Night Gallery went to the hospital with appendicitis." Royce's voice took on a pleading edge. "You're fantastic, and you always go above and beyond your job."

"Maybe you should have made me registrar in the first place."

"If it were only up to me, you know I would in a heartbeat. Hina will be there tonight. She enjoys your sculptural work, and I've told her how great a job you do, but she's never seen you actively working. Coming to help in a pinch is sure to show her that you're better for the position."

He had a point. And Royce had always been there for Cosmo when it counted. He couldn't imagine the harassment he'd have to deal with from Zedd if Royce wasn't there. Heaven's sake, he'd kicked Zedd into a grave for Cosmo, then pulled him back to the party and hovered over him for the rest of the evening to make sure he was okay.

Guilt plunged into his stomach. "I'm sorry. I'm being an asshole. When do you need me there?"

"Yesterday. See you soon."

Shit. Cosmo scrubbed at his face. Micah stopped before him, and Cosmo said, "I'm truly sorry, but I'm going to have to cut our date short. I'm needed for a work event."

"You're not breaking it off because your ex called and threatened you, right?"

"No. Thank god." At least nothing Zedd had done had been that blatant. "I'm apparently the only dependable one at our gallery and not currently at risk for a ruptured appendix. I was very much enjoying our date, but I owe it to the director to be there."

Micah's expression fell. He shifted and rubbed his eyebrow, looking like he was fighting to keep words back. He finally cleared his throat and said, "Maybe we can get together again in the future? Or was this a one-off? I'm not sure I've had sufficient time to woo you."

"I wouldn't worry about failing at that. But just to be certain… Don't forget to call me, hm? Tonight, if you're still up. Or tomorrow. Don't text me ahead of time or leave a message. I want it to be the same as when you call strangers." And the thought of that faux-mystery call was going to sustain Cosmo through whatever cleaning and set up he was ordered to do today.

They packed in haste and headed back to the car. Micah drove Cosmo home, and when they pulled into the complex's parking lot, Cosmo thought about their almost-kiss, and how romantic it would have been sitting on the blanket in the sun, surrounded by mossy headstones. But the moment had passed, and trying to give Micah a kiss goodbye in his idling car with all their picnic supplies between them would be a poor substitution.

Micah squeezed Cosmo's hand. "I hope the event goes well. Don't work too hard."

"Thank you. It was a lovely date." He climbed out of the car and hurried up the sidewalk. A lovely date, but it would be a very long day.

Water beat down on Cosmo's bruised arms, and heat soaked into his sore muscles. He sagged under the stream, tempted to lean against the shower tile and fall asleep. Moving those solid wood tables by himself had been a mistake, but Dahlia really was useless, and next to nothing had been set up. Night Gallery's registrar had been busy avoiding sepsis, but what in the world had everyone else been doing for the past week? It shouldn't have come down to Cosmo. But Royce had heaped gratitude on him, bought him dinner, and Hina called him an invaluable asset to Lemon Disco's art community. The praise and attention didn't do anything for his fatigue, but it felt nice.

He shut off the water and toweled dry. It seemed so much later than eight-thirty. He pulled on a pair of briefs, then flopped into bed and scrolled through Flashbulb, met with dozens of comments from randos telling him how hot he was. It used to be an ego boost, something fun he looked forward to every time he posted a picture, but it had gotten stale long ago and he thought about deleting his account at least once a week. It was tempting to wipe it clean and post only his art, but it didn't garner a fraction of the love his selfies did.

Royce had tagged him in several photos from the charity event, the two of them standing in front of a wall of paintings. Cosmo stood stoically for one picture, his smile pleasant and somewhat fake. In the other, he hung off Royce's arm, head tilted and lips pursed for the camera. Royce had captioned it: *Leave it to @cosmicirony to outshine the exhibits. The night wouldn't have been possible without him.* 🖤

Aw! Royce was so sweet when he wasn't stressed out. Cosmo replied with: 🖤🖤🖤

The phone rang, and "*MICAH*" flashed on the screen.

Cosmo's heart throbbed. He brought the phone to his ear, trying to imagine a stranger on the other end. "Hello?"

"Hi."

"Who is this?"

Micah's husky voice came out both sincere and needy. "I'm an artist. I don't know you, but I know you're beautiful."

Oh my. It was a wonder he got anyone to talk to him at all without thinking he was a pervert. Or maybe they did, and they were into it. They weren't the only ones.

Cosmo leaned back in bed and coiled a lock of damp hair around his finger. "How do you know I'm beautiful?"

"Because all bodies are. I'd like to draw your portrait over the phone. Will you talk to me?"

"I suppose... But shouldn't we introduce ourselves first before getting so chummy?"

"No. Don't tell me your name. I don't want to know. But pronouns are okay."

"Do you say this to everyone you draw?"

"Yes."

This was downright strange, and Cosmo curled his toes in anticipation of whatever came next. "What do you need from me?"

"Describe yourself, please. I'll love it best if you're honest, with details I can picture, but I also don't want to make you embarrassed or dysphoric, so whatever you're comfortable with."

"I have dark, rather voluminous curly hair. It's layered and the back reaches my shirt collar." He imagined Micah's black hole gaze soaking him in, studying each detail of his features. "I'm white with an angular jaw, high cheekbones, and a cleft chin. I've been told I have 'soulful' eyes. I'm five-eight and of slim build." Hesitating, he said, "I know you asked for details that *don't* make me uncomfortable... But I don't like how big my feet are. I used to tell myself it was because all the cute shoes only came in smaller sizes, but I think it's actually dysphoria. I get the same feeling if I don't have at least a little bit of makeup on."

"Thank you for telling me that. Are you okay with describing your hands?"

That was rather specific. Cosmo didn't have unusual hands as far as he could tell. "Well, there are five fingers on each."

Micah chuckled. "Tell me more? Hands are my favorite."

The thought of Micah deriving pleasure from Cosmo's descriptions made him study himself for something to say. "They're narrow with long fingers. Larger than I'd like, but I don't mind as long as my nails are painted. Right now they're a lovely shade of lavender. I have prominent veins and bony wrists... Do you like that?"

Breathing filled the receiver. Micah whispered. "Very much."

Cosmo's cock throbbed, and he squirmed in the sheets. "There's a garnet ring on my index finger, and a Leo zodiac sign tattooed on the side of my middle finger. I have freckles on my knuckles, and deep life lines."

"I want to touch you."

Clenching his thighs, Cosmo said, "Oh, darling, do tell."

"I want to caress the rosy pink knobs of your knuckles. I want to press my lips to your fingertips. I want your calloused palm to slip against mine, the soft webbing of our fingers joined together."

Micah was only talking about hands, but he might as well have undressed Cosmo with his words. "I don't know how you can make that sound so sexy, but I am completely turned on. Is this part of your usual script? Do you say this to others?"

"Only you."

"Are you aroused right now?"

"No." Micah's voice grew thick. "But my heart has a throbbing hard-on for you. I like you so much."

"Aw! That is both cute and vulgar." And Cosmo was at risk of feeling the same. But if he wasn't careful, his heart would have a throbbing puncture instead, a gaping wound where Micah used to be before Zedd chased him away. "Will you describe yourself for *me*? Your forearms, please. Dear lord."

Micah's voice took on an amused lilt. "They're lean and solid, dusted in dark hair. I suppose you like the way the shadows fall across my tendons? The defined ropes of muscle running under my skin?"

The phone grew sweaty in Cosmo's grip. He wiped his hand on the sheets and pressed the phone back against his ear.

"Veins branching like rivers on a map, winding down my wrists, over my hands, and across my knuckles. I want to wrap these arms around you and press you against me. I want to crush you."

Cosmo let out a small moan and pulled at the straining fabric of his briefs.

"Can I text you tomorrow with something weird?" Micah asked.

"God, yes. *Please*."

He chuckled. "Alright. I, uh, think I have enough for my portrait now. Thanks for talking with me. You going to keep thinking about my forearms?"

"I want to think about more than just that. Does that bother you?"

"No. I'm going to draw your hands. Sweet dreams."

He ended the call, imagining Micah's lips against his fingertips. Micah on top of him on that blanket in the graveyard, kissing the wine out of his mouth. His tongue slipping across Cosmo's, glasses fogging with the heat of their quickened breath.

Micah would slide his palms across Cosmo's and pin him to the ground. His always-a-bit-disheveled hair would fall into his eyes as he kissed the tender flesh of Cosmo's throat, sucking it until it bruised…

Oh, but the heavy clouds above them were swollen and gray, and as rain dotted Cosmo's face and lightning needled the sky, they'd rush to the nearby mausoleum for cover. Rain would pour through holes in the roof, bitter wind and dead leaves swirling inside. A pristine casket would sit inside the dim room, mahogany wood with a cherry red finish and brass handles.

He would open the casket and climb inside. Micah would join him and shut the lid. The heat of their bodies and warmth of breath would turn the confined space stuffy, and they were wearing far too much clothing. Gone, then, nothing between Cosmo's bare skin and Micah's.

As Cosmo slid off his underwear to indulge further into the fantasy, the phone jingled with a notification. He smiled. Hopefully it was an in-progress shot of Micah's art.

The text was from an unknown number, and cold dread sank into his stomach as he opened it.

<*You're such a slut. And once he finds out what a party favor you are, he's going to get bored with you like everyone else. But I won't. Because you and I are meant to be.*>

13

THIS USED TO BE THE FUTURE

Micah - Present Day

The phone sat on the drafting table and Micah stood before it, legs wide and fingers twitching like a gunslinger ready to make his draw. He was going to ask Cosmo to come over, and this time, he was going to let him inside. They were going to sit on the brand new couch Micah had used his emergency credit card to buy, and Micah was going to kiss him.

After they'd ended their call the night before, he'd set aside his full-body sketch of Cosmo in lieu of drawing his hands in detail. For more accuracy, he'd pulled up Cosmo's Flashbulb profile and studied some of the pictures. As he'd drawn each crease of his fingers, each white moon on his nails and the highlight on the garnet cabochon of his ring, he'd thought about what Cosmo was most certainly doing at that moment.

Navigating potential new relationships was always tricky. Micah would bring up that he was trans before anything got too serious, and people usually understood. That was a concrete concept they could grasp. But broaching his asexuality often resulted in assumptions and offensive questions that he was tired of hearing.

It had been a relief to learn that neither his identity nor sexuality were a dealbreaker for Cosmo. Micah had a sex drive, and sometimes he'd see a magazine ad of a man in nylons and high heels, or a woman who stared at the viewer like she wanted to step on their face, and he'd feel a tingle of something. But he was pretty sure it was more the concept that interested him than the person's body. It was frustrating that he didn't understand himself as well as he wished.

But oh, how he hoped that when he kissed Cosmo, it would feel more than just wet.

Snatching the phone, he typed: <*Are you ready to hear my weird request?*>

He hit send, but was immediately met with *Message Delivery – Failed*. Hmm. Cosmo must have used up his monthly allowance of emojis and been punished for it.

That was okay, Micah was eager to hear his voice again. He dialed his number, and a piercing three-note tone entered his ear, followed by, "We're sorry, but the number can't be completed as dialed. Please hang up and try again."

A bolt of anxiety jabbed Micah's heart. Had Cosmo blocked his number? That didn't make sense. Their conversation last night had been... Well, it had been *something*, and specifically a something that they'd both enjoyed, even if it was for different reasons.

Micah could go to Cosmo's apartment, but he didn't want to show up unannounced or go anywhere that Cosmo's ex might see him.

His Flashbulb app was still on Cosmo's profile. He navigated to the message box and wrote: <*It's Micah. I tried to call you. Is everything okay?*>

Almost immediately, Cosmo responded: <*My ex texted me* ☹☹☹ *so I had to change my number. He knows about you.*>

How was that possible? The chances of him seeing Cosmo and Micah together at the cemetery or that French bistro seemed slim. It could have been at the gallery or Micah's apartment, though. Micah had come to the gallery with flowers, and Cosmo had accepted them.

This was bullshit. He was not going to let some jealous douchebag get in the way.

<*Are you alright?*> Micah typed. <*Did your ex threaten you? Do you need to go to the police?*>

<*I've tried. They won't do anything to help. I'm freaked out.*>

Asking Cosmo to come over now was out of the question. Micah couldn't risk failing to let him inside. <*You shouldn't be alone. Want to meet somewhere outside the city? How about at your grave on Cherry Lane? Or we could meet in Fairview and sit in the back of a cinema.*> That sounded nice, actually. Micah would put his arm around Cosmo in the dark theater as some special effectstravaganza flashed on the screen. He'd press his nose to Cosmo's hair and whisper that he wasn't going anywhere.

Cosmo's reply appeared: <*I can't see you anymore* 🐱🐱🐱🐱🐱🐱>

No. Micah felt himself shaking his head. He squeezed the phone. No, no, no. They liked each other. It couldn't end like this. <*Your ex isn't going to scare me away. I won't ghost you.*>

<*I'm sorry for dragging you into this.*>

<*You haven't done anything wrong. And *we* aren't wrong. We can figure this out.*>

<*I didn't want this to hurt, but it already does. I'm sorry.*>

<*We can work this out. It'll be okay.*> Micah waited for a response. Every second that went by constricted his throat even more. He wrote, <*Talk to me. Call me so I can hear your voice. Please.*>

He struggled to swallow, his hand clenching around the phone. He whispered, "Cosmo. Please."

The phone screen blurred in his vision, and eventually the screen went to sleep. He hurled it at the wall. It dented the drywall, then clattered across the floor. He yanked at his hair. This wasn't fair! He was so close to letting someone in, in more than one way. So close.

Something dark and consuming reared inside him. He'd been working on pushing it down for nine months. Working on pulling himself *up*. Keeping his head above water, treading until he was strong enough to reach the shore. But the tide was dragging him back, tugging him under, and it was so much easier to just give up and let it take him.

He took off his glasses, crawled into bed, and pulled the sheets over his head.

The phone rang sometime that evening, but it wasn't Cosmo, so he dropped it back to its spot on the floor. When it rang the next day, it still wasn't Cosmo. And the more time that passed, the more Micah stopped checking, and the less he got out of bed, resigned to let the dark sea of depression fill his lungs, swallow him, until he was completely numb.

Days blurred together and time seemed irrelevant. Ah, the irony in that.

His only comfort was the white cat, which he kept thinking of as "Phantom." She'd jump into bed and stare at him with her mismatched shooter marble eyes. If he ignored her, she'd butt her head against his face and mew loudly until he finally got up. He wasn't sure if she needed anything aside from attention, considering that she'd vanish back to her own timeline after a bit, but it had motivated him enough to throw on some sweats and go to the corner store for cat food. That had been at least a week ago, and he hadn't done anything since then except water his plants.

The plastic factory odor still emanated faintly from the couch. Some kind of chemical they used in the dye. Mostly, Micah could only smell himself. He lay with his nose pressed against the cushion, floating in and out of an annoying half-awareness. He needed to sink deeper to forget he existed, but he had to pee, and the sensation wouldn't leave him alone.

Throwing off the blanket, he staggered past a bag of mail Ximena had brought him, and a Tupperware dish full of something he hadn't eaten. It was bad by now. He couldn't remember what day she'd stopped by.

Avoiding his reflection as he passed the bathroom mirror, he relieved himself, then dropped back onto the couch. Something thumped, or rattled, or maybe it was the phone ringing again. Either way, he was too tired to go investigate.

As he slipped back into a half-sleep, he imagined Cosmo padding across the carpet, the couch creaking as he sat down. His teeth floating in the dark like the Cheshire cat.

A hand shook his shoulder. He gasped and sat up. Words clogged in his throat so hard he couldn't swallow. The pulse in his neck jittered. His eyes prickled and watered, but he was afraid to blink.

Stooped before him... was himself. The doppelganger stared at Micah, lines bookending his mouth and glasses slipping down the bridge of his nose.

"Hey. You should get up," Other Micah said.

Was that what his voice really sounded like? It seemed less reedy in his head. And his face was so asymmetrical. God, he'd hoped the thick black frames on that pair of glasses helped disguise his scars better than his other pair, but he was fooling himself. At least the reflection on the lenses helped obscure the fact that his pupil–

"Micah." Other Micah patted his cheek. "Wake up. Hey, c'mon. It's going to get better."

The hair on the back of Micah's neck stood up. "I've done this before."

"No, you– Well, I suppose that's sort of right because *I'm* doing it, and I'm you."

Micah threw off the blanket, his mind insisting that this had already happened. He scrubbed his stubbly face. He should be freaking out, right? That was surely the natural response to meeting a version of yourself from another time. But his initial shock was already being swallowed by the numbing tide. At least the fabric of the universe wasn't being rent apart. Or maybe it was. It was hard to care.

Other Micah sat next to him. "I stood over you for like five minutes, wondering if the fabric of the universe was about to be rent apart."

"I don't understand how you're here. I thought the disturbances I've noticed were from the tenant before me, the cat–"

"Ah. Phantom is mine. Ours." Other Micah shrugged. "She just showed up one day. I asked around, but nobody claimed her, and it seemed like she needed someone. I guess we needed her too."

Micah scrubbed his forehead. His cat all along. No wonder she was so friendly during his first encounter with her.

"What day is it anyway?" Other Micah asked.

"I have no clue." He picked up his watch from the coffee table and snorted. "Friday. The thirteenth."

"Oh." Other Micah slumped against the couch. "That day."

"I don't like the sound of that. What happens today?"

"I don't know." Other Micah glanced at him with his disconcerting pupil. "Cosmo won't say."

His heart leapt. "We talk to him again?"

"Yeah. He's going to text you around six this evening and say he made a mistake in breaking it off. He'll ask you to meet him at that taco truck always parked on the corner of Clementine.

He kind of threw himself into my arms. Our arms... Your arms? You know what I mean." His lips twitched in a smile. "And we find out if it feels more than just wet."

Micah sucked in a sharp breath then glanced at his neglected living room. Mail lay scattered on the floor, moving boxes were still unopened, and one of his pillows had fallen off the couch into a pile of dirty dishes.

Holy hell. He and Cosmo were going to kiss and this place was disgusting and so was he.

Other Micah continued. "But... Something happened that Friday before we met up. Someone did something to him while he was at the taco truck." His nostrils flared, fists balling. "They spooked him. Maybe hurt him."

"Who?"

Other Micah's voice flatlined. "You know who."

Hot anger flooded Micah's limbs. "That motherfu–"

"I guess we can't say for sure it was Zedd, but he's the most likely. Also thought about–"

"Royce?"

"Yeah."

Micah opened his mouth to continue voicing his thoughts, but there was no reason to. He was talking to himself.

Other Micah sighed and said, "Cosmo won't give us details. Just keeps pretending like nothing is wrong. If it *was* Zedd, his plan backfired, because instead of pushing us away, it made Cosmo come running back to our arms. I feel completely useless though, because I don't know how to help the situation."

Micah's mind reeled with the knowledge that Cosmo was hurting, was *going* to be hurt, and the fact that his future self was sitting beside him on the–

"Wait." He sat up straight and stared at Other Micah. "Has it already happened today? No, no, that taco truck doesn't open until five pm." Looking at his watch again, he confirmed that it was only three-thirty. "I can stop it. I can go find Cosmo and make sure that whatever is going to happen, doesn't."

Other Micah's mouth fell open. "You have to! Oh my god. Go take a shower and get down there." He pushed at Micah. "Go, go, go."

Micah leapt off the couch and slipped on a piece of mail. He turned back to Other Micah. "I doubt you'll still be here when

I get out of the shower, but if this doesn't change anything for *your* Cosmo, you hold him close and tell him it's okay not to be okay." He paused. "Same goes for you. Be good to yourself."

"You can't say that to me when you haven't showered in two weeks. Say it to yourself, then go stop whatever is about to happen."

Micah hurried into the shower and shaved with enough haste to nick his chin. He scrubbed the depression off of himself, formulating what he was going to say to get Cosmo to come with him. It sounded like Cosmo was close to wanting to be with Micah anyway. Hopefully showing up and inviting him to go get ice cream or see an art exhibit would be an easy "yes." And if he wanted to leap into Micah's arms in the process, that would be more than alright.

When he got out of the shower, Other Micah was gone. He still had time before he needed to go, so he dumped dirty dishes in the sink and turned on the faucet, then swept through the living room, picking up the clutter and throwing a load of laundry into the washer. He wasn't sure he'd be able to bring Cosmo here and be in the apartment with him at the same time, but if it was life or death, the last thing he wanted to worry about was Cosmo drowning in filth.

Maybe it would be best to start the conversation with what had happened. Cosmo would want to hear all about Micah meeting his other self, and how this new apartment had the future bleeding in instead of the past.

This complex had a serious paranormal problem, but now Micah had an advantage. This was going to fix things between them and prevent something awful from happening, if not to all the Cosmos out there in the block universe, at least to this one.

14

NOTHING BAD EVER HAPPENS TO ME

Cosmo - Pulling the Thread

The nose-stinging scent of chilies and savory meats floated from down the block. Cosmo was going to buy an horchata and a lengua taco. Scratch that. The lengua burrito grande. It was the only tongue-action he was going to be getting for the rest of forever, so he may as well go all out.

After that, he could go to the deli grandpa used to own and buy a bottle of vodka and a paper bag full of Rotfront candies. Then he'd drive to the church at the end of Cherry Lane, lay down in the dirt, and die.

People would be sad about it, briefly. But they'd get over it. His death would be exactly what everyone knew he'd been in life – Duchamp's snow shovel. A bizarre novelty that caught people's attention for a short time, until they grew bored and moved on to something else.

Greasy smoke roiled from the top of the taco truck on the corner, and string lights hanging from patio umbrellas twinkled like gaudy spiderwebs.

A strange intuition suddenly overcame him: he was going to glance over at the decorative brickwork surrounding the flowers, and Micah would be sitting there, waiting for him.

Cosmo turned his head. His stomach dropped. The only thing sitting on the bricks was an empty beer bottle. It was just subconscious hope that his sweet, cozy man who only dreamed of holding hands would be here waiting. Cosmo could message him and beg for forgiveness. Admit how scared he was. And when Micah insisted Zedd wouldn't drive him away, Cosmo could choose to believe it.

The itch of fear in his chest over the thought of Zedd hiding in his closet while he had "phone sex" with Micah had dulled to a background irritation. He'd checked the closets, under the bed, and behind the shower curtain, and no one had been there. The doors had been locked, the windows closed. Zedd must have seen him and Micah together earlier in the day, and just so happened to send that text at a creepily coincidental moment. Or maybe he didn't know about Micah and was only jealous that Cosmo might be with anybody at all.

But a week after the text message, there'd been a letter with no return address in his mailbox. He should have thrown it away without opening it because the single sentence wouldn't leave his mind, and he didn't know if it was a note of romance from Micah or a threat of violence from Zedd.

He could message Micah and ask. No matter the answer, it would give them an excuse to talk.

After pulling out his phone, he opened his Flashbulb messages and stared at Micah's last line from two weeks previous: *<Talk to me. Call me so I can hear your voice. Please.>*

His heart panged. He typed, *<Oh, Micah, I'm so sorry. I>*

A hand gripped his arm, and he gasped, staring into Micah's face. His mind reeled, the ground tilting beneath him. His heart pounded against his ribs, and he forced himself to take a breath.

"Did my pain conjure you?" Cosmo whispered.

Micah nodded without hesitation, which was not what Cosmo was expecting. Goosebumps prickled on his skin. Cosmo had never had a premonition before, and it would be *so* romantic to believe his ache for Micah was pronounced enough for Micah to sense it and come find him. But with Micah's hair more disheveled than normal, the lack of color in his cheeks, and the way his hand trembled on his arm, his vibe was giving Cosmo second-hand panic.

"I know you don't want to see me, but things have gotten extra weird." Micah's voice wobbled. "I want to tell you about it, but let's go somewhere else? Can I buy a lady an ice cream at the Dairy Queen down the block?"

"What kind of weird? Dangerous weird?"

Micah raked back his hair, his gaze darting over Cosmo's shoulder to the patio and taco truck beyond. "I can't let you get hurt."

"Okay." How desperate would he sound if he admitted he wanted to throw himself into Micah's strong arms? That he needed Micah to sweep him away from whatever danger was lurking, whether it was twisted spacetime or just his ex-boyfriend. Burrow into his chest and tell Micah to never let go. "Answer me something first, please. Did you send me a letter that said, *'There's room for two in your grave'*?"

The whites of Micah's eyes flashed, and his grip on Cosmo's arm tightened. "No. Christ. Let's get out of here." His gaze was still glued to a spot behind Cosmo, and Cosmo was afraid to turn around for fear Zedd was standing right behind them.

But when he looked back, he only saw strangers sitting at the tables and benches, eating tacos and scrolling through their phones. And was that– "Royce?"

Micah grunted and started to tug him away. "C'mon. Before he sees you."

"Wait a minute." He thought of Micah asking how friendly of a friend Royce was, and if he made Cosmo *do* things. "I thought you were saying I'm in danger because of Zedd. Are you here because of Royce? You're trying to rescue me from my boss?"

"I don't have specifics about what's going to happen because you wouldn't say–"

"*I* wouldn't say? What is it you want me to say? I've already told you that Royce is my friend. He's never done anything untoward, and he's been a barrier against Zedd." A hot coal lodged in Cosmo's chest. This wasn't what he'd expected at all. "Jealousy is not a good look on you, Micah."

Micah wiped his hands down his face. "I'm not jealous. But I–"

"I have enough of that with Zedd. All anyone thinks I am is a plaything to be tugged back and forth."

"You don't understand. I've heard things about Royce. That he wants sexual favors in exchange for portfolio consideration, but that's–"

"Why is it always Royce that people have a problem with?" He'd always been there when Cosmo needed him as support and a mentor, which was worlds better than his own father had been. "Someone started a rumor that I like having cigarettes put out on my chest. You want to check to see if it's true?" Cosmo unbuttoned his shirt. "It must be, right? Because someone said it!"

"No! Stop that."

Baring his chest, Cosmo stared at Micah, tears forming at the edges of his eyes. "Do you see any burn marks? Better look for yourself because my word isn't any good."

"Cosmo, please," Micah hissed. "This is an emergency. I'll explain on the way." He snatched Cosmo's arm and tried to tug him away. His cheeks reddened as he glanced at their new audience at the tables around them.

Cosmo ripped free of his grip. "It's an emergency? Or am I just embarrassing you? You know, I didn't think anyone in the art scene bought into rumors. It happens to all of us so we have a healthy dose of skepticism. But you don't have rumors about you, huh? In order to get them, you'd have to leave your house once in a while!"

Micah looked like Cosmo had just slid a dagger into his stomach. "Right. Well, this mentally ill, anti-social recluse is still intent on getting you out of harm's way." He snatched the placket of Cosmo's shirt and yanked him forward.

Cosmo slapped Micah across the face hard enough to send his glasses askew. "Stop grabbing me like the misogynistic knight in a fairytale! I'm not your fantasy!"

Putting up his hands, Micah took a step back, mouth agape and chest heaving. His cheek was an angry pink, wire-framed lenses crooked, and there was a look of abject devastation in his eyes.

What the hell had just happened? Cosmo had sunk the knife too deep, thrown Micah's PTSD back in his face, and slapped him like he was Zedd. As Cosmo opened his mouth to apologize, Micah turned on his heel and strode away.

"Micah–"

The beer bottle fell off the decorative edging beside the flowers as Micah hopped up and pushed through the bushes. It bounced off the concrete and rolled toward Cosmo, bumping into his shoe.

Well, good. Cosmo had wanted him to go away. Hadn't he? The amber glass of the beer bottle doubled in his vision. His emotions tugged him in separate directions until he felt like the figures in Dalí's *The Burning Giraffe*, all the drawers of his soul pulled open. The contents were too jumbled to make sense of any of it.

A firm arm slipped around his shoulders, and he startled. Royce's woody aftershave filled his nose, his windbreaker crinkling. "Come sit down with me." He pulled Cosmo toward the taco truck.

Cosmo tried to look back. "Hang on—"

"You're making a scene." Royce sat him down on the bench he'd occupied previously. His voice came out with a hard, commanding edge that wasn't normally directed at Cosmo. "Button your damn shirt. People are staring at you."

It was hard to see the buttons through the blear in his eyes, and his fingers were shaking, but he managed to get his shirt done up again. Royce's expression was unreadable, and Cosmo couldn't bear to have the director disappointed in him.

He hunched his shoulders. "I'm sorry."

Royce's voice softened. "Oh, to be young and gorgeous and have too many men after you."

"It's wretched. I'm so tired. I should just move away and change my name."

Royce rested his hand on Cosmo's shoulder. "I know I won't be around every time to scare these guys away, but I'm here for you. You know that, right?"

"Oh, Royce." Cosmo sniffled, and when Royce tugged him closer, he leaned against him and pressed his nose into Royce's collar. A tiny seed of doubt sprouted in his mind, entertaining the idea that Micah might be right about the director's intentions. But Cosmo immediately crushed the thought. He was not going to let the words of a jealous romantic interest drive a wedge between him and one of his only remaining sources of support. He said to Royce, "You're so good to me. Do you want to go snap Zedd's neck to get rid of one of my man problems?" He looked up at him and batted his lashes. "Pretty please?"

Royce's gaze lingered. "That's... very tempting. But I think what you need right now is some food, hm? What do you want?"

That tongue burrito didn't sound so appealing with his stomach twisted in a knot. Everything felt too monumental right now, too overwhelming. "I want a drink."

"Ah." Royce's eyes crinkled in a smile, creating waterfalls of crow's feet. "Finally going to let me buy you that drink I've been offering for years?"

Cosmo let out a humorless chuckle. "Seems like something always came up, or I wasn't in the mood. But I'm absolutely in the mood now, and I would love it if you joined me."

"Well, there happens to be a bar across the street. But you shouldn't drink on an empty stomach. Want my last taco?"

Cosmo forced down a few bites. They crossed the street and headed into a pub he didn't catch the name of. The scent of beer-soaked wood enveloped him, and the clack of billiard balls came from the other end of the room. He sat on a vinyl seat with a split down the middle and pushed away a sticky napkin.

Royce ordered two mind erasers. What Cosmo needed was a heart eraser. Just scrub away all the feelings inside him until they turned to gummy pink eraser dust and blew away.

The bartender set a fizzy coffee cocktail in a rocks glass before him, and he pounded it back. A rush went to his head, and he blinked at the neon signs behind the bar.

Royce snorted. "I don't think you're supposed to hammer it down like that."

Fire ran into Cosmo's stomach, and he raised his finger to the bartender to request another. "I'm going to do what I like. Are you going to stop me?"

"Not at all. I'll take care of you."

After several more mind erasers, they started to do their job, though he couldn't quite rub out all thoughts of Micah. Cosmo shuddered to think he'd been so close to throwing himself into his arms. He'd thought Micah was different, and it hurt to be this wrong. Using the threat of danger just to get them back together! That was cruel.

Royce gripped Cosmo's elbow. "Are you okay?"

"No. I'm not." Cosmo pushed past empty glasses for a napkin. He pressed it to his eyes. "I'm so sick of the jealousy and possessiveness. I just wanted love."

Royce's coffee liqueur breath tickled his ear. "A gorgeous thing like you should have all the love he wants."

Cosmo pounded the bar. "Damn right."

"Someone needs to give it to you."

"Zedd scares all the good ones away."

Royce's arm slid around Cosmo's back, the overpowering scent of his aftershave lingering. "He doesn't scare me." Lips pressed against Cosmo's neck, and he pulled in a sharp breath. They slid across his throat, sucking at his skin.

Cosmo pulled away and gripped the bar. "Royce, what are you doing?"

"Giving you what you want."

"No. I'm not into it."

"I think you are. Otherwise you wouldn't be getting drunk with me and moaning when I kiss you." He nibbled Cosmo's jaw and squeezed his upper thigh, dangerously close to his groin.

Micah was right.

He pushed at Royce, but couldn't extract himself. "Stop! This is a misunderstanding." And he needed to leave, but he wasn't sure he could stand up on his own. He waved his hand, trying to flag down the bartender, but the man ignored him.

Micah was right.

"What's to misunderstand? You want love," Royce purred. "You want someone who isn't afraid of Zedd. I'm right here, beautiful. I've been here for years. Seeing your heartbreak and pain over people who use you and throw you away. I won't. You know me better than that."

Micah was right. Cosmo was in danger, and he should have listened. Should have left with sweet, kind Micah to go eat ice cream. "No, Royce. You need to stop!"

He gripped Cosmo's jaw hard and kissed the side of his mouth.

"What the fuck is this!" A familiar voice cut between them. "You get your filthy, gnarled meathooks off of him, you petrified piece of shit."

Cosmo turned to look his savior in the face, but his stool wobbled and he flailed for purchase. Acrylic nails dug into his arm, and he was pulled to his feet. Royce growled something indecipherable.

Light florals floated around the woman clutching him, and her hair tickled his cheek. But it couldn't be Déjà; she'd picked up the pieces of Cosmo too many times already. That's why they weren't friends anymore.

She unslung a backpack and rooted inside. "You take one step toward him and I will unload an entire can of mace on you."

Someone else shouted – maybe the bartender – then Cosmo was hauled out the entrance. He staggered onto the sidewalk and rubbed his eyes. Neon light striped Déjà's oversized sunglasses, and her hair was pinned back with sparkly clips shaped like jack-o'-lanterns.

A noise escaped his throat. It really was her. He'd meant to talk to her at that party in August, but she left before he'd had the chance. How did she know he needed her now more than ever?

"Thank you." He threw his arms around her. "Thank you."

"We need to go somewhere else. Do you still live in Climbing Ivy?"

"Yes." Cosmo kept hold of her, his best friend, his anchor. Always his anchor, but he'd drifted away and crashed against the rocks a long time ago. "How did you know I was here?"

"Micah called me." Her heels clacked against the sidewalk. "He was completely distraught."

Cosmo stumbled, the sidewalk a wobbly blur. Oh, Micah. "I – I didn't want Royce to do that."

"I know. And that bartender didn't care at all." She slowed and looked over her shoulder, then urged him on. "It wasn't your fault."

It *was* his fault. And even if Micah had called and begged, why would Déjà want to be involved in this mess? God, how he missed her. Every thought for her, every ache, was held back by the thinnest of dams, but he didn't know what to say. What *could* he say? Too much time had passed. Their wounds had festered and necrotized, and Cosmo didn't know how to heal that.

They reached his door. He pulled out the contents of his pockets until he heard keys clink together, but then they weren't in his hands. Where did they go?

Déjà grumbled beside him, and he steadied himself against the doorframe. He pressed his brow against the wood and shut his eyes, but that was a mistake because it made the feeling of helium in his head more acute.

Keys jingled and the door swung open. Hands pushed him inside. He flopped onto the bed and felt Déjà tug off his shoes.

This night was such a mistake, and now he'd never get to snuggle up to Micah while the man wore that soft, paint-stained sweatshirt. He made do with squeezing a pillow instead, and he must have fallen asleep because when he opened his eyes, sweat plastered his hair to his forehead. His breath was so foul he could smell it with his mouth closed. One of his earrings was jabbing him in the neck, and his head throbbed.

Paper rustled, and he rolled over. Déjà sat on the floor with one of his coffee table books, pursing her lips at the glossy spreads of conceptual art.

The evening came rushing back to him, and shame entered his body like a demon hungry for a host. "Why are you here?"

"Micah called me." She glanced up. "I told you that. You don't remember."

He remembered enough. Too much. After pushing out of bed, he staggered into the bathroom. He took a much-needed shower, letting the hot water beat down on his neck. When he was finished, he pulled on pajamas and sat next to Déjà with a strong cup of coffee.

The highlights on her cheekbones glittered, and a tattoo of quartz crystals graced the side of her neck. She glanced at him. "Feeling better?"

"You're so pretty. I've missed you."

"You told me."

"Sorry. I don't remember that either."

"*'Déjà, you're so pretty and I love you and don't deserve you.'* Which is true." She flipped a page in the book. "*'Déjà, I'm completely taken with Micah. We went to a cemetery and we didn't kiss, but then we had phone sex, sort of, and he wears the cutest, frumpiest sweatshirts. I want him to give me hickies until I look like a peach someone repeatedly dropped on the floor.'*"

Cosmo snorted. "I'm sorry, darling. I'm an absolute mess."

"So nothing has changed in the last three years."

"Truly, it has not." His ache for her had faded, but it had a funny way of appearing suddenly and stabbing him in the heart when he least expected it. The chorus of a song, the sequins on a dress, a painting on the gallery wall… "Maraschino cherries."

"What?"

"Maraschino cherries remind me of you. Because you always ask for three."

"I haven't been to that place forever. Have you?"

He shook his head. He craved their outrageous milkshakes, but it hadn't seemed right to go there without Déjà. "Have you missed me at all?"

She closed the art book and pushed it away, but she didn't stop staring at the space it had occupied. She'd never saved his feelings when it was something he needed to hear, but she was going to tell him *no*, and he shouldn't have asked the question if he couldn't handle the answer.

Sliding over, she pulled him into a hard hug. "So much."

He pressed his forehead to her shoulder and held her tight. There were so many things he wanted to say and ask, and he couldn't remember any of the conversation from before he fell asleep.

She pulled back. "What happened with Royce wasn't your fault, okay?"

The scent of coffee liqueur on Royce's breath, his rough and wrinkled hands all over Cosmo's body – the memory made his stomach churn, and he fought back the urge to vomit. "I led him on."

"No, you didn't."

"With all due respect, you can't know that because you weren't there. I invited him to drink with me. It was my idea. He tried to get me to eat something instead. I pounded back my cocktails and told him I needed love. It was one hundred percent my fault."

"I heard you say 'No! Stop!' And he didn't. Whatever led up to that point doesn't matter. If someone says 'stop,' then you stop. That's it, end of story."

His jaw ached, nose stinging with sudden tears. "But why would Royce expect anything less than for me to put out when I'm... when I'm me?"

"Why do you hate yourself so much?"

"I don't! But if everyone treats me a certain way, then there must be a reason for it! Royce wouldn't have done that unless he thought I wanted it. He's had plenty of opportunities at the gallery when it was just him and me in a back room, and he's never done anything sexual. This evening notwithstanding,

I've felt safer with him around than anyone else. I never have to worry about Zedd showing up at the gallery."

"*It. Does. Not. Matter.* In fact, that makes it worse. He's someone you trust and consider a friend and he violated that. Violated *you*."

The scent of Royce's aftershave – pine, balsam, patchouli – still lingered in Cosmo's nose. He felt Royce's hard grip on his thigh, centimeters from his crotch.

He clutched his elbows and fought against the lump welling in his throat. "Micah knew. He knew it was going to happen, and he knew it was going to be Royce. But I didn't listen."

"I hate to say this, but everyone seemed to believe he was like that but you. Royce used to flirt with you constantly. And remember at your funeral? Your mom looked like she wanted to slit his throat, and she'd only known him for five minutes. This still isn't your fault. I'm just saying that I wish you didn't have to see the way he is the hard way."

Déjà was always right – he may as well have been an actual ghost for as easily as she saw through him. Cosmo had told Royce to stop, and the director had deliberately ignored him. That wasn't Cosmo's fault. But it didn't do anything for the misplaced guilt churning in his stomach. He didn't know how he was supposed to face Royce at work now.

"I should quit the gallery." He meant it the way someone said they *should* work out more or *should* get their Christmas shopping done early. But approval filled Déjà's face and she nodded.

Quitting Identical Dog for a position somewhere else wouldn't be the worst thing. He'd been an art handler for years, and despite his efforts to prove his worth, he wasn't moving up. He shouldn't have had to cut his date with Micah short in order to impress the boss on his day off.

"I suppose… I could text Simone and put out some feelers."

His phone sat on the coffee table amid scattered contents that had been in his pockets. Déjà picked it up and handed it to him. "You should."

Night Gallery probably wasn't a perfect choice for a new job because Simone, the gallerist, collaborated with Identical Dog often and he would still end up seeing Royce, but the familiarity with it would likely make it the easiest transfer.

<Good evening, Simone. This is Cosmo Koslov. 🐱 I must tell you again how fantastic everything looked at the charity event, and I hope it was a huge success.

<I would love to know if you have any positions opening at the gallery??>

He liked Identical Dog. He knew all the hallways and exhibit rooms by heart. The lemon-jasmine scent smelled like home. But he couldn't work there even one more day. And change was less frightening when he had someone to lean on.

Déjà stood and walked to his art desk, inspecting his sculpture pieces with her hands behind her back. They had so much catching up to do. Unless this was a one-time meeting and she would go back to pretending he was a stranger when they saw each other at parties.

His phone jingled with a message from Simone. <Oh, Cosmo… Are you okay?>

He frowned at the text, then reread what he'd sent to her. That was a strange response to his benign question, but it was also nine pm on a Friday. He started to type back that he was fine, but another text appeared.

<Don't you worry about anything. I'll talk to Hina. Alexander is only out temporarily, but I'd love it if you could fill in until he's back. Do let me know if you'd like to work as registrar? After that we can find you something more permanent. I'll inquire at other galleries.>

Cosmo gasped. <Yes! I would love to. 💚💚💚 Thank you so much.> Registrar! It wasn't permanent, but it was a start.

He handed Déjà his phone. She read over the texts and said, "I bet Royce made a pass at her too. Or she's heard about him harassing other employees."

"You think so?" Cosmo had been tight with the director. If the other employees hated Royce, they certainly wouldn't have gone to Cosmo to talk about it. Maybe that rumor about Royce demanding blow jobs in exchange for considering portfolio submissions was true.

His face crumpled and he clutched his elbows.

Déjà sat next to him. "Now we need to make a plan to castrate your boss. Do you still have those nice ceramic knives your mom gave you?"

He winced, then cleaned up the items on the coffee table. "So, did Micah tell you what's going on with his studio? He told me you tried to do a spirit cleansing to get rid of me. You've fully embraced your ghost communing abilities, I see."

"You don't want to talk about Royce anymore." She studied him for a long moment. "Fine. As long as you tell me what happened wasn't your fault. And you'd better mean it."

Swallowing thickly, he said, "It wasn't my fault. But that doesn't make me feel any better about it. Can we please talk about something else now?"

Her face softened, and she squeezed his hand. "I asked Micah to tell me what was going on in the studio, but he never did. He doesn't treat you like trash, does he?"

"Absolutely not."

"He's a little weird."

"Very weird," Cosmo said.

"He has an unusual look."

"Don't you love it?"

"And there's something unsettling about his art that I can't put my finger on."

"Absolutely."

She lightly smacked his forehead. "He's perfect. So why in the hell did you go to a bar with Royce when Micah was right there?"

Cosmo put his face in his hands. "I made such a mess of this."

"Call him and fix it. It's about time you found someone who's good to you."

"I said something very hurtful. There's no way he's still interested."

"You don't know that. He pleaded with me to come help you. He still cares."

Cosmo flopped back on the floor and threw an arm over his face. "About my safety, maybe. Not about dating me."

The silence stretched until Déjà said, "God, you're so hot it disgusts me."

What in the world was she talking about? His face was puffy from drinking too much, and he was wearing ten-year-old pajamas from Walmart. He sat up to find her scrolling through his phone.

"Hey." He tried to snatch it from her, but she leaned away. "You have no business looking at anything on there."

"You handed it to me to look at."

"At my texts to Simone. Not my photos."

"I can't look at photos of you?" Her mouth pulled to one side. "Am I going to see your baked goods in graphic detail if I scroll too far?"

"There's a cream pie in there somewhere."

"Oh, gross." She grimaced and tossed the phone in his lap.

"An actual cream pie. It was good."

The phone rang, and he squeaked.

Déjà pressed her teeth into her bottom lip. "I texted Micah your new number."

"Déjà!" The phone vibrated against the carpet, and he imagined Micah's needy voice on the other end saying, *I don't know you, but I know you're beautiful.*

What was Cosmo going to say? He couldn't let it keep ringing. Picking it up, he pressed it to his ear and said, "Hello, Micah."

Nothing but breathing filled the line, and for a terrible second Cosmo wondered if it wasn't Micah at all but Zedd calling with another creepy message. A throat cleared, and Micah said, "Hi."

Cosmo tugged at the carpet fibers and stared at Déjà, who mouthed, *Come on!*

"You... You showed me the most vulnerable part of yourself. I can't imagine what it's been like for you to go through what you have. That's not pity, just a fact. And this evening I stabbed you right in that soft spot. I'm so sorry."

Micah was silent for so long that Cosmo was sure he'd hung up. He finally said, "I'm sorry too. I shouldn't have pulled you the way I did. Are you okay?"

"I'm fine. Do you forgive me for what I said? And for making a scene?" He cringed. "And for slapping you?"

Déjà made a strangled noise. "You did what?"

"I don't know," Micah said.

It wasn't what Cosmo wanted to hear, but at least it was honest. "You were right about Royce. I should have listened to you."

"Did he–"

"I'm *fine*." Cosmo's words came out too harsh, and Déjà frowned and shook her head. "I really wish I could do this day over again."

Micah laughed, a humorless huff that grew watery at the end, and Cosmo wondered if he'd been crying.

"Why is that funny?"

"Because you've lived this day before," Micah said.

Déjà had scooted so close her ear was practically against the phone, so Cosmo put it on speaker. He said, "Right. I've lived this day before because we're in a static block universe. Some version of me will *always* be living this day. Forgive me if I don't find that humorous right now."

"No. I mean I had actual future knowledge of you living this day. Other Micah didn't have specifics. The things I did this evening didn't happen in his world. But nothing I did stopped the situation with Royce. Except maybe calling Déjà."

Cosmo scrubbed at his arms, a sudden chill penetrating through the sleeves of his pajamas. "*Other* Micah?"

"My future self."

Micah explained briefly what happened, and Cosmo probably should have been creeped out, but he was too hung up on the fact that his other self had acted on the urge to throw himself into Micah's arms. The night would have gone much differently if he'd chosen to leave with him to get ice cream. Instead of picturing a Dairy Queen, he thought of the soda shop he and Déjà used to frequent. Micah sitting beside him in a greasy booth as the neon from the window signs limned everything an electric pink. Sipping milkshakes as Micah explained the situation. Cosmo would lean against him, and Micah would envelop him in his protective embrace.

I want to wrap these arms around you and press you against me. I want to crush you.

An ache filled his chest. He could have had that. But he'd made the wrong choice, and now it might *never* happen.

Déjà had left Cosmo's side. She came back with a plate of white chip cookies he'd made the other day, and she seemed to be trying to fit as many as she could into her mouth at once. Her face was slightly ashen and her gaze unfocused as she stared through the wall and chewed her cookies.

"I know I embarrassed you earlier," Cosmo said into the phone, "but I'm the one feeling very ashamed right now. You must think I'm both cruel and desperate."

"*That's* what you're focused on right now?" Cookie crumbs sprayed from Déjà's mouth. "He just told you he was visited by himself from the future."

"Spacetime is twisted inside the complex." Cosmo waved his hand. "Keep up, darling."

She smacked his arm and bit into another cookie, then coughed and headed into the kitchen. "I need some milk. Or some air. Or a place to lie down."

"I don't think you're cruel or desperate," Micah said. "But I also don't think this thing between us is going to work."

Cosmo's stomach dropped. No, there wouldn't be any soda shop dates or graveyard kisses or anything else with Micah in this future.

"Uh-uh." Déjà's voice came from the kitchen. "I didn't get involved in this just for you to break up with each other."

"What do you want me to say?" Micah's voice strained. "I fell for you, Cosmo, not because we're both young and popular artists who got flirty with each other at a party. No. I'm a struggling, lonely recluse, and you showed up in my studio as a beautiful specter who couldn't hurt me. I fell for the idea of you. The dream of you. I'm too out of the art scene. I'm too old. I'm too – too *broken*."

Cosmo shook his head. "No, you're not. You–"

"It's not like we can sit across from each other sipping outrageous milkshakes and pretend like none of that is between us." Micah choked on his words. "I can't even let you into my apartment for god's sake!"

Wait. Cosmo stiffened. "Why did you mention milkshakes?"

"What?" A loud sniffle came from the phone. "Because you said it. Invited me to some outrageous milkshake place."

"I never said that."

"You must have," Micah said. "Because I was just thinking about how that sounded much more your speed than a Dairy Queen, which further reinforces how out of touch I am."

Breath rushed in and out of Cosmo's chest. "I didn't mention the milkshake place, Micah." He swallowed hard. "I only thought about it."

15

TIME (CLOCK OF THE HEART)

Micah - Snagged Thread

Micah stared at the dark ceiling. The water heater hummed, and the faucet in the bathroom kept a rhythmic *pat-pat* that he'd tried counting to help him fall asleep. It hadn't worked.

His pillow was too warm, and he kept flipping it over hoping for a cool side but he'd done it too many times and now the whole thing was wrinkled and hot and none of the thoughts tumbling around in his head were any that he wanted to entertain. Phantom the cat had suddenly appeared and curled into a white loaf near his feet, and if Other Micah materialized beside him in bed, he was going to unload all his problems whether his other self wanted to hear them or not.

Trying to keep Cosmo out of harm's way hadn't succeeded. Déjà had texted Micah with words he never wanted to see in that arrangement again: *his creepy boss was trying to stick his tongue down Cosmo's throat.*

That pervert of a director violated Cosmo, and the thought made Micah sick to his stomach.

The only thing Micah had managed to do was piss Cosmo off enough to reveal what Micah already knew but didn't want to face – that he and Cosmo were too different to be compatible. Anytime his mind gave him a reprieve from that topic, it shifted to the fact that he had somehow suddenly known about a milkshake place he'd never been to and Cosmo had never mentioned.

He drew the covers up to his chin. The only logical explanation – and he used that term very loosely – was that Other Micah knew about the milkshake place, so now Micah did too.

Déjà had insisted they all go there to sort things out, which seemed like a terrible idea because it was only going to risk Micah getting heartbroken again. He had finally agreed so he could get off the phone and go take out his frustration on a harmless inanimate object, but he was too confused by the milkshake thing to hold any of the fire inside him. And if he'd been hard-pressed to dig out the core of his worries, it wasn't that some new weird thing had happened. He'd already met his future self; how much weirder could it get? It wasn't even that Cosmo's words had jabbed him in a vulnerable spot or that he'd slapped him hard enough to see stars.

The biggest thing on his mind was Cosmo's safety, and his failure to secure it. Trying to remind himself that Cosmo was in charge of his own choices wasn't helpful, because the visual of seeing his own face for the first time after the assault kept appearing every time he closed his eyes. He'd been near unrecognizable, his skin an eggplant purple and dark stitches winding around his eye socket and through his eyebrow.

He hadn't helped himself then, and he'd failed to help Cosmo last night.

By the time late morning rolled around and he slid into a booth in the soda shop in question, he felt like he'd swallowed an anchor. An oldies song he couldn't place floated from the jukebox in the corner. A huge glass of outrageous dairy was the last thing his stomach wanted right now, but greasy corn dogs and fries sounded worse.

"*God*, it's been ages since I've been here." The light cadence of Cosmo's voice made Micah slide out of the diner booth so quickly that he nearly tripped a roller-skating waitress.

Cosmo stood beside Déjà in skin-tight light-wash jeans, a rainbow block print shirt, sculpted clay earrings, and geometric bangle bracelets.

Micah kept his fists pressed to his sides. "Hey." He suddenly wasn't sure which side of the table to sit on. He sat next to Cosmo, then decided that was the wrong choice, but it was too late to switch because Déjà dropped into the seat across from them and set her backpack beside her. Her outfit wasn't quite as flamboyant as Cosmo's, but it still made Micah look like the odd one out. "I don't fit in here. Maybe I should go sit in the tax prep place next door."

Both Déjà and Cosmo glanced at Micah's sweatshirt. It had been a joke, but nobody laughed, and now he was self-conscious. *Smooth, Micah.*

Cosmo leaned against the table and tugged on his curls. "You do not fit in better in a tax prep place. Your unique look is just less surface-level than ours."

Right. Because he couldn't take off his scars like Déjà kicking off her platform goldfish pumps on his rug.

Cosmo pulled a greasy, laminated menu from a rack beside the salt and pepper shakers. He tugged at his bottom lip as he looked it over, exposing charmingly crooked teeth. How perfectly imperfect. Cosmo's unique look was more than surface-level too, although the glittery lime eye shadow at the corners of his eyes was doing something to Micah's insides.

"I'm fine, Micah," Cosmo said. "Stop staring at me."

Cheeks burning, Micah looked away. "It's okay if you're not fine after what happened. Assault isn't something to just be brushed off."

Cosmo kept looking at the menu, but he flinched slightly. "It doesn't deserve to be called that."

"I'm not sure what else to call it if it wasn't consensual."

"It feels wrong to put it in the same category as…"

The same category as Micah and his fucked-up face. "We don't need to break out a measuring stick to see whose trauma is bigger. I hate that it happened to you. The only good thing, I guess, is now you know Royce is a threat. If I'd gotten you to come with me, the non-consensual bar incident wouldn't have happened, but he could have put his hands on you at some other point in time when no one was there to stop it. Which might have been worse."

Cosmo seemed to shrink into the booth more with each of Micah's words. "I'd really rather not talk about it."

Déjà looked ready to unload a prepared speech, but she sighed and said, "Then let's talk about Micah's mind-reading ability."

"That's not what it was," Micah said.

"Future prediction then."

"Not sure that's it either. And if it is, why now?"

Cosmo twisted the bangles on his wrist. "I had a premonition yesterday that you'd be waiting for me at the taco truck. But it didn't happen the way I expected, so I thought it was just wishful thinking."

Wishful thinking. But Cosmo hadn't been wishing for Micah when he exposed his whole chest and demanded Micah check to see if the rumor about him was true.

A waitress stopped at their table, beaming a bubblegum pink smile. "Hello! Are you ready to order or do you need a few minutes?"

Cosmo's gaze was distant. He pushed his menu back into the rack. "A pumpkin shake, please."

"I'll have sweet potato," Déjà said. "With three maraschino cherries."

The waitress looked up from her notepad. "It comes with a toasted marshmallow on top instead of a cherry. Do you want to substitute it?"

"No. In that case, I'd like three marshmallows. It's fine if it costs extra."

Micah reached past Cosmo for a menu. His arm brushed Cosmo's, the warm scent of raspberry and spice overwhelming him. Skimming over the milkshake list but not processing any of the words, Micah looked up at the waitress and said, "Surprise me."

He pulled the paper band off his silverware and rolled it into a tight tube. Once the waitress left, he said, "You know, yesterday, after I failed to get you to come with me, I thought it must mean that no matter how we try to change things, the future is set in stone. But that isn't true, because originally our argument never happened. Maybe... Maybe we only slightly altered something." Other Micah hadn't sat helpless and alone in a Dairy Queen, thinking about his ineptitude until the place closed and the teenage employees kicked him out.

"Did it occur to you that maybe you shouldn't have meddled with the future?" Déjà asked.

"No. It really didn't." Micah flicked his napkin band across the table. "My only thought after the initial shock of meeting myself was keeping Cosmo from getting hurt."

"I don't want him hurt either, but what if you weren't supposed to do that? Maybe it felt like nothing much changed, but you weren't supposed to be there. People saw and interacted with you who shouldn't have. Not just us, but Royce, the people eating by the taco truck, whoever you encountered on the way back home, insects you stepped on…"

"Insects," Micah said. "So, what, I stepped on an ant I shouldn't have and now I've prevented a future president from being born? That seems over the top."

"Does it?" She looked at Cosmo. "You said you knew Micah would be waiting for you yesterday, and he was. And Micah, you knew he had been thinking about milkshakes even though he never said that to you. Something's been altered."

Micah knew Déjà wasn't the source of his sudden anger, so he tried to cram it down, but he couldn't help but say, "And you weren't supposed to be at the bar. We don't know what would have happened if he didn't have anyone there on his side, but I bet it would have been worse. And whether that screwed up the universe or not, I'd do it again to keep him from getting hurt." His voice rose. "I'd run to help Cosmo in *any* universe. In any timeline."

Déjà raised her already dramatically arched eyebrows. Cosmo stared at Micah, his lips parted.

"Besides," Micah muttered, "the premonition of me showing up didn't happen the way he thought it would. What good is a premonition if it's wrong?"

"What flavor is your milkshake going to be?" Cosmo gathered the menus and hugged them to his chest. "You knew we were going to come here, which means in our original future we were here and had milkshakes. So what flavor did you get?"

"Um…" He didn't have any sense of being here before, and couldn't remember any of the shake flavors. Squeezing his eyes shut, he pressed his fingers to his temples and feigned concentration. "Shrimp."

Cosmo grimaced. "*Shrimp?*" He looked at the menus clutched in his fists. "Is that an actual flavor?"

"Shrimp. With pink sprinkles and lemon garnish."

Pushing the menus back into the rack, Cosmo said, "And did you drink this shrimp milkshake?"

"Of course. But I failed to mention that I have a shellfish allergy, so we had a bonus trip to the hospital."

"I know *that* isn't true, because we ate lobster toast together at the bistro." Cosmo rolled his eyes. "And if you'd like my opinion, I think we're now in a parallel universe. If all of time exists at once and always has, that would be the only way to change the trajectory." Cosmo looked at both of them and apparently didn't get the confirmation he was hoping for, because he said, "It makes sense. I read about the many-worlds theory when I was looking up information about spacetime. Supposedly, a new universe is created each time anyone makes *any* decision."

"I don't know," Micah said. "A new universe budding every time I debate whether to brush my teeth or not feels egotistical."

"You should be brushing your teeth twice a day." Cosmo huffed. "And flossing."

"Flossing is against my religion. And I kind of feel like we're making something out of nothing. We don't know if what we experienced were premonitions. If Other Micah shows up again, I can compare notes with him about the future, but that's about it. I kind of hope he doesn't, though. He'll just tell me about some other future event that I'll screw up."

"It's not nothing," Déjà said. "And you shouldn't be ignoring this new ability, even if it seems benign now. This could be serious. You *altered time*. And you're being flippant about it. Don't you think that's a dangerous thing to mess around with?"

"I don't know! I'd say I've never done this before, but maybe I have. Who knows how many Micahs have fucked up how many universes!" God, he needed some fresh air. He was too on edge. "Will you excuse me?"

"Micah–"

He waved off their protests and hurried outside, rounding the side of the building and pacing the sidewalk beside the parking lot. A cardboard drink cup rolled across the asphalt, tumbling in the breeze. He was treading water again, and the dark icy sea always at the fringes of his consciousness was just waiting for him to give up so it could swallow him. It was so tempting to stop fighting and embrace the numbness it would bring.

His car sat nearby, and he considered climbing in and driving home. Texting Cosmo that something had come up, then climbing into bed and never getting back out would be easy. He'd managed to ignore the world for nine months. What was the rest of his life?

As he strode for his car, a strange feeling overcame him that he *should* be at home right now. At home putting the final details on that godawful landscape painting. Focusing on the blades of grass was making his eye hurt, like it often did, so he'd get up to mist his Thai constellation, and–

He rushed back into the soda shop and dropped next to Cosmo. "I– I think I just had another premonition, or whatever we're deciding they are. Maybe they're Other Micah's memories? Because... They're wrong, like your premonition was yesterday. I couldn't predict what flavor of shake I'd get because I never went here with you. I was at home, painting and watering my plants. We had plans to get milkshakes later in the day, but then you got a text that–"

Cosmo's phone vibrated, and he startled, eyes wide. "What's it going to say?"

"I don't know. I just know that you broke off plans with me because of it, and I didn't see you until late in the evening. Do *you* know what it's going to say?"

He shook his head and fought to pull the phone from his tight jeans.

Micah glanced at Déjà. "How weird is this for you? On a scale from one to ten?"

"Considering that I've gotten over my initial shock and can sense ghosts and auras, like a four? No matter how pointless you think this might be, you altered something by intercepting Cosmo yesterday, and by calling me to come help. I mean that as a neutral statement, not an accusation." She lowered her voice, twisting a gothic cameo pendant between her acrylic nails. "I'd like to think I'd help Cosmo in any universe or timeline too, but I don't know if that's true. Just... Pay attention to this sense. I ignored mine for a long time, and I wish I hadn't. That's all."

He nodded. He was bringing his own baggage and experiences to this situation, and Déjà was only doing the same. It couldn't hurt him to stay aware of this sense in case it meant something eventually.

A little of the color left Cosmo's cheeks as he stared at his phone. After tapping out a reply, he said, "Hina, the gallerist, wants me to come remove all my art and supplies from Identical Dog. She liked my sculptures enough to give me a spot in the gallery, but I guess she doesn't like them *that* much."

That was a bummer of a reason for Other Cosmo to cancel plans. Micah said, "I'm sorry. It's probably for the best that you have everything out of there, but I know that sounds like hollow consolation."

"I figured trying to work at Night Gallery would be the easiest, since Hina and Simone are friends. But I get the feeling Hina thinks Simone has stolen me out from under her." He turned up his nose. "Well, if she'd given me a promotion in any of the years I'd been there, maybe I wouldn't be leaving."

"I hope you're treated better at Night Gallery." Micah's phone vibrated in his pocket. He pulled it out and glanced at the text. It was from Déjà: <*chaperone Cosmo while he gets his art! don't let him go alone!!*>

Other Micah hadn't done that, he was quite sure. Cosmo shouldn't have to bear all of this alone, and if Royce was there, the idea of Déjà having to stand up to that pervert was as worrisome as Cosmo doing it.

"I'll go with you," Micah said. "I'd love to see some of your art and know what this poor gallery is depriving itself of."

Cosmo tugged on his polymer clay earring, and there was so much gratitude in his eyes that it made Micah's heart ache. "I'd love that. But what if you don't like my art?"

"I know I will." He soaked in Cosmo's appearance, then tentatively poked one of the glittery bangles on his bony wrist. "You look like a Peter Gabriel video threw up on you."

"Thank you." His smile grew a little bigger. "I'm in a Memphis Milano phase right now."

"He only put on fifteen different outfits trying to decide which one was the cutest." Déjà winked at Micah.

Why was she winking? This look couldn't be for Micah. *Shouldn't* be. Their worlds were too different. What Cosmo had said about Micah's PTSD during their argument had only hurt because it was the truth. He was too similar to his monsteras and his Chinese evergreens; he wasn't acclimated to these conditions. Bring him out of the dark and safety of his apartment and he'd wither and crumble.

If they kept this up, there would only be more arguments where Micah's trauma, or his age, or being out of the art scene was the problem. The fantasy of Cosmo in the comfort of the studio had been perfect, but reality was harsh and messy and wouldn't spare his feelings.

The waitress returned and set a huge ecru-colored milkshake before him. Black sprinkles and pieces of candy corn adorned the whipped cream.

Oh, gross. This was a mistake. "Not shrimp, huh?"

Cosmo gasped. "Candy corn! How delightful." He struggled to suck his pumpkin milkshake through the straw, exaggerating his already defined cheekbones, then gave up and used his spoon.

Déjà picked up her backpack. "I'm going to take mine to go." She slid out of the booth. "Keep me updated on the spacetime stuff, huh? And Cosmo... Maybe we can hang out again sometime."

Oh no, she was leaving them here alone together. Micah gave her a weak goodbye, then turned back to his milkshake. He dug up a spoonful, hoping the candy on top was merely a garnish, but he was met with the overwhelming flavor of marzipan and craft paste. He gagged. There was no pretending he could like that. "I hate candy corn."

Cosmo squinted. "I don't like you."

"It tastes like someone blended a book of stamps with stale sugar cookies."

"Do you like pumpkin pie?" Cosmo carved out a scoop of russet shake and offered it to Micah.

Micah attempted to take the spoon, but Cosmo lightly touched his jaw and pushed the bite into his mouth. Nutmeg and pumpkin melted on his tongue. Cosmo brushed whipped cream from Micah's bottom lip with his thumb; it sent electric pleasure tingling through him, and he threatened to melt just as quickly.

Abort! Abort!

Sitting back, Cosmo slowly licked the remainder off of the spoon. "Did you like that?"

He could have fed Micah a heaping spoonful of mustard from the condiment rack and he would have said yes. "Uh, yeah."

Reaching over, he dug into Micah's milkshake, then sucked the spoon clean. "The sprinkles are turning the whipped cream gray, but it's delicious." He pulled the shake to himself and slid the pumpkin one in front of Micah, then plucked a piece of candy corn from the shake and pushed it between his lips.

Micah jabbed the straw into the pumpkin shake and swirled the cream around. It was a struggle not to think about Cosmo's mouth. And his eyeshadow. And that he'd tried on fifteen different outfits before settling on one he thought Micah would like.

His mind mercifully switched topics when they left and he followed Cosmo's ancient sedan to Identical Dog. No matter what his feelings for Cosmo or his sudden new ability to peek into a window of a future that wasn't his, he couldn't allow himself to screw up Cosmo's safety again. He'd said he was fine, but Micah didn't believe it, and he was determined to be support in the gallery.

They walked inside, enveloped in a soft citrus scent. He squinted his left eye against the harsh fluorescents. A wall of fused glass sculptures greeted them, but he didn't have time to register anything beyond that, because Cosmo strode for the back of the building, his heels clicking on the linoleum. Colorful exhibits passed by in Micah's peripheral vision. He scanned each partition and room they walked by, but there was no sign of Royce.

Cosmo weaved through an installation featuring life-like nude people positioned at various points in the room. They stood upright, but their hair and features pulled toward the ceiling as though gravity had been reversed.

"Wait here." Cosmo opened a back door and disappeared inside.

Though Micah had submitted his portfolio to most of the reputable galleries in the city, he couldn't remember if he'd sent it to Night Gallery specifically. If he had, they hadn't rejected him yet. Thank god he didn't have anything in Identical Dog. Prestigious or not, he didn't want anything to do with this place anymore.

Something clattered from within the back room. Cosmo pushed out a cart, and supplies rattled in the boxes on the bottom. He headed down the hall, and they stopped at a corner partition with resin cubes mounted on pedestals.

Sliced and accordioned animal skulls floated within the resin. In the gaps between the slices were other mediums – dried flowers, fungi, leaves. In the largest cube was a human skull, divided in half. Objects spilled from the brain cavity: loose change, a condom, pills, a house key, a ring with a solitaire stone. How bizarre. The clashing materials unsettled him, and he couldn't stop staring.

Cosmo hefted the cube with the human skull. "It's not real. A museum replica. You can buy real ones on the internet for less than seven hundred dollars, but I find it unsavory. And I don't have that kind of money to be throwing at my art."

"These are yours?" Micah inspected a small skull – possibly a rabbit – and realized the dried flowers and leaves bursting from within the slices were actually candy wrappers. The mushrooms sprouting from a canine were really halved rubber balls, scraps of lace, and tumbled stones.

He bent to another. "This is incredible. I forget what this sort of optical illusion is called, using one medium to represent another."

Cosmo picked up the cube and set it on the cart. "Trompe-l'œil. These are older pieces, when I was still fairly new to working with resin. I didn't pre-seal some of the porous materials properly, and ended up with off-gassing." He pointed to the lace in the faux mushrooms. "You can see the air bubbles."

"Hardly. I wouldn't have noticed had you not pointed it out."

"You're just being nice."

"No, I'm not. I have trouble focusing on fine details with my left eye, especially when the lights are bright."

The cube sagged in Cosmo's arms. "Oh, how sad. I'm sorry for being dismissive." His gaze darted away and he let out an unsteady chuckle. "I wanted my pieces to impress you, but now I'm only thinking about all the flaws you can see."

Micah stopped before Cosmo and resisted the urge to brush the curls from his eyes. "I only see, like, three flaws. Maybe four. Which isn't an automatic deal-breaker, but if you poke me in my good eye your odds with me will be better."

"Lies." Cosmo chuckled. "You don't need vision to know that I'm the hottest creature in existence."

"Got me there." Micah took the cube and set it on the cart. "I am impressed with these, even more so after realizing the trompe-l'œil aspect. They're part science diagram, part pop art. The combination of fragile bone carefully divided, with the almost violent addition of random assemblage is jarring and makes me uncomfortable. I love them."

Cosmo flushed. "Thank you."

"This is a shame." A voice cut between them like rough-grit sandpaper. Cosmo flinched, then snatched one of the remaining skull cubes from its pedestal and put it on the cart.

A tall white man with a cruel line of a mouth stared at Cosmo as though Micah wasn't there at all, his blue gaze icy. He started to walk around the cart, and Micah moved into his path. Royce attempted to side-step, and Micah mirrored him.

Royce's thin lips pressed together until they disappeared, and he let out an exasperated sigh. "There's no need for these theatrics. We both had too much to drink last night, and going behind my back – behind Hina's back – to work for a rival gallery simply because you feel awkward now is childish. You don't need this" – Royce finally glanced at Micah – "*person* to play bodyguard. I know how badly you want to be registrar, and how lonely you are. I'm sure that in the moment, coming on to me felt like it would solve both of those problems. I won't hold it against you."

Angry heat flooded Micah's face, his chest clenching in a tight knot. "You absolute bastard. How dare you twist this into Cosmo's fault?"

Cosmo slammed a resin cube into the cart. He reached for the final sculpture, but it slipped from his hands and struck the floor. The corner exploded, and chunks of resin skittered away. He abandoned it, gripping the cart handle and pushing it forward so quickly that Royce had to leap out of the way.

Micah picked up the damaged sculpture. No matter what Cosmo said, he was sure the rumors about Royce were true, and it wouldn't be surprising if Royce had been withholding promotion from Cosmo until he slept with him. Micah cradled the sculpture to his chest and jabbed a finger at Royce. "I know all about you. I know exactly what you do, and you're mad that it didn't work this time. Don't think for one second that I won't tell every artist I know."

The whites of Royce's eyes flashed, and his nostrils flared. "I have no idea what you're talking about."

"Right. Go prey on someone your equal. Like a cockroach." He turned, but Royce snatched his arm. Micah shoved him into the wall. "You keep your hands off me, old man."

Royce raised his fist, teeth bared in a feral snarl. Cosmo shoved between him and Micah. He stared at Royce, chest heaving, then slapped him hard across the face. Royce let out a clipped exclamation, and Cosmo slapped him again. Royce squeezed his eyes shut, but didn't put up his hands in defense. His cheek flared a vibrant crimson.

Hands pressed against the wall and a vein jumping in his jaw, Royce cracked open his eyes and said, "Cosmo–"

He smacked Royce again, and the sound reverberated off the walls. Turning away, Cosmo shoved the cart down the hall, and Micah hurried to catch up. Supplies and sculptures clattered as the cart weaved drunkenly past the gravity-reversed figures in the installation room. They reached the gallery entrance, and Cosmo rammed the cart through the front doors.

Stopping at his car, he threw open the trunk and packed in the resin cubes. Micah set the boxes of supplies inside, but when Cosmo tried to shut the lid of the trunk, it popped back open. He slammed the lid down, eyes blazing, and it popped open again. The cardboard box dented and crumpled as he tried a third time. He slammed the trunk down over and over, until the box was smashed and the contents surely broken.

He collapsed against Micah and sobbed, balling Micah's sweatshirt in his fists. He pressed his face into his shoulder, his hoarse cries muffled as shudders wracked his body. Micah held him tight and stroked his hair.

Micah had been there. That frustration and anger, the self-blame and feelings of being violated had been his constant companions – his only companions – until he'd destroyed enough art and shed enough tears for depression to take over instead. He couldn't let Cosmo get to that point.

Of course Royce would turn this on Cosmo. *I know how badly you want to be registrar, and how lonely you are*. He knew, and he pounced upon it.

Gasping for breath, Cosmo pulled away, his eyes red and puffy. Streaks of mascara ran down his cheeks. He sniffled hard and wiped his nose, then shook a cigarette from his pack. The lighter trembled in his hands. Micah gently took it from him then held it to his cigarette. Cosmo took a long drag; smoke curled from his nostrils, tears still clinging to his lashes. "Well. That was cathartic. And I'm grateful your adorable sweatshirts are as soft as they look."

Micah pulled it over his head and offered it to Cosmo. Cosmo tugged it on, then pressed his nose to the collar and inhaled. He stared at Micah, then turned the smashed art supply box on its side. After shutting the trunk, he said, "It's mostly sculpting tools, some silicone molds, dust masks. I rather wish there'd been something fragile inside."

"I punched a hole through a stretched canvas and flipped over my drafting table after what happened to me."

"And destroyed a balcony railing."

"'Destroyed' is a strong word. I'm not the Hulk."

Cosmo squeezed Micah's bicep. Micah flexed, and Cosmo smiled weakly, the cigarette bobbing between his lips. "Don't suppose you'll come back to my place, will you? I can show you the sculpture I'm working on."

He couldn't let Cosmo be alone right now. "I'd love to." He climbed into his car and followed Cosmo as he pulled through the parking lot.

In Micah's rearview mirror, Royce walked out of the gallery and stopped at the abandoned cart. He gripped the handle, watching Micah drive away.

16

COME BACK AND STAY

Micah - Snagged Thread

The threshold to Cosmo's apartment was a silver strip of textured metal, dented and scuffed with dirt and bits of dead leaves. Cosmo stood just inside on the front room's low pile carpet – green with rainbow pinstripes. It was a fitting contrast to his purple Oxfords with their shiny toe caps. Micah focused on them, pulled in a breath, and stepped over the threshold.

He straightened and sighed. It was only people in *his* apartment that were the problem. Thank god.

Cosmo smiled and shut the door. "You're okay?"

"Yeah."

"Good." He swept his arm across the front room. "Make yourself at home. I'll fix us a drink."

A bed and large art desk took up much of the space. Against the other wall was a turntable, speaker towers, and a crate of records. All of it looked vintage. '80s postmodern and Memphis Group art in eclectic frames covered so much space that Micah wasn't sure what to look at first. Sketches of divided skulls were tacked above the art desk. Glass jars full of buttons, electronic parts, food wrappers, and fabric scraps sat on top of clear storage drawers. Inside were tubes of paint, bottles of what may have been resin or silicone, brushes, and spools of wire. Sitting on the desk were slices of a skull, encased in resin. Pushed together, they looked like a stack of coasters, or maybe some hideous flavor of aspic dessert.

A hand lightly touched his waist. Cosmo offered him a glass of orange juice. "Thanks." Micah brought the glass to his lips, then paused. "Is it candy corn-flavored?"

Cosmo chuckled. "It's a screwdriver."

"There's a reason candy corn only turns up at Halloween. It's evil."

"You're standing in my bedroom with a cocktail, and you choose to bash candy corn again."

"Am I doing the flirting thing wrong?"

"I'll give you another chance."

Micah sipped his screwdriver and cleared his throat. "It's a delightful, only slightly-cursed confection in cheery fall colors, and the aftertaste of having licked an envelope only lasts for five minutes tops. The chocolate ones taste like death."

Cosmo narrowed his gaze. "I meant flirt with me, not the candy corn."

"Are you jealous?"

"Very. No one ever tells me I taste like death." He drew in a deep breath. "And you don't want to flirt with me anyway, do you? Because you don't like *me*. You like the idea of me. The dream of me. You lied when you said you found me just as fascinating alive as you did when you thought I was a ghost."

"It's not that I like you less now that I know you. It's the opposite. It's just that the dream of you was safer. Easier."

"I'm difficult?" Cosmo huffed. "Ask any past lover, and I'm sure they'd say the same."

"No. You're not. You're captivating and talented. And so beautiful. I have not been able to stop staring at you today. But even so, we can't ignore the things that separate us. I can't pretend that my baggage isn't there, or that where I'm at in my life isn't different from where you are."

"Who said anything about ignoring it? It's part of your package. I get that." Cosmo leaned against his desk and sipped his screwdriver. "Just like my baggage is part of mine. And despite what you think, I don't believe we're that different. I find your art unsettling. You find *my* art unsettling. What more do we need?"

He put up a convincing argument – that, or Micah just badly wanted it to be true. "Promise me something then? Anything else happens, you get another creepy message or Zedd threatens you, don't push me away. I'm not going anywhere just because he or Royce are jealous."

"I promise. But in return, I don't want your mental health to be a reason to push me away either." He poked Micah in the chest. "And stop saying you're too old for me. You're not."

Baby steps when it came to moving forward in life. That's what they'd promised each other. Cosmo wouldn't remember – that conversation was three years ago for him – but Micah had no doubt he would still encourage Micah to go at his own pace. If they could embrace each other's eccentricities, then why not their flaws too?

"Alright. Deal." Micah pointed to the skull on the art desk. "What is it?"

"A badger. I encased the entire skull in resin before slicing through, because I needed thinner slices and didn't want to compromise the structural integrity of the bone. I'm recreating the negative spaces in clay, which I'll then cast and mold in colored resin. Then put all the pieces together and dip it again so it's a solid block."

"So much work goes into your pieces. Will there be a trompe-l'œil aspect to this one too?"

"Yes. The sculpted slices will look like candy."

"I can't wait to see it finished." He glanced at the cubes stacked haphazardly in the center of the coffee table. A long crack spidered through one, and the corner was jagged and cloudy. "Can you fix the damaged one?"

Cosmo shrugged. "Probably, but I'm not sure I care enough to."

"Do you want to talk about what happened?"

"No." Plucking a remote from a small bookcase, he aimed it at the TV above the bed, then flipped through channels. "One of my favorite things about October is all of the classic horror movies play on a loop."

On screen, a man with filthy fingernails slapped a wad of cash onto a table. Someone dropped a sugar cube into a glass of absinthe and urged the man to take the puzzle box sitting between them.

"*Hellraiser!*" Cosmo said.

"I've heard of it. Never seen it."

"I am all sorts of disappointed in you today." Cosmo sat on the bed and patted the space next to him. "It's only just started."

He didn't want to talk through anything, and Micah wasn't going to push him. If company from someone safe while they watched a movie about Hell's BDSM community was what Cosmo needed right now, then so be it.

After kicking off his shoes, Cosmo slid up against the pillows, burrowed in Micah's sweatshirt. Micah sat beside him, then set his drink on the coffee table. The man on TV solved his puzzle box, then screamed as hooks dug into his bare flesh. Cosmo jumped, then gave Micah a sheepish smile. The scene transitioned to a gore-coated floor, racks spinning with bloody body parts.

"Damn it," Micah said. "His torture dungeon is way better than mine."

"You should be taking notes. Although that blood is sure to damage the unsealed hardwood."

The urge to put his arm around Cosmo suddenly overwhelmed Micah. His pulse throbbed, fingers numb at the sudden realization that *this* was the moment. This hour, this interaction, was when he was supposed to kiss Cosmo. Except... It should have been late evening, and they shouldn't have been watching *Hellraiser*.

Cosmo stared at a blank spot on the wall, his mouth parted. "I have that strange sense of premonition again. Do you feel it? It's like déjà vu. Only it's not 'already seen.' More like presque vu: 'almost seen.' The movie is wrong. It's supposed to be–"

"*Psycho*."

Cosmo's eyes widened. "Yes. And we should be drinking wine. It seemed too early right now to open the Merlot, but I thought some OJ with a splash of vodka would be perfect after what happened at the gallery."

"This is so weird." Déjà had told them not to push the sense away, so Micah focused on it instead. It was indeed a feeling of having done something before, but in a way just different enough to be noticeable. It was disorienting, like knowing you set your cup of coffee on the desk moments ago and having it suddenly be gone. "Are we agreeing that these are Other Micah's memories? Other Cosmo's? What *would* have happened to them had I not intercepted you last night?"

"More like, what's currently happening to them. They're still at their point on the timeline string. And us changing the events didn't create a ripple effect that goes through the future, it snagged out a little thread from the string." Cosmo clapped and grinned at Micah. "How's that for a parallel universe theory?"

Goosebumps erupted on Micah's arms, the hair on the back of his neck tingling. The implications of that were hard to fathom. "If you're right, then we're feeling not past or present, but time *adjacent*."

Believing Cosmo was a ghost haunting his studio had been so much simpler.

"I wonder if we'll continue to run parallel, or if the timeline is trying to course-correct. To get us back to where we're 'supposed' to be." Some of the tension left Cosmo's face. "If the thread is being integrated back into the string, that could mean I'm always destined for a future away from Identical Dog. Perhaps even if Déjà hadn't pulled me out of the bar and stayed with me afterward, I would have texted Simone at Night Gallery and asked for a position anyway."

If that thought gave him comfort, Micah wasn't going to dispute it. However, if this was indeed the kind of spacetime fuckery they were dealing with, it could also mean Cosmo was destined to keep working for Identical Dog despite clearing out his things and upsetting both Royce and the gallerist. Being drawn back by a predestined future. Ice water flooded Micah's veins. That wasn't the kind of course-correcting they needed.

"Micah?" Cosmo tugged on a lock of his hair, a shy smile playing on his lips. "I said, I think you're supposed to put your arm around me. We *are* trying to get the timeline back to the way it should be, right?"

But what if the way it "should" be was something they didn't want? How big of a snag in the thread of the future could they make?

Cosmo was still watching him expectantly, and if he kept up this train of thought, he was going to miss the opportunity for something he *did* want. When this had happened originally, he wouldn't have been preoccupied with the "presque vu" ability. They'd been watching *Psycho* and drinking wine, the connection and moment perfect enough to draw them together.

He slid his arm across Cosmo's shoulders and tugged him close. Cosmo's strong scent of berries, bergamot, and clove surrounded Micah, and he nuzzled closer. Cosmo's hair teased his cheek, his throat so close to Micah's lips that he could feel the heat.

On screen, trees rustled in the breeze before a sunset-painted sky to an accompaniment of ominous music. It didn't matter if this moment wasn't exactly the same. And there was something comforting in knowing that no matter what universe they were in, every Micah and every Cosmo would fall for each other.

He ran his fingers across the tendons in Cosmo's hand. He stroked the valleys of his knuckles. These were hands he'd drawn in detail but never caressed. Glittery bangles clacked together on Cosmo's wrist as he brought Cosmo's hand to his lips. He softly kissed the channels of veins winding under his skin, then the creases of each finger. Cosmo pulled in a sharp breath and turned toward him.

The lime eyeshadow at the edges of his agate eyes shimmered in the light, and a faint trail of mascara had dried on his cheeks. Micah kissed it away. Cosmo's fingers drifted across his jaw and into his hair. He arched his neck and guided Micah there. When Micah's lips pressed against his throat, Cosmo let out a small groan and twisted closer.

Micah peppered kisses across his skin, and the longer he lingered in one spot, the harder Cosmo clutched him, his breath whistling through his nose. He looked up, then pressed his lips to Cosmo's. Pleasure snapped through him, all his joints reduced to gelatin. Cosmo's teeth grazed the corner of his mouth as he kissed back, hungry and urgent. His tongue darted between Micah's lips, trailing the taste of spiked fruit.

Oh, fuck. This absolutely felt more than just wet.

"I've wanted this so bad." Cosmo's hands slid over Micah's stomach and across his chest. He pulled Micah's sweatshirt over his head, then pushed the bracelets off his wrists and dumped it all on the floor. Spirals of hair mutinied from his thick curls, his pupils wide and lips parted. His voice was breathless and expectant, the same as it had been on the phone when Micah asked him to describe himself. "What are you waiting for? Kiss me again."

Micah did. He called back the memory of that striped sweater with the oversized neckline, and how warm Cosmo's flesh had been when he first touched him, believing he was a ghost. He'd watched that recording so many times, advancing it frame by frame.

His lips brushed Cosmo's ear as he said, "You're vibrant and strange and you smell like frost-kissed berries in a dark, leaf-littered forest. One misstep, one turn the wrong way, and I'm hopelessly lost."

"Oh god." Cosmo pushed up the back of Micah's shirt, then dragged his fingers down, his nails sending an electric tingle through Micah's skin.

"You taste like overripe fruit that's fallen from the tree. Your flesh is sweet, warm, and soft, and you intoxicate me." Micah nipped at Cosmo's throat. "You make me delirious. I want to sink my teeth into you. I want to consume you."

Cosmo moaned. He slid his hands down the back of Micah's jeans and squeezed his ass. "More. Tell me more."

He wanted to tell Cosmo how much he wished they could do this in Micah's apartment. The couch still smelled factory-new, but the only one to make a depression there was Micah. His kitchen was clean, filled with more than enough dishes for him alone. The bed was made, and big enough for two.

The threshold of his door looked exactly like Cosmo's, a dented strip of dust-caked metal. But it was an impenetrable barrier, trapping Micah inside and keeping everyone else out. He needed Cosmo to sit on the couch, to use his dishes, to lie on his bed.

Blinking through the sudden blear, he said, "The door of my heart is wide open for you. Please come inside. You don't even need to wipe your feet first. Leave tracks all over me. Come inside and stay."

Cosmo pulled off his shirt so vigorously he might have popped a button. Above his nipple was a tattoo of a dagger piercing a paint palette, framed by a banner that said *KILL YOUR IMPOSTOR SYNDROME*.

"Oh. Uh." Micah pressed his teeth into his bottom lip and pulled back.

"What?"

Damn it. How he hated this conversation. "It's a little soon for me to want to... I'd rather just kiss and snuggle with you until the sun explodes."

Cosmo stared for a moment, eyebrows furrowed, then picked up his shirt from the floor and pulled it back on. "I got caught up in the moment and wasn't thinking."

"I'm sorry. It frustrates me too."

"I'm not frustrated, and don't you dare apologize. I just don't want to misstep. I don't know enough about the nuances of asexuality, so I need you to tell me when we aren't on the same page about things. If we spent more time together, would that make you more interested?"

"Like am I demisexual? Maybe? I think gray-ace might be more accurate. But yes, more time would help. This is just a little fast for me." He took Cosmo's hand and rubbed the pads of his fingers. "I don't ever experience sexual attraction the way allosexual people seem to, but I still think about certain things with people I'm interested in: kissing them, touching their hands... I might feel some kind of diluted sexual attraction under certain circumstances. I'm still not sure about that. And sometimes kissing and touching and sex feels good, sometimes it feels like nothing. Might as well be a handshake."

A dramatic blast of music came from the TV, and a woman screamed. Cosmo jumped and clung to Micah. On screen, an undead man with extra-juicy skin scuttled across the floor toward the woman. Cosmo put a hand over his eyes but peeked through his fingers.

Micah chuckled. "Are you scared?"

"This part is gross. He's so... *gooshy.* And the way he crawls across the floor..." Cosmo shuddered.

"Should we change it to something else?"

"Heavens no." Cosmo drew up his knees and huddled beside Micah. "But you can put your arm around me again."

"I can do that." He nuzzled Cosmo's cheek. "I'm sorry if it isn't enough."

"Shush. You're enough. Besides, that corpse on screen has definitely killed my boner."

"He doesn't turn you on? I mean, he's very wet."

"Ugh." Cosmo feigned a gag.

Micah's thoughts drifted away from the movie, pulled back every so often by Cosmo's suppressed shrieks and his fingers digging into Micah's arms. It was hard to pay attention with the taste of Cosmo on his lips, with tangled timelines, and how much he yearned for Cosmo to be able to sit on *his* bed, in *his* apartment.

"Want to do something really weird with me?" Micah asked.

"Are you trying to turn me on again?"

"I need you to haunt me. Be my ghost."

"How?"

"Show up at my apartment unannounced, and come inside without asking."

Cosmo stiffened. "I won't do that."

"Please? You said you didn't want my mental health to push you away. Help me? I need to practice letting someone inside if I'm ever going to beat this phobia."

"But that isn't what you're asking for. I believe in consent." He cocked an eyebrow. "I never come inside without permission."

Oh lord. "I'm giving you consent. Welcoming someone across my threshold is too much for me, but I think this will work."

"I couldn't bear to give you a panic attack."

"I don't know who else to ask. And if it's going to work with anyone, it will be you." Cosmo was going to tell him to get a therapist, just like everyone else did. He was going to say consensual non-consent was disgusting and he didn't want any part. "Just think of it as creepy role-playing."

Cosmo drew his nails along Micah's inner forearm and let out a deep sigh. "What shall I do?"

"Come over. But don't tell me when. Tomorrow, four days from now, a week. I'll leave a key under the flower pot. I'm in number twenty-six."

"Alright, but I wish I had a sense of whether or not this would work. This would be a good time for presque vu to show up."

It would. Micah left soft kisses on Cosmo's temple, fishing for that sense of "almost seen." If it could help him predict future events on *this* timeline, that would be something. Though he came up empty, Cosmo entering his apartment had to work, because Micah was determined not to spend all of his futures alone.

17

EVERY BREATH YOU TAKE

Cosmo - Snagged Thread

It was clear this sweatshirt wasn't Cosmo's.

He stood in front of the mirror and pulled the collar up to his nose. After three days, the scent was starting to wear off. It wasn't perfumed with the sexy notes of jasmine and amber of that cemetery cologne, but smelled like fresh linen and Micah's skin. Cosmo inhaled deeply.

It was slightly too big. The neckline gaped, sleeves swallowing Cosmo's wrists. He rolled up the cuffs, but that made the ill-fit even more obvious. And it was so slouchy and casual. It didn't go with anything in Cosmo's closet. This powder blue number pulled from a department store athletics section. Micah had probably owned it for years. Oil paint in various hues crusted the cotton, and there was a small hole in one cuff that Cosmo needed to stop touching or he'd worry his thumb through it.

His hair was behaving today, his eyeliner was perfect, and the dusky pink lipstick picked up the cool tones in his skin. He'd found a pair of earrings in the back of the jewelry box that he'd forgotten about, and that pimple that had been on his forehead was finally gone. He looked chic and beautiful – and the sweatshirt ruined his entire aesthetic.

With a grin, he opened the camera on his phone. Pouting his lips, he turned his head until he found the angle that most perfectly showed off his jawline. Wait, no. The sweatshirt wasn't enough. He needed a shot where the purple hickey on his throat was also visible.

He arched his neck and gave the camera a smoldering gaze, then snapped a dozen photos. They all looked so good.

Instinctively, he hit the *Share* button, and nearly tapped Flashbulb before realizing what he was doing. But what was he so afraid of? Zedd might have scared away his past loves, but Micah had already proved he wasn't going anywhere. Cosmo was happy, and he wanted the world to know.

After selecting three photos, he added filters and loaded them onto Flashbulb.

Comments popped up immediately.

😺😺😺

Whaaaaa. So pretty! Looks like someone had fun.
Omg. Who???
I want to be that sweatshirt. 🔥 🔥 👀
Damn, baby. Are you trading outerwear for hard smooches? Because I have a leather jacket that would look great on you.

Normally these sorts of comments gave him a boost, but a needle of irritation pierced through the enjoyment. He replied: *Tempting offer, but I'm only stealing one man's clothing right now. And maybe if he's verrrrrry nice, I'll give his sweatshirt back.* 😏😏😈🍆🍆🍆😻😻

Leaning back against the door, he pressed the phone to his chest and sighed. It vibrated, and the notifications bar filled with more comments.

Slut.
Whore.
Zedd was nothing but good to you.
I hope you fall down the stairs and break your neck.

Cosmo made a noise in his throat. He'd expected this, but not so quickly. What asshole was stalking his Flashbulb? He squinted at the profile picture. It was from one of Snake Milk's concerts; green light burned through smoke machine fog as Zedd wailed into the microphone. The drummer held his sticks aloft in the background, and the bassist looked like he was about to trip over a power cord. Zedd had been blocked for a long time, but this account was set to private. It could be any one of the band members.

Screw it. He had more pictures on his phone – ones from the afternoon spent watching *Hellraiser* with Micah, and he was going to upload all of them.

Micah - Snagged Thread

Thank you for submitting your portfolio to Wegmann's Gallery. While your art is beautiful, it isn't the right fit for our current collection, so we're going to pass.

Micah thumped his head against the desk. He was going to have to take on more commissions of barns so he didn't completely max out his credit card. Either that or cave and tell prospective clients that yes, he could draw their kid from a photo for fifty bucks, and yes, he promised that it wouldn't look at all "disturbing" the way some of his portraits did.

A knock came at the door, and he startled. Speaking of. That landscape painting hadn't worked to summon Beelzebub, but Micah still knew what Hell felt like. It was finally finished and dry enough to the touch to let the client take it home. He would get his second chunk of the commission money and never have to squint at tiny blades of grass again.

He'd told the client that he could bring it to her, but she'd insisted Micah's place was on the way.

As he stood, adrenaline engulfed him. His mind screeched warnings of danger. He stopped, feet rooted to the carpet. His heart hammered against his ribs, eyes wide as he tried to understand where this feeling was coming from. He hadn't even opened the door yet.

She was going to step inside. He'd turn his back to grab the painting, and she'd walk inside without being invited.

Though that fear always lurked in the back of his mind, this wasn't paranoia. It was that sense of what Cosmo called "presque vu." It had already happened to Other Micah in *his* universe.

The knock came at the door again, and Micah broke from his trance. He grabbed a nearby easel, propped it near the door, and set the painting on top. Sensing when something about the future wasn't quite lining up the way it should didn't seem like much more than an interesting party trick, but if it saved him a panic attack, he was going to relish in the power.

Shaking out his hands, blew out a slow breath and opened the door. The client stood on the balcony, smiling sweetly with her purse clutched in her hands.

"Hi. How are you?" Hopefully his grin didn't look as unsteady as it felt.

"I'm fine, thank you. Is that it behind you? I can't wait to see it in person." She put a hand on the doorframe and stepped on the threshold.

Micah's nerves vibrated, his mind shrieking out a chorus of *No! Bad! Go away!* "I'll bring it outside. It looks so much better in natural lighting." He picked up the landscape, then tried to angle it to fit out the door, but the corner bumped into the wall. "Shit. Hang on, I–"

The woman stepped onto the carpet, reaching. "Let me help."

"No!" The edge of the canvas rammed against the doorframe as he widened his stance, trying to block the doorway with his body.

The woman recoiled, pressing herself into the balcony railing.

He turned the painting and slid outside with it, then he strained to reach his doorknob. The canvas slipped from his grip, and he fought to catch it before it hit the ground. The client yanked it from his hands.

God, this whole ordeal was terrible from start to finish. Micah snatched the knob and slammed the door shut, then turned to the client. "Sorry about that. It's a little unwieldy. I didn't damage it, did I? If I did, I can fix it."

She held up the painting, angling it from side to side. "It looks okay. But that's why I was going to help you."

"I appreciate that, but I'm only halfway done chopping up my neighbor and fitting him into a duffel bag." The laugh that came out of his throat sounded deranged. "It's a real mess in there right now."

Color drained from the client's face, and she tightened her grip on the painting.

"That was a joke." Cosmo would have been amused. But Cosmo wasn't a soccer mom who commissioned paintings of barns in grassy fields. Micah cleared his throat. "Sorry. My humor is getting a little too in the spirit of the season."

The tension in the woman's face relaxed. "Right. Halloween is coming up." She forced a chuckle, then pulled a wallet out of her purse. "I bet you're great at scaring the trick-or-treaters."

"I don't know. I haven't been disfigured that long."

"Oh, no." Her eyes widened. "I didn't mean it like that."

He really needed to get better at self-deprecating jokes. "That was a–"

"I just mean because you're an artist, and creative people always have great costumes and decorations, right?" She pulled a stack of hundreds from her wallet and furiously counted through. "And if you like Halloween, then you probably get really into it. But if you're embracing how you look for a costume, then that's great. I think that's commendable. Uh, not that you look scary. You look... You're very talented, and the painting is beautiful." She pressed the hundreds into his hand. "There's one extra there. It's a tip because... You're very talented."

She hefted the painting, waving off his offers of assistance, then hurried down the stairs.

That went well.

After heading back inside and locking the door, he stopped at the bathroom mirror and forced himself to look at his reflection. He'd never been great at selfies, and the only pictures of him after the assault were taken by the police.

This look had worked for Bowie, though. Micah pulled off his sweatshirt, tamed his hair, then held up his phone. He snapped a few photos, then cringed as he scrolled through the gallery. Delete, delete, delete.

Opening Flashbulb, he navigated to Cosmo's profile. His stomach fluttered at the sight of the most recent photos. They were taken when he and Cosmo had watched *Hellraiser*. Micah's face wasn't in the Flashbulb pictures, but there were his fingers, intertwined with Cosmo's. There was Cosmo, his head resting on Micah's shoulder.

He scrolled down and sucked in a breath. Cosmo had posed in Micah's sweatshirt, pouting for the camera with a hickey clearly visible on his neck. Three hundred likes and so many comments.

As many lewd replies populated the post as Cosmo's others, and he left just as many kiss emojis in reply, but his comments had taken on a viciously snarky edge.

Someone wrote: *You're taking up too much room in my spank bank.* 😉 Cosmo replied, *Consider this a cease-and-desist, darling. Give your poor meat a rest.* 🍆🍆🍆

Micah snorted.

Another commenter left: *I want to be that sweatshirt.* 🔥 🔥 🧥
Cosmo wrote, *Please have a little more ambition in life.* 🌶

Cheeks aching from how hard he was grinning, Micah scrolled through the comments on each shot. Ice sleeted through him as he stopped on the photo of his and Cosmo's hands.

They all leave you eventually, you cheap slut. But I won't.
They all leave you eventually, you cheap slut. But I won't.
They all leave you eventually, you cheap slut. But I won't.
They all leave you eventually, you cheap slut. But I won't.
They all leave you eventually, you cheap slut. But I won't.

Micah swallowed hard. The commenter's account was brand new, with only five followers. The profile pic was of some punk band. Hadn't Cosmo mentioned his ex was a singer? Zedd probably created a throwaway profile every time he got wind of Cosmo being with someone new. But it wouldn't work this time.

After screenshotting the comments and hitting the *Report* flag for each one, he left a comment of his own:

For you, my love, I would watch hours of infomercials.
For you, my love, I would pull on wet socks.
For you, my love, I would endure ten paper cuts.
For you, my love, I would drink bathroom tap water.
I'm here for you, my love, and I'm not going anywhere.

Even if Zedd's messages were removed from Flashbulb and his account suspended, he'd probably make another one and see Micah's comments. He'd probably click on Micah's profile and try to figure out who'd stolen Cosmo's heart. Good.

Micah took more selfies. They didn't look any better than the previous ones, but that was no longer the point. After adding some artsy filters, he loaded them onto Flashbulb, then walked to the drafting table and snapped photos of all of his portraits and sketches of Cosmo. He added them to his account and tagged Cosmo's profile.

He glared at Zedd's disgusting comments. "Look upon this anisocoric bicon and despair, loser. I'm not going anywhere."

A soft *meow* came from somewhere nearby. Micah expected Phantom to materialize and weave through his legs like she often did. He turned around; the room was empty. The *meow* came again, a strained and pitiful sound, and he realized it was coming from outside. When he opened the door, a flash of dingy white fur disappeared behind an empty flowerpot sitting on the balcony.

"How'd you get out here? You, missy, are an inside cat." He'd never really thought of himself as a cat person, but she brought him comfort during her unpredictable appearances, and he could only imagine how upset his other self would be if something happened to her.

He stepped around the flowerpot, and Phantom darted away from him and through the open apartment door. She immediately went to her water dish in the kitchen and drank greedily. Her fur was clumped with dried mud and burrs, and dirty tear tracks ran from her eyes. Bits of dried blood coated the inside of one of her ears.

Micah knelt down to check her ear, and she scurried down the hall and dove under his bed.

"What in the world happened to you? You even lost your... Oh." He straightened, staring at the clods of mud on the tile. She didn't lose her collar. He hadn't given her one yet. The frightened, filthy cat beneath his bed was real, and this was the first time they'd met.

His other self hadn't mentioned what a poor state she was in when she first turned up. As much as he wanted to, he resisted the urge to follow her into the bedroom and pull her into her arms. Instead, he opened a can of cat food and scraped it into her dish. When she returned to the kitchen and started eating, he kept his distance. Hopefully with her belly full and a warm place to sleep, she'd grow comfortable enough to let him clean her up a bit later.

He folded his arms and leaned against the counter. "Welcome home."

Cosmo - Snagged Thread

The familiarity of Night Gallery made sliding into the temporary position as registrar much easier than a first day at a new job normally was. It helped that Cosmo had experience doing half of the required duties during his time as Identical Dog's art handler.

It was impossible to forget that he should *not* have been doing those duties as the art handler, because his new director, Clarence, scrunched his face and shook his head every time Cosmo mentioned some aspect of his experience. Clarence had muttered the phrase "how unbecoming" half a dozen times, and it was only noon.

Clarence stood at the computer, squinting through his thick glasses as he trudged through instructions about a program Cosmo already knew how to use. The light from the monitor settled into the creases of his face and made him look much older than the forty-something he probably was.

Simone was wandering the gallery and kept appearing at random times to ensure Cosmo was doing okay, but she wouldn't always be here, and Cosmo would be working under the direction of Clarence most of the time.

He suddenly felt the phantom sensation of Royce's crinkly windbreaker against his face as he'd leaned in, hoping for a bit of emotional support from a friend. If he'd had any sense at all, he wouldn't have become close enough to consider his boss a friend. The idea that Royce never had been, despite coming to Cosmo's funeral, to birthday parties, to his rescue whenever Zedd showed up, dumped a sour sickness into his gut and made him feel both oblivious and stupid. He knew he needed to give himself some grace; he would never call another person stupid for ending up in a situation where someone violated them. He needed to be kinder to himself. But that feeling of guilt that he'd brought this upon himself, that maybe he deserved it, was *so loud* that it was difficult to drown out.

The director tapped at the keyboard, and Cosmo eyed the wedding band on his finger. "You're married?"

"Hm? Yes."

"Happily?"

Clarence frowned. "Is this your idea of small talk?"

"Are you queer?"

A flush crawled up the director's neck and he sputtered. "Are you hitting on me? I don't have anything against people like you, but I'm straight. And happily married. I find your questions very unbecoming and would prefer you don't ask things like that again."

"I'm not hitting on you." Cosmo brushed curls from his eyes and folded his arms. "I just wanted to make sure that– I'll feel better if – if you aren't interested in me."

"Why would that..." Clarence turned his attention back to the monitor. "Right. You'll find that unlike *some* galleries, we're capable of conducting ourselves in a professional, sexual harassment-free manner."

He knew. Somehow, he knew what had happened. Maybe the whole gallery did.

Cosmo suddenly felt like someone had peeled open his chest and exposed every dirty thing that made him up. "May I take a short break to smoke?"

"This isn't the time."

"Then may I use the restroom?"

"Which is it you need to do? Smoke or use the restroom?"

Cosmo clenched his jaw. Neither one would get rid of the cramp in his stomach, but he couldn't stand here a second longer. "Please."

Clarence sighed. "Five minutes."

Striding around the counter, Cosmo hurried past exhibits, pushed through the bathroom door and locked himself in a stall. He leaned against the side and squeezed his eyes shut. Nothing was wrong. The gallery was beautiful, Simone was kind, and Clarence was offended by the mere suggestion of him being queer.

And if everyone here knew what had happened between Cosmo and Royce, that wasn't any more awkward than having a public argument with Zedd or sleeping with someone once and running into them at a party weeks later.

Everything was fine. Even so, abandoning this job to go home and take a scalding shower was tempting. What were the odds that Clarence would believe their *new* registrar had appendicitis too?

His phone jingled with notifications: *m.wildsmith tagged you in a post. m.wildsmith commented: "For you, my love, I would..."*

Oh, Micah. The ache in Cosmo's stomach soothed a little as he swiped open Flashbulb and tapped on the comment. His laugh bounced through the empty restroom. Micah would pull on wet socks for Cosmo, would he? How dreadful. Clearly there was no lover who would sacrifice more.

Simone's voice carried into the restroom. "Cosmo, are you okay?"

He tucked the phone away and left the stall. "I'm fine."

"Are you sure? I'd like to come in, but I don't want to make you uncomfortable."

"Gender is a construct. And I'm fully clothed. You can come in." He stopped before the mirror and smoothed rebellious strands of hair.

She peeked inside, then walked up to the sink. She reminded Cosmo of a much curvier version of Grace Jones, and whether in the gallery or in a bathroom she looked like an art piece herself. "You're feeling ill?"

"The only thing making me ill is that people here know my dirty laundry."

She frowned, heavy crystal earrings wagging on her lobes. "Clarence is a busybody."

"How unbecoming."

"Your reasons for leaving Identical Dog shouldn't be anyone's business, and I'll talk to Clarence about feeding the rumor mill. If you have any more issues with him, please text me. I want you to be comfortable here."

His voice came out strained. "I'm fine. And the gallery is lovely. I'm sure I'll enjoy it here."

"Someone dropped this off for you." Simone squeezed an envelope, glanced at the front of it, but didn't offer it. "It doesn't say who it's from, and the message written on the outside is a little creepy."

No doubt she was worried it was from Royce, but it was more likely to be from Zedd.

There's room for two in your grave.

In fact, Zedd and Royce were probably colluding to make Cosmo's life miserable.

He eyed the envelope. "If it says I'm a slut, please toss it in the trash."

"No, nothing like that."

Cosmo peered at the words: *Taste our pleasures. We have such sights to show you!*

He grinned, sagging against the sink in relief. "It's from the guy I'm seeing." The sentence felt strange in his mouth – he hadn't been with a guy since Zedd – but strange in a way that kicked his heart into a higher gear and made him eagerly tear open the envelope. "We watched *Hellraiser* the other day. Micah is such a doll. This is probably a dinner invitation, or a wholesome letter wishing me a good day, or–"

Cosmo slid out a fifty-dollar gift certificate to Carnal Delights, that sex toy shop by the car wash on Main. He squeaked and stuffed the certificate back into the envelope. What a completely inappropriate thing to send on Cosmo's first day on the job! How was he supposed to concentrate on work with a naughty gift from Micah in his back pocket?

The joy inside him swelled until there was no room left for anything else. He'd have to send Micah something in return.

If Simone noticed the nature of Cosmo's gift, she made no indication, her gaze fixed at a blank spot on the wall. "Micah... Does he happen to be a portrait artist?"

"Yes. He's exceptional."

"I was just reviewing his portfolio this morning. His drawings have the precision of Albrecht Dürer, but with the unsettling quality of Alfred Kubin."

"Oh my god, you're so right!" Cosmo tucked away the envelope and pulled out his phone. He opened a photo of the portrait Micah had let him keep. "He's done some of me, and I can't get over them."

"His other pieces are great, but this is fantastic. He has more?"

Micah had tagged Cosmo in a Flashbulb post, but Cosmo had been too distracted by his pledge to endure papercuts and bathroom tap water to see what it was. He opened Micah's profile, and his breath caught. Selfies! Micah stared into the camera almost aggressively, defiantly, his lips pinched. His white tee hugged his strong shoulders and revealed more than a little chest hair.

With some difficulty, he scrolled past the selfies and found the rest of the portraits Micah had done of Cosmo. He handed Simone the phone. Her eyes lit up, and she tugged on her earring. "Fantastic. Fantastic. He should have included these in his portfolio."

Cosmo imagined Micah's art on display in Night Gallery, and how viewers' heads would turn when they realized the fabulous and disquieting portraits were of none other than the gallery's new registrar. "Oh! Can you imagine if there were portraits of the gallery staff on display?"

Simone gasped. "That would be so fun for the next reception. Does he take commissions?"

"He does. I'm not certain how booked he is right now, but I'm sure he would love to participate. He has a lot of practice drawing life models." Cosmo clapped his hands and bounced on the balls of his feet. "You could pose for him!"

He didn't want to put words in Micah's mouth, but he'd mentioned living off his commissions, and life drawing being his bread and butter.

"I'll give him a call about his portfolio and set something up." Simone turned to the mirror and pouted, patting the sides of her gumby fade. "As long as he can make my portrait look as beautiful as yours. I feel bloated."

Cosmo resisted the urge to screech with joy. "He makes everyone look beautiful, which is part of the allure of his art. And you're a vision, regardless."

"You're sweet." She headed for the door. "I think this is enough girl-talk in the bathroom, hm? We have things to do."

"Of course." He closed out of Flashbulb and tapped out a text to Micah:

<*Omgoddddddd. Thank you for the absolutely salacious gift!! I can't wait to find something that tickles my fancy.* 🍆🍆😋😋😋🍓 🍓💥💥 *Maybe I can find something we'd both enjoy??? Btw, don't put down your phone because you have an important call coming your way.* 🐍>

This would be an incredible way for Micah to build up his clientele and get back into the gallery scene. And how wonderful it would be for him to draw a live model again.

With extra vigor in his step, he headed back into the gallery to find Clarence. Even if he had to suffer through more tutorials he already knew by heart, thinking about that gift certificate in his back pocket was going to help pass the time. Oh, Micah.

As he reached the end of the hall, he froze mid-step, overwhelmed by the sudden sense that Zedd was here. He was going to come around the corner, one of his eyes blacked and both of them blazing, snatch Cosmo by the arms and slam him into the wall.

His chest heaving, Cosmo backpedaled, a hand to his throat. Not here too. Was there nothing Zedd couldn't taint?

He couldn't get into a fight with Zedd in a new place of work. And he sincerely doubted Clarence had the fire and defensiveness Royce did to drive his ex away.

Cosmo's stomach dropped. He didn't want to think about Royce. *Or* Zedd.

The envelope crinkled as Cosmo felt for it. He thought of the hickey on his neck, of Micah whispering that he wanted Cosmo to leave tracks all over his heart. Zedd was *not* going to ruin this, no matter how angry he was. This was Cosmo's life, and he wasn't beholden to anyone.

Stepping around the corner and steadying himself against the wall, he strained for the tell-tale clomp of Zedd's leather boots, but was met only with the soft chatter of visitors admiring an exhibit. Maybe he wouldn't show. That sense of presque vu meant something had changed slightly. Zedd had confronted Cosmo on the original timeline, but maybe he wouldn't show in the parallel one here. Or maybe, like the first kiss with Micah, the events would arrive at a different time, and Zedd would pop up tomorrow. Or the next day. Or the day after that.

Cosmo made a noise in his throat. Why was Zedd so upset anyway? Over the Flashbulb pictures? He reached harder into the adjacent memory, fishing for the words Zedd hurled.

Zedd's hot breath buffeted his face, his eyes watery and jaw tight as he pressed Cosmo into the wall. *Just stop. Tell him to stop, and I'll leave you alone. I swear to God.* An involuntary shiver ran through Cosmo's body as he tried to shake away the memory of his other self. This again. Goddamn it. Screw him! Micah wasn't going to stop seeing Cosmo, and that was a fact Zedd would have to deal with.

A hand grazed Cosmo's elbow, and he screamed. The sound echoed, and visitors turned his way.

Clarence frowned at him, then pushed his glasses up the bridge of his nose. "If you're quite finished, er, standing in the hallway, we have work to get done."

18

ARTISTS ONLY

Micah - Snagged Thread

The phone rang for a second time. Normally Micah never hesitated to pick up – a call meant someone on the other end to talk to, no matter who it was. But Cosmo had known this call was coming, and Micah didn't think it had anything to do with presque vu.

"Important" could mean any number of things. Cosmo had so many connections to the art world; it could be a potential new commission. His stomach clenched – or maybe it was a therapy appointment.

He couldn't just let it ring. "Hello?"

"Hi, is this Micah Wildsmith?"

"Yes."

"Micah, my name is Simone Green, gallerist of Night Gallery. How are you today?"

Oh god. Did something happen? "I'm– I'm good. Is Cosmo okay?"

"What? Oh! Yes, he's fine. I hope I didn't give you a scare. I'm calling because I've reviewed your portfolio and love your work. Cosmo showed me additional portraits on your Flashbulb, and they're fabulous. I'd like to offer you representation. Night Gallery has a loyal…"

A gallery wanted to represent him. Finally! Simone mentioned the particulars of their clientele, commission profits, how his art would be displayed and the exposure and support he could expect, but all Micah could think was that he should have sent Cosmo a hundred-dollar gift certificate instead.

Knowing Cosmo had talked Micah up and influenced Simone's decision added an extra layer of anxiety to seem impressive, and he'd already creeped out his landscape client today.

"Does that sound like it would be a good fit for you?" Simone asked. "If so, I'd love for you to come down at your earliest convenience and look over the contract."

"Uh, yes. That sounds great. I can be there today." He couldn't remember what cut of the commissions she'd said the gallery would get, but it was likely standard, and galleries marked up artwork much higher than a freelance artist would, so even after fees, the artist often made more than they would on their own. It would all be in the contract anyway.

"In addition, we have an artist reception next week that Cosmo thinks you'd be perfect for. I would love to have you live draw me during the event, and this would be a paid commission of–"

Micah dropped the phone. It hit the desk and tumbled across the carpet. His heartbeat crashed in his ears. He couldn't draw live models anymore. Hadn't he told Cosmo that? Surely he did. Why else would Micah be on the phone, begging random people to describe themselves? It was true that he hadn't actually tried to draw an in-person model again since the assault, but the very idea made him break out in a cold sweat.

Simone's voice drifted from the phone. "Micah? Are you still there?"

He picked it up, trying to keep his voice steady. "I'm here, yes. Sorry. Listen, I appreciate the offer, but I think drawing you in a public setting is going to be a little out of my comfort zone."

"Oh..." Her voice sank. "That's too bad. I don't want to pressure you at all, but perhaps we can talk about it more when you get here? All of our clientele are lovely and laidback, and I'm sure we could work out something to make it as stress-free as possible."

Shit. Shit. Cosmo had told Simone that Micah was perfect for this, and now he was making himself look like a bad fit. He might not lose the offer of rep, but he didn't want to do anything that would reflect poorly on Cosmo. He'd only just started there. Micah had never been one to believe in a predetermined destiny, but that didn't mean it wasn't how the universe worked. They shouldn't have been able to make a parallel universe – a snagged thread. If that thread was trying to course-correct, and Cosmo wasn't supposed to be working for Night Gallery, destiny might try to pull him back to working under Royce, no matter how hard he tried to leave.

"Oh, Christ."

"I'm sorry, what was that?" Simone said.

"Uh, yes, okay. Let's talk about it when I come to review the contract."

"Fantastic! It's a week away, so plenty of time to prepare."

Plenty of time. Right. He shook out his numb hands. "See you in a bit. And thank you. I'm very excited."

She chuckled. "Don't thank me. Thank Cosmo."

After checking on Phantom, who seemed content to stay beneath his bed for the time being, Micah drove to Night Gallery in his best suit and a fit of indigestion. He had to hold it together. If he didn't go through with this, once Night Gallery's actual registrar came back, they might let Cosmo go. Royce would undoubtedly find out, and it wasn't a leap to picture him pouncing on Cosmo when he was vulnerable, convincing him to come back to Identical Dog.

Micah swallowed, grimaced, and pulled into the gallery parking lot.

Checking his appearance in the rearview mirror was a mistake. His bangs were already mutinying from his coiffe, and he'd taken on a pallid, sweaty sheen. After dabbing his brow with a napkin from the glove box and taking a long pull from a bottle of water, he left the car and walked inside.

A white man a bit older than Micah stood at the reception desk, squinting at a computer monitor. Micah gave his name and the man introduced himself as Clarence, the gallery's director. Micah followed him into an office, and after a moment, they were joined by Simone. She sat behind a desk and pulled out a folder. A resin cube sat atop a stack of papers on the corner of the desk. Inside was a partitioned bird skull bursting with seeds and tiny plant sprouts that were probably actually beads and knotted bits of thread.

The sculpture anchored Micah, and he reminded himself that he could do this. It was hard to focus on the conversation about their gallery and what sort of collaboration and networking they offered, but it wasn't dissimilar from the last gallery Micah had been in, so he nodded his head and hoped he looked enthusiastic.

The commission fees and terms were reasonable, so Micah signed the contract. He patted the resin cube on the corner of the desk for a bit of physical reassurance, and said, "You have one of his pieces."

"Oh, yes. One of his first. He's so talented." Simone smiled. "And I can't get over the portraits you've done of him. I hope you can make me look as good."

Micah turned the resin sculpture, sliding his fingers across the slick surface, but didn't dare pick it up. Instead, he studied Simone's features. She had wide-set eyes with feathery lashes and eyebrows plucked to oblivion, drawn back on in a shade darker than her bister complexion. Her hair was a high flat top cut at a slant, with a fade around the sides. Her white suit jacket created hard angles of her hourglass figure. "You're a study in contrasts. Geometric hair and pencil-thin brows on a soft, heart-shaped face. A suit with a dramatic cut struggling to contain generous curves. Long, chitinous nails on rounded fingers."

Clarence frowned. "Did you just comment on her weight and compare her fingernails to beetles?"

"I love him!" Simone stood from behind the desk and grinned. "Such fascinating perspective. You'll have to tell me what to wear for the portrait."

"We're not doing a nude, then, right? Sometimes it's what people want and many of the portraits in my portfolio are because–"

She laughed. "I do *not* have that much confidence."

"You should. All bodies are beautiful."

"I appreciate the sentiment, but getting naked in front of a hundred attendees at the event is more than I'm willing to do."

"Right." Because this was going to be in public. Drawing in front of others had never bothered him before, but the risk of freezing up and panicking when it was just Simone was bad enough. If he made a scene in front of an entire crowd, it would be a disaster.

Simone frowned, searching his face. "Are you okay?"

His throat was closing hard enough he was certain he'd choke on his own tongue. A cold sweat broke out on his brow. Simone stared at him with concern. He turned his attention to Cosmo's sculpture on the desk, thinking about the corner exploding and chunks of resin skittering across the floor in Identical Dog.

All he needed to do right now was say yes to this event. Baby steps. Sweat itched at the collar of his shirt. He gave her a smile that felt more like he was merely peeling back his lips, and said, "I'm fine. Just a little overwhelmed."

"The atmosphere will be very casual, I promise. But not 'no clothes' casual." She laughed. "And any accommodations you need, just say the word." She strode around the desk, then air-kissed both his cheeks. "I'm looking forward to working with you, Micah. Clarence can take care of any questions you have and give you details about your exhibit."

"Thank you. Will you excuse me for a moment?" He left the room, limbs stiff, and strode quickly for the restrooms. He pushed through the door, slammed open the stall, and vomited into the bowl. Sweat coated his brow, his hands shaky as he gripped the seat. The end of his tie floated in the putrid water.

Past-Micah – not the depressed and unwashed man who'd been sleeping on the couch less than a week ago, but Micah from before the assault – would have been overjoyed at this opportunity. The idea of drawing a gallerist during an event, with so many potential new clients watching, would have sent him into a fit of excitement. How incredible for his career! He could build up his base of clientele and fans, and would surely meet plenty of new artists. Past-Micah would call Everett with the news. Past-Micah would ask someone to record the event so he could share the footage with Mom and Dad.

Micah ripped off his soggy tie, wiped his mouth, and flushed the toilet. He gargled with the tap water, splashed some on his face, and scrubbed off his tie, then wrapped it in a wad of paper towels and stuffed it in his pocket.

Now that he was part of a gallery, he'd have to attend receptions and art fairs and charity events. If he was able to draw Simone, other people would commission him for the same. He'd have to let them inside the studio to draw them. Fixing his career wasn't quite incentive enough to ask for help. After all, he'd spent the past nine months hiding away at home while his life spiraled down the drain, and it wouldn't be hard to do that again. But the idea of failure reflecting negatively on Cosmo meant Micah *had* to pull himself together. Cosmo had promised to slip into Micah's apartment and be a "ghost" for him, but he hadn't done it yet, and they were running out of time to practice.

Micah needed a therapist.

The urge to vomit rose again, but he clenched his stomach and called Everett.

Keyboard clacks filled the speaker. Everett looked at the screen and frowned. "Jesus, you look like shit."

"I feel like shit."

"What's going on? You sick?"

"I need a therapist. I need you to call one of the ones from that list for me. Please. Set up some appointments for as soon as you can."

Everett blinked like he hadn't heard Micah correctly. "Uh, yeah. Of course." He laughed uncertainly. "You're sure? I mean, you are, right? You're really going to go?"

"Yes, I'll go."

"Okay. I'll do it right now. Call you back when it's set up. Hang in there."

Micah drew in a deep breath, wiped off his smeared glasses, and left the bathroom. Cosmo drifted through a hallway, and despite his queasiness, Micah's stomach fluttered in a good way. He took a few steadying breaths, enchanted by the cut of Cosmo's silhouette against a huge Bauhaus-inspired painting on the wall behind him.

Cosmo stopped to inspect a shoe scuff on the baseboard. He rubbed at it, frowning.

Stopping beside him, Micah said, "Do they have you spit-shining this—"

Cosmo shrieked and fell into the wall, a hand clutched to his heart. He stared at Micah, his chest heaving, then threw his arms around him. "Oh, you scared my soul straight out of my body."

It was tempting to make a joke, but Micah's queasy stomach coupled with Cosmo's tremble pushed the urge away. He rubbed Cosmo's goose-bumped arms. "Did something happen?"

"No." Cosmo pulled away, brushing hair from his eyes. "Just a little on edge."

"Why?"

"Good god, you look atrocious. Simone didn't reject your portfolio, did she?"

"No. I signed the contract and agreed to the event. I'm just very nervous."

"Oh."

The concern didn't leave Cosmo's face, so Micah added, "But I'm excited. I'm part of a gallery again! Thank you so much for your help. You didn't need to put yourself on the line like that."

"Simone was the one who brought you up. I didn't even know you'd submitted your portfolio here. But the idea to have you draw her was mine." He smiled and leaned in for a kiss.

Micah was *not* about to kiss Cosmo with puke on his breath. He dodged Cosmo's lips, pressed his hand against the small of Cosmo's back, and pecked at his neck.

Cosmo let out a small gasp. "You are positively naughty today. After work, do you want to help me pick out something fun with the gift you got me?"

The only thing that sounded fun right now was lying on the floor. "I wouldn't know where to begin."

"You mean you don't own anything even for your own... mm, personal aid?"

"I have a vibrator with dead batteries."

Cosmo laughed. "Poor baby. I'll find something."

"I bought that certificate for you to use, not me. Are you sure you're okay? Nothing's wrong?"

"You know how jumpy I get sometimes." He waved his hand like Micah's concern was obstructing his vision, then gave him a light peck on the lips before Micah could stop him. "You should go celebrate. I'm so happy for you."

"I'd hope that my art speaks for itself, but I appreciate any arm-twisting you did on my behalf. Thank you." His phone vibrated, and he pulled it out. "My brother. I should take this."

Cosmo nodded, but continued to stare at Micah. "Of course. Talk to you soon?"

"Yeah. See you later." The phone continued to ring. Micah bit his lip, then cupped Cosmo's cheek and caressed the edge of his jaw.

Cosmo sighed, his eyelids fluttering, and leaned into the touch. "I must get back to work now." But even as he said it, he took a step forward and gripped the lapels of Micah's suit jacket.

The phone stopped ringing, then started again. Micah reluctantly pulled back and whispered goodbye, leaving Cosmo with a dazed dreaminess in his expression.

He answered the call as he headed through the lobby and pushed through the front doors. "Hi."

Everett held his phone properly, fluorescent office lighting crowning his hair. "All done. You've got an appointment with Dr. Yoshioka on November twentieth at ten am. That's the soonest I could get you in."

His stomach plummeted. That was weeks away. It would help in the long run, but was too late for the event. Shit. Not that one or two sessions probably would have helped enough to keep him from panicking at the reception, but now he'd have to find some other way to practice. Baby steps weren't going to cut it. "Thanks for doing that."

"You bet. Do you need me to call you that day to keep you accountable so you actually go?"

"That's probably not a bad idea."

"Will do." Everett's smile wavered. He set down his phone, blew his nose, and picked it back up. "I'm so proud of you, little brother."

"You better not be crying."

"Who's crying? Nobody's crying." Everett's voice broke on the last syllable. "Talk to you later. Love you."

"Love you too." The call ended, and Micah put away his phone. The tie in his pocket was starting to dampen his shirt; he pulled his suit lapel away and rubbed at the wet spot.

A car drove through the parking lot, slowing as it went past Cosmo's sedan. It parked, and a white man in a leather jacket and sunglasses climbed out. Why did he look familiar?

Adrenaline surged through Micah's limbs. It was Zedd. He was wearing that leather jacket in the profile photo of that Flashbulb account that had been leaving Cosmo nasty comments.

Zedd pulled a pack of cigarettes out of his back pocket as he strode toward the gallery. He tried to pull out a cigarette, then dropped the pack. Picking it up, he managed to get one out and light it, but his hands shook, and two of his fingers were in metal splints.

He strode up to the doors, but Micah blocked his path. Zedd took a step back, smoke curling from his nostrils. He looked Micah up and down, then said, "Right," and flicked his cigarette onto the sidewalk. "No smoking, huh."

"You're not coming in."

Zedd pushed up his sunglasses. He had a black eye, the flesh beneath his eye swollen and purple. "Excuse me?"

"You want both your eyes to match? If not, I suggest you turn around and get back in your car." Micah was not going to let this douche harass Cosmo today. And standing up to Zedd gave Micah extra satisfaction because it would be a direct incident of Zedd *not* scaring Micah away the way he did with Cosmo's past partners.

Narrowing his gaze, Zedd said, "And who are you supposed to be, random man? This art gallery needs a bouncer? Get the hell out of my way."

"Is there room for two in your grave, Zedd?"

The color drained from Zedd's face. He stared at Micah, wide-eyed, his throat working. He stepped back, stumbling, then turned and ran. When he reached his car, he jumped inside and peeled out of the parking lot. Someone laid on their horn as he cut them off. The light turned red, and Zedd ran straight through.

19

VISIONS IN BLUE

Cosmo - Snagged Thread

Armed with a dry erase marker and a strong sense that he was doing something wrong, Cosmo climbed the stairs to the second floor of Micah's apartment complex. Light glowed beyond Micah's Venetian blinds, but it was dim, coming from the hallway or kitchen.

The flowerpot at the corner of the balcony had nothing in it but some soil and rocks, and Cosmo wondered if Micah had set it up here specifically so he had something to put a key under beside the obvious welcome mat. The fact that he was leaving a key outside at all had to be extremely vulnerable for someone so terrified of anyone coming inside their place.

He lifted the pot and picked up the key.

Pressing his brow to the cold glass, he squinted through the slats in the blinds. Opening the door and walking inside in full view of Micah would be disastrous and not at all ghostly.

After unlocking the door, Cosmo carefully twisted open the knob and strained for sound. A heater hummed from the living room, and the scent of laundry soap and new furniture wafted around him. A white cat sat on the couch, its tail twitching. It hunched into itself, staring at him.

A hiss of water came from down the hall, then the creak of the tub. Perfect. Cosmo slipped inside and locked the door behind him. The living room was sparse aside from the couch and the potted plants; several milk crates of items still sat in a corner. On the drafting table were new sketches of Cosmo – some of his hands, and a full body one of him in the outfit he'd worn on their cemetery date.

A voice came from the bathroom, off-key lyrics to something very familiar. Was Micah singing… Soft Cell?

Cosmo put a hand over his mouth and squeezed his eyes shut. How adorable. He knew exactly what to write with the marker now. Except he'd planned on writing it on the bathroom mirror, and that would be impossible with condensation fogging the glass. And much too awkward with Micah inside in the shower.

After creeping down the hall, he peered into the bedroom. Micah looked like the exact kind of man to own a bed with a cozy quilt, and Cosmo was not disappointed. An oval mirror sat above the dresser, and he stopped before it.

The water shut off in the bathroom. Shit. Micah must be the type to believe in three-minute showers.

Cosmo leaned past books, a bottle of cologne, and Micah's wire-framed glasses, and scrawled on the mirror:

THEY SAY I'M DYING AND I DO IT SO WELL

He capped the marker and hurried from the room. The bathroom door opened behind him, and he dared a glance back as he turned the corner into the living room. Micah stood in the hall, a sheen of water on his back and his delicious bare ass exposed. Cosmo let out a squeak, then slapped his hand over his mouth and flattened against the wall.

Instead of the footsteps receding toward the bedroom, they grew closer. Cosmo would have to reveal himself soon, but the message on the mirror was supposed to soften the blow and help Micah prepare. He probably couldn't see much without his glasses, and Cosmo lurking in the living room as a blurry figure while Micah was stark naked was going to be the opposite of helpful.

Cosmo tucked himself into a dark corner behind the drafting table and held his breath. Micah's frowning face was just visible around the side of the table. He was different without glasses, his scars much more obvious. Coupled with his slicked hair, he looked like a sexy villain from an espionage film. Which was a lazy stereotype, and Cosmo felt bad for even thinking it.

Micah turned from the room. A door creaked down the hall. Cosmo counted the seconds, waiting for Micah to see the mirror and say something to the effect of, *I know you're here.*

When Cosmo counted to seventy, he pried himself from the corner and stretched his aching legs. Maybe Micah's eyesight was worse than Cosmo thought, and he'd gotten dressed without noticing the message.

Cosmo slipped through the hall and peered into the bedroom. Micah stood before the mirror in his briefs and glasses, his hands clenched into white-knuckled fists on an open dresser drawer. Breath rushed in and out of his heaving chest. He stared, unblinking, at the message on the mirror, and the terror in his reflection made Cosmo's heart crumble.

This was a horrible idea. Maybe he could leave before he made it–

Micah's gaze snapped to Cosmo's reflection in the mirror. He whimpered, his throat working, eyes pleading for help, but Cosmo didn't know how to help this.

What had their last "ghostly" interaction been? Micah had been sleeping in bed when Cosmo came in to gather the last of his belongings upon moving out. He'd sat on the bed next to Micah and they'd joked that the only spirits they had were their own.

Be my ghost.

Cosmo slapped off the light switch and walked into the room. He whispered, "Hello, handsome."

Micah was a dark silhouette at the dresser, his frantic breathing filling the space between them. Cosmo ran his fingers down Micah's arm, and Micah made a small noise. Prying his hand loose from the dresser was easier than Cosmo expected.

"I don't want to be chained to an empty grave on Cherry Lane. I want to stay here, with you."

Tension blazed from Micah like the heat of a cremation furnace. Cosmo tried to tug him toward the bed.

Micah's feet held firm. His lips parted like a dying fish. "Leave."

"What?"

"Leave." His silhouetted expression begged for it. He looked like an animal being taken to slaughter, and Cosmo wished he could step back in time and refuse to follow through on this plan.

He dropped Micah's hand and strode from the room. He walked outside, closed the door, and gripped the cold balcony railing until the metal dug into the flesh of his palms, trying to imagine what Micah must be feeling.

Earlier in the day, he'd gone to Fieldstone's to look at the shoes. The department store already had Christmas decor out, which was completely vulgar because it wasn't even Halloween yet, but that didn't stop Cosmo from looking at the glass ornaments and jarred candles. He'd picked up the green one and brought it to his nose. He didn't even think about it, even though he'd looked at the label. The sugar cookie one smelled like sugar cookies. The cinnamon one smelled like cinnamon. The pine one should have smelled like pine, like Christmas trees. But the aggressive scent of Royce's aftershave constricted around him, and Cosmo dropped the candle. It shattered on the floor, and everyone turned his way. Instead of paying for it and helping to clean it up, he'd just walked out. He hadn't even apologized.

Halfway to his car, in the middle of the parking lot, he'd broken down and called Mom. It was a wonder she could understand anything through his sobs. No doubt she would have murdered Royce had she been in town. Cosmo had forgotten, actually, that she'd left on a cruise with the woman she'd been casually seeing, and wouldn't be back for a week and half. He could have called Micah or Déjà – and perhaps they would have been the more obvious choices since they already knew about the situation with Royce – but in that moment, all Cosmo had wanted was his mother.

Glancing back at Micah's door, he shook out a cigarette and lit it. What he felt when smelling that pine candle and unloading everything on Mom was surely only a fraction of what Micah was going through, and the thought made his heart ache. Cosmo wanted to pull him into the bed and wrap him in that cozy quilt. He wanted to stroke Micah's hair until his tremors abated and his breathing slowed. Until everything was okay and it didn't hurt anymore.

Leaving didn't feel right, but Micah had told him to. The cherry on the end of his cigarette glowed and crackled as he took a drag. When he smoked it to the filter, he'd go.

Dead leaves shivered on the branches, and a cat trotted across the parking lot. Music thumped from one of the apartments below, and raucous laughter split through the chorus. Cosmo considered his cigarette, but it was going to keep burning down whether he smoked it or not. He took a quick puff and strained for any noise from within the apartment. Micah was probably shivering in the sheets. Or maybe he'd punched his fist through the bedroom mirror in frustration and was now cleaning up the mess.

The cigarette inched down to the filter, a column of gray ash hanging from the end. He tapped it off, then took a final drag. After stubbing it out on the ground, he headed down the walkway toward the stairs.

He paused in front of number twenty-one. If he walked inside right now, he might see past-Micah. He could still be a ghost and warn him about the attack yet to come. If the attack never happened, Micah wouldn't have to suffer with PTSD. But there was no way to know how a warning of the future would alter things, and they'd already made a mess of the timeline once. Besides, if presque vu was indication of the timeline trying to course-correct, that might mean that Micah's destiny was always to be assaulted, no matter how he tried to change things. With Cosmo's luck, his attempt at being helpful would only result in Micah getting attacked somewhere else or in a different manner, with possibly a worse outcome than the original. Cosmo had hurt him enough.

A door creaked, and he looked back. Micah peeked out, his mouth pulled in a hard line. Cosmo's stomach clenched. He hurried back up the walk, then stopped before the door. Micah stood on the carpet inside, dressed in a pair of heather gray sweatpants and a crisp white tee, which molded to the contours of his chest and the soft slope of his stomach. His wet hair stuck to his forehead, and he held the doorframe in a grip so hard Cosmo expected him to rip off the molding.

Micah's throat flexed. "I'm sorry."

"Don't be sorry."

"But I am. I failed again. I don't understand why this is so hard."

Cosmo fished for something to say that wouldn't be printed on a trite motivational poster. "*I'm* the one who should be sorry. You asked me to, but I–"

"It was a bad idea all around. Not your fault."

Gravel scraped beneath Cosmo's shoes as he shuffled his feet. "When you first started drawing portraits, were you good at it?"

"God, no. All my faces lacked depth because I didn't know how to shade right, and I couldn't draw curly hair to save my life."

"Those first attempts were failures, but you didn't give up, obviously. My hair looks fantastic in all of the portraits you've done of me. There's always 'the gap,' right? That space between our skill and our taste that we have to cross in order to get better. You can see when something falls short, but you don't yet have the skill to know how to fix it."

Micah's cheeks inflated, and he blew out a breath. "I'm not sure you can apply art theories to my trauma."

"I can, and I am." Cosmo stared at the silver strip of metal dividing them. "This threshold isn't a force field, the balcony beyond part of a separate world. It isn't a portal that only opens when the planets of your mind align."

Micah scoffed. "That's exactly what it is."

"It's not. It's something that needs practice, and with practice comes failure. You just try again, when you're ready."

Standing firmly on the carpet, Micah took Cosmo's hands and stared down at their feet. Cosmo inched forward, ever so slightly, until the caps of his shoes were on top of the threshold.

Micah squeezed his fingers. "Stop. Don't."

Cosmo backed away, then sat beside the door. Micah stepped out and closed it, then slid down next to him.

"During my short-lived time with a therapist, she told me I needed to practice prolonged exposure therapy, gradually reintroducing things into my life that I'd been avoiding," Micah said. "When I saw your handwriting on the mirror, for a split second it made my heart flutter, until the knowledge kicked in that you aren't a ghost. This wasn't very gradual, I guess, and I'm sorry I asked you to come do it."

"I got to see your absolutely fantastic ass, so it was worth it."

Micah chuckled. "Good thing you're a ghost and not a werewolf, huh? Can't have you transforming at the sight of my full moon. You'd get hair all over my new couch, and the cat already has that job covered. Where were you hiding? In the closet?"

"Darling, I came out of there way back in kindergarten when I wore a tiara to school and declared myself a princess. And then later on the principal called my mother in for a talk because I was kissing both the girls *and* the boys."

Wet hair fell into Micah's eyes as he tilted his head back. "I knew I was a boy when I was a kid, even though I didn't have the vocabulary to explain it. My parents understood better than I did why I hacked off all my hair and got upset when relatives gave me dolls or dresses for my birthday. We read books, had a lot of conversations, but unfortunately, we lived in a state where transition for minors was criminalized. So I was forced to go through a puberty I didn't want."

"God. I'm so sorry." Cosmo was realizing more and more that certain things he was uncomfortable with were really indicators of gender dysphoria, but he didn't have any desire for medical transition. He couldn't imagine what it would be like to have to endure a forced puberty with the wrong hormones.

Micah waved a hand, but his face didn't have as much casual dismissal as the gesture. "It's one of those things that I don't think about often because it only gets me worked up. We moved when I was seventeen, and I was able to physically transition. But my romantic attraction took me a lot longer to figure out than my identity, and being ace had a lot to do with it. In junior high, my brother – Everett – stole a porno mag from our dad. When he started showing me the pictures, he realized I didn't look very excited, and he asked me if I even liked girls. I insisted I did. I had a crush on a girl in art class. But I admitted to Everett that I had the same butterflies in my stomach for a boy in biology. At the time, it didn't occur to either of us that I could be bi or pan, so – very logically – he asked me what I thought about when I jacked off, because surely that would clear it up. I said, 'video games.'"

Cosmo laughed. A chilly wind gusted across the balcony. He scrubbed at his arms and tucked his hands into his armpits.

"You're cold." Micah thudded his head back against the door. "I hate this. I should be able to let you inside."

"Or you could just warm me up."

Micah reached back and opened the door. Warm air drifted

out around them. He brushed back Cosmo's hair and gave him a slow kiss. Micah smelled of clean and shampoo perfume, his cheeks freshly shaven and velvet soft.

Cosmo savored his lips and said, "You're a fruit."

"Hey now."

"You taste like soft, sweet-fleshed grapes, pounded and fermented into a vintage wine. There's just enough tartness and bite to your kisses to make me lightheaded."

"Being fermented isn't really my kink, but I am enjoying the metaphors."

A faint ringing came from somewhere nearby. Cosmo pulled out his phone. Dozens of Flashbulb messages and likes filled the notification bar.

Let me eat your 🍑

Take some pics without the sweatshirt. Take some without the clothes.

Cosmo scoffed and swiped the comments away.

"Something wrong?" Micah asked.

"Just people being gross on my Flashbulb photos."

"That seems to happen a lot. Uh, not that I've scrolled through all your pictures."

"They're just jealous I'm seeing someone new."

"As they should be," Micah said. "We just can't let anyone know you're dead, or I'll get charged with necrophilia."

Cosmo slid backward until his ass was on the carpet, the cold metal of the threshold leaching into his thighs. "I suppose we can keep that detail to ourselves."

Micah eyed Cosmo's backside inside the apartment, then scooted back himself, just a little. "You're still wearing my sweatshirt, I see."

"You can't have it back."

He grinned. "Wasn't going to ask."

Cosmo scooted back a little further, and Micah matched him. He glanced back at the living room they were slowly making their way into. Panic flashed in Micah's eyes. He swallowed, his breath shallow, and said, "I can't do any more right now."

They were technically both inside the apartment, only their lower legs on the step beyond. Cosmo lay back on the carpet and tugged Micah down with him. "Can we stay like this for a moment?"

Micah trembled, his chest heaving. He stared at the ceiling like his gaze was the only thing holding it in place. "Okay."

"You squeeze my hand if you need me to leave but can't get any words out."

Fingers twisted loosely through Cosmo's, and Micah clamped his eyes shut. "Thank you for helping me."

"Of course."

"I think I'm going to need more help. It's about the gallery event. You stuck your neck out for me and I don't want to let you down, but I – I'm worried I won't do my best."

He couldn't tell if Micah was afraid his artwork wouldn't come out well, or if he meant he was out of practice with the networking aspect. Before Cosmo could ask, a phone rang again. Micah's finger tickled his palm, and he said, "Sounds like my phone. Be right back." He stood, then crossed through the living room and walked down the hall.

Cosmo stepped outside and leaned against the doorframe. He could handle schmoozing potential clients at the gallery on Micah's behalf. It might make Micah seem more intriguing, this incredibly talented artist too intent on his figure drawing of Night Gallery's gallerist to pause and talk to onlookers.

The ringing grew louder. A pillow slid off the couch and crashed into a stack of dishes that Cosmo was certain hadn't been there a moment ago. He blinked and did a double take. Micah lay on the couch, adjusting the blankets drawn up around him. His hair was a greasy tangle, and he had several weeks of beard growth.

What in the world? "Uh, Micah?"

Cosmo meant to call this timeline's Micah, but the doppelganger on the couch stirred and rubbed his eyes. "Hello?"

A voice drifted, and someone else materialized out of nothing and entered the room. *Another Micah*? There were three of them inside the apartment now? Wait, no. This man was so similar he could almost be a twin, but he was taller, there was a faint shot of gray at his temples, and his features and glasses were slightly different. It had to be Micah's brother.

Everett squeezed Other Micah's shoulder. "I'm gonna order takeout. But I'll tell the delivery person not to knock. Have them leave it on the step and text me that it's here." He bent down and picked up the dishes on the floor. "Bet your landlady wants these back."

Was this a past event? Perhaps after Micah's assault? No, that couldn't be since Micah hadn't lived in this apartment back then. It had to be a future one.

Other Micah looked around the room like he hadn't heard Everett at all. "I thought... I thought I heard him."

Everett sighed, then sat on the couch and pulled Other Micah into a hug. Other Micah's voice was muffled against his brother's neck as he said, "I swear it was him."

Pulling off his glasses, Everett wiped his eyes and put a hand to his forehead like Other Micah's words were causing him physical pain. "It's going to be okay. How about you have a shower, hm? I'll order something with a criminal amount of cheese, then we'll eat and... It'll be okay."

Other Micah stood from the couch, such an expression of defeat in his face that Cosmo resisted the urge to rush inside and squeeze him tight. But he wouldn't have had time to anyway, because frantic particles engulfed Micah and Everett, and they disappeared.

Everett's disembodied voice drifted. "Don't bother looking for your razor. It's not in there."

"Jesus. That's not necessary," Other Micah said. "You hide my knives too?"

"We'll eat with our hands like the animals we are."

Cosmo thumped his head against the doorframe. Poor Micah. What had happened to warrant him falling into such a depression?

Footsteps padded down the hall, and present-Micah stopped in the living room and shook his phone. "Sorry about that. Was looking for the source of the ringing, then my phone *did* ring. It was Rye Williams. Do you know Rye? Surrealist furniture artist who makes chairs you can't sit in? They live in the apartment below this one. I guess they've heard that I complain when music is too loud, so they wanted to make sure theirs wasn't. I told them to invite me to whatever party they have going on, and I won't complain. So they did." He snorted, then stepped outside and slid his arm around Cosmo's waist. "It's a Halloween party. I wasn't really serious about wanting to be invited, but... It might be fun? I haven't been to a party in who knows how long."

"Oh." Cosmo had been so distracted by everything going on that he hadn't made the connection that the music and laughter below the balcony was coming from Rye's party. "I got an invitation to that."

Micah searched Cosmo's face. "You okay?"

"Sure. Yeah." The Micah of right now was coercing people into inviting him to parties. He was prepping for a gallery reception. He was practicing letting Cosmo into the apartment, even if it was hard and he couldn't do it yet. Such a far cry from the defeated man sleeping on the couch. "Can I ask... Do depressive episodes still happen to you often?"

"Uh, that would imply that they've ever gone away." He slid down against the wall, then pulled Cosmo into his lap. "It was the worst in the first months after my assault. I eventually got out of it, but I'm still sensitive to setbacks. I'm glad you didn't see me last week after you broke up with me."

Cosmo cringed. Oh no. When Other Micah had woken up on the couch, he'd said, *I thought I heard him*. Where was Cosmo? He had no plans to break up with Micah again. He wanted to drown in this sweatshirt, drown in Micah, no matter how many harassing comments he got from Zedd and his friends. He opened his mouth to tell Micah what he'd seen, but Micah spoke first.

"Are you thinking about Royce? Is it hard to get out of bed now? We can talk about it, if you want."

"What? No." He'd talked to Mom, and that was enough for now. "I'm fine. It's not the first time someone kissed me without consent. Honestly, if I'm going to be upset about each of those times, I might as well never leave my house again."

"This time it was your boss, though. And he tried to turn it back on you. Make it seem like you were at fault."

Royce had deserved every slap Cosmo had given him, but knowing that didn't make the guilt go away. "You should be worrying about yourself."

Micah tensed slightly. "What's that supposed to mean?"

"That came out rude. It's just that..." Cosmo glanced into the apartment at the empty couch and clean floor where there had previously been a stack of dirty dishes. He ran the back of his hand down Micah's smooth, freshly-shaven cheek. "I saw something. When you went looking for your phone. I saw – I saw *you*, depressed. The living room a mess. And your brother was helping you up to go take a shower."

Micah's face turned ashen. His throat worked, then he turned back toward the living room. "It took you this long to tell me that?"

Cosmo hunched his shoulders. "I can't help but think it's somehow my fault. I don't know what would make me–"

"No, no." He turned back and leveled his gaze, his glasses slipping down the bridge of his nose. "I'm sure it's not you. When I get like that, sometimes it's not even a big thing that causes it. It's depression. It doesn't need a reason to show up." He blew out a slow breath. "Must be pretty bad for Everett to come help, though. And these timeline intrusions are getting annoying. I didn't mind with you. At least you're cute. Now I'm just faced with my unwashed future self."

"I know I can't make it go away, but you're making progress on things and I am more than happy to continue helping you with it. If you backslide and your brother needs to remind you to shower and eat, that's going to be a sad turn of events, but it doesn't negate your efforts. Setbacks don't mean defeat."

"My muse *and* my life coach. How did I get so lucky?"

Cosmo presumed that was defensive sarcasm, but when he looked into Micah's face, all he saw was sincerity. It should have been reassuring. Cosmo wasn't a flake. He was dependable, always there when loved ones or a job needed him.

So where was he in Other Micah's future?

20

SOMEBODY'S WATCHING ME

Micah - Snagged Thread

Orange string lights twinkled in the window of Rye's apartment, and carved pumpkins flanked the step. Music throbbed from inside. Ximena stood on the sidewalk, arms folded, as an older man droned on about something. As soon as she spotted Micah and Cosmo, she exclaimed, "Oh, there you are! Let's go take a look at that leaky sink, hm?"

Before Micah could ask what she meant, she gripped him by the elbow and pulled him down the sidewalk. Cosmo quickened his pace to keep up with them, then looked over his shoulder. "Gary is still here, huh?"

"Who's Gary?" Micah asked.

"Dreadful man. He used to live next me," Cosmo said. "I drastically cut down on my smoking simply because I didn't want to step outside, knowing he'd inevitably want to talk to me. It got so bad that I begged Ximena to let me move into a different unit. She moved him instead."

Ximena nodded. "I would not be surprised to learn that he's stuck in his own personal time loop, because he complains about the same things over and over."

Micah laughed. "I suppose I should consider myself lucky that I've never been roped into one of his conversations."

After slowing her pace, Ximena looked back and loosened

her grip on his arm. Gary had wandered away from the building, slowly heading toward the one across the parking lot. She said, "It seems safe now. But if he starts heading toward you – run."

She left their side, enough urgency in her step to indicate she didn't feel safe quite yet. Micah and Cosmo doubled back for Rye's apartment, and Micah said, "Who knew the scariest thing you'd encounter this close to Halloween would be a dude named Gary?"

"You kid, but you haven't had the misfortune of talking to him yet," Cosmo replied.

They reached Rye's door without incident, and Rye opened it before they could knock. Their hair was lime green this month, and they had on a tight red bodysuit with a pointed tail and horns, a stick-on goatee, and glittery red eyeshadow. Micah felt underdressed in his jeans and tee shirt, but at least he'd changed out of his sweatpants.

"Cosmo! Glad you could make it." They pulled him into a hug, then their gaze jumped between him and Micah. They offered Micah their hand. "Hey. Um, sorry I didn't give you an invitation when I was handing them out to everyone else last week. I figured you wouldn't have come. Glad you're here, though. You two know each other, huh?"

Micah shook Rye's hand, then tugged Cosmo close, hoping it looked intimate but not possessive. "Well, the art world is quite small."

"True! Come have a drink." Rye ushered them in, and they waded through pirates, serial killers, pregnant nuns, and presidents. Vibrant violin and organ music filled the room.

Cosmo smiled and waved to practically everyone around them. "This sounds like vampire ballroom music."

"I knew I was going to need those plastic fangs," Micah said.

"That sounds fun," Cosmo purred. He slid his arms around Micah's waist and shuffled in a circle. Micah thought of their time on Cosmo's bed, his lips gently savoring Cosmo's flesh like it was a ripe peach, and he had to keep his knees from turning to jelly.

Cosmo rested his head on Micah's shoulder as the music wove around them. "Hold me tighter."

Micah gripped him close. He wasn't sure if Cosmo was struggling with the same depression Micah was prone to, but his self-worth had certainly taken a hit after what happened with Royce, and it wasn't fair. "You keep saying you're fine, and I know you're not. *I* wasn't. I felt... I felt so *foolish* for ignoring my gut and letting someone who I had a weird feeling about into my place. It made me think I deserved what happened to me. Make bad decisions, get consequences that match."

Cosmo started to protest, but Micah said, "I don't feel like that anymore. But climbing out of that guilt was hard. And I want you to know you're worth more than your negative thoughts. For you, my love, I would stub my toe on a bed frame five nights in a row. For you, my love, I would drink coffee that was slightly too hot. For you, my love, I would dice a pepper and rub my eyes." He swayed with Cosmo, his lips brushing Cosmo's ear. "I would do all kinds of specific and mildly painful things for you."

"You're a strange man."

"I want to give you everything you deserve."

Cosmo's Adam's apple bobbed, his gaze searching Micah's face. "And what would that be?"

Micah wasn't a poet. He wasn't a writer. Hopefully his portraits exposed the soul of the person he drew, but they couldn't say all he wanted to say to Cosmo, and words didn't seem sufficient. "You deserve love. And respect. You deserve for every secret desire of your heart to come to pass. And I don't know what those are, but I'd very much like to find out."

Partiers bumped into them, but Micah barely noticed. Tears had formed at the edges of Cosmo's eyes, and Micah would have given anything to take them away.

"I want... I want you to eat my baking," Cosmo said thickly.

"Damn, you're sexy. I can do that."

"I want to have late-night conversations with you on the balcony."

"We can. Tonight even."

"And I want you to read books to me in bed."

"Okay, you'd better stop now or I'm going to take you right here in this crowded living room."

"Lies."

Micah stopped dancing. He brushed his thumb along Cosmo's cheek and wiped away a tear. "The things you want are simple. They're easy." He clenched his jaw, his throat working. "And it hurts me to know that no one has ever given them to you before. I will eat every cookie you bake. I'll read you every book. You deserve to be treated like the queen you are."

Cosmo sank against Micah and shut his eyes. "Do you know Marcel Duchamp's *Prelude to a Broken Arm*?"

"Was that part of his *Readymades* series? *Fountain* and all that?"

"Yes. The snow shovel. What do you think of it?"

"Eh..." Micah hesitated, unsure of what answer Cosmo wanted. "I like some conceptual art if it really makes you think, but I can't say it's my favorite."

"It's an absurd novelty."

"I'm not into absurd novelties. I love art that's genuine. Passionate. Deep." He caressed the nape of Cosmo's neck, his other hand pressed protectively against the small of his back.

Cosmo nodded, his eyes full of hope. Micah didn't know what Duchamp had to do with anything right now, but it was apparently the right answer. The song changed, howling wolves and creeping notes ramping up into the dramatic synth of "Thriller," which would probably be played at every Halloween party until the end of time. The partiers with their latex masks and red Solo cups took on a new energy, and someone's plastic cutlass smacked into Micah's thigh.

He swayed with the music and nipped at Cosmo's lips. "You gonna bake me cookies this week?"

"Not cookies. I'm going to fill you up with my banana bread."

"That sounds really dirty."

"It's cream-filled."

"You're making this up."

"It'll give you a leg-cramping orgasm. It's that good."

Micah raised his eyebrows with a smirk. "I'll gird my loins." Maybe that would be a good time for Cosmo to help Micah practice for the gallery reception, if he was still willing. But the first step was being able to let Cosmo inside the apartment, which Micah hadn't been able to do yet. His reaction to Cosmo coming in unannounced had been much worse than he'd hoped. If he couldn't get Cosmo inside, then the rest of his ideas for practice wouldn't matter, and he was certain the reception would go horribly.

Cosmo suddenly pulled out his phone and opened the screen. If it was more disgusting Flashbulb notifications, Micah was going to pluck the phone from his hands and drop it in the punch bowl.

"Everything alright?"

"Goddamn it." Cosmo sighed and showed Micah the phone.

It was a text from Déjà: <*Went to ur apt to drop something off, and there's a really fukkin creepy note taped to your door. I want to believe it's a Halloween prank, but it's only on ur door. PLEASE tell me Zedd isn't still harassing u.*>

God, that guy never stopped. Cosmo shouldered past dancers, the phone pressed to his ear, and Micah hurried to keep up. The music quieted as they stepped outside. A chilly wind licked around them.

"Darling, are you still at my apartment?" Cosmo said. "I don't want you there alone. Not after what he did to you at my funeral… He sent me one last week. Guess I'll have to take this one to the police too." He shut his eyes and pinched the bridge of his nose. He turned to Micah. "The note says, '*I hope there's enough space in your body locker.*'"

"Shit." Micah rubbed his forehead. "I didn't want to worry you, but I should have told you that he was at Night Gallery the other day. He came up to the doors and I wouldn't let him in. When I quoted his last threat back to his face he got scared and left. I didn't realize you'd been going to the police about it."

"Micah! So my presque vu *was* correct. He was going to come inside and slam me against the wall. But you stopped him and didn't tell me." A series of expressions flashed across his face, and Micah expected to be chastised for not saying anything.

Instead, Cosmo twined their fingers together and said, "The police have been spectacularly unhelpful so far. I'd rather have you around. Will you come home with me? I'll cook you something."

"How can I say no to that? Are you scared? I won't let you be alone. I should have given Zedd a black eye to match his other one."

Déjà's voice drifted from the phone. "What's going on? What did Micah say? Something about Zedd at the gallery?"

Cosmo switched the phone to his other ear. "Sorry. Yes, the sentient garbage can I used to date showed up at Night Gallery."

"Let me get my jacket, and I'll meet you at your car. We can go back to your place, but I think you should call the police too." Micah hurried down the sidewalk, then turned for the stairs that would take him up to his level. He needed more than a jacket. If Zedd was showing up at Cosmo's place to leave threats at his door, then they had to prepare for it to escalate.

He needed vigilance, he needed a flashlight, and he might need a weapon.

Cosmo - Snagged Thread

Cold metal from the car door handle dug into Cosmo's fingers. As much as he relished the idea of him and his new beloved alone in the kitchen, Cosmo offering Micah a spoon of vodka sauce to taste or – goodness – feeding him a forkful of pasta, he didn't want Déjà to feel scared and alone either. He spoke into the phone. "Are you going home? Or would you like to have dinner with Micah and me? I'm cooking."

Déjà hesitated. "I'm invested in this drama now, even though I know I shouldn't be. But I don't want to cramp your style."

"You could never. You amplify it by your mere presence."

"Save your flirts for Micah." There was a smile in her voice. "Meet you here."

Cosmo hung up. If Mom were in town, no doubt she would insist he stay with her for the time being. He had no choice but to head back home, but it was still a huge relief to know he had two people nearby who cared about him and his safety. His relationships with Déjà and Micah weren't flawless; there would be more arguments and hurt feelings because that was life. But they wouldn't ever betray his trust the way Royce had.

"Something In My House" hammered from Rye's apartment. The tangerine string lights twinkled, and candles inside the jack-o'-lanterns on the step wobbled in the breeze. Since Déjà wasn't at the party, it seemed like things between her and Rye hadn't worked out, which was terribly sad. They seemed like they would have made a good fit.

Micah came out of his apartment on the floor above, wearing a jacket, a small luggage bag in one hand. When he stopped at the car, Cosmo asked, "What's in the bag? Rope? A set of knives? Duct tape? We'll need a shovel too. Zedd's grave isn't going to dig itself."

"Duct tape, yeah. But there's only one knife. A phone charger." A flush crawled up Micah's neck. "Also a couple books. I wasn't sure what you like. And... my toothbrush."

Butterflies swarmed in Cosmo's stomach. His toothbrush? "Dinner, murder, *and* a sleepover? That's quite a full night."

"Does it turn you on to think about me sitting in a chair in the dark, keeping watch while you sleep? Because that's what I was picturing."

"Yes, it does." Though that wasn't at all what Cosmo had meant by "sleepover."

"I just want to be prepared in case this is worse than we think and you want me to stay with you. Don't want you to be alone. Did you call the police yet? I'd suggest you spend the evening in my place, but, well..."

"I'll call them after I see the note. And you're coming home with me. Toothbrush and all." Cosmo climbed into the driver seat. Micah was going overboard by bringing a weapon, but Cosmo wasn't going to tell him to tone it down. When he slid in, Cosmo said, "Is there really a knife in there? I have knives, you know."

Poor Micah couldn't possibly have any blood left in his body with all of it rushing to his face. "It's my, uh, comfort knife. I keep it taped under my art desk."

Cosmo pulled out of the parking lot and merged with the evening traffic. "Do you always take it with you when you go somewhere? I'm asking sincerely, not to be judgmental."

"I doubt it would be a good idea to keep it strapped to my ankle when I'm out getting groceries. No, it stays in my place, and I know Zedd only taped a note to your door, but I'll feel better with it nearby."

"Okay."

Micah pulled at a stray thread on his seatbelt. "It's weird to have a comfort knife."

"Since when has weird been a bad thing?" Cosmo flashed him a smile. "I'm going to make penne alla vodka. You like pasta, don't you?"

"Definitely. Especially if it has a criminal amount of–"

"Cheese?"

"Yeah. I only cook easy stuff for myself: eggs, stir fry vegetables from a bag, canned soup. But as you can see" – Micah patted the modest paunch of his stomach – "if someone offers me carbs or cheese, I take it. Ximena was determined to fatten me up in the months after I came back from the hospital. I probably would have starved without her because I didn't have the motivation to make anything for myself."

Cosmo reached over and squeezed Micah's knee. "I'm glad someone was looking out for you... Do you see Everett often?"

"We talk a lot, but I don't see him much in person. It's hard when you're two thousand miles away from each other." Micah looked out the window as restaurants and car dealerships drifted by. "He took time off and flew out after the assault to take care of me, but that was the only time he's been to visit since I've moved to Lemon Disco. I know he wanted to stay longer, but he had work obligations. My parents didn't want me to stay here at all. Wanted me to move back."

If it took something that big for Everett to get time off work and see Micah then that didn't bode well for what Other Micah was going through on the future timeline. And what kind of callous asshole did that make Cosmo to not be there for him when he needed it so badly?

"I'm going to cook you so much pasta," Cosmo said.

Micah chuckled.

They pulled up to Cosmo's complex. The arc sodium light over the sidewalk was off, shadows and high juniper bushes shrouding the building. Tiny plastic pumpkin lights glowed dimly from someone's window, but the other apartments were dark. It felt more ominous than it should have, and the knife in Micah's bag was lending them both comfort now.

Déjà hopped out of her car and met them on the sidewalk. A thick three-ringed binder was tucked under her arm. She eyed Cosmo's door like Zedd was hiding in the bushes beside it. Which Cosmo wouldn't put past him, but there were three of them against him, and Micah had already scared Zedd away once.

Micah looked as apprehensive as Déjà, clutching his luggage bag to his chest. Cosmo marched past them both and tore the note from the door. It was a little hard to read in the twilight, but Zedd had written in big angry Sharpie letters.

Cosmo cleared his throat and read aloud, "*'I hope there's enough space in your body locker to fit in the guard dogs you have wrapped around your finger.'*" He pursed his lips at the page. "Clearly he means Royce and Micah. *'You win. I don't want to be anywhere near you. Keep your boyfriends away from me, and I'll stay away from you.'*"

It took reading the note three more times before the words finally sunk in. Cosmo looked up. "I win? I win!" He laughed and bounced on the balls of his feet. "Micah! You scared Zedd away for good."

Micah scratched his head, a furrow between his brows. He took the note from Cosmo and chewed on his bottom lip as he looked it over. "I didn't really do that much. And mentioning a body locker still seems like a threat."

"Oh, that. No, he's referencing a conversation we had back when I was planning my funeral party." Cosmo kissed his cheek. "You might not think you did much, but you did what no one else could in the last three years."

"Damn, Micah." Déjà punched his shoulder. "Way to go." She snatched Cosmo's arm and pulled him into a hug. "Thank god!"

"I guess he did look pretty scared when I told him to leave the gallery. He ran all the way back to his car," Micah said. "Still doesn't make sense, though. He had a black eye and his fingers were in splints. What are the odds your new director kicked his ass?"

"Clarence? Please. Zedd is always injuring himself at his gigs. He plays with fireworks and falls off the stage. No, it was all you, Micah, and I know exactly why." Cosmo took the note, then unlocked the door and ushered them inside. He took Micah's luggage bag and set it on the bed. "I hate to say this, because it's horribly unfair to both me and my past lovers, but it's because you're the first man I've dated since Zedd. I was with a trans femme person before this, and two women previous to her. None of them lasted long because Zedd didn't see them as threats. He should have because I thought for sure Marla would gut him like a fish. She didn't. She ghosted me like the others. And I thought you would too."

"Never." Micah locked the door, then tested the front window. After drawing the curtain, he opened his luggage bag and pulled out an alarmingly large filet knife and a roll of duct tape. He glanced at Cosmo, then taped the knife under the coffee table.

Déjà made a slight noise and looked like she was trying to school her face into a neutral expression. Cosmo leaned to her ear. "Stop staring. It's his 'comfort knife.'"

"And he brought it for *you*? Aww."

Cosmo could think of all kinds of comforts to give Micah in return, if he was interested. Starting with pasta. He switched on the TV, and Pinhead's pasty, nail-studded face splashed across the screen. "*Hellraiser* again. Oh, but this is one of the awful straight-to-DVD installments." He handed the remote to Déjà. "Change it to whatever and make yourselves at home. I'm going to start dinner. Don't ask to help. I'm cooking for you."

Déjà kicked off her heels, then sat on the bed and flipped channels. "Not sure I can make myself more at home than Micah just did by taping a knife under the table. You two are so cute it's sickening. You know that, right?"

Micah scrubbed at his arm, sat on the bed beside Déjà, then stood and peered through the curtain again. Cosmo sighed, then set a pot of salted water on to boil and took out the cutting board. Maybe Micah would relax once he had some food in him and was satisfied that Zedd wasn't lurking. This should be a celebration!

Cosmo crushed cloves of garlic with the flat of a knife, then minced them and began peeling the skin off the shallots. Thank goodness he made this dish regularly enough to have all the ingredients needed for a bigger batch. Though he wasn't sure if the amount of cheese in the fridge counted as "criminal."

When the water started to boil, he poured in the penne and pulled out a skillet for the sauce.

Déjà stopped in the kitchen and leaned against the wall, staring at her phone. She tucked a lock of black hair behind her ear. "Were you at Rye's party?"

"Yes. Micah and I danced, and he made so many romantic pledges that I'm going to have to make a list on the fridge to keep track of which ones he's fulfilled."

"I thought that was your hair I spotted in this pic." She frowned and swiped across the screen.

Cosmo wasn't sure he should ask, especially since he thought he knew the answer, but he said, "You and Rye did get together, didn't you? But you broke up."

She glanced up at him, her eyes suddenly watery. "Yeah. Couple months ago. You know how it goes. You get into a fight over something ridiculous that doesn't even matter, then you say things you don't mean just to hurt them. They do it back to you, and before you know it you're alone on your couch eating ice cream out of the tub."

Yes, Cosmo knew exactly how that felt.

"Or standing in front of the open fridge eating shredded cheese out of the bag." Micah stopped beside Cosmo, then pulled a wooden spoon from the utensils container and stirred the noodles.

Déjà chuckled. "I've done that too."

Apparently no one had heard Cosmo when he said he wanted to work alone in the kitchen, but he could hardly be upset that they were here keeping him company.

There'd been times when Cosmo had waited for one of his inamorates to reach out first after an argument, to apologize, and he would have taken them back. But they didn't, and Cosmo had believed that meant they didn't want to have anything to do with him. That had happened with Déjà too. But maybe they'd all been waiting for *him* to reach out.

On the other timeline, Cosmo had thrown himself into Micah's arms after their breakup. On this snagged thread, it had been Micah finding Cosmo. They both still wanted each other.

"Do you still love Rye?" Cosmo asked.

Déjà shrugged, but a tear rolled down her cheek. She blinked rapidly, her false lashes wet. Cosmo set down his chopping knife and pulled her into a tight hug. "Call them. The longer you let this go on, the harder it will be to repair. Or go crash their party. I won't be offended if you leave before dinner. It just means Micah will have to eat more pasta."

Micah made a shooing gesture at Déjà and whispered, "Go, go, go."

Her laugh was part sob. She wiped her eyes. "I'm sorry. I'm being such a bummer. I–"

"*Please.*" Cosmo put his hand on his hip. "I have cried on you more times than I can count. You have every right."

"It's just that... Rye plans their Halloween parties months in advance. We were going to be a retro angel and devil couple. And" – Déjà's chest hitched – "and I told Rye I wanted to be the angel, but they didn't want to be the devil because it was this skin-tight, itchy bodysuit and they have sensory issues. I said they could wear something more comfortable, but they just wanted me to be the devil instead. We argued about it, and the fight was *so stupid*. After that, it seems like the stupid fights just started to increase. And I don't know why I decided to look at their pics from the party tonight; maybe I thought it would make me angrier at them and the breakup would hurt less. But – But they're wearing the devil costume. Why would they–" Her words dissolved into harsh sobs.

"Will you watch the pasta for me?" Cosmo asked Micah.

He ushered Déjà back into the front room and sat with her on the bed as she cried into his shoulder. He rubbed her back until her shudders ebbed.

Micah disappeared into the bathroom, then came back with a box of tissues, which he set on the coffee table and nudged toward Déjà. "Clearly Rye has joined a demonic cult that requires members to endure wedgies and getting glitter stuck in their eye. There's no other explanation."

Déjà laughed. She pulled a tissue from the box and dabbed at her face. "Why do such odd things come out of your mouth?"

"Don't go trying to rescue them. You'll only risk getting indoctrinated into a world of scratchy polyester and having your tail get closed in doors. I've seen this before."

Cosmo bit his lip and stared at Micah with what must have been a bit too much desire, because Micah smiled shyly and scrubbed the back of his neck. He excused himself to go stir the pasta.

Pulling out her phone, Déjà said, "I'm willing to risk it." She typed something out, then blew out a breath and picked up the three-ringed binder she'd brought in from her car. "I can't leave yet, though. I have something to show you."

The binder had a tiny oil painting affixed to the front: an unsettling anatomical blob – one of her ghosts – sitting in a fancy goblet surrounded by grapes and pears. She said, "My mom thought I'd be into scrapbooking because it's 'artsy.'"

Cosmo gagged. "Ew. There's nothing wrong with craft hobbies, but they aren't the same thing as fine art. You told her that, of course."

"You've never met my mom. I'm not going to tell her that. Anyway, I've had this book and all the ephemera sitting in my closet for a long time, and I finally thought of a use for it."

"You filled it with your art?" He hadn't seen anything new of hers in years. "I can't wait to see!"

"There are some little pieces, yeah, but that's not the focus." She ran her hand across the cover. "Do you remember how everyone filled that cremation urn with notes to you at your funeral party? You never took them home. I don't know if you even read them."

He'd been so upset at the time that he'd abandoned all of the decor and party supplies, including an ice cooler and a card table. "I didn't. I forgot about that, actually."

"I went back to the church the next day." Her expression fell, wet lashes fluttering. "I sat there and cried over losing you as I read all the notes from that urn. I wanted to give them to you, but I was also pissed and tired, so I never did. I think it's about time you got them back, though."

She cracked open the book and set it in his lap. Strips of paper ran in rows down the decorative page. An ink sketch of a decrepit church beneath a glittering moon sat at the bottom of the page.

Some people make art, but you <u>are</u> art. You embody the creative spirit we all strive for.

We've only met a couple of times, but you are kind and sweet, and I wish I had half of your style.

I have no doubt your mind is a fascinating place to be. You're a fixture of the art scene, and I can't wait to see what you do in the future.

You have a good soul, and I wish nothing but good things for you. I hope all your dreams come true.

Don't ever stop being yourself, Cosmo.

The notes distorted in Cosmo's vision. People had written about his mind, and his creativity, and his *soul*. They were the antithesis of every comment on his Flashbulb pics. "Thank you. You put so much–" The words lodged in his throat. He pressed the heels of his hands into his eyes until he saw stars.

Déjà said, "You have to promise me that when you start to feel shit about yourself, you open this book and read those notes."

Cosmo nodded. "This is such a lovely gift. Micah, come see this."

It was all he'd wanted from his funeral party. He'd needed that reminder that people cared, and instead he'd gotten into a fist fight with Zedd, and Déjà had broken up their friendship. Even with time being tangled, he couldn't go back and fix that. That version of himself would always feel worthless and alone, wanted only for his external beauty. But it was hard to believe he had no inner worth when there was physical evidence to the contrary.

Maybe he would read one note every day and commit it to memory.

Micah sat on the bed beside Cosmo and looked over the notes. He smiled and kissed Cosmo's temple. "Those are lovely. And they're all true."

Déjà's phone vibrated on the coffee table. She picked it up and pressed it to her generous bosom, then blew out a slow breath and looked at the screen. Her face contorted, eyes filling with tears, and Cosmo hoped Micah didn't make another satanic cult joke because it wasn't going to be funny this time around.

Her breath ratcheted, and she snatched a tissue from the box.

Cosmo sighed. She'd been there for him so many times when it had been him furiously pressing tissues to his face, but seeing her in pain hurt almost as much.

He started to pull her close, but she said, "Rye says they're a mess without me. That they think about me every day."

"Aww!" Happy tears, then. That was so much better. When Cosmo had met Micah at the soda shop after their argument, he wasn't sure if their relationship still had a chance. Micah had said as much on the phone. But he'd fidgeted and blushed and had looked like he'd melt sooner than the milkshakes, so Cosmo was grateful he'd been overt in trying to get Micah back. It didn't seem like Déjà would need to do much to repair things either.

She scrolled up on her phone's screen, then snorted and dabbed her eyes. "Rye says they desperately wish I'd been around to tell them not to make the punch red at the party because Kevin just spilled it all over the carpet."

Cosmo headed into the kitchen and rummaged through the fridge. He handed Déjà a can of club soda. "This might help. Now go. Get your beloved back. Micah and I will be just fine here alone. Won't we?"

Micah nodded, but he pressed his hand beneath the coffee table where he'd taped his knife. Was he still not convinced Zedd was gone for good?

Déjà flicked her hair over her shoulder, pushed up her cleavage, then headed for the door. "Wish me luck."

"I don't think you need it, but good luck, darling."

"Let me walk you to your car," Micah said.

She frowned, her hand on the doorknob. "It's only twenty feet away."

"And you can't run from Jason Voorhees in stilettos."

Maybe Cosmo needed to change the TV to something more wholesome. "Those are wedge heels, Micah."

"Oh. My mistake. You're fine, then." He opened the door and ushered Déjà out. "But just in case."

Cosmo went back to finish dinner – he hadn't even chopped the shallots yet – and eyed Zedd's note on the counter. Micah was being paranoid, and Cosmo wouldn't hold it against the poor love since he had history with being attacked in his home, but every second Micah was outside was dialing up Cosmo's doubt. He needed to convince Micah everything was fine otherwise they'd *both* be reaching for that knife under the coffee table.

21

MY HEART GOES BANG (GET ME TO THE DOCTOR)

Micah - Snagged Thread

The night air smelled heavily of damp leaves and pot as Déjà climbed into her car. It was too dark out here, the silence so thick Micah was aware of his breathing and heartbeat. He glanced back at the warm glow coming from behind Cosmo's curtains, which looked like an invitation to be singled out among all the other darkened windows. Zedd had conceded, but it felt like a trick. Something was wrong with this situation, and it was frustrating that Micah couldn't figure out what it was.

He startled as Déjà turned on her car. She rolled down the window and leaned her elbow on the sill. "Thanks, white knight, but I don't think we're going to have to run from Jason or Pinhead tonight."

"Who said I wanted to run from Pinhead? He's kinda hot."

"It's the leather, huh?" She flipped down the sun visor and stared into the mirror, applying a fresh coat of red-hot lipstick.

"Everyone looks good in leather. Suits. Lingerie."

"Gonna disagree simply because I don't want to see Pinhead in a babydoll and heels, but Cosmo has all kinds of outfits that I'm sure he'd wear for you if you were interested."

Oh, now that was an image. He realized Déjà was saying his name. "Sorry. I went somewhere for a moment."

"Clearly." She grinned. "You're good for each other. He makes you want to live again."

The statement took Micah aback. His eyes watered, a sudden lump in his throat. "What? Why would you presume–"

"I'm not presuming. And I don't mean that love has magically cured your mental health. That's would cheapen what you've struggled with. I'm sure it's been a hard road to recovery. But Cosmo is motivating you. All that murky red and black in your magnetic field is being drowned out with ribbons of bright green and orange. And Cosmo's magenta aura is the supernova it's always been."

Micah glanced at Cosmo's apartment. "What does magenta mean?"

"Someone free-spirited. Artistic. A little bit shocking in their non-conformity."

"I like that color. Hey" – he squeezed her hand – "good luck with Rye."

"Am I overdoing it with the cleavage? Don't want to look desperate."

Déjà had an ample amount of, well, everything, and her dress complimented her shape, but she'd pulled the neckline low enough to expose the lacy edges of a black bra. The thought of Cosmo in lingerie threatened to make Micah's heart stop, but he was useless in this scenario.

"You're asking the wrong person. Sorry."

She laughed and rolled up her window, then pulled out of the parking space. Micah hurried back up the steps, glancing at the dark bushes before opening the door and locking it behind him.

Cosmo stood at the sink, running water over a colander of pasta. "Was about to go out there to rescue you."

"You've seen horror movies, so you should know that's a terrible idea."

Cosmo scraped garlic and shallots off the cutting board with the edge of a knife and into a skillet, where they sizzled and released a savory fragrance that made Micah's stomach groan. "You still seem on edge. Are you getting presque vu that something is going to happen?"

"No."

"Are you thinking about... About what happened to *you*?"

Micah tensed. He had been but only in the general sense that he didn't want Cosmo hurt. "I'm just worried that the note from Zedd is some kind of trick."

"Darling, he's not clever enough for tricks. He has no subtlety. If he said I've won and he's leaving me alone, then it's the truth. Do you want to make a bet?" Cosmo pulled out his phone and tapped the Flashbulb app. "I'll bet you that there isn't a single harassing comment from one of his throwaway accounts that's dated *after* you threatened him at the gallery. If I'm wrong... I'll delete my account."

Micah raised his eyebrows. Magenta aura or not, he hadn't expected Cosmo to wager that. Not when it seemed to be something he enjoyed so much. "And if you're right?"

"Then you spend the night in my bed," Cosmo whispered. Micah sucked in a breath, and Cosmo said, "It doesn't have to be anything sexual. I just want you to stay with me tonight even without a threat to my safety. Wouldn't want you to have brought your toothbrush for nothing."

"I'll take that bet."

"Good." Cosmo added a can of tomato paste to his skillet of sizzling aromatics, then tapped his notifications. He clucked his tongue. "I'm a 'frigid twink' am I? That's a new one."

Micah scowled. "Is that from Zedd?"

"No, just some rando who didn't take kindly to my snarky reply. The last comment from that account with Zedd's band pic is dated the same day you were at the gallery. And none of the other comments mention Zedd." He showed Micah the screen. "See? The comments stopped."

"What about your DMs?" Micah asked.

Pulling a bottle of vodka from a cabinet, Cosmo said, "DMs weren't a part of our original bet."

He wasn't sure why that mattered when they were trying to make sure Cosmo was truly safe from Zedd, but Micah had a card up his sleeve. "Then I'll sweeten it. If I'm wrong, not only will I stay with you tonight, I'll go to therapy."

"Oh, we're getting serious now." Cosmo set down the vodka and swiped a lock of hair from his eyes. "That's asking too much. It's not something you should be pushed into."

"C'mon. My parents would take that bet in a heartbeat. Well, the me going to therapy part. I don't think they'd want me to spend the night in their bed. I outgrew that decades ago."

"Alright, but if you change your mind, I won't hold you to it."

Micah stirred the simmering sauce on the stove as Cosmo tapped at his phone and handed Micah other ingredients: heavy cream, a cube of butter, Parmesan cheese.

"Well, I have a lot of bots asking me to become an 'ambassador' for their queer clothing line. And for twenty-nine ninety-nine I can buy ten thousand subscribers. How about that?" Cosmo frowned and clicked on a message.

"Is it Zedd?"

"Hard to say. They have a default profile picture, no followers, and no bio." After staring at the message, Cosmo stiffened. His mouth flattened into a hard line, then he handed the phone to Micah. "Don't you dare click those pictures. You'll lose your appetite."

The message said, *Don't you know how much I want to take care of you? I'll do it so well.*

Below the message was a series of blurred photos that all warned him they might contain sensitive content. Ew. Micah knew what those were without clicking. The very last message, dated today, said, *What do I have to do to get your attention?*

Just a bunch of unsolicited dick pics. Even Micah got messages like that, though in his case it was usually a "lonely" woman who wanted to send him nudes – certainly for a price.

It could be Zedd, but there were so many random throwaway accounts on the internet that there was no way to know for certain. He hoped Zedd's note really was as surface level as it seemed. The idea that Micah had scared him away for good, had protected Cosmo and kept him safe, made pride swell beneath his ribs.

He wrapped his arms around Cosmo's waist. "Alright. I'm convinced. I cheated on our bet, though. I was already planning to go to therapy. I have an appointment set up."

Cosmo gasped and stopped stirring the vodka sauce. "That's wonderful! I'm so happy to hear that. I know you had issues with therapy before, but hopefully you just need to find a therapist who is the right fit for you."

He'd been told that before – by Everett, by Mom and Dad, even by Ximena – and it made sense, of course. But what if there *wasn't* a therapist out there who was the right fit for him? What if he hated all of them?

Micah didn't need to work himself up over non-existent problems again. Especially not right now. "Yeah. I'm just going to focus on making it to this first appointment, then assess from there."

"When is it?"

"Not as soon as I need, but it's better than never, right?"

"Absolutely. And I'm much happier to hear you're going to go on your own volition and not because you lost a bet. But I must confess that I cheated too." He set down his spoon, then tapped at his phone. "I just deleted my account anyway."

"Really? You won't miss it?"

"I might at first, but it's better this way. It felt like such a necessary source of validation, but all the lewd comments were getting to me, you know? I don't need that kind of attention. I take screenshots of all of the weird messages and comments I receive in case the police need them, but I'm tired of fielding them. It will be easier without the account."

"You're worth so much more than the sum of comments from internet strangers. You deserve love for your inner beauty." He brushed curls from Cosmo's neck then kissed his throat, savoring the beat of Cosmo's pulse against his lips.

Cosmo let out a soft moan and dug his fingers into Micah's hair. "Dessert before dinner is not allowed." He let Micah's lips linger a moment longer before pulling away and pointing at a cabinet. "Be a love and pull down a couple of plates for us, will you?"

Instead of a dining table, which there wasn't room for in the tiny studio, a high counter sat in a small nook off of the kitchen, with two stools side by side. They wouldn't be able to eat facing each other, but if they were at Micah's, their choices would have been the couch or the floor.

Cosmo plated the food, and Micah set silverware and napkins at the counter. They sat down, and Micah took a large bite of penne drenched in sauce. He groaned as the rich, acidic flavor filled his mouth. He should have let it cool down a bit, but it was delicious. "Oh my god. Amazing. You won't end up with any leftovers because I'm going to wake up in the night and eat it all."

"Good!" Cosmo's phone vibrated. He checked it and said, "Déjà said she and Rye are talking. It's going well."

"That's great to hear. I hope it works out for her." He focused on making a dent in the heaping pile of pasta before him.

Cosmo's bare foot suddenly slid against his ankle and beneath his pant leg. Micah swallowed thickly and stuffed a forkful of pasta in his mouth. Despite what Cosmo promised about nothing needing to be sexual between them tonight, the idea of spending the night in his bed made Micah's stomach clench. He had no doubt Cosmo would respect his boundaries; his nerves stemmed from the idea that maybe tonight, with Cosmo, he didn't want any.

Even if there was zero risk of Zedd showing up, Micah wanted to be as close as possible to Cosmo. He wanted to hold on and never let go.

Cosmo's toes were still sliding beneath Micah's pant leg. Micah pushed away his plate. "As delicious as this is, I don't think I can eat anymore right now."

"Am I making you flustered?" Cosmo pulled his foot away. "I'll stop."

"Don't stop. But maybe we can go sit somewhere more comfortable?"

"Yes." Cosmo stacked their dishes and hurried into the kitchen. He portioned things into containers and dumped pans in the sink.

Micah took off his shoes and sat on the bed, trying to push away the nervous ache in his stomach. At least it was for a good reason this time.

Déjà had switched the TV to a home improvement channel, and the hosts were *ooh*ing over glittery Styrofoam pumpkins with rustic bows. Cosmo stopped beside the bed and wrinkled his nose at the TV, then handed Micah a tall glass of what was probably a screwdriver.

"I don't know how it was when you lived there, but there haven't ever been many trick-or-treaters since I've lived at the complex," Micah said, "but this year I'm going to have to shut off all the lights and put a sign on the door asking people not to knock. Maybe I could just set a bowl of candy outside."

"I hate that you have to worry about those things."

"No pity. You promised." Micah sipped his drink. "But I'd love your help again if you can come to my place tomorrow?"

Cosmo switched off the TV, then pulled a record from its sleeve and set it on the turntable. "Of course. I'm happy to." He turned on the receiver and set the stylus on the record. Funky synth filled the room, followed by Prince's falsetto commentary on all the gossip surrounding him. He sat back down on the bed. "You don't mind some music, do you?"

"You're asking permission three years too late. No Soft Cell?" Micah slid his toes up Cosmo's ankle and watched as Cosmo's eyes widened slightly.

"Listen, future ghost, I was living in that studio long before you. From my perspective, you were haunting *me*. Always on the phone with your French telemarketers and lurking as a shadowy figure in the hallway."

The bed creaked as Micah pressed Cosmo back against the pillows and kissed him softly. "I'm not going to complain with any earnestness because I don't want to jinx it and have the universe take you away. I'm not letting you go anywhere."

Cosmo's lips parted, and he slid his hands around Micah's waist. There was guarded hope in his voice as he said, "And what are you going to do with me now that you have me?"

"I want to be close to you. As close as I can get. It's hard for me to pick apart exactly where that feeling is coming from. If it's purely romantic or if there's some low-grade sexual attraction mixed in. Maybe we can just… see where this goes?"

Cosmo's voice was barely a whisper. "Yes. Yes, let's. I'll follow your lead."

Dark curls hung in Cosmo's eyes, and Micah swept them away. He left a peck on each shimmery eyelid, down his cheek, and kissed the lingering hint of citrus from his dianthus lips. "I want to be inside you. In your blood. Your veins. I want to haunt the valves of your heart, the way you haunt mine."

Cosmo grabbed a fistful of Micah's hair, tugged his head close, and hissed in his ear. "You already are. This chapel is dedicated to you."

Micah lost himself in Cosmo's leaded glass gaze and the warmth of his hallowed halls. "You're my muse. You inspire me, motivate me. You make me want to put the broken pieces of myself back together."

It had only been two months since the first message on Micah's mirror appeared, but three years had passed for Cosmo. Micah wanted to make up for all the empty moments that had occurred before they met in person. He was intent to learn every desire in Cosmo's heart and make sure they happened.

Sometime during the night, Micah's eyes flew open, his pulse racing. Someone had tapped on the window.

No. Wait. It was presque vu. It hadn't happened. But it had on the other timeline. He hadn't sensed anything off during the other events of the day, which meant that this moment, for whatever reason, was slightly shifted from where it was supposed to be. Maybe it was Déjà's butterfly effect or some other cosmic reason Micah didn't have time to figure out right now.

Cosmo slept on his back, one arm thrown over his face and his mouth open slightly. Snatching his glasses off the coffee table, Micah blinked in the darkness and strained for more sound. After groping through the clothes on the floor, he found his jeans and pulled them on, then peeled the knife from under the table.

Zedd's note was a trick to lull them into a sense of false security. It had to be. Why would someone be tapping on the window in the middle of the night? But the only thing that note had guaranteed was that Micah spent the night holding Cosmo close.

"Your plan backfired, asshole," Micah whispered.

A soft *tap-tap* came at the window, and he jumped and squeezed the knife handle. Okay, he had the upper hand here. What was going to happen next? The doorknob would jiggle. The light from a weak flashlight would cut through the darkness outside the window, but Micah had ensured the curtains were drawn tight; there was no way for the person to see inside.

He could jump up right now and fling open the door, brandishing the knife. No, that was a terrible idea. Then the door would be wide open, and Cosmo would be exposed. Zedd would shove past Micah, walk over the threshold and inside.

That thought made Micah's chest seize up and his joints rust. No, no, no. What happened to Micah was *not* going to happen to Cosmo.

The doorknob jiggled, and Micah squeaked and dropped the knife. Jesus! Even if he didn't open the door, he should at least shout through it that he was calling the cops and scare Zedd away. But he was frozen to the spot, still imagining Zedd's motorcycle boots clomping over the threshold.

A flashlight beam wavered outside and tried shining through the window. He held his breath, waiting for something else to happen, but after a moment the flashlight clicked off and footsteps crunched through brush. A car door slammed.

The sound broke Micah from his paralysis. He crept to the window and parted the curtain with trembling fingers, but only caught a glimpse of glowing taillights as a car pulled away.

22

THE SUN ALWAYS SHINES ON T.V.

Micah - Snagged Thread

Today was a new day, and instead of asking himself what could go wrong, Micah was forcing himself to wonder what could go *right*.

Telling Cosmo that Zedd had been slinking around and testing the doorknob in the middle of the night hadn't gone right. He'd been convinced Micah had only dreamed it, insisting that he was a very light sleeper and if someone had knocked at the window or Micah had gotten up for any reason, that Cosmo would have woken up. And he *had* woken when Micah got out of bed later to use the bathroom. But none of what happened had felt like a dream.

Despite his dubiousness, Cosmo said he'd take the newest note to the police, and he'd promised to text Micah throughout the day so Micah knew he was okay until they were together again. Which would be sometime soon. Micah was going to practice letting him inside. There was still the potential for something to go right.

His phone vibrated with a text. <*Hellooooo darling. 🌿 I'm outside, and I have a hot, girthy, cream-filled banana bread for you.* 🍌 ✨>

Micah chuckled and opened the door. "My mouth is ready."

Cosmo stood on the step wearing an orange cardigan and plaid pants, a pan of bread in his hands. He cocked his eyebrow and smirked. "I like the sound of that. And I have good news! Here, take the bread."

After setting the pan of bread on the kitchen counter – it smelled heavenly – he joined Cosmo outside. A cigarette jutted from Cosmo's lips as he leaned against the railing, his gaze on the gray sky. His cheekbones shimmered with some kind of highlighter that matched his cardigan, and little cartoon decals of ghosts and pumpkins adorned his nails. He looked like the patron spirit of Autumn, and if he tasted like pumpkin spice, Micah wouldn't be surprised.

Smoke rolled out of Cosmo's nostrils. "So, I got my nails done."

Bringing Cosmo's fingers to his lips, Micah kissed each one, even though they smelled like cigarettes now. "I noticed. Very cute. Is that your good news?"

"No. Afterward, I went to the police with Zedd's note and I told them what you said about him skulking around. They said it probably wasn't him. It was either them – the police, I mean – or the pranksters they've been looking for. I guess the popular social media dare right now is to knock on someone's window at night, and if they open the door, they're hit with condiment packets from Jojo's. You know, the ones everyone hates because all you need to do is breathe on them for them to explode and get all over you?"

"Good lord. Don't kids have, like, homework they should be doing?"

"Did *you* do your homework?"

"No." And as much as Micah was afraid to concede and let his guard down, it *was* almost Halloween. Scaring people into opening the door in the middle of the night wasn't funny, but Micah was grateful he hadn't lunged over the threshold with a filet knife.

Cosmo held up his finger. "I begged the police to go talk to Zedd anyway. They tried, but he wasn't home. Neighbor said they hadn't seen him since yesterday afternoon when he was loading band equipment into the drummer's van. He was off to go do a gig in Fairview. I'm sure it's the same venue he's always at there, where they play late into the night."

It was hard to refute that. And Micah had been intent to focus on what could go right today. "I never thought teens pegging people with ranch packets would be something to be grateful for, but I'll take it."

Cosmo stubbed out his cigarette. "Do you feel better?"

He blew a deep breath through his nose. "Yeah." Now he needed to address the fact that they were still standing on the balcony.

He thought about how he'd played with Cosmo's hair as he read to him in bed the night before, both of them content, their bodies wrapped up in each other. Thought of their heartbeats pounding into each other, of Cosmo's spiced berry scent and slender fingers. Dancing, tears dragging mascara down Cosmo's cheek as Micah promised to give him all the love he deserved.

Before he could think it through, he gripped Cosmo's wrist and pulled him over the threshold and into the apartment. He slammed the door shut and locked it, every muscle tensed to protect the eggshell fragility of his conviction against the roaring panic he was certain would come. But it didn't. There were no klaxons of *Bad! Stop!* No sensation of having the wind knocked out of him or his feet cemented to the floor.

Cosmo stood stiffly beside him with a look of shock on his face. "Uh. Okay..."

Tension unspooled from his shoulders. He'd done it. They were both standing inside like it was nothing. Like it was normal. For nine months, he'd been bested by that dented and dusty threshold. For nine months, he couldn't let someone walk over that strip of metal. But he hadn't been focused on the threshold this time, only about all the things Cosmo made him feel. There'd been no time for his brain to unleash the monster of panic, just like when he'd run into the studio to rescue Cosmo from past-Ximena's exploding lightbulbs.

The solution seemed so easy. A red-hot coal burned in Micah's chest. He should have been able to let Cosmo in from the beginning. It shouldn't have been this hard. And the knowledge that it was still only Cosmo this worked with made the coal in his center smolder even more.

Cosmo searched his face. "It – It worked?"

"It worked."

Cosmo bounced on the balls of his feet and clapped his hands. "Darling!"

Resisting the urge to drive his fist through something, he gave Cosmo a gentle peck on the lips and tried to feel some of the joy Cosmo was clearly experiencing for him.

The scent of banana, cinnamon, and cream cheese filled the kitchen. Micah pulled down a plate, then paused as he reached for a knife. He needed two plates. He had company, and he needed two plates. His fantasies were as simple in theory as Cosmo's, but just as difficult in practice. Why? Why was it so difficult?

"Look at us!" Cosmo said. "You let me in without a problem and now we're eating my baking. I am so proud of you."

Clenching his jaw, Micah shook his head and said, "You shouldn't be."

"Why ever not?"

Micah scowled at the door, at that stupid goddamn threshold. "Because it shouldn't have been this hard for me to do in the first place! I'm so far from having my shit together. You didn't see the state I was in after my assault." He flung an arm toward the empty couch. "For Christ's sake, I told you how I looked just a week ago after you broke up with me. It was disgusting. It's a miracle that couch doesn't smell like armpits. After your assault, you didn't crawl into a bed and stay there for three months. You didn't stop showering or cleaning or eating."

Cosmo's eyes widened. "What happened to me wasn't—"

"I know you're hurting. But you got out of the bad situation you were in. I'm proud of that. You confessed to me the things you want and deserve, and now we're doing them. I'm proud of you for that too."

"I'm not allowed to be proud of *you* for making progress?"

Micah opened his mouth, then closed it again. He rubbed his forehead, eyes shut, unsure of what to say.

Cosmo said, "I realize that seeing your progress isn't as easy as comparing one of your old drawings to a new one, but I'll bet it would be just as dramatic if you could. And not only have you let me inside without panicking, you've got your reception at Night Gallery—"

"I puked my guts out in the gallery restroom over the idea of having to sketch Simone in front of an audience," he blurted. "I'm going to panic and fail."

"What? But–"

"You vouched for me, and I don't want to do anything that would jeopardize your job there. You can't go back to Identical Dog."

Cosmo stiffened. "Right. My worthless ass is going to go crawling back to Royce because I couldn't possibly get a job at some other gallery. The only thing I have working for me is my looks."

"I didn't mean it like that."

"Didn't you?" Cosmo's mouth twisted, and he hugged his arms to his chest. "It's what everyone else thinks, so why shouldn't you?"

"I swear I didn't. I've just been thinking about us being on this snagged thread, and how..." He shook his head. Neither of them knew how this parallel universe business worked, and it was foolish to presume it would try to pull Cosmo back to Identical Dog to correct the timeline when he was standing right here telling Micah it wouldn't happen. "I'm sorry. I'm being an asshole." He walked outside and rested his elbows on the balcony railing. The scent of laundry soap mingled with exhaust, and a chihuahua peed on the tire of a car before trotting away. Someone hacked and coughed from a nearby unit, and a conversation drifted in what might have been Thai.

The fire that had been smoldering in his chest had died, washed away by the realization that he was letting his mental health push Cosmo away again. He walked back in, vaguely noticing that he hadn't hesitated, even though he knew Cosmo was inside.

Cosmo sat on the couch, squeezing an accent pillow. He didn't look up when Micah approached, but whispered, "I'm sorry. I shouldn't have told Simone that you would sketch her without knowing if it was okay first."

"I'm sorry too. I let you in without a problem, and it made me so angry with myself for some reason. You didn't deserve to have that directed at you. You've had nothing but good intentions, and of course you could get a job at some other gallery." He sank onto the couch and slid his arm around Cosmo. "The couch doesn't smell like armpits, right?"

Cosmo pressed his face to the pillow, then wrinkled his nose. "It's a little ripe."

"Damn it."

"I'm joking. It smells fine. Did we just have another fight?"

"I guess we kind of did." So much for things continuing to go right today.

"Then I'm getting better at this. Normally all my arguments with partners end in fist fights or things being thrown over balconies."

Micah cringed. "I suppose it depends a lot on who you're arguing with."

"Shh. I'm proud of myself for not hurling the banana bread into the parking lot. Don't spoil my moment."

"If you had, I would have eaten it off of the road." And he vowed never to get into that kind of argument with Cosmo. He wasn't ever going to be like Zedd.

"No need for that." Cosmo stared at the carpet between his feet. "Do you still want a piece?"

"Absolutely." Micah didn't want to ruin this moment for Cosmo. He was going to take a huge bite of the bread and tell him it was the most delicious thing he'd ever eaten. Even if it was full of spiders. Or candy corn.

After walking into the kitchen, Cosmo cut into the bread and served them both a slice. A wide ribbon of cream ran through the center. Before Micah could pick up the slice, Cosmo broke off a chunk and fed it to him. Cream cheese and soft, spiced bread melted on his tongue. He moaned and sagged against the counter.

Cosmo watched, a small smile playing at his lips. "You like it?"

"God." Micah chewed, cream sticking to his gums. "It's incredible."

"Oh good!" He pulled off another piece and pushed it into Micah's mouth, even though Micah hadn't yet swallowed the first bite.

Once Micah was certain Cosmo wouldn't have to give him the Heimlich maneuver, he poured himself a glass of milk and said, "I can't believe your ex didn't like your baking. I can't believe that anyone wouldn't like it. The coffee shop on the corner has the best muffins, but I'm ruined now. They're going to taste like dirt compared to this."

"I can make muffins too."

"Marry me."

Cosmo smiled. He cocked his head, toying with the hem of Micah's shirt. "If the event is stressing you out, I'll tell Simone right now that you can't do it. You can draw her from a photo or something instead."

"No, please don't do that. I think I can do it if you help me practice. Will you pose for me? Let me draw you? Or are you too mad at me?"

Cosmo tugged on one earring. "I think the conclusion we can come to is we're both that GIF of a flaming dumpster floating down a flooded street, but we're helping each other get better. We should both be proud of that, don't you think?"

Micah nodded. He would never scoff at Cosmo's achievements, no matter how small they seemed to be from an outside perspective, and he needed to allow himself the same understanding.

"I'd love to help you out with this."

"Great." Micah sighed. "I don't need to do the whole portrait. Just the act of having you pose in the living room while I start sketching will be enough to help."

He headed into the living room, pulled out his pad of drawing paper, and set it on the easel. He took his pencils from the drafting table and dropped them into the little plastic cup on the easel tray. This used to be a ritual he enjoyed. Sharpen his pencils, wiggle the easel around to face the front room, roll up his chair. *Please get comfortable. Tell me something about you. Do you have kids? Pets?*

"Micah?"

He looked up. "Huh?"

"I said, 'what do I need to do?' Do you want me to pose a certain way or stand in a particular spot?"

"Right there is fine. Can you shift most of your weight to one leg?"

Cosmo was a natural at poses, which had been clear from his Flashbulb pictures. He shifted, his hip jutting out and adding visual interest to the line of his body. Light from the front window picked up amber highlights in his hair. Micah gripped a pencil, his mind trying to drift to places he normally avoided.

The man's name had been Derek, and Micah didn't ever want to know their names now. He'd come inside and said, *You have so many plants. The first time I ever walked by, I thought a woman lived here.* It had caught Micah off-guard, needling a part of him that still worried about being perceived as a gender he wasn't, until he decided the comment was just plain sexist and odd. *The first time I ever walked by.*

But he'd brushed it off and set up his drawing tools anyway.

Cosmo had pulled off his cardigan and opened the first two buttons of his shirt. He saucily slid the shirt off one shoulder and winked. "Should I take it off?"

"Um... Yes, sure." He was trying to have fun with this, to put Micah at ease. "Your pants too, if you want."

Grinning, Cosmo pulled off his shirt. His ribs flexed beneath his fair skin, and a thin silver necklace chain sparkled against his collarbones. His arms were lean, shoulders and elbows and wrists all sharp angles. Veins snaked up his hands and into his forearms. He unbuttoned his pants and pushed them off.

Micah needed to concentrate on Cosmo. On his task at hand. He didn't need to think about Derek, or how eager he'd been to get started.

He didn't need to think about Derek asking for a glass of water, and as Micah turned to fetch it, Derek ripped the replica sculpture of *Comedian* from the wall and smashed it into Micah's face. His glasses had shattered, and a piece of the lens went straight into his eye. Then Derek hit him again. The worst part was never understanding why Derek had done it. He hadn't tried to rape Micah. He hadn't stolen his wallet or his electronics. His family had suggested it was a hate crime, but Micah passed well enough as a cis man that he didn't know how Derek would have known he was trans. His thoughts only circled back to the idea that there was no motivation – it had been violence for violence's sake – and the notion kept him awake more nights than the pain in his face had.

Cosmo plucked the pencil from Micah's hand. "We should stop."

"What? No."

"You're clearly upset."

Whatever Micah had looked like just then, it hadn't been the result Cosmo was aiming for. Micah took his pencil back and loosely started a sketch. "I'm okay. Please."

For a moment, Cosmo just stood there, but Micah kept drawing, so he walked back into the center of the room, standing at the edge of a blade of light streaming through the curtains. Pink indentations remained on his calves after he peeled off his socks. His knees were prominent knobs, and dark hair ran across his thighs.

Micah forced his shoulders to relax, his hand sketching more from muscle memory than conscious effort. He drew the jut of Cosmo's hips, his narrow waist, and his navel.

"Can you tell how flat my ass is from this angle?"

"Do you want me to give you a more generous one?" Micah asked.

"No. That would be a lie." Cosmo smirked. "Just make sure you get my banana bread right, okay?"

The tip of Micah's pencil broke against the paper.

Cosmo walked to the easel and clucked his tongue. He slid his hand along Micah's neck. "You don't seem like you panicked doing this, but you also don't look like you're having a good time."

Micah thought about the sharp metallic tang of blood in his mouth, of trying to scream but nothing coming out, each blow of the sculpture making him more confused and sluggish until he couldn't fight back at all. "Maybe I don't want to draw anymore."

"Should I get dressed?"

"Yeah."

After donning his clothes, Cosmo sat on the couch, and Micah joined him. Cosmo pulled Micah's head into his lap. "Your assault broke you." It was a whisper of a question, neither pity nor callousness in Cosmo's voice as he ran his nails along Micah's scalp.

"Quite literally. Fractured my eye socket. But yeah, I feel like a dropped vase. The mess is long gone, but for nearly a year I've been crawling around on the kitchen floor, trying to find all the scattered pieces. But one's under the fridge and a couple got thrown away, and even put back together, you can see all the seams that make me."

"You're a beautiful vase, though. I'm glad you exist."

A lump formed in Micah's throat. He squeezed Cosmo's hand and kissed his knuckles. "Thank you."

"I'm an urn with a huge crack running down the side, and all my ashes have fallen out and blown away in the wind," Cosmo said.

"Then you're the perfect empty vessel to fill with good things now. Late night conversations, books in bed, graveyard dates... Cookies."

"You'd fill a funeral urn with cookies?"

"You know I would." Micah's nose stung. He sat up and squeezed Cosmo hard. "I'm glad you exist too."

"I–" Cosmo's breath tickled his ear, his voice hitching. "I keep thinking about Royce. The smell of his aftershave. His windbreaker. His hands. Telling me I wanted it."

Micah held him harder. "I'm so sorry."

"But you know, I do feel better after deleting my Flashbulb account. I think it contributed a lot to me feeling like I'm worthless. Which we both know isn't true. We've already established that I'm your muse – a cracked urn full of cookies."

"I'll fill you with whatever you want."

He expected Cosmo to suggest something dirty, but his eyes were full of hope. "With love?"

"Oh, yes." Micah trailed a finger down Cosmo's sternum and stopped at his heart. "So much that the lid is never going to fit back on."

23

THE KILLING MOON

Cosmo - Snagged Thread

People drifted through the gallery halls with their tiny flutes of champagne, remarking on Eddy Marquez's vision for his peculiar still lifes of bloody cuts of beef. They mused that he'd surely been going through something traumatic and dark to create such pieces, and hopefully the poor man was getting out of his depressive episode. The truth was Eddy was a butcher and had merely found it to be convenient subject matter. Although that in itself probably spoke to his state of mind.

As Night Gallery's newest artist, Micah's exhibit was directly up front by the refreshment table, and for once, Cosmo wished he was the art handler. The handler had done a fine job of mounting the portraits, but Cosmo could have been the one framing and displaying Micah's art with care.

Pulling the pocket square from his jacket, he rubbed a fingerprint from the glass over one of the drawings.

Someone behind him exclaimed, "Oh, I love these. Wait, they're of you!"

A cluster of people had gathered, their gazes jumping from the portraits to Cosmo. He put a hand under his chin and batted his lashes. "Aren't they fabulous?" The only thing these people loved more than art was gossip, and Cosmo had gotten permission to spill this particular secret. He leaned forward, teeth pressing into his lip. "You didn't hear this from me, but nearly all of these portraits were done over the phone. Micah talks to random strangers – telemarketers, restaurant hostesses, sex line operators – and gets them to describe themselves for him."

A woman gasped, and the people around her murmured. "How strange."

"Isn't it, though? He's very eccentric."

"Is that how he drew you? If so, he did an amazing job."

"He saw me very briefly during a chance encounter, and was so enamored with my look that he was compelled to draw me. He's done my portrait over the phone too, and I must say that it was a thrilling experience."

"I've never heard of such a thing. What a unique way to draw someone. Their own perceptions of themselves must come out in the drawings. Almost like he's drawing their inner selves."

Cosmo grinned. "That's why they're all so beautiful."

The woman plucked a business card from the holder beside the exhibit. "He'd draw me this way, wouldn't he?"

"Well... It's supposed to be a secret, but I'm sure if you asked him nicely, he'd love to do this sort of commission for you."

Other people reached for business cards, and by the time they drifted away to another exhibit, half of the cards were gone. Micah was going to have all the phone calls he could handle.

Cosmo had seen his beau only for a moment before Simone whisked him away to discuss her portrait. Hopefully his initial nerves would wear off as he sank into the routine of drawing.

When Cosmo had been standing in the living room, slowly stripping, Micah's gaze kept flitting away, roaming over some memory only he could see. His breath had quickened, hand visibly shaking as he wielded his pencil.

He wanted to take that pain away from Micah as much as Micah wanted to take away Cosmo's. Hopefully Micah would call his brother after the event was over and brag about how well he did.

Checking his watch, Cosmo excused himself from chatting patrons and walked down the halls. After peering into Simone's empty office, he stopped at the easel set up near the reception area, but Micah wasn't there either. He was supposed to be on in less than fifteen minutes.

Loud retching came from the bathroom. The soles of Micah's loafers peeked from beneath a stall door.

Shit. "Oh, honey. Okay." He pulled out his phone. "I'll tell Simone you can't do this."

"No!" Micah's voice was hoarse and desperate. He coughed. "No, I have to."

"You don't, and if Simone knew it was making you so anxious you were puking up the hors d'oeuvres, she would tell you the same."

The toilet flushed, and the stall door slammed open. Micah's face was pale and sweaty, his glasses dangling from his hand and tie tossed over one shoulder. He splashed water on his face, gargled, and raked back his hair.

"The first time I came back to your place, I could tell how badly you wanted to be able to let me inside," Cosmo said. "But a desire for something isn't always enough to power through. You needed time and practice to get me into your apartment. And now I can stand inside without hurting you. This is just another hurdle that requires more time."

Micah blotted his brow with a paper towel. "Or an alternative? Maybe I could sketch you again instead of Simone, if you were up for it. Clothed, this time."

It seemed better to call the whole thing off, but if Micah needed to do this for his own sense of accomplishment, then so be it.

After sending a message to Simone, Cosmo tucked Micah's tie back into his vest, straightened his collar, and kissed his clammy brow.

His phone jingled with a reply, and he read it aloud. "*'I'm so sorry to hear that. I was looking forward to my portrait, but this night was supposed to be a fun way for Micah to meet potential clients, not cause him stress. If it's better for him to draw you instead, that's totally fine. Did you ever meet Franchesca? She couldn't paint unless she had 3 cups of decaf coffee, her favorite slippers, and daytime court shows playing in the background. She did a live painting event and we had to find her a laptop and play Judge Judy before she'd get started.'*"

Cosmo tapped his lips. "I *did* meet Franchesca. She was lovely."

"I'm glad she's accommodating, but I know you can't be my Emotional Support Lover for everything I do."

"I'm your muse, remember, so that seems perfectly appropriate." He tucked his phone away and headed for the door. "I think I saw some seltzer water. I'll snatch you some quick. Meet you at the easel."

Slipping through attendees and managing to avoid getting sucked into any conversations, Cosmo stopped at the refreshment table and skimmed past the carpaccio and assortment of cheeses. A few remaining flutes of champagne sat out but probably wouldn't help Micah's stomach.

The chatter faded as he headed down exhibit halls to the break room. Much less fancy fare of day-old bagels and a Tupperware tub of brownies Clarence's wife had made sat on one of the tables. Poking his head into the fridge, he pushed past forgotten condiment packets and coffee creamer.

"I *know* I saw seltzer somewhere."

A shadow loomed, and a hand offered Cosmo a bottle of seltzer water over the top of the fridge door.

"Thank you! Where was it?"

"On the counter," Royce said.

Cosmo straightened so fast that he banged his head on the freezer handle, but he barely felt it. He clutched the bottle to his chest and backed away, blood pounding in his temples. "You have some nerve."

Royce stared with pursed lips, his expression that of a person who had something to say that they'd rather not. "If Simone knew I was here, she'd throw me out on my ass. And I hate that it's come to that. She and Hina used to be such good friends, and Hina doesn't even talk about Simone anymore. The galleries have become rivals, and it's all your fault."

Cosmo's chest felt like it had been run through with a red-hot poker. "I need to go." He tried to hurry around Royce, but Royce stepped into his path and held out his arms. His fucking tie was crooked – always crooked – and the sight of it made Cosmo want to sock the man in the face.

"Just a moment. I'd been hoping to smooth things over. I even got you a gift."

"I don't want your gifts." What Cosmo wanted was *out of this room*, even if he had to dive through Royce's legs. He couldn't stand here a second longer.

"I know how dramatic and emotional you can get, and I should have thought about that when you told me in the bar that you needed love. Kissing you then was terrible timing, and being drunk is not an excuse. I'm sorry it upset you so much."

Royce stepped forward, pinning Cosmo between the counter and the table of bagels. No one was in the back part of the gallery right now. Cosmo hadn't passed anyone in the halls. They were all too busy sipping their champagne and pocketing Micah's business cards.

Deep furrows cut into Royce's brow. "Then you blocked me from your Flashbulb. I made a new profile, and I sent messages to your DMs with pictures of my gift, but instead of replying you deleted your account. That was hurtful and unnecessary. You sex yourself up and pout into the camera in your tiny shorts that showcase every curve of your package, all for the attention of random strangers. But when someone who's been your friend for years wants to give you the love you deserve, you push him away? Why are you a slut for everyone but me?"

Realization crashed through Cosmo. It was Royce. The whole time, it had been Royce calling him a slut. He'd made an account with Zedd as his profile pic so it looked like the harassment was coming from him. Royce in his DMs, sending him pictures of... what exactly? Cosmo didn't want to know.

He balled his fists, nostrils flared. It was easy to feel like the one to blame, the one to lead Royce on, but it wasn't true. This wasn't his fault. He'd trusted Royce, and the director had kept going even after Cosmo told him to stop. "I know how beautiful I am. But I dress the way I do for *myself*. My clothes aren't an invitation for you to put your hands on me."

"And you dislike the attention so much that you reply to every comment with kisses and hearts? You can pretend to be demure for your new boyfriend, but you and I both know who you really are."

He always thought Royce had chased Zedd away because he cared about Cosmo, not because he wanted Cosmo all for himself. And Cosmo had never seen Zedd threatening any of his past loves firsthand. He hadn't been sure how Zedd even knew about Marla or anyone else. But Royce had known. Probably half of the harassment attributed to Zedd had been Royce making it up.

He loomed over Cosmo, his gaze icy. "I'm still going to give you my present, but I don't think it's any good now. He's been in my trunk for four days."

Cosmo screamed. Royce slapped a hand over his mouth and yanked him toward the door. Cosmo sank his teeth into Royce's finger and twisted in his grip, jabbing elbows and kicking feet. Something jammed into his side; electricity popped and agony raced through Cosmo's body. His fingers spasmed, muscles full of fire ants. Something hard looped around his wrists; he yanked away and tried to free his hands, but couldn't pull them apart.

He staggered forward, unsure which bleary hallway was the right one. Everything was a fuzz of white and harsh fluorescents. Cool air buffeted his face as he shouldered through a door. Wrong way.

Royce grabbed a fistful of Cosmo's hair and shoved him outside. He hissed, "Scream and I'll stun you again. You'll go right into the trunk with Zedd."

Cosmo sobbed. Zedd's black eye and broken fingers, his note swearing he'd leave Cosmo alone. It had been Royce's doing. Royce skulking around his apartment with a flashlight and testing the doorknob.

Asphalt scraped under his shoes, his uncoordinated legs useless and weak. Royce's pine aftershave filled Cosmo's nose. Snot and tears ran down his face, his restrained arms full of itchy adrenaline he couldn't use. The lights of the gallery receded, and Royce's car loomed ahead. No. No, no, no. Cosmo was *not* getting stuffed in the trunk with his ex-boyfriend's rotting corpse.

He twisted hard and broke free of Royce's grasp, then slammed his head into the director's nose. Royce gasped and put a hand to his face.

Cosmo ran.

"Help!" He stumbled, his ankle caving, and he shouldn't have worn these shoes.

Royce yanked him backward, a hand over his mouth, and dragged him to the car. Blood ran in a river from the director's nose. He pulled a gag around Cosmo's mouth, then popped open the trunk. A vaguely body-shaped object wrapped in a tarp took up much of the space. Cosmo's scream was muffled by his gag. He shook his head furiously.

"My gift to you," Royce snarled. "The bane of your existence, strangled and snuffed out, just like you asked of me. Enjoy." He hauled Cosmo inside and slammed the lid. Darkness swallowed him. The sickly sweet smell of decay filled the trunk. Cosmo gagged and concentrated on not vomiting. The engine rumbled, and the car pulled forward.

He slid as far to the edge of the trunk as he could and groped for an emergency handle, but it was too hard to feel for anything, especially in the dark. The rough carpet liner scratched at his cheek, and he was grateful that for a moment the sharp scent of motor oil overpowered the stench of rot. The zip tie around his wrists caught on something pointy. He worked against the metal, trying to saw the plastic apart.

A dusty memory surfaced of being at a birthday party as a kid. There'd been a pinata, all the kids taking turns whacking the poor paper mâché donkey with a baseball bat. Candy rained from a split in the donkey's belly. Cosmo wanted all of it. He dove into the grass beneath the swinging bat, snatching up bubblegum, taffy, and even those gross little chocolate balls with the candy shells that came in a clear wrapper. Someone yelled at him to get out of the way, to wait until the pinata broke open, but if he did that, the other kids would take it all.

On his second dive for candy, the bat slammed into his forehead. He ran up to Mom, bawling. She scooped ice out of a cooler, wrapped it in a napkin, and pressed it to his growing goose egg. *Was that a good idea?* she'd asked. He'd sobbed and shaken his head. *Are you going to do it again?* No, he was not.

Some people were sensible. They listened to logic and to the good advice from their friends. Then there was Cosmo, who had to learn everything the hard way. If he'd listened to Déjà, if he'd advocated for himself more, maybe this wouldn't have happened. He could have quit Identical Dog at the first hint of Royce holding him back. He could have told Royce to get bent when he'd demanded Cosmo cut his date short to help set up for the charity. He could have had enough self-love to admit that he did deserve Micah. They would never have broken up, and Cosmo wouldn't have been walking up to a taco truck hollow and miserable.

None of that insight did him any good now, because he was going to die a horrible, painful death, and that wasn't pessimism. It was presque vu. And now he knew why he wasn't in Micah's future. Why Everett needed to hide Micah's razor and order him takeout with a criminal amount of cheese.

No Cosmo in any universe was going to get a happy ending, because he was going to be stabbed to death in the decrepit church that hosted his funeral party. He'd probably end up in the same grave as Zedd.

There's room for two in your grave.

And after he died, he was going to haunt Déjà, and he was going to haunt Micah. Not to torment them, but to tell them how very sorry he was.

Micah – Pulling the Thread

Cosmo is gone.

The thought assaulted Micah as he arranged his pencils on the easel and nodded politely to something he didn't hear from one of the onlookers.

Cosmo is gone. It cramped his stomach and sent a tingly panic shooting through his fingers. The worst part was he didn't know why he'd had the thought or what it meant.

The only place Cosmo had gone was to fetch seltzer, but they *were* about to start, and he wasn't out here yet.

Micah excused himself and headed down the hall. It was just his anxiety – he was under too much pressure with the event. Any moment, he'd find his love heading his way with a can of bubbly water, or maybe he'd gotten caught up in a conversation about one of the exhibits.

His dread increased with every step. Clarence stood beside Micah's portraits with a group of people. He flagged Micah down and said, "There's our man of the hour. We were just remarking how–"

"Have you seen Cosmo?"

"No, but–"

Micah hurried past. *Cosmo is gone.*

Presque vu flooded him with a sudden memory from the other timeline. Goosebumps erupted on his arms. This had happened before. He'd find a box of bagels spilled across the floor of the break room, and a bottle of seltzer in the hall. And when he found scattered zip ties and spattered blood in a parking space outside, he was going to call the cops. Except when this happened in the adjacent universe, no one had known where Royce had taken Cosmo. They wouldn't know until days later when it was far too late.

He shoved through the back door and sprinted for his car. With trembling hands, he dialed 911, then hopped into the driver's seat and peeled out of the parking lot.

"Lemon Disco Police Department. What's the address of the emergency?"

"My boyfriend has been abducted!" Micah ran over a curb and sped through a yellow light. "He's being taken to the old church on Cherry Lane. Please hurry; he's going to kill him!"

But there was still time. They'd changed things in this universe already, and if Micah got there before it was too late, he could change this. He'd snag another thread from the string of time. He'd yank the fucking thing out as hard as he could.

The emergency operator asked him for his phone number and name. His hands cramped around the steering wheel, accelerator mashed all the way to the floor. The buildings thinned out, making way for farm fields and cow pastures. His headlights sliced through the dark, momentarily flashing on cars ahead until he sped around them.

"Where are you now?" the operator asked.

"I'm on my way to the church."

"Sir, it's not advised for you to put yourself in danger–"

"He's going to kill him!" Micah's voice fractured. "Please, Christ, you have to get there *now*."

Royce had probably murdered that ceramics artist too, the one he wanted sexual favors from who was eventually found dead in her bathtub.

There wasn't anything to use as a weapon in the car, but if Micah got to the church before the police did, he'd improvise. That's what people did. They strangled women with shower curtain ties and beat men with wall sculptures.

He searched his mind for more details of the impending events – if he knew exactly where Royce would be with Cosmo, he could figure out how to approach to catch the bastard by surprise – but the only other future memory beyond the blanket of dread was of Micah sitting in the shower with his clothes on, icy water beating down on his face, until Everett walked into the room and hauled him out.

There was no time to mourn the fate of Other Micah. The road sign for Cherry Lane loomed. Micah pulled into a sharp turn, and the car skated on loose gravel. The phone flew from his hand and clattered across the floor. He slammed into a mailbox, and it bounced off the windshield.

A red taillight glowed ahead. At first he thought it was a motorcycle, but then the other light flashed on momentarily. *Blinkblinkblink – blink – blink – blink – blinkblinkblink.* Micah's heart leapt. Oh, his baby was smart.

His first instinct was to rear-end Royce's car, but he couldn't do that with Cosmo in the trunk. He hung back. Cosmo would be safe until they stopped.

Darkened houses and barns passed from view. Reflective mile markers flew by. The flashing taillight burned into Micah's retinas. It suddenly went dark, and the car sped up. Shit. Micah floored the accelerator. If Royce knew someone was on to him, he'd keep driving until he lost them.

He pulled up alongside Royce, then drifted into his lane. Royce laid on his horn and tried to weave around Micah, but Micah yanked the steering wheel to the right and slammed into the side of the other car. The side mirror shattered. Royce tried to cut ahead, swiping the nose of Micah's car, but fishtailed and swerved onto the shoulder. The car veered down the embankment, bounced violently, and crashed into a utility pole. The pole listed and glass sprayed from the windshield as the front end of the car crumpled. Smoke billowed in the beams of the headlights.

Micah hammered the brakes, and ice scrapers and water bottles flew into the front seat.

The trunk of Royce's car popped open, and Cosmo clambered out. He dropped into the grass, then ran into the field. Micah's heart lurched. He jumped out of the car and vaulted down the ditch. Rocks and brush slashed at his arms, and sweet-smelling rot drifted on the cold breeze.

He hadn't saved himself from Derek. Every Micah would let Derek in, turn to get him a glass of water, and get smashed in the face with a ceramic sculpture over and over.

He hadn't saved Cosmo from Royce. Not at the bar, and not at the abandoned church on the other timeline.

But the universe was giving him a do-over. This time, he would do what his other selves couldn't. He loved Cosmo, and he wasn't going to fail.

Royce's silhouetted figure stumbled out of the car. He turned and sprinted after Cosmo. Light winked off the blade in his hand. Cosmo screamed, the sound cutting above the crash of Micah's heartbeat and the trill of crickets. Cosmo fell, scrambled up, and veered for a house in the distance. Micah gained on them, and just as Royce looked back, he tackled him.

The blade flew from his grip. He reached for it, but Micah slammed his fist into Royce's face. Blood flew from his mouth. He tried to pull away, but Micah snatched his tie and yanked on it. Royce let out a strangled cry. This absolute piece of shit had hurt Cosmo enough, and Micah might not be able to do anything about Cosmo's other self, but he could save this one.

Hauling back hard on the tie, he punched Royce again and again. Micah's glasses flew into the dirt as Royce clawed at his face. He jabbed a thumb into Micah's paralyzed eye, and white-hot pain burst in his vision.

Micah cried out and shielded his eye. A knee jabbed into his chest, dirt and rocks scraping beneath him, and Royce smashed his fist into Micah's jaw. Blood flooded his mouth.

Fingers wrapped his throat, Royce's eyes blazing and lips peeled back in a red snarl. Micah threw frantic fists, but his chest was full of razor blades, his body trying to seize up. *No!* He had to fight back. If not for himself, for Cosmo. Gasping, he clawed at Royce's hands, but the man's fingers dug harder into Micah's windpipe. White stars burst in his vision.

Fight back! Get up! You have to—

A rock crashed into Royce's head with a sickly crack. Cosmo wrapped his arm around the director's throat and hauled him back, his eyes wild. "You should have killed me when you had the chance!" His voice was ragged and strained, face streaked with dirt and blood. "Because the only one who'll be warming a grave now is you!"

Cosmo shoved him into the dirt and slammed his fist into Royce's face. Micah kicked him in the balls with the force of nine months of frustrated rage. Royce gasped and choked, hands flying to his crotch. Where was that switchblade?

Sirens wailed, lighting up the night. A cop car slid to a stop, and an officer jumped out and skidded down the embankment.

Micah waved his hands. "Over here! I placed the 911 call!" He backed up as the officer trained his gun and flashlight on Royce.

Shivering, Cosmo clutched his elbows and clenched his teeth. Micah wrapped his arms around him and held him as tightly as he could.

"This time was different," Cosmo murmured into Micah's neck.

This time was different.

24

NEVER GONNA GIVE YOU UP

Micah - Snagged Thread

Light Christmas music drifted as Micah walked down a long aisle of international candy. The snow in his hair was melting and running down the collar of his coat, his cheeks still bitten from the December wind. Going to a Christmas tree farm had been a huge mistake. He hadn't known that the smell of pine reminded Cosmo of Royce, but it still felt like Micah needed to make up for it somehow.

This international market advertised having fake trees, but they hadn't made it far enough through the store to find them yet. Despite Cosmo voicing their distaste for "suburban mom" decor, they kept stopping to look at ornaments and gingerbread house kits. Micah was afraid he might lose his beloved among the decor because Cosmo's fair isle patterned leggings might as well have been camouflage against all the throw pillows.

Cosmo opened the glass door of a cooler at the end of the candy aisle, then let out a tiny gasp. "Syrok! I haven't had this in years. My grandpa sold it at his deli." Picking up a narrow box, they waved it at Micah. "It's curd cheese coated in chocolate. A little like yogurt or cheesecake. I must get one."

Micah stopped at the cooler then swiped all of the boxes of syrok into his shopping basket. He shrugged at Cosmo's confused expression. "I know it doesn't make up for our last stop, but a dozen tiny Russian cheesecakes can't hurt, right?"

Cosmo shrank into their coat, pressing their nose against the collar. Their curls were tucked beneath a knit hat, but even without an ever-present lock of hair hanging in their face, it was hard to read their expression. "Micah..." Christmas music filled in the silence between their words. "I need to tell you something. When you asked me to come with you this weekend to pick out a little tree, I – I experienced presque vu. I thought maybe it was my imagination, but when we went to the tree farm, it happened again."

That didn't make sense. Micah had felt something at the tree farm, but he'd brushed it off as childhood nostalgia. And he'd been too distracted by Cosmo's reaction to the scent of the trees to notice anything else. He still got presque vu occasionally, but only during conversations with his brother. His best guess was that Other Micah had moved away, maybe to live with Everett. Cosmo's presque vu had stopped entirely – because on the other timeline Cosmo was dead. "How is that possible?"

Cosmo's teeth dug into their lip. "Because we're going to make another parallel universe. You're going to help me, and it's going to work. It already has if I'm alive and helping you tie a pine tree to the top of your car on some other timeline." Their eyes grew glossy, their voice barely a whisper. "In that universe, I'm never abducted. And darling, you don't have any scars on your face."

Goosebumps pebbled Micah's arms. His chest heaved, and he nearly dropped the shopping basket. His past self was still carrying out his life from three years ago in apartment twenty-one. Still participating in art fairs and dating Courtney and welcoming life models into his studio. He hadn't let Derek in yet. Didn't know Derek was a threat.

Pulling in a deep breath of cinnamon and potpourri, he said, "What do we need to do?"

"We write it all down in a notebook. Warn our other selves about what's to come."

It was a huge risk. They'd be changing the entire trajectory of two lives. "I don't know. My assault has shaped every decision I've made afterward. If I never become an anxious shut-in desperate for connection, there's a good chance I'll never meet you at all.

Making sure you're alive and safe is more important than whether or not we have a romantic relationship, but if I don't know you, how am I going to give you a notebook of warnings?"

"But we've already met. The only reason your past self lives in that studio is because I saw you in the bathroom as a ghost, and it frightened me into moving *out*. Thus enabling you to move in. If you're never assaulted, maybe you won't fall for me in the same way, but if we're both artists active in galleries and the art community, surely we'll run into each other at some point. Especially if your other self has a notebook of future events. You'll be looking for me."

There was so much confidence in Cosmo's face. Micah hadn't noticed the presque vu the way Cosmo had, and he wasn't sure their theories about how spacetime worked were even correct, but presque vu had given Micah enough future knowledge to stop Cosmo's death. A whole notebook of warnings would have the power to do so much more. And besides...

"There's a comfort in knowing that no matter what universe we're in, every Micah and every Cosmo will fall for each other." He cupped Cosmo's cheek and gave them a soft kiss. "I thought that before, and I still believe it. Let's buy your candy and a plastic tree and figure this out."

Micah pushed his key into the knob of apartment twenty-one and creaked open the door. Ximena hadn't rented the studio to anyone else, but it no longer felt like his, especially with the lack of furniture. And he couldn't shake the sense that he was intruding – because he was.

Clutching at his arm, Cosmo whispered, "You're certain you saw something on the camera?"

"No, I heard him. He was talking to Courtney. My ex-girlfriend. His *future* ex." The conversation had been indistinct, but he'd clearly heard past-Micah say the word "ghosts." Which meant that Micah's intrusions into the studio weren't going unnoticed. They just needed to time it when the veil of crossed timelines was thin enough to see each other.

Courtney's voice drifted. It had a hollow quality like she was on speakerphone. "–such thing as ghosts. It's all a product of human imagination, the way we naturally try to pick shapes out of clouds or figures from the shadows."

"Or Jesus from a grilled cheese sandwich?" past-Micah replied.

He was never going to get used to hearing his own voice. And past-Micah should have known Courtney wouldn't believe him. Should have called Everett instead.

"Exactly," Courtney said. "Hey, you wanna come over tonight? I'll order takeout, and we can play cards or something."

"Eh, I'm kind of busy."

Cosmo cringed. "Ouch."

Micah leaned to his ear. "They're on their way out. Don't feel bad. The only comment she ever made toward my art was 'It's nice.'"

Pressing a hand to their mouth, Cosmo feigned nausea and hissed a little too loudly, "Dump her."

Micah walked into the room, and his shin slammed into something hard. "Ow!" A coffee table had materialized in the center of the room. The past was dangerous. He tucked his composition notebook under one arm and rubbed his shin. "My leg is going to look like a piece of discount fruit tomorrow."

Cosmo smacked him, and Micah straightened. Past-Micah stood in the hall, mouth agape, with water and soap bubbles dripping from his hands. He'd always called Courtney while washing the dishes.

Past-Micah's throat worked, his chest heaving. Micah thought about the faint imprint of future memory he'd had of sitting in the freezing shower stream in all of his clothes, completely broken by Cosmo's death, and Everett hauling him out of the tub. He resisted the urge to give his past self a hug. That future wasn't going to happen. Not on this timeline.

"We're not ghosts." Micah pushed his glasses up the bridge of his nose. "More like time travelers from a couple years in the future."

Past-Micah blinked and seemed to regain a bit of his composure. "Did you come to give me lottery numbers?"

"No." Micah stepped forward and offered him the notebook. "I don't know how much time we have, but everything is in there. We only wrote down things we thought you *needed* to know, and" – his gaze drifted to Cosmo – "I promise there are no spoilers for the good parts."

After wiping off his hands, past-Micah took the notebook gingerly and traced the words *To Micah and Cosmo* on the cover. He looked up. "Are you Cosmo?"

Cosmo smiled and gave a little wave. "You're cute without the scars too. Please don't lose that notebook. The warnings inside are very important."

Past-Micah flipped it open and stared at the pages. Micah imagined what he was seeing: bold red marker that screamed, *HIS NAME IS DEREK. DO NOT LET HIM IN.*

Cosmo planted a gentle kiss on past-Micah's cheek, which immediately turned a deep shade of pink. "Take care of yourself, darling."

And Cosmo. They were taking care of them too. Micah still didn't understand what the note taped to the last page of book meant, only that it was a message Cosmo had to learn the "hard way."

Frantic motes engulfed past-Micah's face. Micah reached through the mist swallowing him and squeezed his shoulder. "Don't let Cosmo know you hate candy corn."

Cosmo said, "We should have come back in time to give you some taste."

The coffee table evaporated, and past-Micah's phantasmal voice drifted. "Candy corn tastes like you're eating a greeting card."

Micah opened the door and stepped out onto the balcony. "It really does. And not a fancy Hallmark one."

"I feel ganged up on," Cosmo huffed.

Micah took their hand and led them back to the apartment. Pinpricks of snow floated from the sky, melting as they hit the ground. He stopped at the door, then cupped Cosmo's cheek and pecked their lips. "Are you okay?"

Drawing in a deep breath, Cosmo nodded. "It's going to work. It already has."

Deciding what exactly to write down in the notebook had taken so many nights of arguing and talking over things that neither of them even wanted to discuss in therapy, let alone at the kitchen table. There were descriptions of Derek and the dates Micah would meet him, spacetime theories and details Other Micah might need, and they'd gathered evidence that connected Royce to the murder of the ceramics artist Micah used to know.

Even though it wasn't conclusive, hopefully it would be enough for their other selves to tip off the police with.

This would be the biggest snagged thread of all, and only Other Micah and Other Cosmo would know how drastically it changed things, but sometimes that sensation of presque vu still flared up for both of them, often when they were together, indicating that in this thread and the new one they'd just created they were still safe and in love.

When they walked inside the apartment, Everett looked up from his laptop, which he was awkwardly trying to type on with Phantom in his lap. "Did you see him this time?"

"We did." Even with Royce in prison, things were far from being wrapped up, but a heavy weight had been lifted from Micah's chest.

Cosmo plucked a teardrop-shaped Christmas ornament from the box and hung it on a branch. After they'd set it up, they'd complained that it smelled like nothing, and even if it couldn't smell like pine, it needed to be Christmas-y. They'd bought a can of cinnamon scent and unloaded it onto the tree.

"Everett, please tell me you're the sensible brother," Cosmo said. "Agree with me that candy corn is delicious."

Everett closed his laptop and set it on the couch. "It's not my favorite candy, but I like it. Especially the chocolate ones."

"Ugh." Micah plugged in the string lights on the tree. A kaleidoscope of colors twinkled from the branches. "At least we can all agree that candy canes are great."

"I... don't like peppermint," Cosmo said.

Micah clutched his wounded heart. At least Cosmo had good taste in pies. The eggnog pumpkin ones were sure to be delicious, and the two cinnamon apple pies currently warming in the oven made the apartment smell like the world's best bakery. A third apple pie sat on the counter, wrapped in cellophane and tied with a wide green bow. Cosmo had said they didn't want to leave it in their car, but they hadn't mentioned who it was for. Micah peeked at the tag, but he didn't recognize the names.

"It's for Zedd's parents," Cosmo said quietly.

Micah nodded. Cosmo hadn't attended Zedd's funeral, but they had chipped in for flowers and had a couple of brief phone conversations with his father.

Cosmo tugged on one of their polymer clay Santa earrings. "I doubt they'll want me to stay long; they don't hate me, but I also don't think my presence is helpful for them. I found some old photos of Zedd in a shoebox, though, so I'm going to take those over with the pie."

"You have such a big heart. I'm sure they'll appreciate the photos. Hopefully the pie too."

A knock came at the door. Micah crossed to it and peered through the peephole. All the guests were here. His Christmas party was going to be tiny, but having five guests in his place at once would feel like a crowd. They probably wouldn't stick around for Cosmo's "Killer Claus" movie later, but that was okay. Micah's favorite part of watching horror movies with Cosmo was the way they shrieked in a mixture of fear and enjoyment and clutched Micah's arm. If their terror-snuggling grossed Everett out, he could go back to his emails.

Hesitating only a moment, he swung open the door and said, "Hi! Merry Christmas."

Déjà, Rye, and Ximena stood on the step, their arms laden with food and gifts. Déjà leaned forward in her oversized sunglasses and air kissed Micah's cheeks.

"Feliz Navidad, mijo!" Ximena scooped him into a hug, pulling him half out the door.

Micah welcomed them inside. They stepped beyond the threshold.

He closed the door and smiled.

EPILOGUE

Cosmo - Snagged Thread

Cosmo's hand shook as he brought a cigarette to his lips. He wasn't sure if he wanted to keep crying or just throw up all the milkshake sloshing around in his stomach, but this cemetery was suitable for neither. Leaves on the trees in gold and vermilion blurred into an autumnal smear as he tried to blink the tears from his vision. At least he'd worn waterproof mascara today.

"I just want" – he sniffled and took a drag – "I just want some Cosmo, in some universe, to not be treated like shit. Is that really so much to ask? Even if it's not me. Just *some* Cosmo." A composition notebook sat in his lap, the cover closed so he didn't distort the handwriting with his tears. Micah had warned him the information inside was heavy, and Cosmo had initially refused to look, insisting that if he didn't read it yet, that meant he'd get another date with Micah. In reality, he'd delayed looking because he'd been terrified to know.

It was so much worse than he'd expected.

Smoke rolled out of his nose, and he wiped his wet lashes. "Who knows how many parallel universes are out there. Do you think I'm treated like shit in all of them?"

"No, I don't." The wind tousled Micah's hair, blowing his bangs across his forehead. Bits of dirt and leaves dusted the knees of his jeans, his back resting against a listing headstone. "I know for a fact that the Cosmo who wrote in that notebook isn't treated like shit."

"How can you know that?"

Micah tentatively folded his hand over Cosmo's. "Because he's with me. Other me. And I would never treat you like shit."

Cosmo sorely wanted to believe that their counterparts on the other timeline were happy together, that Micah treated him as something other than an absurd Dadaesque novelty, something other than a transient interest to be enjoyed for a brief time and thrown away. But if every one of Cosmo's other selves went crawling back to Zedd again and again, if every one of them ignored warnings about Royce, then he was doomed to be miserable in every universe.

"I could quit my job and move away, or I could call a police station and tell them that Royce–" Cosmo choked and tapped the notebook for emphasis. "I died originally. Why do you think that is? Some people are sensible, Micah. They listen to logic and to the good advice from their friends. Then there's me. I fall back into the same habits until they bury me alive."

Micah adjusted his glasses and said, "Are you saying you deserve what Royce did to you? Is *planning* to do to you?"

"No! But I threw my own funeral just to move on from Zedd. I need something dramatic in order to change. And I need... I can't do it alone."

"You're not alone. And I think having your self from another universe deliver you a warning for the future is pretty damn dramatic. Other Cosmo clearly has enough love for himself, for you, to have written all of this out so it doesn't happen again. And I think he knew you'd react this way, because there's a message in the book you need to see."

Cosmo had seen all he needed to. He couldn't stomach reading any more of his screw-ups that would end in dire consequences. But Micah took the notebook and thumbed to the very back. A folded piece of stationery was taped to the page, and above it, written in sparkly green gel pen in Cosmo's handwriting was: *For Cosmo, who has to learn the hard way.*

He scoffed and stubbed out his cigarette, then lifted the flap of stationery. His vision doubled as he stared at lines running across, and he let out a small sob and pressed his hand over his mouth.

You are the vision and surrealism of a Salvador Dalí
You are the haunting dramatism of a Francis Bacon
You are the fleeting and fragile flesh of a Zdzisław Beksiński
But there is one thing you are not
YOU ARE NOT A SNOW SHOVEL ♡

Cosmo wouldn't have been able to write that message to himself with any sincerity. But his other self had, and maybe that was enough for now. He could keep the note with him and choose to believe it. Choose to remember that he was worth more until he was able to write it back to himself with conviction.

Micah's voice was as soft as the cemetery wind. "Can I put my arm around you?"

Cosmo could give up, resign himself to the idea that a happy ending was never in the cards for him, or he could follow what his heart wanted, choose to believe he deserved *that*. And if Micah treated him like shit – which he didn't actually expect – then he'd leave and move on to something better. *You are not a snow shovel.*

As he leaned in, Micah enveloped him with strong arms. The scent of laundry soap and clean skin filled his senses, and that paint-stained sweatshirt was just as soft as he knew it would be. The idea that in some other cemetery, in some other universe, their other selves might be doing this very thing was actually rather romantic.

"Do you want to go home?" Micah asked.

"I'm not sure I feel safe there." Quitting his job at Identical Dog; calling the police and warning them about Royce; maybe staying with Mom for a while; weren't things he was looking forward to doing, but the sooner the better. "Would you mind terribly if we went back to your place for a bit while I sort things out?"

"Not at all. I have stale, teeth-fracturing candy corn waiting for you."

"What a delightful gift."

The color in Micah's cheeks deepened, and he gave Cosmo a shy smile. "Other Micah mentioned that you like it, so I went right out and bought some. But I didn't think it would take so long for us to meet. Figured we would have run into each other at an exhibit or party long before we did."

"I'm surprised you were able to keep from eating the whole bag of candy corn while waiting for me to show up."

Micah wrinkled his nose, then replaced it with a grin. "Rock-solid willpower right here." He stood and held out his hand. Cosmo clasped it, and Micah pulled him to his feet.

"How is your willpower against baked goods?" Cosmo asked.

"Non-existent."

"Good. I'm going to bake you some red velvet white chip cookies. You won't know what hit you." He tucked the notebook under his arm then laced his fingers through Micah's. Sunflowers flourished between pitted headstones, and a forgotten jack-o'-lantern gave them a toothy grin as they passed. They followed the winding trail through fallen leaves, heading out of the graves and into the light.

ACKNOWLEDGEMENTS

Shake Out the Ghosts was inspired by a late night conversation about spacetime and the concept of "future ghosts." That idea lodged in my brain and wouldn't leave, and I knew it would be the seed of my next book. This story was my most difficult to get right (so far) and took a solid year of editing and some convoluted timeline diagrams before it ever landed in my agent's inbox. But I'm convinced this book is also my best (so far).

A huge thank you to the following people who helped make it possible:

My incredible agent, Ren Balcombe, and all of Janklow & Nesbit who helped behind the scenes.

My editors, Gemma Creffield and Desola Coker, and their endless enthusiasm for everything I write. Gigi St John, Caroline Lambe, April Northall, Amy Portsmouth, Raeesa Saint, Eleanor Teasdale, and everyone at Angry Robot Books.

My critique partners, who I hope I'm friends with in every universe: Shelly Campbell, Keshe Chow, Essa Hansen, Darby Harn, and Jennifer Lane.

To Art History 100, for introducing me to Francis Bacon's *Painting, 1946*. And to Soft Cell and Dead or Alive, which I listened to enough to drive any mortal out of their mind.